Using Them All

10 FreeUse Hotwife Stories

Lacey Cross

Contents

Taking Them All

Freeuse Wedding Party

Lacey Cross

CHAPTER 1

My husband, Jonas, and I have an agreement that I can fuck whoever I want, whenever, as long as I come home and give him all the juicy details. So when one of my best friends invites me to her second bachelorette party at a ski lodge in the mountains, I'm not that excited since I don't like to ski. But it's whatever, I'm sure I can find a little action over the weekend. Some lonely guy who fancies cuddling up by the fire in his room and slipping his cock inside me while the snow drifts against the window. Then I'll come home to Jonas, and he'll fuck me as I tell him all the filthy things I did over the weekend.

Sighing, I watch Vanessa, the bride-to-be, teeter off into the bedroom after a long gab session between the four of us who came on the trip. Our cabin has one bedroom with two sets of bunk beds, and Vanessa and I are the last ones left awake.

Right before she closes the bedroom door, she slurs, "Goodnight, Nadia," and I softly call out goodnight. Not that the others are going to wake up with how much booze they downed.

I'm the only one who didn't drink, so I'm wide awake at midnight. Scanning the room, I snicker at how we trashed the place in just a few hours. The cabin is decorated with sturdy, rustic furniture, and it was immaculate when we got here. Now it's littered with empty Champagne bottles and streamers from party poppers. I could be nice and clean up for everyone, but, nah, they can help me in the morning.

I didn't realize that the lodge was only going to have individual cabins. There's no common room or bar for me to meet a random older gentleman who knows how to treat a woman right. Not being able to find a guy to hook up with annoys my buzzing pussy. Man, I shaved and everything for this trip. What a waste. I'm not sure I would have come if I had known I was going to be trapped in a cabin for the weekend. I'm not going skiing with them tomorrow, so what am I even doing here?

This weekend getaway was a last-minute decision, so not all of the bridesmaids are here. Vanessa requested one last trip as a single woman and tossed the plan together. I could have said I was busy, but my slutty pussy thought she was going to get sex, so I said yes.

I slip my hands down the front of my tiny, cotton shorts and panties and rub my pussy. Vanessa was half passed out, so she's probably already asleep, and the other two went to bed hours ago. They didn't wake up when Vanessa was singing at the top of her lungs, so I know a little moaning from me won't disturb them.

Dipping my finger into my wet pussy, I gather the moisture to use as lubrication against my clit. The wooden chair isn't comfortable, but it'll have to do. I scoot my ass to the edge and rest my head on the back of the chair so I can close my eyes and go to town on my clit. My moans aren't quiet as I caress my clit in circles. Each brush of my finger creeps me closer to my orgasm, and I daydream that my husband is on his knees between my legs, licking my clit and fingering me. I know what I'm asking for when I get home. I'll tell him it was a waste of a trip and I deserve a good pussy licking.

My thigh muscles tense, and I arch my back as the pleasure builds. I'm breathing in quick puffs and continuous moans. When I speed up my rubbing, it tips me over the edge. I gasp as the waves of bliss wash over me, but it's a tiny orgasm and the peak is short-lived. Ugh, a powerful orgasm would have made me sleepy and instead I'm even more awake.

Pulling my hands from my shorts, I wipe my fingers on the fabric and sigh. If I were at home, my husband would take care of my neediness. He's always good about that, and I love him dearly. We have a great sex life. If he wasn't so hot for me to sleep with other guys and tell him about it, I wouldn't do it. Don't get me wrong, I have fun, but I'd never cheat on my husband. But he loves it, and the rough fucking he always gives me after I describe blowing some other guy, or how my pussy was pounded so hard I saw stars, is fabulous.

The small living room is sweltering from the dying embers in the log fireplace. It was warm before my orgasm and now I'm sweaty and miserable. I flutter the edge of my tank top, so it billows out and creates a tiny breeze, but it doesn't help. Shit, I need to cool down.

Getting up, I step outside the cabin and the door gently clicks shut behind me. I groan happily at the slap of icy wind. I'm only going to be out here for a few more seconds, which is good since I'm standing on a small wooden porch in my bare feet, tiny shorts, and tank top. Once I cool down, I'll welcome the warmth of the room.

The lodge has six cabins, all close together, and four of them have no lights on. But the one directly across from me looks like a party cabin. The lights are blazing, and 90s rock music blasts through an open window. Thankfully, we couldn't hear the music through the thick walls of our cabin. The noise level reminds me of college and the parties I attended at the frat houses. I wish the people in the cabin well, whatever they're celebrating, but I have to get inside before I freeze to death.

When I grip the doorknob, it doesn't turn. Staring at the door in disbelief, I take a few seconds to comprehend that I'm locked out. OH FUCK.

I beat on the door frantically. Vanessa better open this door right quick. I shouldn't have even come outside in this outfit. The icy wood against my feet makes me bang harder on the door. I stop knocking and try to listen to see if I can hear any movement, but the thick walls and door prevent me from being able to tell. Wait, how long does it take for someone to freeze to death?

I curl my toes, and I can already tell they're too cold. Maybe if I knock long enough, Vanessa will open the door. But will it be before I lose anything to frostbite? It only takes me a split second to decide what to do. Before I give it too much thought, I'm dashing down the snowy walkway, straight for the party cabin. The snow has been falling for hours and the untouched path makes it easy to keep my footing. My bare feet sink into the fluffy whiteness as I speed walk as quickly as possible while still being careful not to trip.

Stumbling up the porch, I bang on the cabin door, and it's almost immediately answered.

A massive, ginger-haired guy with a beard blinks at me before calling over his shoulder, "Hey, who hired a stripper to come all the way up here?"

I open my mouth to tell him I'm not a freaking stripper when he grips my shoulder and tugs me into the cabin. "Come inside. You're crazy to be standing out there without shoes on and in that skimpy outfit."

The warmth of the room smacks me in the face, and I almost sigh in happiness. Oh, thank God. Ginger Man, as I've now dubbed him, draws me to the couch in front of the fireplace, pushes me down, and sits beside me. He pulls my feet into his lap and rubs them between his warm hands.

My red toenails and lightly tanned skin contrast against his ivory tone. His hands are enormous and make my tiny feet appear even smaller. The longer he rubs them, the more it's like a foot massage. I close my eyes, sink into the couch cushions, and moan softly. Keeping my eyes closed, I enjoy the massage while my other senses take over. Someone turned down the music, and the hum of voices tells me there are several people here–at least five, maybe more. There's enough talking that I can't hear everything going on at once, and I have to concentrate to isolate the voices. Clearly, there's a card game going on, since every few seconds a table gets thumped, people laugh, and other people groan. Another group of guys is close by, discussing time travel theory.

"So, who ordered the stripper?" Ginger Man calls out again, and a chorus of "Not me" and "I don't know" rings out.

"Maybe it was Ron?" a deep voice suggests, and a bunch of people agree that it sounds like something Ron would do.

Wait, are they all men? I open my eyes, peek over the side of the couch, and count ten guys with a quick glance. I snuggle back down on the couch and watch Ginger Man rubbing my feet.

Hey, this guy is pretty damn sexy. I've always had a thing for bigger men because I love feeling small and helpless when they pin me down. Add in the red hair and beard, and I'm sold. My pussy flutters and reminds me that my last orgasm wasn't the best.

"So..." Ginger Man smiles at me. "Are you going to strip for us?"

His hands turn into more of a caress, and I almost groan at how erotic it feels. Here I was, wishing I could find a guy to fuck tonight, and the universe handed me more men than I can handle...

Or did it?

My body zings alive, and my nipples pucker as I imagine fucking multiple men tonight. Can I really do this? My husband said whoever, whenever. A splash of wetness leaks from my pussy. Oh, hell yeah, let's do this. It's going to be the sluttiest thing I've ever done in my life, but I'm going to fuck them all.

I remove my feet from his hands and curl them under me as I shift onto my knees. Smiling seductively, I purr at Ginger Man, "Ron didn't hire a stripper..." I don't actually know who this Ron person is, but I go with it and continue, "Ron hired a freeuse slut for anyone to use."

My voice was loud enough that the guys discussing time travel stopped talking. "Well, holy fuck," one of them murmurs.

"Me first!" chimes in a second guy, and a thrill runs through me, straight to my clit.

I'm already breathing heavily, and my tingling pussy makes me yearn to straddle Ginger Man and grind against him. Ginger Man stares at me for a few seconds, and a ball of lust lodges in my gut while my breasts ache to be touched. Someone argues in the background about deserving to be first.

"Shut up!" Ginger Man bellows, and the entire room quiets. "I'm first," he states in a tone that leaves no room for disagreement.

Several people murmur in approval, and longing blossoms in my core. I'm not sure I've ever desired to be fucked as much as I need this guy to fuck me right now. Is he going to take me to the back room? This cabin is larger than the one I'm in and has several doors leading to other rooms. We could go into a bedroom, and the guys could come in one at a time.

"Get on your hands and knees," Ginger Man commands.

My eyes widen. Uh... I open my mouth to protest, and he gives me a wicked smile. "You said Ron paid you to be a freeuse slut. Is there a problem?"

I close my mouth and shake my head. My entire body vibrates from sexual tension. Holy fuck, am I really going to do this? I stand up and sink to my knees on a fake sheepskin rug in front of the fireplace. When Ginger Man kneels behind me and tugs my shorts and panties down, excitement pulses through me and rushes straight to my shaved cunt. Looks like I really *am* going to do this.

He groans. "Look at that pretty pussy, you guys. All shaved and wet for us."

Oh fuck, that's hot. My mind blips out, and I shake my ass at him, daring him to fuck me. Instead of using his cock, he rubs my velvety folds with a finger and presses one inside my pussy. I moan at the invasion. God, his finger is thick. If that's one finger, what will his cock feel like?

He slips a second finger in, stretching me out even more, and I grind back against his hand. He laughs and finger fucks me slowly while lust almost overwhelms me. When he shoves in a third finger, I'm so amazingly full, I think I'm going to explode and come all over his hand, but I don't.

"Guys, she's so warm and tight. Do you think I should show her what my cock feels like?"

A chorus of guys call out "Yes" and "Do it," and knowing there are men watching us is crazy hot. All I can see is the fireplace, and I'm afraid to peek behind me. I might freeze up with a ton of eyes staring at me. It's better to imagine it. I assume it's true, but I don't know for a fact.

Clothes rustle behind me and then the tip of a cock rubs up and down my slit. The head is thick and bulbous, and I bet his shaft is huge. He grabs onto my hip with one massive hand and steadies me while he presses his cock against my entrance.

"You ready for this, slut?" he growls.

I squeal as he applies pressure. As the head slips in, it stretches me out. "Ohhh god, yes," I moan, and he plunges straight to my core with no further warning.

"Fuuuuuck!" I cry out from the exquisite pleasure that borders on pain because of how enormous he is.

Holy hell. I knew he'd be big, but I wasn't expecting THIS big. My head whirls as he pummels into my pussy.

His voice is almost jolly when he talks to the room. "You know what the best thing about a freeuse slut is, boys?"

Someone asks him, "What?" and he whacks against my cunt so vigorously, his balls slap against my clit.

"Fuck!" I can't hold back, and I'm swearing with each thrust.

"You can use her, and you don't have to wait for her to come."

Ugh, what? My pussy clenches around him and I'm so close to coming that I consider begging. He gives a loud grunt, and I can tell he's about to erupt. His shaft pulsates, and he clasps my waist with both hands and yanks me against him, grinding his cock deep inside. His head rubs my magical spot, and with a few brushes of the tip, I explode.

"Ohhhhh fuuuuuuucck," I scream as he blows his load inside my pussy, and waves of rapture overwhelm me. His cock jerks and his hot cum paints my inner walls. He pulls out with a loud, wet sound and his seed gushes out and drips down my thighs.

Leaning my head down on my forearms with my ass in the air, I try to catch my breath as aftershocks of pleasure ripple through my core. I'm not paying attention until another cock probes my slickness.

Oh, shit. I'm not sure what I was expecting, but someone replacing Ginger Man immediately wasn't a thought. The next dude slams into me and starts bulldozing my pussy.

"Hey, you're right," the dude fucking me states. "I can come whenever, and she won't complain."

I rest my face on my forearms, ready to grumble that I will complain, but the pleasure in my core builds again. Am I going to have another orgasm already? This guy's cock isn't as large, but he's enthusiastic and hitting a pleasant spot repeatedly.

Another climax builds, and right before I come, the dude fucking me spurts his load with a loud groan while the room cheers him on. How many of these guys are going to fuck me?

I don't even realize the guy left my ass until a strong spank makes me squeak, "Hey!"

"Get back up on all fours, slut," a deep voice commands, and I obey without question.

I gasp when another cock probes my sodden hole. This new guy fucks me slowly. I wasn't expecting gentleness, and the pleasure is more intense because I can feel every one of his long strokes.

"I hope Ron paid well. You're going to be used all night long," he declares, and the zing of delight from his words almost tips me over the edge again. Oh, fuck. ALL night? Am I up for this?

He gives a few experimental strong whacks against my pussy, and I cry out from the sharp pleasure. Jesus Christ, I'm about to come again. A warm glow envelops me, and my brain gets fuzzy. Each stroke is better than the last, and I'm floating in a place where time doesn't matter.

The guy clutches my long brown hair in his fist and pulls my head back while he drills into me, hard and deep.

"Come for me," he demands, and my body obeys with no thought.

I cry out as my third orgasm of the night hits me like a train wreck, and I convulse around his cock. He spanks me again, and I collapse onto my arms as he yells like he scored a goal with his orgasm. My entire body vibrates, and my pussy flutters as more cum coats my walls. When he pulls out, our combined juices rush down my leg.

I'm a mess, and I barely notice the next guy press into my pussy. I lose count of the men who fuck me, and I don't know how many orgasms I have after my sixth. It's a stream of pleasure, each orgasm building on the last. At some point, a guy decides to fuck my mouth, and it's the first time I get to see who's connected to the cocks. This guy is average looking, but his cock isn't. He's got a thick, meaty shaft, and I lick my lips eagerly.

As he eases his cock down my throat, I taste myself on him, so I know he's already fucked me. He uses my mouth while another guy drills into my pussy, and his shaft muffles my moans. He blows his load sooner than I expect, and I'm not able to swallow it fast enough. Cum and spit drip down my chin when he removes himself from my mouth, and he's immediately replaced with another guy.

On and on it goes. Once that first guy realized they could get a blowjob, the rest join in and go for round two with my mouth. I welcome each one and suck on them greedily. I can tell they all fucked me because I'm cleaning my juices off their cocks. The guys pounding behind me create a nice back-and-forth movement between me and the cocks in my mouth, and each whack against my sodden hole shoves the cocks deeper down my throat. My screams of pleasure when I orgasm are stifled, and all I hear now is the crackling of the fire, cheering from everyone as they watch, and the groans and moans of various men as they fuck me with abandon.

I'm lost in a haze of desire, and I don't know how many cocks I suck. Each one is different: thick, slim, short, cut, uncut. After so many in a row, they all blend together. I don't even have time to wipe the cum off my face, and some of the men grip my head and smear jizz up into my hairline. This is, by far, the filthiest thing I've done in my entire life, and I'm eager to get home and tell my husband and get my reward for being such a slut.

Eventually, I'm flipped over, and a gigantic body covers me while an enormous cock slides into my sore pussy. It's Ginger Man again, and he fucks me slowly while kissing me. Our tongues swirl together, and I cling to his massive shoulders. My pussy squeezes around him, tiny aftershocks from all my orgasms. His breath is ragged as we rock together.

"Do you need more cum?" he groans.

All I can do is murmur, "Please."

He kisses me again as his cock pulsates and fills me. My pussy clenches, and another soft climax runs through me, gentle waves after so many sharp peaks. He fucks me through my orgasm, and when he finally pulls out, the room is silent.

Sudden cheering and the chorus of claps make me smile dreamily. Jesus, my hubby is going to love this story.

Ginger Man helps me stand, pulls my panties and shorts back up for me, and leads me to the couch. Someone brings me a bottle of water, and another person hands me a thick wad of cash. The room is still spinning, and I'm uncertain what this is for. I glance at Ginger Man with the question in my eyes, and he grins at me.

"It's your tip."

I try to hand it back to him. I don't want their money, and since I'm not really a stripper, I wasn't thinking about a tip. He takes it back, and instead of setting it aside, he shoves it down the front of my shorts and grins at me.

"Keep it. I insist."

A strong rap on the door makes everyone jump, and one man opens it. Vanessa is standing there.

"Have you guys seen..." She spots me sitting on the couch and her eyes widen.

I can guess how filthy and used I look, but I don't care.

"Hi." I wave at her weakly, and Ginger Man guides me to the door.

Everyone says goodbye, and some praise me and say they had a fabulous time. Ginger Man hands me an enormous pair of men's slippers to wear home, and I promise to leave them on the porch in the morning. Vanessa is silent as she helps me back to our cabin. When we walk in, I turn to her. She looks like she's going to say something, but I hold up my hand.

"I must sleep. We'll talk later."

She nods, and I stumble into the bedroom and launch myself onto the lower bunk. When my husband said whoever, whenever... I hope he meant ten guys. I fall asleep with a smile on my face.

Chapter 2

The next morning, while the other bridesmaids are outside playing in the snow, I tell Vanessa the story. Her shock and delight have me going into great detail, and I swear her to secrecy. The rest of the weekend, I feel her eyes on me, and I catch her staring toward the men's cabin with a pensive look. I'm not sure what she's thinking, but I can tell it's not directed at me, so I don't let it concern me much. I'm too worked up and excited about seeing my husband soon, and I daydream about what will happen since I'm not totally sure what to expect. He'll probably be shocked, like Vanessa, and then horny... or at least I hope that's how it goes.

I want to return the slippers to the guys and sneakily give them their cash back before we leave the lodge. It felt dishonest for me to keep the tip money. I worked hard for them, but their hot, sticky cum was enough payment. I tuck the money into the toe of one slipper and put them in a plastic bag. Creeping over to their cabin, I leave the bag on the porch for them to find later.

I don't get home until Monday afternoon while my husband is at work, and I text him to let him know I'm back. I'm already wet and greedy for his cock. No matter how many other guys I fuck, my husband is my rock, and nothing compares to the love I feel when he fills me with his seed and leaves me with a gushing creampie.

Nadia

I'm home!

Jonas

I can't wait to see you, baby. I hope you had a fun trip.

I giggle as I type.

Nadia

I have a story for you. I exercised my "anyone, anywhere" free pass.

Jonas

Oh, really? I'm intrigued. Tell me more.

Hmm, what should I tell him? Nope, I'm making him wait.

Nadia

You don't get the story until you're home and inside me. But I'll tell you a tidbit. It involved more than one cock.

He takes a while to reply. Work must be busy.

Jonas

OK, baby, but I expect you naked and in bed when I get home.

Ohhh, heck yeah.

Nadia

Yes, sir!

I don't normally call him 'sir,' so I send him a winking emoji along with the message. He replies with a GIF of a teddy bear blowing me kisses.

Sighing happily, I glance at the clock on my phone. Ugh, there are still three hours until he gets off work. My pussy buzzes angrily. Yeah, it's going to be a long afternoon.

I'm naked and lying on top of the covers when he walks into the bedroom after work. I couldn't wait, and I rubbed my clit a little in anticipation, forcing myself to stop when I got too close to coming. He'll be able to slide right inside me and fuck me hard. I'm more than ready for him.

Jonas grins when he sees me. "Good. You're right where I want you."

I pat the bed next to me. "Join me, and I'll tell you the story."

"Hold that thought. I'll be right back."

I pout as he leaves the bedroom, and my pussy quivers. I hear him go into the bathroom, but he doesn't take long. When he comes back, he's naked, and his thick cock juts straight out. I swear it gives me a little wave as he approaches the bed. Wetness leaks from my pussy, and I roll one of my nipples between my fingers while Jonas settles in next to me. I'm almost too turned on to tell him what happened. I long to climb on top of him and ride him until I cream all over his cock, but he deserves story time first.

He leans into me and softly brushes his lips against mine before applying pressure and coaxing them open. He tastes like coffee, and I groan as our tongues dance. His cock is heavy and thick as it presses against the softness of my tummy. I reach down to stroke him, and tendrils of delight light up my core the longer we kiss.

His cock is wet with pre-cum, and I use it as lubricant to slide my fingers firmly up and down his length. I take my time with it, so he doesn't get too excited. I'm vibrating with desire and desperate for him to fuck me, but I force myself to take things slow, so I don't deprive him of any pleasure.

He breaks off the kiss and nibbles down the column of my neck, heading straight for my tits. He starts with small kisses on my nipple for a moment before taking the entire tip into his mouth.

"Tell me what you did," he demands around my breast as he continues to suck and pull on my nipple.

Fuck, it's hard to think when he's doing that. Okay, focus, Nadia. I groan when he pinches the other nipple–hard.

Shiiit. Okay... Okay... must concentrate. Since he's teasing me, I'm going to turn the tables on him. "Guess how many guys I fucked this weekend?"

That makes him pause since he already knows it was more than one. "Uh... three?"

He goes back to sucking on my breast, and I giggle. "Higher."

He pulls back and stares at me. "Four?"

"Higher."

His eyes go round. "FIVE?"

"Higher." I give him a mysterious smile and tug on his cock.

His cock grows harder, and I feel a shiver run through his body. "Nadia, just tell me how many." His tone says he's done with our guessing game.

Kissing him briefly, I move my mouth to his ear and whisper. "I don't know, but I think it was ten. Sometimes I had two at once... and the rest would watch."

I lean back so I can see his face, trying to assess what he's thinking. A flicker of shock passes over him, but his eyes quickly turn feral.

"How many orgasms did you have?"

"Um... I lost count."

He crawls on top of me, tugging my legs open. I'm not fighting him. In fact, I help by spreading them as wide as I can. He fits the head of his cock against my pussy but doesn't sink in.

"Nadia, you know what happens when you fuck other guys, right?"

I nod. "Uh-huh, you get to use me and come as many times as I did. Without trying to make me come."

He flashes a wicked grin. "So should we call it ten orgasms?"

Oh, shit. Even if he fucked me twice per day, that means I'm not coming for almost a week. I use my cutest voice possible, the one I know he can't resist. "Um... I think it was six?"

He laughs. "You don't seem too sure of that number."

Thank God it's not how many times the men came since I believe most of them came twice: once in my pussy, and once in my mouth.

"No... no... I'm SURE it was six." I blink at him innocently and hope he buys my act.

"Hmm, okay... if you're sure."

"Oh, yes, I'm... fuuuuuuck." He slams into me, straight to my core, and a massive spike of pleasure rushes through me.

He whacks against me. "Nadia, you are a thirsty little cum slut."

"Oh, God. Yes, I am."

When he grabs my wrists and pins them above my head, I close my eyes and take my punishment. He whacks against me, and each thrust shoots spirals of bliss through my core. The rule is that if I come, fine, but he's not waiting for me. Chances are good I'm going to come at this rate.

He's panting, and his voice is rough. "Did you like fucking all those men?"

My clit throbs, and I need to come so badly. I cry out when he thrusts extra hard and whimper, "Yes, it felt so good."

"Did you think of me while they used you?"

Ohhh, there we go. Love for my husband floods through me. "Yes," I gasp as a zing of bliss almost makes me come. "I always think of you. Everything I do is for you."

He groans, lets go of my wrists, and pushes my knees up to my chest. "I'm going to fill you up and you're going to be dripping for days."

He jackhammers into me, and when he hits the perfect spot, my orgasm rips through me. I squeal and shudder while my pussy clenches around his cock. Knowing I came drives him into a frenzy, and he slams into me repeatedly.

He comes with a growl, and his cock spasms. "I love you," he groans as he shoots load after load of hot cum deep inside me. His body twitches against me, and he slows down his thrusts before withdrawing and lowering my legs. We're both in a daze as he collapses next to me and cuddles close.

My heart races, and it takes a while for my breathing to calm down. Our bodies are slick with sweat, but we don't move. He doesn't speak, and when I look at him, he's got a glazed, sexually satisfied glow.

This is how it always is after I've been with another guy. It's going to be several days of a gloriously possessive and insatiable husband, and it's why I enjoy being a hotwife. None of this would be fun without my husband. Sure, the sex is great. But while the men are fucking me, I think of how Jonas will react later, and it increases the pleasure in the moment. I always come harder knowing my husband is going to get a thrill from hearing about my slutty adventures.

After a bit, I can tell he's coming back to his senses because he caresses my hand and kisses my shoulder.

I turn my head to look at him and whisper, "I love you."

His eyes glint when he replies, "That's one."

Giggling, I give him a peck on the mouth. "Yep, five more to go."

It's going to be a fun few days at my house.

The End

BORROWING THE BRIDE

FREEUSE WEDDING PARTY

LACEY CROSS

Chapter 1

We're not superstitious, so Mason and I didn't sleep separately the night before our wedding. When I wake up the morning of our big day, Mason is on his side, already awake, and has his head propped up with a hand while he studies me. Normally I might find this creepy, but lately I've been doing a similar thing while he sleeps. I flush as happiness ripples over me. It's surreal that the day has finally arrived.

Mason and I have been together for six years and engaged for the last two. He dragged his feet so long to set a date for the wedding, my mother was positive we were heading for a breakup. She wasn't far off base. I didn't tell anyone, but we hit a rough patch a year ago and broke up for two weeks. He wasn't sure he believed in the institution of marriage, and I told him if he wanted to be with me, he better start believing in it fast. My ultimatum led to the breakup, but two weeks apart was more than enough time for us to realize we were both being idiots.

When we finally talked after our separation, I told him I realized that I didn't need a stupid piece of paper to prove we belong together. And he told me he realized that if it was just a dumb piece of paper, he'd rather get married than be without me.

I sleepily murmur, "Good morning," and he leans forward to brush his lips against mine.

My body hums alive, and I wish we had time for a morning romp. I peek over his shoulder at the alarm clock—shit, nope. My alarm is going off in minutes.

"Good morning, babydoll. You ready for today?" It's a serious question, but the twinkle in his eyes shows me he knows I'm ready. I've been ecstatic for days now.

Yawning into a smile, I can't resist teasing him. "Maybe. It depends on what you got me as a wedding gift."

His devilish grin in response might have concerned me any other day, but he can't cause too much trouble since most of today is scheduled down to the minute. Our wedding planner is very precise.

He kisses me on the nose. "I have two gifts today."

Uh oh. I only got him one. I'm cautious with my "Two?" They better be small. I got him the expensive telescope he's been drooling over. It's a marvelous gift, but hopefully he didn't go overboard.

He nudges me onto my back and kisses me deeply for a few moments, and a punch of desire burns in my core. I moan as he nibbles his way down my neck. "Your first gift is that today is a freeuse day."

My pussy clenches with need. Ohhh, what's this? Ever since the short breakup, we've been trying to spice things up in the bedroom. We've experimented with freeuse, where he spends a day using me however he wants. I revel in it. We've also been talking about me being a hotwife... after we're married. I joked that we had to wait because I wasn't a wife yet, but I'm sure we'll try that soon. I have a kink about feeling like a sex toy and just a hole to be used, so freeuse days are always fun. It's not something I want all the time, but occasionally it's thrilling and naughty to be objectified.

Excitement swirls in my core when he slips a hand under my nightshirt and plays with my nipples. If he intended to get me horny this morning, he succeeded. I'm groggy and the haze of lust makes it difficult to think, but we can't do freeuse right now.

"Mason..."

He sucks lightly on my neck as shivers run down my spine. "Yes, Vanessa?"

Fuck, he better not give me a hickey. I shove on his head. "We have a schedule. We can't do freeuse today."

He stops sucking and peers up at me. "Sure we can. I promise not to mess up the schedule. Does that work?"

My wet pussy says it works very well. Fuck it. I laugh at him. "Okay, I'm yours for our wedding day then."

"You're mine every day," he announces as he swoops down to kiss and lick my neck again.

The loud beeping of my alarm clock makes me giggle as I shut it off. "Okay, enough of that. It's time to get up!"

It might be mean of me, but his groan gives me great satisfaction as we both get out of bed for the big day.

The ceremony is perfect, despite the inevitable tiny mishap that always seems to happen. Stephanie, a bridesmaid, forgot her shoes at home and had to beg her cousin to switch shoes with her so she didn't wear flip-flops during the ceremony.

The hotel is gorgeous, and the decorations are exactly what I selected. The devotion I feel for Mason as I walk down the aisle tells me I'm making the right choice. There's no hesitation on his part during our vows, and I can see adoration written all over his face.

Our reception will serve dinner and feature an open bar with live music. While the groomsmen usher the guests to the reception hall, Mason and I duck into a bathroom to freshen up. I plan to wear my wedding dress for part of the night and then change into something more comfortable.

The bathroom is fairly large, with four stalls and a vanity with a row of sinks below the mirror. I'm at the sink fixing my makeup and watching Mason take an "out of order" sign that is leaning against the wall, open the A-frame sign, and set it right in front of the door outside the bathroom. It's a little unnecessary since we won't be in here long, but whatever, that's Mason.

He's relaxed and happy as he moves behind me and kisses my neck. "Well, we're married."

Mmmm, I adore it when he nibbles and kisses right there. He always knows the perfect spot. Gentle waves of delight radiate through me from his touch.

I wash my hands and smile softly. "Yep."

Without warning, he shoves my shoulder to the counter, and I swallow my gasp. Oh shit, he's fucking me right now? My legs quiver and all gentleness leaves my body as passion takes over. This is dirty and hot.

He yanks up my white wedding dress and bunches the lace and tulle around my waist, and I squirm with need at the rough treatment. I'm wearing white, satin panties, and he rubs my pussy for a moment as a damp patch grows with each stroke. Shit, this is going to be something to remember from our wedding day. He wants me to ignore what he's doing, but it's tough to do that when my face is against the bathroom counter.

His voice is deceptively casual. "What was your favorite part of the ceremony?"

Pings of bliss shoot to my toes, and I try not to moan. Uh, how am I supposed to think while he's driving me wild with his fingers? I wrack my brain.

When he speeds up, I blurt out, "The vows."

I'm proud of myself for coming up with a quick answer.

He fumbles with opening his pants before pushing aside my panties. When the head of his cock fits against my wet slit, I almost lose it and moan from the joy.

"So, what was it about them that made it your favorite part?"

Damn him. He presses the tip inside me and all thoughts drain from my head from the delight.

He pulls out. "I'm waiting."

Ugh. Okay, I can do this. "I liked the—" He slams his cock inside me, and I can't hold in my cry of elation. "Ohhhhh, god."

He sets a frantic pace, as if he's in a competition of who can come the quickest, and the assault on my pussy has me breathless and dizzy.

"Vanessa... I'm still waiting."

I grip the edge of the counter and hold on as he plows into me relentlessly. How is he not winded? "I liked..." I almost lose my train of thought again from ecstasy as he slams into me. "... Liked your personalized vows."

Pings of bliss flutter from my core, and right when I get close to my orgasm, he groans out, "Oh fuck, babygirl, I'm coming!" and fills my pussy with his warm cum.

He slowly fucks me as he comes down from his orgasm and when he withdraws, he slaps my ass. "I'm done with you. Let's get back to the reception."

My entire body cries out in displeasure and I'm desperately horny. Holy shit, why did I agree to freeuse today? I'm so out of it, he has to help adjust my panties and straighten my dress. I'm flustered and dazed when I look in the mirror.

Mason must sense that I'm nervous about my appearance. He kisses my cheek and whispers, "You look beautiful, and having my cum dripping out of you is going to make you feel even sluttier than being used in the restroom."

Our combined juices leak out of me, and my nipples harden. Shit, he's right.

The reception is a blur of sexual excitement and laughter, and I wish Mason would take me upstairs and fuck me right now because I need to come so badly. I didn't think I would get edged on my wedding day. But, sadly, we have to stay long enough for dinner and to cut the cake. The catering company did an incredible job: the salmon is delicious, and the cake looks like it's right out of a magazine. Even so, all I can think about is fucking my new husband.

After they clear our plates, Mason leans over to me. "Do you want to know what your second gift is?"

Ooooh, it's gift time! The telescope is waiting at home, but I can tell him what it is, if he wants to know. "Sure, tell me."

He moves closer and his whisper tickles my ear. "Now that we're married, you're a hotwife."

I'm unsure what to say for a moment. What sort of gift is this? Like, ohhh sure, someday I'll fuck other guys and get my kicks, but it doesn't seem like much of a gift since we already discussed doing it after the wedding. At least my telescope is an actual gift.

It doesn't matter though, I love him even without a tangible gift. I smile indulgently at him. "Okay, I'll be your hotwife anytime you want. Do you want to know what yours is? It's at home."

"Well, don't you want to hear what the rest of your gift is?"

Oh, there's more. I give him a quick peck on the lips. "What's the rest?"

"See the table over there?"

He points to the table where all four groomsmen are sitting and laughing. His best friend, Aaron, catches my eye, and I swear his eyes smolder. My nipples harden, and I feel a blush creep up my face.

Okay, that's odd. "Yeah, I see the table with your friends."

"They are your wedding gift."

My pussy clenches from desire, but I'm confused. He can't mean what I think he does. "Uh… what?"

He kisses my ear, and his voice is husky. "In an hour, we're going to leave the party, and they're going to join us in our room to fuck you and turn you into a hotwife. I want your first time to be with people I trust."

My mind blanks for a moment, and I stare at him wide-eyed. I should probably thank Nadia for this.

A few weeks ago, on a bachelorette weekend in the mountains, one bridesmaid, Nadia, visited the neighboring cabin and, by her account, had a pretty thrilling time with ten men. When I got home, it was all I could think about. I dreamed about fucking multiple men, and when Mason and I made love, I imagined other guys in the room. I eventually told Mason about my slutty fantasy, and he asked if I'd do it if he arranged it. In a moment of horniness, I said yes, but only after we were married. I didn't expect it to happen on our wedding night.

Mason reaches for my hand in my lap and squeezes it. "Do you want to fuck four men as your gift?"

Every fiber of my being screams with delight, but only a whisper comes out.

"Yes."

<h1 style="text-align: center;">CHAPTER 2</h1>

Before we leave the reception, I gather my bridesmaids together to thank them and dish about my wedding present. Nadia gives me a high five, but everyone else is shocked. I'm glad at least one friend supports my kinky plans.

When I rejoin Mason, once we decide it's acceptable for us to duck out of the reception, we sneak upstairs. In the elevator, he gives me the option of having tonight recorded on video, and there is zero hesitation with my yes. Proof of me fucking four guys that I can rewatch in the future? Hell, yes.

In the room, he tells me to take a nice, long, relaxing shower because Jose, a groomsman, is loaning us his video equipment for the night, and he's going to come help set it up. I'd rather not witness two men fiddling with electronics, so I'm happy to hide in the bathroom. I also want to gather my thoughts before the afterparty starts.

The shower refreshes me, and I'm practically vibrating with need as I put on the white lingerie set that I bought especially for tonight. It's a sheer negligée with a wisp of fabric that they called a G-string but is mainly a joke, along with the matching robe. I kept my blonde hair in a topknot in the shower, so it didn't get wet, but I know it's eventually going to fall down during the evening if I'm fucking four guys. I eye my hair critically in the mirror before unwinding it and putting it in a ponytail. This is so dirty, and Mason's bedroom shenanigans this morning kept me on a low simmer all day. Add in the actual edging in the bathroom before the reception, and I'm like a match ready to be lit on fire.

Spreading my fingers on my left hand, I admire the glint of my newly acquired wedding band. Thank God, I'm finally married. I wasn't sure it was ever going to happen, and it almost didn't. After our two-week breakup we did couples counseling, during which he admitted to hooking up with multiple women while we were apart. I'd spent the time with my face in a carton of cookie dough ice cream, sobbing, and binge-watching romantic comedies.

It took me a little while to accept that everyone processes hurt in their own way, but it still perturbed me when I found out he had a threesome with twins. We had never discussed bringing a third into the bedroom, though if we had, I would have wanted it to be another man. That led us to discussing me being a hotwife or having a threesome. Mason claims he gets super hot at the thought of me with other men, but I need to see it to believe it. I guess I'll find out tonight.

Smoothing the fabric of the robe down my thighs, I adjust the bow I made with my robe's belt to make sure it's perfect. It's been a long day, and I expected to be exhausted by now. Instead, I'm energized and looking forward to the wedding gift from my husband.

I fight the urge to reapply my makeup. There really is no point since I'm about to get thoroughly fucked. Butterflies dance in my stomach, and I'm trembling when I smile at myself in the mirror before leaving the bathroom. Am I insane for doing this?

The honeymoon suite is a wedding gift from his parents, and it's nicer than any room I've ever rented before. There is a separate master bedroom with two large, overstuffed chairs in a corner. The king-size bed dominates the room, and the mirrors on the wall opposite the bed are low enough that we can watch ourselves fucking. I giggled as soon as I saw the mirrors earlier. The room is exactly what I would want for my wedding night.

As I walk out of the bathroom, I see Mason over by the window with Jose, setting up a video recorder. An unexpected third person catches my eye and startles me. "Shit, Stephanie. I didn't see you there."

Stephanie, the bridesmaid who forgot her shoes, gives a frosty smile. "I helped Jose carry the equipment from his car."

I perch on the edge of the bed and feel a flash of annoyance. Something about Stephanie's expression irks me. Is she judging me? She's rigid and obviously uncomfortable as she shifts impatiently. I shouldn't have spilled the beans to all the bridesmaids about Mason's wedding present to me.

Stephanie scowls at Jose. "You almost done?"

Dang, what burr got up her ass? And where is her hunky husband? She's continually raving about her spectacular marriage and her sexy, wonderful husband who will do anything for her. Why is she up here with Jose and not with Mr. Perfect?

Jose's melodic tone entrances me. "We're about finished — be patient."

He could talk to me every day, and I'd never tire of hearing his voice. It hits a little differently tonight, knowing he's going to fuck me. My pussy gets wet as I imagine him whispering sweet nothings while he's plowing into me.

Jose startles me when he whoops out a "Done!" and I can sense Stephanie's sigh of relief.

Oh yeah, Little Miss Perfect Marriage is judging my harlot soul for wanting to fuck all the groomsmen, but I don't care. This is my life. If I wanted to get railed by an entire football team, it would still be none of her business.

Mason follows Jose and Stephanie towards the door. When he passes me, he bends over to kiss my neck and whispers, "I'll be right back with the men."

My pussy buzzes and my nipples harden while my brain freezes from how hot this is. Since I can't think, all I do is give him a brief nod as they leave me alone. The soft click of the hotel room door jolts me out of my stupor. Holy fuck, it's almost time.

Chapter 3

I have too much energy to sit still, so I jump up and pace in front of the bed. It's not long before I hear the door open and all the groomsmen come in, laughing at some joke. Jose and Mason are the last ones into the room, and the three in front all stop when they see me.

"Wow." Aaron whistles softly. "You're gorgeous."

A jolt of lust has me trembling. Since he's Mason's best friend, he sees me more often than the other guys. I was afraid this would be awkward, but the appreciation in his glance makes my pussy throb. I've always been curious about whether he was good in bed. He's an incredibly kind person, and I assume he's a giving bedmate and focuses on the woman's fulfillment. Tonight is my chance to find out.

Leo and David are twins, and I'm secretly pleased that I get to fuck twins. It only seems fair, since Mason did. Not that anyone is keeping score, but it feels like the universe is balancing our sexual exploits. Leo and David are identical, but they're easy to tell apart. David has an active job, so he's fit, while Leo has a desk job and has a soft dad bod. I don't know them that well, but I trust Mason to choose the right guys for me.

Mason weaves between the men and comes in close to kiss me passionately. His tongue plunders into my mouth, and I'm lightheaded. I sway towards him while he continues to ravage me. When he brings a hand up to my breast, cups it, and gives it a light squeeze, knowing the men are watching causes an illicit thrill to zip between my legs.

He breaks off the kiss and murmurs, "I'll be in the room the entire time. Okay?"

I nod breathlessly as he shrugs out of his tuxedo coat and sits in one of the oversized chairs. Neediness consumes me as he loosens his bowtie and uncuffs his sleeves so he can roll them up. He's methodical in his process, and I watch him while all the groomsmen stand there, drinking me in with thirsty eyes but not speaking. After Mason unbuttons his shirt and untucks it from his pants, he leans back, linking his hands and resting them on his stomach. What's going on?

He grins at me before addressing the men. "I want you all to undress her slowly. Give me a good show since I'm sharing my freeuse slut with you tonight."

My pussy clenches, and moisture leaks down my inner thigh at his words. Ohhhh fuck, he's taking part? When he sat down, I assumed he was going to watch and stay silent. He knows being called a slut drives me wild, but he's never done it in front of other people. His words ping a part of my brain, and I really do feel like a slut. One who wants the men to use any hole they desire to fill.

The men surround me, leaving room for Mason to see me clearly. Was this all pre-planned? My head spins as Jose plucks the bow of my robe open while the twins move behind me. One of them kisses my neck, and I tilt my head to the side to give him better access.

Four sets of hands roam my body, and I close my eyes and groan from the pleasure. Holy fuck, this is erotic. Since I can't see, I don't know who is doing what, and someone pushes my robe down. It falls to the floor, and moist lips press against my now-bare shoulder.

Since Jose was in front of me, I assume it's his hands that cup my breasts and tweak my nipples. Someone runs a hand down my front and inside my panties, and I spread my legs apart so he can slip his fingers between my wet folds. Bliss builds in my core, and I moan as a thumb caresses my clit softly.

"Kiss her," Mason demands, and my eyes fly open as Jose brushes his lips against mine.

I was right. It's Jose's hands on my breasts, and as he deepens the kiss, I melt towards him. Someone behind me pulls up my negligee, and multiple hands massage my ass. I sigh in ecstasy as the person rubbing my clit speeds up. The longer the kiss goes on with Jose, the wetter I get. I didn't think it was possible to get more turned on, but I'm desperate to be fucked and growing needier by the moment.

This is fucking amazing. I close my eyes again, letting the sensations surge over me. The twins are being thorough in their exploration, and when one of them slides a digit into my wet pussy from behind, I squeal into Jose's mouth. He breaks off the kiss with a laugh, and he helps someone remove my negligee over my head.

This time, when Mason gives direction, I don't open my eyes. "Remove her panties."

Fingers hook into both sides of the fabric and drag them down my legs. They're so tiny, I don't even bother stepping out of them.

"Isn't my wife lovely?"

The guys murmur agreements, but it's Aaron's "Yes, she is" directly in front of me that makes me open my eyes.

I hadn't noticed that Jose moved to the side, and Aaron's mesmerizing brown eyes bore into mine. My breath catches, and my body tingles. Aaron's dress shirt is open, and he removed his undershirt at some point. His dark-brown skin contrasts with the whiteness of the shirt, and I want to stroke his well-defined chest. I raise my hands and almost touch him, then drop them again. I'm not sure I'm allowed to do anything but stand here.

I sneak a look at Mason, intending to question him, and get another shock. Mason has his thick cock out, and he's stroking while staring straight at me. Oh fuck, that's hot.

He smiles at me. "Babydoll, did you want to touch him?"

Fuck yes, I do. I keep my voice neutral when I reply — in case he doesn't want me to be too enthusiastic. "May I please?"

His grin gets bigger. "Yes. Take his shirt off and kiss his chest."

I lock onto Aaron's gaze again as I nudge his shirt off his shoulders and tug it down his arms. I drop it on the floor with all of my clothes. The other guys are stripping, but I barely notice. I've only got eyes for Aaron as I run my hands up his chest. His skin is warm and soft, and his muscles jump as I lean in to plant a kiss next to one of his nipples. Mason can't see what I'm doing, and I dart my tongue out to give him a lick as well.

"Now remove his pants," Mason groans, and more wetness leaks down my thigh.

Does he enjoy watching me undress his best friend? As I unbuckle Aaron's belt and unzip his pants, the other guys caress me again. A quick look at them tells me that everyone is undressed except Aaron and Mason. I wish I could be in Mason's position and watch the men play with me, but I guess that's what the video is for. I'll be able to relive this and remember how it felt... and it's so fucking fabulous.

It's only six hands on my body, but it's complicated to keep track of them. One is between my legs and brushing my clit from the front, and another hand is coming at my pussy from the back and finger fucking me with two digits. Someone has both hands wrapped around me and is playing with my nipples. Longing builds in my core and I sway on my feet as the sensations threaten to overwhelm me. I have to shake my head to focus on my task of stripping Aaron.

As I sweep Aaron's pants down, I hook onto his boxers and take them off at the same time. His thick cock springs free, and he takes a step closer to me so that the tip grazes my belly. He's got a gorgeous, well-shaped shaft with a slight upward curve to it. If I didn't have all these hands fondling me, I would sink to my knees and beg to suck him.

Mason's voice cracks. "Do you like his cock, babydoll?"

Before I answer, I look at Mason. He's stroking his shaft slowly, with a lust-glazed hunger in his eyes. Oh yeah, he's loving this.

Beaming sweetly at him, I purr, "It's magnificent. May I rub it?"

"Yes," he breathes, and I don't wait for further instruction. Using both hands, I caress Aaron's length and gently cup his balls. Aaron's gulp of air tells me he wasn't expecting a thorough inspection, and he closes his eyes, clearly enjoying every stroke.

I'm momentarily distracted because one twin starts kissing any part of my body he can reach, and I tilt my head to give him access to my neck. All the men touching me drives me close to an orgasm. I rock my hips, forcing the fingers in my pussy to fuck me faster. I can't handle much more of this. He better let me have a cock inside of me soon.

Mason clears his throat. "So, my little freeuse slut. I have a surprise for you tonight."

What's this? I blink at Mason. Getting fucked by four guys isn't enough of a surprise?

He smiles wickedly. "I bet you didn't know that David enjoys tying his girlfriends up."

Oh, hell yes. I'm getting tied up along with all this? I stay calm as I reply, "No, I didn't."

My eyes widen as everyone stops what they're doing, and Aaron takes my hands and holds them together. This all seems choreographed, like Mason went over the evening with everyone. The groomsmen are all being careful to leave a clear line of sight for Mason and the video camera next to him. He's not telling them exactly what to do and they seem to know. They're not talking unless asked a question, so that must have been part of the discussion. It's like we're all Mason's puppets tonight, and it's erotic knowing this wasn't a last-minute gift he thought of this morning. Hmm, how long ago did he plan this?

When David shows up at my side with a cord and begins binding my wrists in front of me, I'm 100 percent positive this was all pre-planned. He makes quick work of tying my wrists up and tests that the binding isn't too tight. Now that David is visible, I inspect his cock to see what he's packing. No one would blame me for being curious.

He's an adequate size, with thick veins standing out that I wish I could skim my fingers over. But with my hands bound, I don't think I'm going to be touching anything. I squeeze my thighs together, thinking of him sliding inside me. Do identical twins have identical cocks? Now I'm curious to see Leo, but he's behind me so I have to wait until he moves.

Mason continues to stroke himself, and I keep peeking over at him. All these hands on me and knowing I'm going to be fucked by four men makes me want Mason even more. This is going to feel amazing, but I really need my new husband's cock inside me tonight as well. I'm hoping he plans to use me after the other men are done.

"Do you guys think my freeuse slut is ready to be fucked?"

I focus on Aaron when they all respond with various forms of agreement, and his eyes glow with desire. Did he want to fuck me before given this chance, or did he only want me after Mason made the offer? I'll probably never know, but he's a very willing participant. Shit, this better not make doing things with him awkward in the future. But even if it does, I don't think I would say no to tonight. I'm flushed and trembling with need for all these men.

"Babygirl, I want you to get on the bed on your back. David will secure your wrists to the headboard. Use your safeword if you need us to stop. Understand?"

I break off eye contact with Aaron and shine all my love towards Mason. "Yes, I understand."

Crawling on the bed to the center, I wiggle my ass and get a nice, sexual zing from knowing the guys are watching me. I'm almost blinded by my hunger, and everything is hazy. I'm beyond caring about anything except getting a cock inside me. The foreplay of them undressing me ramped me up to a ten on the neediness scale, and I might combust the moment someone fucks me.

As soon as I'm settled on the bed, David climbs up by my head and raises my wrists. He uses more cord to attach my already-bound-together wrists to the headboard. His cock wags close to my face, and I could probably shift and suck on it. Raising my head, I glance at Mason and he's watching me intently. I give my dear husband a huge grin, turn my head, and lick David's cock.

David jerks, and his sharp intake of breath almost makes me giggle. I peek to see Mason's response to my antics.

He's not stroking, and his eyes narrow. He studies me for a moment before commanding, "Suck on it."

Mmmm, yeah, he doesn't have to force me to do this. David moves a little closer, making it easier for me to engulf the tip. He's salty with pre-cum, and I swirl my tongue on the underside of his cock while he presses in further. He kneels next to me, so he can fuck my mouth with shallow thrusts while two pairs of hands tug my legs open. I'm too busy with David, so I don't pay attention to who is doing what at the end of the bed, but it's Aaron who climbs between my legs.

Bending my knees, I open myself as wide as I can while Aaron fits the head of his cock against my slick opening. I moan, "Ohhhh, god," around David's shaft as Aaron sinks into me. The pleasure is so intense my vision blurs and the room tilts. Aaron is thicker than Mason, so when Aaron props himself up on his arms and drills into my pussy, his cock stretches me out more than I've ever been before.

As Aaron speeds up, so does David. I thought I wanted all four guys to unload in my pussy, but the longer David fucks my mouth, the more I'm craving him to blow his load in my throat. It's not really about where they come, it's more about how dirty and slutty I'll feel from them using various holes. I'm not sure if the guys realize that tonight is all about me. Mason might be the director, but he's doing this for me. This is only happening because Nadia's experience in the cabin was such an enormous turn-on.

The guys might not be speaking, but as David and Aaron fuck me, they moan loudly, and hearing two men enjoying me at the same time spirals me closer to my orgasm. I didn't explode immediately when Aaron entered me, but I'm not going to last long. Aaron picks up speed, and it seems like he's going to come soon. I'm chanting "Fuck me," but since David's cock is in my throat all the way to the base, it's garbled nonsense.

When I try to move my legs to wrap around Aaron, two people grab my ankles and hold my feet down to the bed. Helplessness washes over me, and I arch my back as electricity shoots to my toes. Oh god. Being totally restrained with a guy fucking my mouth and another in my pussy is the right type of dirty. I close my eyes as my orgasm hits me, and I cry out around David's shaft as my entire body convulses from rapture.

David groans and his cock pulses against my tongue while spurts of his cum coat the back of my throat, and a few seconds later, Aaron shouts out his own "Oh god" as he unloads his cum deep into my pussy. He whacks against my sodden hole a few more times before pulling out, and I eagerly lick and suck on David, cleaning him off. I'm not hating David's cum, but Mason tastes better.

When David pulls out and gets off the bed, I lift my head to make sure Mason is okay with everything. He's still stroking his cock, but he's got the pained look on his face he always gets when he's trying not to come. Oh yeah, he's still doing fine.

The men let go of my ankles, and Jose mounts the bed. Instead of leaving my legs down, he presses them up towards my chest as he slides into my pussy. "Ohhh, fuck," I groan as he hammers into me. Jose is an enthusiastic lover. He's fucking me so hard and fast, I have to close my eyes to avoid becoming overwhelmed by everything. Each stroke shoots pleasure down to my toes, and I'm quickly ramping up to a second orgasm. I keep expecting Leo to come fuck my face after his brother did, but to my disappointment, he doesn't.

I flex my hips and meet Jose's thrusts, trying to force him as deep as he can go. I need him to hold on until I come again, and I'm begging "More, please" over and over. This might be the hottest thing I've done in my life. I can't think of any sexual experience that tops this.

Tension coils in my belly, and my breath runs ragged. A rush of joy causes stars to twinkle at the edge of my vision. The twins move to each side of me on the bed and suck on my nipples. The combined assault of their mouths and Jose's cock is more than I can take, and my second orgasm rips through me.

I squeal and moan in delight as I buck my hips, and my body trembles with the strength of my climax. Time holds no meaning as Jose continues to fuck me. His rhythm is punishing, and the sounds of him slapping into my wet pussy fill the room along with his groans. He comes with a roar, and Leo kisses me deeply as Jose spasms and fills me with his cum.

I open my eyes when he withdraws his cock, and the combined wetness from the two men slips out of me and runs down my crack. I want to squirm from how filthy it feels. Jesus Christ, I've had the cum of three men on my wedding night, none of which are my husband. This is so fucking slutty, and I love it.

The twins are still on the bed with me, and I look towards Leo, assuming it's his turn. He smiles and rolls me onto my side facing away from him. David tweaks and plays with my nipples and kisses me again. Our tongues twist together, and Leo lies behind me with his cock poking my ass. He better not be trying to fuck that hole without lube. Thankfully, when he readjusts, I can tell he's going for my pussy.

Raising my leg, Leo slides into me, and we both moan from the pleasure. This is one of my favorite cuddle-fuck positions, and I curl my leg behind his to keep my thighs spread. He grabs my hip and drills into me while David sucks on my nipple again.

I'm chanting "Oh, fuck" while the smack of my skin against Leo mingles with his moans. I try to see how Mason is taking this, but David is in my way, so I close my eyes and enjoy the men using me. David holds onto my breast, so it doesn't jiggle with Leo's vigorous thrusts, and the perfect amount of suction from his mouth sends tingles straight to my pussy, where his brother is bucking against me wildly. Right when I'm on the brink of another orgasm, Leo groans, and his sticky seed coats my cave walls.

Ugh, fuck. I was soooo close to coming. I mewl out in distress when he pulls out. This better not be over. I need to come again.

David presses my shoulder. I roll onto my back, and he moves his mouth to my other nipple as Aaron gets on the bed between my legs again. Uhh, what the fuck? The men get seconds?

Mason must have sensed my confusion. "That's right, use my slut all you want, guys. She's yours for the taking tonight."

Ohhhh, fuck. I don't know why I assumed each guy only got one go at me. I close my eyes as Aaron slides into me again. He's fully erect, and knowing he's fucking two other guys' cum back into me is so filthy, I explode around his cock, and my brain switches off.

Ecstasy bursts through me, and everything becomes a blur as the guys continue to use me. At one point, I suck on Leo's cock while his brother fucks me. Their cocks are similar enough that if they were at the same fitness level, I don't think I would have been able to tell the difference between them in the dark.

I don't know how long everything goes on, but it seems like they use me for hours. I lose track of my orgasms after the fifth one, and by the end, it's waves of unending rapture. When they stop, I barely notice. Someone unties me and the room gets quiet. I settle onto my stomach and fall asleep, totally spent.

I'm woken up as Mason slides his cock into me. He covers my body with his and uses his body weight to press me down into the bed. My pussy is tender from the continual poundings, but his gentle prods as he stretches me only give me pleasure. He and I have an agreement that he can fuck me in my sleep during freeuse days, so I'm not surprised that he's doing just that. It hits a pretty big kink of mine, and I moan softly and murmur his name as he slowly fucks me.

"Vanessa, you know I love you so much. Don't you?"

Between moans, I murmur, "Yes, Mason."

Layers of pressure build in my core, and every part of me buzzes with bliss. He could fuck me all night long if he wanted, and I wouldn't complain. He rocks against me, and each nudge deep inside me pushes me towards a gentle climax. I peak again right before he comes, and I cry out as I quiver from the intense orgasm.

He groans when he knows I've come, and his cock pulses as he fills me with his cum. He relaxes over me, and his shaft spasms, releasing every drop inside my pussy. When he finally slips out, he kisses my neck and rolls to his side, taking me with him until we're spooning.

I'm immediately half asleep again, but he jostles me a little to wake me up.

"Vanessa... babygirl, are you okay?"

I smile dreamily, even though he can't see it. "Mmm, yes. Best present ever."

He chuckles and snuggles me tighter. "Well, don't get any bright ideas of doing this again. I'm not sure I want to share you with more than one guy at a time."

His statement wakes me, and I almost giggle. Who does he think he's fooling? The pure lust I saw on his face while the guys were pawing me told me he was all in for what was going on.

I take his hand and kiss his palm. "I know. It was a one-time deal."

"Yeah," he says gruffly. "You're mine."

I nibble on one of his fingers playfully before responding. "Yes... yours." I don't add that he's mine now as well. That's what being married to me means.

He kisses my neck, and I hum with approval. He and I both know there is no way in hell this won't happen again. But next time, I'm going to make him ask for it. This new hotwife knows how to play the long game.

As he relaxes fully, and I melt back into him, I think about the video of tonight and how much fun it's going to be to watch over and over again.

Oh yeah, best wedding gift ever.

The End

PLEASING THE CROWD

FREEUSE WEDDING PARTY

LACEY CROSS

Chapter 1

My phone beeps that I have a text message, but I ignore it. Who in the fuck is texting me at 8 a.m. on a Saturday? No one I need to talk to, that's for damn sure. My husband, Cameron, and I had to get up early today because we have our second wedding of the weekend to attend. After the shitty week I've had, attending yet another frivolous, waste-of-money event isn't high on my to-do list.

I was a bridesmaid yesterday for my friend, Vanessa. Her sugar daddy's parents are so rich, they had a live band and an open bar with unlimited drinks. The amount of booze downed last night could have easily paid our rent for three months. Thank God I'm not a bridesmaid tonight — I wouldn't have been able to afford another dress.

I lean on the counter and stare in the mirror. Luckily, I don't look as tired as I feel. Earlier this morning, I pulled my long brown hair into a high ponytail and put on stretch pants and a tank top, intending to do a little housecleaning after breakfast. A fight with Cameron changed my plans, and I've been hiding in the bathroom for 30 minutes to avoid him. We've been bickering all week, and I don't want to admit what the real problem is.

I'm so fucking jealous of my friends getting married. It's not even funny.

My stomach tightens, and I grip the edge of the counter, wishing it was Monday already so I could put this shitty weekend behind me. I don't want to keep fighting, but how do I explain to my loving husband that I'm resentful that we didn't have a big wedding when it was my idea to elope at the courthouse?

Cameron and I have been together for five years, and he proposed two years ago. We planned to save up for a wedding since neither of our parents could help financially, but after a year went by and we still had very little put aside, I knew if I wanted to be his wife in this century, I had to give up my dreams of anything more than a potluck reception in my aunt's backyard.

We eloped, and a week later we had a reception for anyone who was willing to bring food and their own beer. I would've loved to have the huge wedding, bridesmaids, and a bachelorette weekend where everything was all about me. Our potluck reception at my aunt's house was a year ago, and now it seems like all my friends are getting married. Each joyful event I attend makes my lack of a wedding sting even more.

And I was a bitch to Vanessa last night, which doesn't help my mood this morning. She's the friend who had the amazing bachelorette weekend that was all about her. It was in a mountain cabin, and one of the other bridesmaids, Nadia, ended up fucking like ten guys in the cabin next to us, or some crazy shit like that.

I didn't even know Nadia had an open marriage, and it blew my mind when I found out. The way she described it was crazy hot, and it's all I've thought about since the trip. I love Cameron, but I'd like ten guys using me for a night and giving me more orgasms than I can count. Cameron would never go for it, so I can't even bring it up. Once your wife says she wants to fuck ten guys, where do you go from there? We'd probably end up divorced.

To top it all off, not only did Vanessa have the wedding of my dreams, but halfway through the reception, she gossiped to all us bridesmaids that her husband was 'gifting' her to all the groomsmen after the ceremony. I mutter to myself as jealousy burns in my stomach. Like, Jesus Christ... I can't even make this shit up.

After Vanessa told us the plans with the groomsmen, I kept checking them out and imagining it was me. Cameron got tipsy and horny, so he kept taunting me and saying he was going to use me and edge me when we got home. I planned to imagine a fantasy of me with all the groomsmen while Cameron did whatever he wanted to my eager pussy. He ruined it all by drinking too much and getting sick. A friend took him home while I stayed and finished my bridesmaid duties. I saw Vanessa right before she got to fuck all the groomsmen, and she looked stunning in a white lingerie set. Her husband even set up a video camera so they could watch it later. Why can't that be my life?

When my phone beeps again, I glance at the screen.

Ugh, it's Cameron.

I hop up on the counter and plant my ass without checking the message. I might just camp out in the bathroom all morning. Fuck him. At least our apartment has two bathrooms. He can use the other one until I feel like vacating this one. My phone has enough battery life, I could stay here for hours.

A knock on the bathroom door makes me jump.

"Stephanie, can we talk?"

I snort in reply. Guess he decided to stop texting me from across the apartment. We're only fighting because I'm in a bad mood. He just mentioned that he wouldn't drink tonight, and I got snotty after thinking about last night again. He snapped back at me, and now, here I am... hiding in the bathroom.

I sigh loudly. Shit, I'm not being fair. I married a wonderful man, and it's not his fault we both come from poor families. Even if we had saved up thousands for a wedding, we would have been smarter to put it down on a house or something else instead of blowing it on a big party. These are the same arguments I've been telling myself for months, but it still doesn't help the jealousy that consumes me at every wedding I attend.

Cameron knocks again. "Stephanie... baby, please, can we work this out? I'm sorry I got sick last night. I wanted to dance with you all night long. You looked so lovely."

Fuuuck, he thinks I'm mad because he got sick? He sounds so adorable and pathetic. I can already feel my anger draining away as I slide off the counter and open the bathroom door.

Cameron is standing there holding a bouquet of pink carnations that he obviously just bought at the grocery store around the corner. He got the cheap flowers because he knew I'd get even more pissy if he wasted money on expensive ones that wouldn't last as long. And pink is my favorite color.

My heart melts as I stare into his pleading puppy-dog eyes. Yeah, I can't stay mad at him.

"Oh Cam, I'm not angry because you got sick. I would have liked to dance with you, but it was free booze. Everyone was drinking too much."

He looks taken aback. "Then why are we fighting?"

I take the flowers from him and move past him to hide the flush of shame I can feel creeping up my cheeks. After setting the flowers on the counter, I dig a vase out from under the sink and fill it up with water.

I keep my tone neutral, not wanting to risk starting another fight. "It's been a long week. I told you work was stressful."

Work was actually less hectic than normal, but I don't want to admit to him the real reason I was so grumpy. I keep my back to him as I adjust the flowers in the vase, and he slides up behind me to kiss the back of my neck. I hold in a moan, close my eyes, and continue to arrange the flowers.

I may not fuck other men, but that doesn't mean our sex life is vanilla. Cameron heard that Vanessa and her new husband have freeuse days, and he and I have been trying that. From Friday to Sunday night was supposed to be freeuse for him, but his drinking messed up those plans.

As he presses his hardness against my ass, I imagine five guys in the doorway, watching. One thing that's funny about our relationship is that we both can go from annoyed to fucking in the blink of an eye. It makes for some fantastic angry sex, but almost all of my grouchiness faded once I saw the flowers. He's obviously not letting our tiff this morning stop anything.

Cameron nibbles on my neck. "Did you hear what Mason's wedding present to Vanessa was last night?"

I fight the urge to tip my head to give him better access and murmur, "Uh-huh, she fucked all the groomsmen."

He presses my shoulder towards the counter. I give zero resistance and lower my chest while my pussy tingles. Oh yeah, we're about to get fucked.

He grinds his cock into my ass. "Isn't that insane?"

"Yes... insane," I pant as pleasure swirls in my belly.

Fuck it, I can't pretend to ignore him anymore. I put my palms on the counter to gain leverage and thrust back as hard as I can.

When Cameron drags my stretch pants and panties down to my knees, I moan loudly. He's not usually this straight to the point with no foreplay unless we're having hot, quick, angry sex.

He backs off, and I watch him over my shoulder as he undoes his jeans. As he shoves them down, I take a step back and bend over fully, using the counter to support my head and forearms. Since my pants are only down as far as my knees, I can't spread my legs very wide, but Cameron doesn't care. He slides a finger into my pussy, and I gasp at the sudden contact. I'm so wet already, and I almost tell him I don't need warming up and to shove it in me, but I stop myself. Why would I tell him to stop pleasuring me? That's crazy talk.

Cameron spreads moisture from my pussy to my clit, and I moan as he brushes circles around my swollen bean.

His voice is husky. "I didn't know Vanessa was such a slut that she'd want to get fucked by a bunch of guys at the same time."

I can't tell if his tone is admiration for Vanessa or slut shaming, so I keep my opinion to myself. Yeah, it's slutty... amazingly slutty. I would have traded places with her in a heartbeat. Some of those groomsmen were smoking hot.

He moves his hand back to my pussy and finger fucks me roughly. "Do you think it's slutty that she had all those guys fucking her last night?"

My head reels, and it's difficult to determine how to respond. He's pleasuring me and talking about multiple men and one woman. How do I take this? When he adds in two more fingers, the thickness drives me wild, and I groan with longing.

Shit, let's just see what he says. "Yeah, Cam, a woman taking so many men at once is nothing but a little slut."

He removes his fingers and replaces them with his cock, slamming into me and shoving me against the counter. "Yeah, a slut who wants to be used."

He grasps my hips and hammers into me, and I hold on to the lip of the sink. I'm not wearing a bra under my tank top, and my breasts swing wildly with each vigorous thrust.

When he hits a sensitive spot, I gasp out, "A filthy whore who wants all her holes stuffed at once."

We haven't tried anal yet, but he loves it when I mention it in our dirty talk.

"Yeah," he huffs as he plows into me. "Such a filthy whore."

I can tell neither of us is talking about Vanessa anymore — not that I ever was. It was always me getting pounded by all the guys in my head, but I'm not sure who he's thinking about. Is it me, or is it a vague, generic, slutty woman?

Spikes of bliss travel through me, and I'm creeping towards my orgasm. I'm not sure if I prefer the fantasy of multiple men doing me at once, or if I prefer the idea of them in the doorway watching. Either way, this is a fantastic visual in my head, and it's helping me climax faster.

Cameron speeds up. "Tell me something, Stephanie...." I moan in response, and he continues. "Would you let me watch a guy fuck your pussy while you sucked on another guy's cock?"

Ohhh, god, would I. I'm not sure how enthusiastic I should sound, but when he smacks my ass, I squeal out a loud "Yes!" from the shock.

He keeps drilling into me. "Would you let my basketball buddies all take turns with you?"

The room tilts and my brain freezes. I forget how many friends he plays basketball with, but it's at least five guys.

He spanks me again, hard. The pain lights up my pussy, and I almost come. I groan, "Ohhh, fuck!"

"Would you, baby? Would you want to fuck all my friends?"

I'm close to coming, so I slip a hand down to caress my clit while he slams home several times, on the brink of his own orgasm.

"Tell me, Steph. Would you?"

His long groan makes one thing crystal clear. He's imagining me fucking all his friends, and the idea of it is about to make him come.

Knowing this is his fantasy, my orgasm jolts through me, and I cry out in a stream of words. "God, yes. I'd be your filthy whore and fuck all your friends all night long. Let them use whatever hole they want."

Euphoria surges over me while Cameron groans, "Such a dirty slut," as he explodes and paints my cave walls with his warm cum.

He fucks me for a few more thrusts as my pussy quivers around him, and my body shudders from the aftershocks of bliss. When he pulls out, he adjusts my panties and stretch pants back over my ass and holds onto me as he gently lowers us both to the floor. I sprawl half on top of him while we both try to catch our breath. As I rest my head on his chest, I can hear his heart rate slow down. Dang, I should get him to fantasize about me fucking other men more often.

We're both quiet for a bit, and he finally speaks. "Would you ever want to really do that?"

I debate for half a second before answering truthfully. "Yes, I would."

"How about tonight?"

What the fuck? His tone of voice is dry, so I can't tell if he's for real. I lean up on my arms and check his expression.

He's not joking.

Oh, hell yeah, I'm taking this chance before he changes his mind. I'm about to blurt out 'Yes' but change my tactic.

I keep my voice flirty. "Hmm, I don't know. Can they all wear suits so I can pretend I'm a bride?"

He snorts in amusement. "Yes, I could arrange that. We could do it after the reception tonight. Your own groomsmen."

Ohhhh, fuck yes!

I lay my head back on his chest and smile. "Okay, Daddy. Make it so."

He chuckles when he hears me say Daddy. I only use it when I really, really want something.

Chapter 2

I'm a wet mess the rest of the morning and afternoon. Cameron claims he has a lot of planning to do, and whenever I see him, he's hunched over his phone, his fingers racing like he's taking a typing test. If I wasn't so turned on, I'd be annoyed that he was ignoring me.

Do his friends even want to fuck me? Wait, are they even all single? Not that it's any of my business. I'm not the relationship police, and non-monogamy is becoming more popular in our age bracket.

I've never been invited to his basketball games, but that was okay—I like the fact that he has interests of his own that he doesn't need me for. I've always assumed his basketball buddies were casual friends he didn't see outside of the games, but apparently he's close enough to them that he seems to think they'll fuck me on short notice. If he dangles this carrot in front of me and doesn't deliver some men in suits, me and my pussy are going to be extremely disappointed.

I'm bursting to discuss this marvelous, new, slutty life with my best friend, Jasmine, and I wander into my bedroom for some privacy to call her. She was a bridesmaid for Vanessa too, and I'll see her at tonight's wedding since we run in one big circle of friends, but I need to talk to her now. I flop on the bed and clutch my phone to my ear.

Jasmine picks up after a couple of rings, and I can tell she's chewing gum from the snap of a bubble when she answers. "Yo, bitch. What's up?"

I fucking adore Jasmine. Half the time she looks and talks like she's the biggest bimbo on the planet. In reality, she's brilliant and working on her doctorate degree in psychology. She once told me she gets her kicks from men thinking she's a bimbo, and that's how she hooked up with her husband, Sebastian. He thought he was getting lucky and having a one-night stand with a hot, blonde airhead, but she ended up wrapping him around her little finger before he knew what hit him. He's a decent guy and is utterly devoted to her, so more power to them.

When she pops her gum in my ear again, I smile. "Jas, you're never going to believe the morning I had."

"Oh yeah? Tell me yours, and I'll tell you mine."

I explain the fight and everything leading up to Cameron fucking me senseless and me agreeing to sleep with his basketball buddies. The longer I talk, the more I think I sound crazy, and my stomach knots.

When I'm done explaining everything, Jasmine's screech of "No fucking way!" is so loud, I have to tear the phone from my ear.

I smile at her antics. Her reactions never disappoint me. "I'm serious. He's organizing it right now."

She's quiet for a minute. "Why do you think all our friends are experimenting with freeuse and group sex? Is a couple more likely to try it if their friends are doing it?"

Uh oh, she's focusing on the wrong thing. "Hey, Jasmine, listen for a second."

"Hmmm?" She still sounds distracted.

The knot in my stomach hardens. "Do you think I'm crazy to do this? Should I be asking you to talk me off the ledge? You're smart. Level with me here."

Her musical laugh relaxes me. "Steph, I can't say what's right for you. If at any point you don't want to do it anymore, call it off. But Nadia is living her best life fucking whoever she wants, so why can't we?"

My pussy buzzes at the thought of Nadia at the ski lodge with the 10 guys in the cabin. Yeah, it's still hot and I want to do it. Wait, is Jasmine thinking of fucking other guys as well? She said "Why can't 'we'."

"Jas, are you and Sebastian opening your marriage?" She giggles again, and the merry tinkle makes me smile; it's so damn contagious.

She gushes, "Oh no, but we're trying freeuse. Someone filled Sebastian's head with glorious stories at the wedding last night. He's already fucked me once today, and he's at the gym right now. He's always horny after he works out, so I'm expecting another pounding when he gets home."

She gives me graphic details about what happened to her in the kitchen this morning, and I'm oddly turned on. Should I be horny while thinking of my best friend fucking her husband? I want to rub my pussy through my panties, but no way in hell am I going to masturbate at the thought of Jasmine spread out on a table.

My clit throbs, and I swallow the excessive saliva in my mouth. What the hell is happening to me? I'm a sex-crazed version of myself. Fuck, I better get multiple cocks inside me tonight. I'm going to go insane with lust if I don't find an outlet soon.

Jasmine interrupts my thoughts. "Ohhh, I gotta go. I just heard the garage door. Love you!"

I barely have time to say goodbye before she disconnects. Heh, fine. Goodbye to you too. I roll onto my side, set the phone on the bed, and trace the outline of a rose on our floral comforter. I get lost in a daydream of being bent over the kitchen table while a parade of guys use me from behind. This isn't just a slutty thought. Deep down, I really am a slut.

Cameron strolls into the bedroom. "Hey, baby?"

I glance up at him in a sexual daze without responding. He stops and his eyes narrow while he studies me.

His face relaxes into a smile. "Someone appears to be all turned on. Were you thinking about all my friends fucking you?"

"Yes," I gasp out as he climbs into the bed behind me and rolls me onto my stomach. There is no foreplay. He yanks my pants and panties down just far enough to get access to my pussy. I'm so wet his cock slides right in, and we both moan as he sinks inside me. A zip of intense pleasure ripples from my pussy when he bottoms out.

His weight presses me down into the bed as he slowly fucks me, never pulling out all the way. The room spins with each nudge against my pussy. Shit, what if he doesn't let me come? Our freeuse weekend agreement was that he could fuck me all he wanted and not even let me come. Since I already had an orgasm this morning, it seems more likely he'd stop as soon as he blows his load into me right now.

Cameron places a firm hand on my shoulder and speeds up. "God, your tight pussy is so fucking wet."

I whimper as he uses me. Waves of delight build as he whacks against my pussy.

He fucks me in a quick, desperate rhythm that has me clawing at the comforter. "You were so fucking eager for my cock. This is what you want, isn't it?"

When I don't respond, he demands, "Isn't it?"

"Yes," I moan. "Fuck yes."

My climax is within reach, and his words are driving me closer to the abyss. When he slows down again, I can tell he's about to come.

He growls, "I married a filthy slut who wants to be used."

"Yes," I mewl out as I try to bump back against him in a desperate attempt to orgasm. If he'd hold on for a few more minutes, I could come.

"Steph, you'll do anything for this cock, won't you?"

Oh fuck, he's really getting into the dirty talk today. This is fabulous. "Yes... anything. God, please, can I come?"

He laughs harshly at my response and continues to drill into me slowly. "You'll even let me fuck your tight little ass if I want to. Admit it."

Ohhhh, shit. The pulse of rapture from my pussy almost overwhelms me, and I'm rushing towards my orgasm. I cry out, "Yes, anything. Please let me come."

With one final plunge, he roars and floods my pussy with its second load of cum today. Oh, holy fuck. I'm not going to come. Biting the comforter, I try to hide my moan of distress.

My entire body is lit up and every nerve ending pings as he stretches out next to me. My brain is mush, and I fight back tears. I was so damn close to coming; this is horrible. Whose idea was it to let him use me all he wanted this weekend?

I'm tense, and my body shudders from the stolen orgasm. A maelstrom of discontent swirls in my brain, and I take a moment to realize he's rubbing my back.

"Relax, baby. It will be okay. I promise."

He continues to snuggle me and murmur sweet nothings while I come down from my frenzy.

Eventually I take a deep breath and tease him. "If there haven't been multiple cocks in me by the end of the night, I'm going to be crabby."

He kisses the back of my head. "Oh, it's all arranged. You're going to have more cocks than you know what to do with."

Hmmm... we'll see about that. I don't voice the thought and snuggle closer to him, enjoying his warmth.

Chapter 3

Before we leave for the wedding, Cameron tells me that his friends will be at our house when we get back. He doesn't say how many he invited, and I don't ask since I want the surprise. God, I hope it's more than two. I want so many cocks there's a flood of cum all over me tonight. I don't know if this will ever happen again, so it needs to be good enough to satisfy me for years.

I'm sure the wedding is amazing, but my mind is a million miles away through the entire ceremony. Cameron holds my hand and occasionally gives me the side-eye, grins, and squeezes my fingers. We cut out from the reception as soon as the party is in full swing.

Jasmine catches me as we're leaving, and she hugs me with a hurried, "Goodbye and have fun!"

She's flushed and trembling, but before I can ask her what is going on, she whispers she'll see me tomorrow and runs off. Huh, something is definitely going on with her. I'll have to call her tomorrow.

My body is buzzing in the car, and I swear the drive home takes twice as long as it should. The house is quiet as we let ourselves in. Where are the guys?

I kick my high heels off. I'm about to question Cameron, but he speaks first. "The guys are in the den. Go get ready, and text me when you're done. I want to go talk to them."

He takes a few steps down the hall towards the den before turning back to me. He tips my chin up and kisses me deeply while my bare toes curl into the carpet.

"Steph, have fun tonight. I want to watch you come multiple times."

My nipples harden at his words, and I want to rub my thighs together. I give him a saucy "Yes, Daddy," and he laughs as heads to the den.

Once he's out of sight, I rush upstairs to the master bathroom, turn the shower on, and speed strip. I want a quick rinse before the men dirty me up again. I toss my hair in a bun so it doesn't get wet, and within a few minutes, I'm in the bedroom drying off.

I know exactly what I'm going to wear tonight. If I want to pretend to be a bride, I'm going to use the white lingerie I wore after our wedding a year ago. Even though we weren't having the big ceremony, I still wanted something special. I splurged on the most gorgeous, sheer teddy I could find. I haven't worn it since, which makes tonight seem like it really is my wedding night.

There isn't much to the outfit; it has molded lace cups with a front hook that brings the sides of the sheer fabric panel together. Someone could easily part the fabric and run their hands along my stomach. It ends at my hips, and there are matching g-string panties. I decide to skip them since I don't want to risk one of the men ripping the panties in their haste. If anyone is going to tear them off me, I want it to be Cameron.

I pace the room as my stomach flutters. Everyone is downstairs, waiting for my text, but I want to savor the anticipation for a few more minutes. Eyeing the bedroom critically, I decide the lamps should be on. I dawdle while making the room perfect by removing the throw pillows from the bed and turning the lamps on before dimming the overhead light. I'm not sure how to prepare my room for multiple men to fuck me.

Wait, maybe we should have done this in the spare room. Will I ever be able to make love with Cameron again without thinking about the other guys who fucked me in our bed? My pussy clenches, and a shiver runs down my spine. Hell, maybe that would be a good thing. It would add a little zing to our nights. Shit, I'm overthinking everything.

Sitting on the end of the bed, I admire myself in the full-length mirror on the opposite wall as I test out various poses for how I want to sit when all the men walk into the room. I'm looking and feeling sexy tonight, and I cross my legs and lean on one arm while I text Cameron.

Stephanie

I'm ready.

He doesn't respond to my message, but within a minute I hear the guys laughing and joking as they head upstairs towards the master bedroom. A thrill runs through me, and I catch my breath. That's more than just a couple of guys making that much noise.

Cameron leads the way, and five men in suits file in behind him. They stand behind Cameron, all facing me. Two of them look nervous and shift their weight from foot to foot.

I take the time to smile at each one of them and say, "Hi guys. Thanks for coming."

A naughty thrill zings through me. Holy fuck, I'm going to have six cocks in me tonight. I don't know anyone's names, but does it matter? The idea of five anonymous cocks inside me is dirty and awesome.

We all stare at each other in silence, and my heart races while wetness leaks from my pussy. Heh, panties might have been a good idea after all. Am I supposed to start the party?

Cameron clears his throat. "Stephanie, you have a choice tonight."

Ohhh, I get to decide something?

"Do you want to be blindfolded?"

Oh, fuck yeah! I'm about to blurt out my "Yes," but I hesitate and reconsider. If I'm blindfolded, I won't be able to see his enjoyment. I blink at him while my mind races. But it would be easier to imagine a slutty wedding fantasy where I'm a bride getting railed by all these men if I'm blindfolded.

Hell, let's do it. I grin. "Yes, please."

His eyes crinkle up at me. "Okay, I want you to lie in the middle of the bed."

Uncrossing my legs slowly, I stand up before crawling onto the bed. I feel six pairs of eyes following my every movement, and I'm breathless with need. Knowing they'll all have their hands on me soon is erotic as all fuck. I snake my way to the center and stretch out flat on my back, resting my hands on my stomach.

Cameron comes to the head of the bed and sits on the edge next to me. He pulls a long silky blindfold from his pocket before leaning over and kissing me softly.

"I love you, Steph."

Contentment washes over me at his words and I know he's going to do whatever he can to make tonight wonderful for me. I murmur, "I love you too," as he covers my eyes. I tilt up my head so he can wrap it around the back and secure it. He doubled up the fabric, and with the dim lights, I can't see anything. I wave a hand in front of my face to double check. Nope, not a thing.

The sound of rustling clothes fills the room, and Cameron leans over me and unhooks the front of my lingerie. He pushes the fabric to the side and exposes my breasts to the cool air and the men's vision. Since I'm not wearing panties, I'm essentially naked.

Cameron takes control. "Steph, spread your legs. Let the guys get a good look at you."

Shit, that's hot. I'm so turned on, they're going to get quite an eyeful. I spread my legs, and even though I can't see anybody, knowing they're all probably looking at my pussy causes an odd mixed feeling of vulnerability and eroticism. The mattress dips at my feet, like someone got on the bed. Oh, I guess we're starting.

Cameron leans close to my ear and whispers to me, "I want you to imagine that we just got married in the most beautiful ceremony. You were the gorgeous, blushing bride of your dreams."

Oh, fuck yeah, I can get into this fantasy. As he talks, I picture everything he's saying.

He continues. "The reception was perfect, and everyone had a great time. You and I snuck off early so we weren't exhausted."

Someone crawls between my legs and nudges them open even further so he can kneel between them. The tip of a cock runs up and down my wet slit, and I tremble from desire, imagining Cameron is about to fuck me for the first time as a married couple.

Cameron whispers more. "I blindfolded you so you could experience the pleasure and shut your mind off. Can you do that for me, Steph?"

I silently nod as the guy between my legs sinks his cock into me. Every inch stretches my pussy walls as he fills me, and I groan from the bliss. He's a lot thicker than Cameron, so it's difficult to stay in the fantasy that this is my wedding night. This is not Cameron in my pussy. The guy pulls my legs up as he thrusts slow and deep.

The bed on the other side of me dips, and someone leans over me as a wet mouth attaches to my nipple.

"Ohhhh, god," I moan, and Cameron takes the nipple closest to him in his mouth, swirling his tongue around the sensitive peak.

The onslaught of ecstasy from two men at my breasts and a guy with a gigantic cock in my pussy almost short circuits my brain. I arch my back and grip the comforter in my hands as bliss ripples up and down my body.

Cameron stops sucking on my nipple and kisses his way up my neck and whispers in my ear some more. "You looked so innocent and sweet in your wedding dress. But you and I both know you're just a filthy little slut. Don't we?"

I wasn't expecting the switch from loving to dirty talk, and my body hums in response. I speak in a normal tone so the other men can hear me clearly. "Yes, I'm a filthy slut who wants to be used."

The guy in my pussy takes my announcement to heart and speeds up, while the guy sucking on my tit tugs on my nipple with his mouth while I groan.

Cameron chuckles and uses a normal tone of voice again. "Well, in that case, open your mouth wide. Brad is going to shove his cock down your throat, and you're going to show everyone how well you can suck while getting your pussy pounded."

My mouth falls open from shock, but Cameron takes that as obedience, and he nudges the side of my head. I turn my face away from him as the bed jostles and a guy kneels next to me. As I wrap my lips around his fat cockhead and suck, my brain really does switch off. I become the fucktoy I wanted to be tonight.

The guy's cock is salty with pre-cum, and I gurgle happily around his thickness as the guy in my pussy speeds up more. He's plowing into me, knocking me around on the bed. The guy in my mouth buries his cock to the hilt, and I relax my throat so I don't gag on him. He pulls out and I try to keep the suction up so he can't remove his cock. He rewards me by sliding it back down my throat.

Cameron plays with my nipple, and I move a hand up to try and stroke his cock through his pants. "Oh no you don't." He laughs and pushes my hand away from his crotch.

I try to pout, but with the thick cock in my mouth, it's impossible. The pleasure builds, and I'm getting close to my orgasm. The massive cock inside me jerks a few times and a warmth floods my pussy. Ohhh, he came! The guy fucks me for a moment longer, pumping everything he's got before he climbs off.

The guy's cum slides out of me, and Cameron reaches down between my legs and massages some of it into my clit. I moan "Oh my god" around the cock in my mouth as his fingers create pings of bliss in my core.

"You like that, my slut?" Cameron growls.

I mewl out a tiny "Yes" as best I can, while someone else climbs between my legs.

This next guy doesn't tease me or wait, and I cry out from the sudden invasion of his savage thrusts. He's not as thick as the last guy, but he's still a good size, and he hammers away at my pussy while the guy in my mouth speeds up his face fucking. The first spurt of his cum hits the back of my throat as he groans.

I lick and suck for all I'm worth, trying to get all the cum. The guy at my breasts stops sucking, and when the cock from my mouth pulls out, I can tell the guy who was at my breast is next in line to use my mouth.

The absolute filthiness of the situation tips me over the edge as another cock eases between my lips. I buck and scream with pleasure as he fills my throat with his shaft, and the guy between my legs enthusiastically fucks me as the orgasm ripples through me from my fingers to my toes. It's a strong one, and the aftershocks continue while my mouth and pussy get used.

Cameron whispers in my ear again. "Just think, baby. I could roll you over and fuck your ass right now, and all you would do is beg me to use you harder. Wouldn't you?"

I try to nod and say yes, but the cock in my mouth prevents me. Cameron laughs, as if he can see my predicament.

His voice is thick with desire. "In fact, Steph, you're such a fucking whore you'd let us all fuck your ass and you'd beg for seconds."

While the two guys fuck me, I imagine all the men lining up to use my ass. Oh god, he's right. What's worse... I want it. It's the ultimate way to be a fucktoy for the night. If this cock wasn't in my mouth, I would beg for it. Would Cameron let it happen?

My head whirls and another orgasm rips through me unexpectedly. I convulse from the energy and cry out around the cock in my mouth as the dude blows his load deep in my throat. I'm beyond caring about anything, and I lap and suck on this guy's cock while holding back my gleeful whimpers as the dude in my pussy fucks me rougher than anyone has ever fucked me.

When he shoves my knees to my chest, I welcome the position change. The angle makes the pleasure sharper as ecstasy courses through my body. The room fills with a chorus of moans and groans, and I'm chanting "Fuck me" as the guy removes his cock from my mouth. Within moments, the guy between my legs deposits his load of cum in my pussy as he growls out with his release.

Cameron grips my chin and turns my face towards him as he kisses me deeply, sucking at my lips and tongue that just cleaned off the other guy's cum. Oh hell, that's hot.

It barely registers when another guy climbs on the bed, and he keeps my knees up to my chest as he drills into my pussy. I thought the first guy was huge, but this new guy makes the first guy seem small. I groan as he stretches my pussy beyond anything I've ever felt before. It's a painful pleasure that I welcome. I never want this guy to stop fucking me.

I scream out a stream of obscenities as the dude hammers at my pussy. The delight is too intense, and I explode around his cock within a minute.

"Ohhhh, fuuuuuck," I scream as I come apart.

My pussy squeezes around him as he fucks me furiously, each thrust sending a heavy pair of balls whacking against my ass. A dangerous, alarming desire flits along the edge of my consciousness. I don't know that I want this to be only one time. This is so fucking incredible.

The gigantic dude in my pussy roars and paints my cave walls with load after load of hot cum. I'm a bundle of lust and desperate for more. I'm not surprised when he's immediately replaced with another guy. How many guys have fucked me? I think it was two in my mouth, and three or four in my pussy… If it's four, that means someone is coming back for more. A fuzziness washes over me when I realize they could keep using me like this for hours.

Cameron whispers, "I love you," and gets up on his knees. The familiar scent of him fills me as he pushes his cock between my lips and fucks my mouth at the exact pace and depth he knows I can withstand. He's the roughest of them, and I welcome his thrusts in my throat as the new guy in my pussy fucks me with abandon.

Someone's finger is on my clit, and I whimper around Cameron's cock as I edge close to another orgasm. Holy fuck, how many is this now? I try to count as I come again; this one is almost painful in intensity. They seem to build on each other, and as the blast overwhelms me, I scream out and stop thinking all together.

I'm floating in a daze and barely notice that Cameron doesn't come before he pulls out. Every inch of my body is teased and played with.

When someone fingers my ass, Cameron growls, "Stop. That's mine someday." The guy quickly removes his hand.

It's possible hours pass. Time has no meaning, but eventually the room goes silent as everyone but Cameron leaves. He tugs the blindfold off, and I blink in the soft lighting. He covers me and slides his cock between my sore and used folds as the soft joy surprises me.

He fucks me slowly and passionately, mixing all the men's cum with my juices as he drives his cock into my wet hole. He kisses me and murmurs that he loves me. I'm beyond coming again, but I welcome his orgasm when he finally climaxes with a groan.

He collapses on me and kisses my neck while I relax into the bed, totally spent.

"Steph, you were perfect and so goddamn lovely."

I try to lift an arm to caress his back, but I have no energy.

He twists off me. "You need a drink."

He helps me sit up, and a bottle of cool water touches my lips. I sip greedily, and after he sets it on the nightstand, he helps me nibble on some crackers he'd brought upstairs for this purpose.

The snack and water revive me a little, but I'm utterly exhausted and more in love with my husband than I've ever been in our entire marriage. This night was magnificent, and Cameron made it that way.

We snuggle, facing one another, and he brushes his thumb across my cheek. "Steph, you okay?"

I yawn and giggle. "Oh, yeah. I just need sleep... Was everyone pleased?"

He kisses my forehead. "Oh yeah, you definitely pleased them all. Now sleep, my princess, we can talk more in the morning."

I smile, already partway asleep. "Cameron?" I mumble.

"Yes, baby?"

I can tell I'm about to zonk out, but I want him to know something first. "Think it's time for you to claim my ass."

He laughs at that and pulls me closer to him. "Oh yeah, you're going to beg for it first. We'll talk about that in the morning as well."

"Sounds good," I mutter and fall asleep.

The End

Gratifying the Guys

Freeuse Wedding Party

Lacey Cross

CHAPTER 1

The smell of bacon lures me towards the kitchen while my mouth waters. My husband, Sebastian, woke up before me, and he's creating the delicious aroma throughout the house. Since he's going to the gym today, I didn't expect him to make breakfast — and definitely not bacon, since we usually only have it on the days we're staying home and being couch potatoes.

I'm happy he's still home, and I pull at the neckline of my t-shirt and bounce in my sneakers as I stroll into the kitchen. I've got an abundance of excess energy this morning, and I figured Sebastian had already left for the gym, so I'd planned to get a quick run in while he was gone. Now all I want to do is attack a pile of bacon and skip the run.

Sebastian's facing away from me, and I get a sexy view of his tight ass in his gray boxer briefs. All he's wearing are boxers and an apron.

Lust simmers in my gut as I press against him, fondle his buns, and kiss the back of his neck. "What's up, buttercup?"

I squeeze each ass cheek, and he moans, "You hungry?"

He asks as if he didn't already know he was going to share. We've been together six years now, and I don't think I've ever turned down bacon. I peek around his shoulder and he's dishing up two plates with scrambled eggs and toast. Mmm, yeah, that looks tasty, but so does his cute butt. It's a toss-up which I want more.

"I'm *starving*," I tease, exaggerating my words. "But *not* for food."

He laughs, moves out of my grasp, and carries the plates to the table. "Jasmine — babydoll — behave. We have a busy day."

I follow him and notice he'd already set glasses of water down for us before I got to the kitchen.

I fake grumble as I sit down. "Why did two of our friends choose the same weekend to get married?"

I'm not expecting him to answer, and he kisses my forehead before taking a seat and ravenously attacking his eggs and bacon. He doesn't seem interested in a quick fuck this morning. Bummer. Every Friday we usually fool around and fall asleep in a tangle of sweaty limbs, but that didn't happen last night. Vanessa, one of my closest friends, got married, and I was a bridesmaid with duties that kept me busy. By the time we got home from the wedding, we were exhausted and crashed.

We have another wedding to attend tonight, but thankfully I'm not in the bridal party. The plan is to drag Sebastian to the dance floor and grind against him long enough to convince him to cut out early. It's been a long week of no nookie. I'm working on my doctorate degree in psychology, so between my schooling and him working, this babydoll needs to get stuffed tonight.

I eat slowly, watching him in my peripheral vision. I want to untie that silly apron, climb into his lap, and go to town on Willy — the pet name I gave his cock because it makes me giggle every time I say it.

"Did you like the wedding last night?" he asks.

I shrug. "It was fun. Vanessa and Mason looked happy."

I take a sip of water and almost spit it out at his next question.

"Do you know what freeuse is?" he asks casually, like he just heard about a new trend on social media.

My mind goes blank. I know exactly what it is from Vanessa and my other friend, Nadia, but what does he know about it?

"Um, yes... But I've never done it or even thought of doing it, so..."

Yeah, that's a lie. As soon as Nadia told me she and her husband had been messing around with freeuse weekends, I researched the kink. I've been fantasizing about doing it with Sebastian. I'm just so dang busy, I don't have time to give up a weekend to let him use me whenever he wants.

He shovels the last bite of egg into his mouth and gets up to put his dirty dishes in the sink. When he comes back to the table, he leans in, his lips mere inches from my ear, and he speaks softly. "Would you like to be my freeuse slut?"

His breath on my neck sends a shiver through me and I match the tone of his voice, whispering, "Yes."

I'm not done eating, but the food is all but forgotten as I tilt my head up. He searches my face, as if he's trying to determine whether I'm serious. A low hum of desire burns in me. I'll do whatever it takes to get his wonderful cock inside me today. He peers down at my chest and then back up, making me fidget.

"The guys were talking about it at the wedding. Can we try it today?" he asks hoarsely.

Knowing he was probably talking to Nadia's husband, and possibly the groomsmen from last night who fucked Vanessa, gives me a rush. I've heard the tales from the women's side of the story, and I wonder what their hubbies told Sebastian. Not that it matters, as long as he fucks me.

My voice sounds breathy when I answer. "Yes, but only today. I have classwork to finish tomorrow."

Even as I tell him I'm busy, I know that if he woke me up tomorrow morning by fucking me, I'd lie there, loving it.

He kisses my temple. "Then finish eating so I can use you."

I grin and take a big bite of egg, chewing dramatically. I expect him to go do something else, but he stays where he is, watching me like a hawk. A flush creeps up my neck, and it's difficult to swallow. Is he going to stand there the entire time? It seems like he's toying with me, and my pussy throbs in response to remind me we enjoy being toyed with.

There's no way I'm going to finish my food, so I stand up and push my chair in. He'll probably drag me to the bedroom as soon as I set the plate in the sink. Before I can pick up my dishes, he steps behind me and applies pressure to my shoulder, forcing me to bend over the table, directly onto my dirty plate. Uh, what the fuck?

He removes the glass of water and sets it on the counter, and I stay smooshed into the plate. This is a new experience. He's never shoved me into food before. Is this even sexy?

When he comes back, he forces his hardness against my ass. His hands slide under my shirt around the sides, and he lifts me up a little and cups my breasts through my sports bra. Okay, I take it back. This is hot. I whimper, and my pussy lights up as he removes his hands from my shirt and presses me back down onto the wooden surface. Why is this turning me on?

I wiggle against one of his hands as he skims it over my stretch pants and rubs between my legs. I gasp when he spanks me, hard, and the sharp pleasure makes me tingle.

"Don't move. Pretend like I'm not doing anything."

Um… I'm squished against my unfinished breakfast, and I'm supposed to pretend nothing out of the ordinary is going on?

He nudges his cock against my ass again and I arch my back and moan loudly, "Please."

When he slaps my ass again, I whimper. Oh shit! He's gonna do it again. My body trembles as anticipation builds.

"Babydoll, you don't seem to understand. You're my fucktoy today, and I told you to pretend nothing is going on."

Desire ripples through me. I think too much all the time, and the rare occasions I can let go and become a fucktoy are amazing. Maybe freeuse will get me in the right mindset to shut my brain off.

His fingers slip into the waistband of my pants and panties and drag them down. He only gets them as far as my knees before stopping. I'm still wearing my running shoes, so getting them off my feet would have been a challenge. I moan from arousal as he slides his hand between my legs and rubs my clit.

He presses two fingers into my pussy. "Do you realize the power you gave me today?"

I moan louder, but don't answer.

He continues. "I'm going to use you whenever I want, however I want, wherever I want, and you're going to just take it."

Oh, fuck, that's hot. My head spins as he finger fucks me roughly. Spikes of bliss swirl in my stomach, and I peep out in distress when he pulls his hand away. Dammit, it was just getting good.

He tugs on my shoulder, indicating he wants me to stand, and the plate sticks to my shirt for a moment and clatters to the table as I rise. My shirt is a fucking mess, and I almost laugh while he turns me around to face him. He lifts my chin with his hand and stares at me intensely as he steps close enough that his cock presses against my stomach. While I was bent over, he removed the apron and pulled his boxers down far enough to free Willy, and his skin is warm and smooth.

Sebastian crushes his lips to mine, and I open up and welcome his seeking tongue. He holds me against him, kissing me with such passion, and I feel dizzy from the lack of oxygen.

When he breaks off the kiss, he says, "You are a freeuse slut. Now say it."

I nod as a shimmer of yearning grips me. I need his cock so badly.

"Say it," he commands.

"I'm a freeuse slut."

"Good girl."

I almost moan at his approval. I glance over my shoulder at the mess we made of the table and squeal when he picks me up and sets me on the edge. He removes my sneakers, one by one, dropping them to the floor with a thud, and pulls my pants and panties off the rest of the way.

"Put your foot on the chair and spread your legs," he orders, and I immediately obey.

I'm usually the dominant one in our sexual play, and I'm loving this side of him. Who knew my sweet buttercup had a tiger lurking in him?

He rubs my clit with his fingers again, and I cry out. I'm already wet and desperate for him. He pushes two fingers inside me, and I jerk against him, aching for more. He pushes my knees further apart and removes his hand, replacing it with the tip of his cock. As he sinks into me, my body instinctively clenches around him.

"Oh god!"

He grins wickedly at my reaction. "Does my freeuse slut like this?"

Calling me his freeuse slut and not by my name sinks me further into the mindset I crave.

"Yes," I groan as I grip the edge of the table and rotate my hips, trying to rub his shaft against my cave walls.

He pushes me down until I'm on my back as he strokes in and out. My dirty plate is half under me, but I don't care. My whole body is buzzing as pleasure builds in my core, and I whimper with each movement.

He grabs ahold of my hips as he speeds up and starts talking dirty.

"Does my fucktoy like this?" He doesn't give me time to respond as he hammers against me. "Your pussy feels so damn good."

I moan, "Yes."

"Is my slut ready to come?"

I squeeze my eyes shut and hold on to the edge of the table firmly, rocking my hips with every deep plunge of his cock.

I'm so close, and when he thrusts harder, I moan, "Yesssss," in one long breath. I don't want him to stop, and I chant "Fuck me" as my thigh muscles tense, welcoming the bliss.

He's fucking me so hard, the table squeaks, and my sighs and moans join his panting as I spiral higher and higher.

I'm almost lost in delight when he says, "Come for me, babydoll."

I scream out, "Oh... my... god!" as my orgasm rips through me.

My heart is racing as I luxuriate in the sweet sensation. A few more strokes later, he groans and his cock twitches while he blows his load. He shudders and pumps into me as I drift in a haze of sexual delight. When he pulls out, I take a few seconds to realize he's done with me.

I lift my lashes and he's gazing down at me with love.

"Wow," I murmur softly.

"Babydoll, this is only the beginning. I've got all day to use you."

Desire races through my veins as I grin at him. "Sounds good to me."

He helps me to a sitting position and kisses my forehead. "I'm going to get cleaned up and go to the gym. Be a good girl while I'm gone."

As he leaves the kitchen, I study his sexy, naked ass, and cheerfully call out, "Aye aye, Captain."

My pussy throbs with the aftermath of my climax. Well, hell, if freeuse includes me having orgasms, I'm down for this every Friday or Saturday. Heck, we could call it Freeuse Friday. Mmm, yeah.

The food smeared across the table catches my attention, and I look down at my t-shirt and can't hold in my bark of laughter. Okay, I need to clean up the kitchen and shower. I'm one filthy slut.

CHAPTER 2

I tidy the kitchen and pop in a piece of spearmint gum from a pack on the counter. When Sebastian comes in to give me a quick kiss on his way out the door to the gym, he murmurs, "Mmm, minty," and tries to steal the gum from my mouth. Laughing, I swat him away. God, I love that goofball.

Taking my time in the shower, I daydream about how many times he's going to use me today. He usually comes home from the gym horny, so I bet I get it at least one more time before the wedding. Once I'm out of the shower and dry, I toss on my favorite sundress and prowl around the house with excess energy. I need to find something to do before Sebastian gets home since all I can think about is him walking in the door and bending me over the nearest surface.

When my phone rings, I see it's my best friend Stephanie calling, and I smile as I answer.

"Yo, bitch. What's up?"

I purposely pop my gum in her ear, hoping she laughs at me. When she says I'm never going to believe the morning she's had, I plop down on the couch. Oh, hell yeah, this is just the distraction I need. I'm still daydreaming about Sebastian coming home and fucking me, and I almost miss it when she tells me that her husband is going to have her fuck all his basketball friends tonight.

I screech, "No fucking way!" into the phone, and she sounds amused by my reaction.

What the hell? She's now my third friend who is doing a freeuse day that turned into some slutty gangbang. My pussy buzzes, and I space out, daydreaming about being double stuffed. Shit, that's hot. Where's my gangbang offer? I hold in a snort. No way in hell Sebastian would ever go for that, and I don't really need it since I'm having fun with this freeuse thing.

Stephanie and I chat for a bit. She sounds insecure about whether she's doing the right thing, and I assure her it's fine. Why didn't the guys tell Sebastian how wonderful it was to have their wife fuck a bunch of other dudes? Why focus only on the freeuse part? My pussy throbs again, and I rub my thighs together. Yeah, I need to stop thinking about a bunch of guys using me like a fucktoy. This is a quick road to nowhere.

I'm filling Stephanie in on the details of my kitchen romp when I hear Sebastian get home. Heck yeah, fun times are about to begin again.

I rush into the phone, "Ohhh, I gotta go. I just heard the garage door. Love you!" I disconnect the call right as Sebastian walks into the living room.

I grin at him. "Hi, sweet cheeks."

He comes over for a kiss. "Hi, babydoll. Did you miss me?"

"I missed you *soooo* much. I almost died of loneliness."

He sits on the couch next to me, and I rest against him.

"Hah, somehow I doubt it."

When he turns the TV on, I toss him the side-eye. Why isn't he fucking me yet?

"Did you get a good workout?"

He rolls his shoulders as he chooses a stand-up comedy show to stream. "I did. I'll be sore tomorrow, but it was worth it."

Hmm... fine, I guess we'll watch TV. We only have a couple of hours before we have to get ready for the wedding. But if it's his freeuse day, I have to just let him do whatever he wants... even if it isn't doing me. I cuddle closer to him, and he tugs me up into his lap so I'm sitting sideways with my legs stretched out along the cushions. A thrill runs through me. Ohhh, maybe I'm wrong, and he's going for it. He wraps his arms around me, pulling me close, and I feel him relax.

I wait expectantly for a solid minute, but he gets engrossed in the show. Ugh, fuck. Laying my head on his shoulder, I nuzzle his neck and breathe in deeply, taking in his scent. Some people find it odd when I say it, but I love the smell of Sebastian when he gets home from the gym. I try not to geek out on people about the psychology of how the scent of your partner relaxes you, but the quirks of the brain amaze me. But no matter the reason, if he comes home sweaty, I love cuddling with him as long as I can shower before I leave the house.

I give him a couple of neck kisses and turn my attention to the show. It's not my favorite comedian, but it's still funny, and I get sucked in and giggle along with Sebastian's deep laughs. I'm comfortable and don't pay attention to his hand tracing slow circles on my bare shoulder. The sundress I'm wearing leaves my shoulders and arms bare, so he has clear access to rub the length of my arm up to my neck.

After several minutes of stroking my skin, he repositions his legs and my ass comes into contact with his growing erection. I notice him glance down the valley of my cleavage and then back up to the TV. Well, well, well, he's not uninterested after all. My stomach flutters at the thought.

Sebastian's hand moves between my shoulder blades and traces the length of my spine. As his fingers trail down my back through the fabric of my dress, I shiver, and a gush of wetness hits my panties. This better be going in the direction I think it is. He keeps one hand on my back and places his other on my thigh. His fingers creep up my leg, giving me goosebumps, and I shift my body slightly to spread my legs wider and give him better access.

When he says, "Don't stop watching," my mind goes fuzzy as I try to concentrate on the show.

He moves his hand up, rubbing me through my panties, and I hold in a moan as my vision glazes over. Does he really expect me to watch the TV? I gasp when his fingers slide underneath the band of my panties to tease my slit, dipping inside my folds and sliding back out. I can't help myself; I try to grind against his hand.

"Babydoll, what are you doing?"

His tone says I'm misbehaving, so I peek up at him. He's watching the show, but I need him to fuck me, so I don't care if I'm being bad. He's hard enough, so I'm confident he's going to give me what I want no matter what I do.

I'm flippant in my reply. "I think you know."

The corners of his mouth twitch and he presses his lips to my hair. "You're such a naughty girl."

I writhe and moan, "Yes, now please fuck me."

Without looking away from the TV, he bounces me in his lap, causing his cock to rub against my pussy, and I moan louder.

His chuckle vibrates against my ear. "Keep that up, and I won't."

"Please, just fuck me already," I whimper in frustration.

"Tell me what you want, babydoll."

Didn't I just tell him? I shimmy my hips. "Fuck me, please."

"I think you forgot something. This isn't about what you want. Now keep watching the show."

Oh, fuck. I press my lips together to contain a whine and pretend to watch the show. He continues to bounce me in his lap, and I hold in my gasps and ignore the need to grind against him. Within a few minutes, I can't take much more of the torture. What sort of shitty freeuse day is this? Isn't he supposed to use me?

"Stand up a moment," he demands, and I'm disoriented as I do what he asks.

He takes his cock out of his sweatpants, slides his hands up the sides of my hips, and yanks my panties down. Mmm, yeah, this is getting good. They fall to the floor and I step out of them as he tugs me back into his lap, positioning me straight onto his cock. The tip slides inside me and gravity takes over, bringing me down until I'm balls deep.

"Ohhhh, god," I moan as delight ripples through me.

"Now watch the show, babydoll. This isn't about your enjoyment."

Fuck. Did the guys at the wedding tell him to treat me this way, or is this natural for him? I'm loving it, and keep my eyes trained on the TV as he holds onto my hips and forces me to rotate against his cock. I keep my hands in my lap, trying to pretend I'm not doing anything out of the ordinary. A small part of me feels like a dirty little whore from how he's treating me, and it turns me on even more. I shiver with excitement and bite my lip. I'm going to come soon at this rate.

Sebastian flexes his hips, speeding up his thrusts. Since he's not letting me move, he's staying fully sheathed, and the tip of his cock massages the pleasure points deep in my pussy. It's driving me wilder than if he was doing long strokes in and out.

The bliss builds, and I finally crack, wiggling against him with a groan. I undulate against his cock, trying to get him deeper inside me. The friction causes me to cry out loudly. I'm almost there. Just another minute.

He must be able to tell I'm about to climax because he wraps my hair around his fist, pulls my head up, and growls, "Watch the show, babydoll! Don't you dare come!"

Shit. I cry out again, and I quiver in anticipation as he thrusts harder and faster. He pulls me down against him until he's slamming into me. I feel his cock twitch right before he explodes. Ohhh, fuck... I haven't come!

He groans and pumps his seed deep inside me, and I whimper when the pleasure ends abruptly. I sag back onto his lap, and my pussy spasms from the denied orgasm. I'm crazy turned on and in shock that it's over. He lets go of my hair and rests his forehead on my back, sighing softly.

"Are you okay?" he murmurs into my hair.

"Yeah, but... I didn't finish," I whisper.

He lifts his head, brushes my hair to the side, and kisses the back of my neck. "I know, babydoll. But this is freeuse. Do you want to stop?"

I frown and look down at my hands, confused, and I'm not sure how I want to answer. "Am I going to come again today?"

He's quiet for a minute, as if he's thinking. "I'll tell you what, let's make a deal."

What's this? I perk up as he continues.

"I want you to do your old bimbo routine at the wedding tonight and get a bunch of guys panting after you. Then I'll bring you home and fuck you so hard you'll see stars."

I'm nodding before he even finishes, and my pussy clenches around his softening shaft. "Deal."

Chapter 3

The rest of the afternoon is a blur of activity as we both shower and get ready for the wedding. I planned to wear comfortable shoes to dance in, but now that I need guys drooling over me, I switch them out for some sexy, spiked heels. My dress is a gray, form-fitting number with a thigh slit; my toned runner's legs are one of my best features, so the dress looks amazing on me. I keep my long, platinum-blonde hair down in soft waves, and I'm extra careful with my makeup. When I'm done, I look and feel sexy.

In my early 20s, I used to get my kicks out of making guys think I was a bimbo. Sometimes I just wanted mindless sex and would choose a hot jock who looked like he was good for a night of fun, never letting on that everything I was doing was calculated to get him to fuck me. When we were done — usually a seedy encounter in a dirty bathroom — he thought he just scored with a hot bimbo, and I was content from my orgasm. I didn't realize what I was doing was a kink until later when I was researching a college project.

The funniest part is that it led me to Sebastian. He was one of my filthy bathroom conquests, but after he fucked me against the wall and gave me a mind-blowing orgasm, he turned apologetic like he had just done the most horrible thing ever by losing control. He was an adorable, lost puppy, but as soon as he started spiraling and said something about how he took advantage of me, I dropped the bimbo act. We ended up talking for hours at a bar, and we've been together ever since.

Occasionally, for fun, I pretend to be a bimbo again with him, and I found out that sex is more fulfilling when the person doesn't really think of you that way and you both know it's just an act. And hey, it keeps the spice alive. He's never asked me to act this way towards other people though, so tonight is something different. My pussy is still buzzing from the lack of orgasms, so I'm going to do whatever it takes to get that hard fucking, and I better see those stars he promised.

The wedding ceremony is beautiful and sentimental, but Sebastian's fingers caressing the skin of my thigh exposed by the slit in my dress distracts me the entire time. It's amusing that all the guests seem to be the same people we keep seeing at all these weddings. We're just one big group of friends, and only the relatives change. It already seems like eons ago, but Vanessa's wedding was only last night. Mason and Vanessa are off on some fancy, tropical honeymoon, but the rest of the wedding party is here.

Knowing that the groomsmen fucked her last night, I study them curiously. I wonder how many times they all came. Hell, how many times did SHE come? With that many cocks plowing into her, I'd guess it was at least three or four times. Maybe some of them came over her. Ooooh, maybe it turned into a circle jerk with her on the floor. Fuck, that's hot, especially if she was in her wedding dress. I twist in my seat, trying to find some relief for the ache between my legs, and I can tell that I'm flushed. It's not from the crowded, warm room, but if anyone noticed, they might think it was.

When the ceremony ends, people get up to head into the hotel's reception hall, but Sebastian leans over and whispers in my ear. "You seemed a little worked up during the ceremony. What were you thinking about?"

My brain freezes, and my lips part. Do I tell him I was thinking about a circle jerk and wondering how many orgasms Vanessa had last night? I'm not sure he's ready to hear every filthy thought in my head, so I shrug and play it cool. "Nothing."

He shoots me a roguish grin. "No, it wasn't nothing. If you want to come tonight, you'll tell me."

Ugh. I could lie... fuck it, why bother? I turn towards him, give a slow smile, and this time it's me who moves in close to his ear. I kiss his earlobe, and gently tug the flesh between my teeth, knowing it makes him shiver.

My breath is a soft puff when I purr. "I was imagining a circle jerk of men ejaculating on me."

He pulls back and gapes at me. "Were they jerking each other off, or only themselves?"

I have to hold in my laugh. That's the first thing that pops into his head?

"I wasn't paying attention. I was waiting for the splashes of cum to coat me."

He looks like he's digesting the thought, and then he shrugs. "I bet they were only touching themselves."

Oh my God, his wife says she's daydreaming about a group of guys coming all over her, and all he can think about is whether the dudes are crossing swords? Shit, this is why I love him.

I slide my hand into his and squeeze it. "Sweet cheeks, let's go dance, so I can play the bimbo and get fucked hard."

He stands and gives me an answering grin. "I just needed a moment to process. Come to find out, I married a slut who wants to be covered in cum."

I laugh loudly. "Oh honey..." I pull him towards the exit. "I haven't even told you about my double-stuff fantasy from earlier. You married a super slut."

The reception has barely started, but I excuse myself and leave Sebastian at a table while I follow a pack of women to the restroom. I'm not watching where I'm going and run into someone coming out of the bathroom.

I wobble and almost tip into the wall, blindly apologizing. "Oh shit, I'm sorry!"

A light, feminine laugh that I'd recognize anywhere rings out. "Don't worry about it, Jasmine. I'm impressed you can walk in those heels."

Millie, one of my close friends, grins at me. She was another one of Vanessa's bridesmaids. I hadn't noticed she was here tonight, despite knowing she planned to attend. She and her husband must have been sitting behind us.

I rotate my leg to show off the thigh slit and my sexy shoes. "I'm seducing Sebastian tonight. This outfit is my secret weapon."

"Somehow I doubt you need much help to seduce him." She laughs again, and I lower my voice.

"We're playing with a freeuse day."

She tilts her head and raises an eyebrow. "That's different from usual?"

"Yep. I'm going to put on a bimbo show to get him worked up, and then he can fuck me as hard as he wants." I smile at her. "It should be interesting."

Her brow furrows slightly. "Well, I hope you get your orgasm. Freeuse sounds fun for the user, but not so much for the usee."

I giggle. "Yeah, I already didn't come once today. I'm banking on me being so turned on that I explode as soon as he fucks me again."

I can tell she's puzzled as we say goodbye. Not everyone understands the appeal of being used like a sex toy, and that's fine. It's good I didn't mention the circle jerk fantasy.

After a glass of wine and a slow dance of rubbing against Sebastian, he pulls me off the dance floor and out to a quiet side hallway. He kisses me softly, and I sway towards him. This is nice, but I can't spend all night snogging him. I haven't found an opportunity yet to follow his instructions.

"Don't you want me to flirt with other guys?"

"Mmm, yes. I want you to be my horny slut tonight, so I'm working you up."

God, why do I love it so much when he calls me filthy things?

Leaning in, I give him a hard kiss. "Then let's go back to the party so I can slut it up."

He laughs. "One thing first. I'm going to sit and watch you flirt with other guys, but while you're doing it, I want you to think about the guy standing over you and jerking off."

All thoughts drain from my head while I stare at him and blink. When I can think again, my senses buzz alive with a whoosh. My nipples pucker, and I feel myself growing more wet. My entire body tingles. Holy fuck, that's dirty and I love it.

He must be able to tell he stunned me for a moment because he laughs again and kisses my nose. "Can you do that for me?"

I nod. Fuck yeah, I can. "It's going to be rough, but a girl's gotta do what a girl's gotta do."

He cups my ass and squeezes it. "Go find someone to flirt with while I visit the restroom."

Nodding and smiling, I take a deep breath and turn away from him to go find a potential flirt-buddy.

Once I'm out of his sight, I run into Cameron and Stephanie leaving early. She's living her best life because I know she is having sex with a bunch of guys tonight. I'm having fun with Sebastian and this playful side of him, but would he ever consider sharing me? I think I need to ease him into the idea. He's the type of guy who likes to think about things for a while and isn't one to jump headfirst into anything... unless it's fucking a bimbo in the bathroom years ago, but even then, he felt horrible afterwards.

I down another glass of wine and grab the closest cute guy I can find to dance with. The next hour is a blur of flirting and dancing, but I'm hyper aware of all the guys looking at me. I'm attracting interest because of my outfit and how free I am with my attention. I make sure that every time I dance with a guy, it's within Sebastian's view from the table where he's sitting, and I purposely touch the men's shoulders or brush against them as we're dancing. None of the guys seem aware of what I'm doing, which is fine with me, but the longer it goes on, the more Sebastian looks hot under the collar. He's getting turned on by this, and knowing that gets me even more excited. It's an amusing feedback loop of eroticism.

I'm dancing with one of Sebastian's closest friends, Brian, when I realize my husband isn't sitting and watching me anymore. Where did he go? I look around the crowd of people and spot him resting against the wall near one exit, talking with two guys. Both of them are wearing suits. They look familiar, but their backs are to me so I can't tell who they are at first. Oh wait, I know who they are. They're the groomsmen who fucked Vanessa last night.

A vision of them spurting cum all over her makes my heart race, and I feel my face heat. It seems fucked up to be picturing my friend getting jizzed on. I plan on asking her how she liked her night with the guys the next time I talk to her, and hopefully I don't run off at the mouth and ask whether she was covered in cum in the end.

I'm distracted by my naughty thoughts when Brian and I stop dancing. I step away, smiling at him, and as we weave through the crowd of couples dancing, my gaze drifts past him. It lands on the two groomsmen. Dang, they're handsome guys. Vanessa got lucky.

One of them — David — turns to look at me, and his eyes meet mine. His mouth splits into a wide grin, and I'm immediately paranoid. What is Sebastian telling them? Is he saying that I'm his freeuse slut tonight?

I hope he is.

My breathing quickens. Is this crazy? I want my husband to spread it around that I'm his freeuse slut. I probably need therapy. Just because I'm getting a doctorate in psychology doesn't mean I'm not just as messed up as the next person.

I watch them talk for a moment, and I daydream again. This time it's not Vanessa getting covered in cum. It's me. Yeah... I'm such a slut. I'm getting turned on even more thinking about my husband sharing me.

David's mouth moves like he's saying something to Sebastian, but he keeps his eyes glued to mine. He beams a smile at me, and when I smile back, he turns to Sebastian and the other guy. I try to focus on Brian, but I can't stop staring at the men talking to Sebastian. My legs tremble, making me wobble in my shoes.

"Jasmine, you okay?" Brian's hand touches my arm, and he pulls me out of my perverted trance.

I think the wine and dancing got to my head because I shake my head and blurt out, "I was just daydreaming about my husband sharing me with other guys."

"Oh." He frowns and rubs his chin. "I didn't know you guys had an open marriage."

"We don't..." I let my voice trail off.

He sighs and I can tell he's disappointed. "Guess Sebastian gets you all to himself tonight."

Wait, what? This is Sebastian's best friend. My mouth flops open like a fish, and I don't know how to respond. Brian wishes he could fuck me? But... But... What? Did Sebastian say something to him?

I glance over at Sebastian, who is still talking with his friends. He's animated, and his eyes sparkle. He looks like he's having a great conversation. God, I need to sit down.

Brian follows me as I beeline to the nearest table and slide into a chair.

"Are you okay?" he asks.

I wave him off. "I'm fine, just a little tipsy."

He looks towards Sebastian. "If you're sure you're fine, I'm going to go talk with the guys."

I tell him to go have fun, and I rest my elbow on the table and put my chin in my hand. This night has taken a very odd turn. I feel like a voyeur, watching my husband and wondering what they're all saying. I'm secretly hoping it's about me and my sluttiness. I mean, I have been fantasizing about him sharing me with other guys. It's not like it'll really happen, so why does it feel so wrong in a deliciously naughty way?

I'm still daydreaming when Sebastian joins me. He bends down, gives me a deep kiss, and pulls me to my feet.

"Jasmine, I've got a new offer for you."

I tilt my head back in surprise. "What?"

"If you really want a bunch of guys to come all over you, I have volunteers."

My pussy clenches, and a ripple of desire swirls low in my belly. I shake my head. Fuck, I'm dreaming and just imagined Sebastian offering to share me.

When I don't reply, a huge grin spreads across his face, and he raises his eyebrows suggestively at me. "Come on, Jasmine. You said you wanted a bunch of guys to cover you with cum, right?"

A blush creeps up my face. Did I actually say that, or did I tell him I was imagining Vanessa covered in cum? Shit, now I don't remember. Obviously, he understood I was thinking about myself.

I nod but say nothing. I'm too flabbergasted by the turn of events, and I don't want to admit how much I want him to share me in case he's teasing me.

He leans closer, and I can smell the cologne he wears. It smells masculine and spicy.

He holds my waist and pulls me towards him. "Say it, Jasmine. Say you want my friends to cover you with cum."

His breath tickles my neck, and I shiver.

"Yes," I whisper. "I want your friends to come all over me."

Sebastian croons, "Good slut," and kisses me softly. "You've been a good girl tonight. I think you deserve a reward."

I like the way he's thinking. He pulls me out of the room, into the hallway, and keeps walking. Where is he taking me?

He pauses in front of a door. "Babydoll, my friends are waiting on the other side of this door. Do you really want this?"

I swallow hard. My heart races and my skin tingles. I want this so badly.

"Yes, please." I squeeze his arm and nod.

His eyes crinkle with amusement. "Do you want more than a circle jerk?"

My mouth forms an O. Uh... I take a few seconds to reply. "What do you mean, more?"

He licks his lips and grins wickedly. "I've been imagining watching them fuck you. Free pass tonight. Do you want it?"

Holy shit! "Just for tonight, right? This changes nothing?"

That makes him laugh. "Oh, it changes something. I'm going to have an amazing memory to jack off to."

This seems crazy and totally unlike him. Who knows if he'll ever be in this mood again. Fuck it, I'm not passing up this chance.

"I'm game if you are."

He kisses my nose. "As long as I get to watch them fuck you, I'm game."

Oh, I'm totally on board with this. I take his hand and squeeze it. "Bring it on."

CHAPTER 4

Four guys wait in the room for us: Brian, David, David's twin brother, Leo, and their other friend, Aaron. I hadn't seen Aaron at the reception, so I don't know how he got involved with this, but I'm not going to question my good fortune. He's gorgeous, and I always thought he seemed like a sweetheart of a guy.

The room is a fancy office with a couch along one wall. I'm fairly certain we're not supposed to be in here and I don't know how they got the key. But, again, no questions. This is better than a dirty bathroom, so I'm not one to be picky.

The guys all look at me, and I suddenly feel shy. What do I say to them? Welcome to my pussy, I hope you enjoy it? Yeah... no.

I squeak out, "Hi, guys."

Sebastian closes the door and locks it, then walks over to the desk and pulls the office chair to a corner before sitting down.

"Babydoll, give me a striptease."

He motions to me, and I walk over and stand in front of him.

"Remove your clothes."

I take a deep breath and turn, presenting my back to Sebastian so he can unzip my dress. It feels like it takes forever for him to work the zipper, and when he finally does, the sound is louder than normal. I turn back around to face him again and shrug my dress off, letting it pool on the floor before kicking it aside.

Sebastian's voice is rough. "All of them."

I unfasten my strapless bra and toss it on top of my dress. I slide my panties down, bending over to step out of them carefully because I still have my high heels on. The men behind me are getting a very graphic view of my wet pussy, and it makes me feel like even more of a slut.

I'm naked except for my shoes. I stand up straight, waiting to see if he tells me to take them off as well. He doesn't.

"Turn around." His voice is deep and powerful.

This feels so naughty, but I love it. Turning around, I face the other men and shake my ass at Sebastian. He fondles me for a moment.

"Damn, babydoll, you're so fucking sexy. Now go suck on David's cock."

A delicious hunger for the forbidden quickens my pulse at his words. Fuuuuck, that's hot.

David sits down on the couch and unzips his pants, pulling his cock out. I can't fucking believe I'm about to suck off one of Sebastian's friends. I kneel between David's legs and grip the base of his shaft, hovering my mouth over the tip. David presses my head down gently, and I fit my lips around his cock, needing no further encouragement. His shaft is pleasantly thick, and I waste no time getting into it as I bob up and down on him, sucking greedily, making sure everyone sees me deep-throating his cock.

I hear one guy groan, and it makes me more excited. For all I know, this could just be a normal weekend night for them all, but this is something I've never done before, and the experience is surreal. When I woke up this morning, I never imagined the evening would end this way.

I suck him for a while, and he moves his hips, fucking my throat.

"Fuck yeah, Jasmine. You're so good." David's voice is husky, and I can hear the excitement in his tone.

I moan around his cock, loving the feel of him in my mouth. As I suck him, I rub the base of his shaft with one hand and slip my other hand between my legs. I'm dripping wet, and I groan as my fingers find my clit. I'm desperate to come, but the party just started.

Sebastian calls out, "I think someone needs to fuck her while she's being such a good girl sucking on David."

My body stiffens from shock at his words, and I catch movement out of the corner of my eye as Aaron moves behind me, kneeling down. I hear clothes rustle and a zipper. Oh fuck, this really is going to happen. My pussy clenches and I moan louder around David's cock.

I can't believe I'm going to be fucked by another man in front of my husband. Aaron caresses my ass, and I stop rubbing my clit and reposition my knees to spread open further for him.

David grabs the back of my head and fucks my face as Aaron pulls my hips towards him. He reaches through my legs and slips his fingers inside me, pumping slowly. I whimper and swirl my tongue around the cock in my mouth. I'm so close to coming, but I need more.

"Fucking hell, you're so wet," he says.

Aaron slides his fingers out of me and reaches to the front of me to grab my tits. He squeezes them roughly, and I cry out around the shaft in my throat.

"I'm going to fuck you now." He runs his fingers through my hair and pulls my head back, forcing me to release David's cock from my mouth. Shit, I thought Aaron was going to be the gentle one.

"Ohhh god, yes." I try to move my hips towards him, wanting his cock in me.

Aaron lets go of my hair, holds onto my hips, and with one swift thrust, he impales me. Aaron's cock is huge — bigger than I expect — and I scream in surprise when intense pleasure rockets through me as he stretches me apart.

"Fuck yeah, Jasmine." He pounds into me harder, and I affix my lips around David's cock again.

I want to be spit-roasted and ping-ponged between them. I want to be ridden hard and taken by all the men. I want to be used like a cocksleeve. And in the end, I want them to jerk off on me. Fuck, I want this so bad.

David's hands are on the sides of my head, holding me still while Aaron fucks me hard and fast. I'm spinning out of control, and I can barely breathe. When Aaron slams into me extra hard, a rush of elation floods me as I climax.

"Oh fuck!" I scream, but it's garbled by David's cock.

Aaron groans and pulls out right before he comes. David releases my head and removes his cock from my mouth. Neither of them filled me with their cum. I sit up. Ugh, what is going on?

Sebastian claps. "Nice show."

I give him a questioning look over my shoulder.

He smiles. "No one gets to come until the end. They're going to use you for as long as they can and then you're going to get your wish of being covered in their cum."

I shake my head. "I'm not going to last that long."

He laughs. "That's fine. Your goal is to come as many times as you can. They're the only ones who can't."

Oh, fuck yes. Multiple orgasms for me!

Sebastian still plays director. "Get up and bend over the desk."

Yeah, I like where this is going. Luckily, the desk is mostly clear. I bend over it and give a silent apology to whoever's office this is.

"Now spread your legs wide."

I space them apart, knowing how obscene this looks. My pussy is so wet, I can feel the drops running down my inner thighs. I love how turned on I am, knowing I have four hot men lined up to use me.

Leo stands behind me and rubs my ass cheeks. "You're fucking perfect, Jasmine," he murmurs.

I whimper, enjoying his hands on my body. I've always had a soft spot in my heart for Leo. He's David's twin, but David is the fit one and Leo reminds me of just a normal dad type, albeit a pretty dang cute one.

His cock is already hard and out of his pants as he brushes it against my butt. He holds onto my ass cheeks and separates them, and I imagine he's examining me. I squirm from embarrassment. Somehow, it's worse when I think someone is inspecting my holes.

When he dips a finger into my pussy, as if he's testing my wetness, I moan and bump against him. He quickly replaces his finger with the tip of his cock, and I barely have time to register the change before he plunges his length into my eager pussy. I arch my back from the pleasure and try to hold in a groan. He grabs onto my waist as he drills into me, and I whimper as he goes deeper.

"This feels amazing," he pants.

I give a tiny nod, even though he probably can't see it, and push my butt towards him, wanting him to fuck me harder. He takes the hint, ramming into me, and I gasp as he shoves me against the desk. My nipples scrape the surface and I stretch my arms straight out so I can hold on to the far edge. My legs quiver as he hammers into my pussy, each thrust jolting me against the desk.

"Ohhh, god," I moan, and my pussy clenches around his cock as he works me into a frenzy.

I lose track of time as he uses me like the fucktoy I am. Each whack against my pussy spirals me higher and higher. The desk creaks as he slaps against me, and the other guys moan as if they're beating off while watching Leo plow into me.

I almost come from the thought, and when my husband calls out, "Come for us, babydoll," Leo's grunt and hard thrusts tip me over the edge.

My whole body shakes as I scream from the intense orgasm, and multiple guys groan with me. Leo fucks me for a bit longer before abruptly pulling out. The room tilts, and I'm lightheaded as more wetness leaks down my leg. It's only my juices since Leo didn't come.

Resting the side of my face against the surface of the desk, I wait for whoever is next. I think Brian is the only one who hasn't taken a turn with me yet, and I glance over my shoulder as he approaches. I don't have time to congratulate myself on being correct because his cock is out and pressing against my sodden hole. He slowly works it into me, and I whimper as my cave walls stretch around him.

When he holds onto my hips and fucks me at a steady pace, a tremor of awareness runs through me. Brian is the one man I never dared allow myself to think about fucking. He's Sebastian's best friend, and we get together with him regularly. Of all my husband's friends, he is the most off-limits, and I fit around his cock like it was made for me. His cock is bigger than my husband's, and the curve of it massages the perfect spot deep inside. I'm going to climax quickly and there's no way to stop it. Oh fuck, now I'm going to be thinking about this every time I see him. It might have been better not knowing how well we fit together.

A strong slap on my ass breaks my thought process, and I buck my hips and cry out from the pain. Why am I being spanked? Brian speeds up the pace of his thrusts and spanks the other cheek. Ohhh, shit. I've never been one to crave being spanked, but somehow, with Brian, it feels natural. Yeah, this is dangerous.

Gripping the edge of the desk, I focus on the sensations swirling inside me. I'm still sensitive from my last orgasm, so I know there's no way I'll make it more than a few minutes without coming again. I grind my hips back into him, desperate for release.

"Fuck me harder," I beg, and he does.

Brian thrusts his hips faster and harder, and I throw my head back from the sheer joy his cock is creating inside me. I can feel the heat rising in my body as I prepare to come again. I squeeze tight around him and rotate my ass, wishing I could milk all his cum out of him. Originally, I wanted them to come on me, but now the idea of him filling me up sounds even better.

Brian groans and pounds into me harder. "Oh fuck, Jasmine, I'm gonna come."

I tense up, waiting for him to explode.

"Stop!" Sebastian growls.

Oh, shit. That's right. He can't come! At the very last second, Brian pulls out and stumbles away, cursing at himself for his lack of control.

Since Brian didn't actually come, Sebastian seems amused and chuckles, "That was a close one."

He gets out of his chair and stands behind me. Uh, is he going to fuck me in front of everyone? My body tenses up, expecting the head of his cock to probe my pussy at any second, but he slides his fingers inside me instead, and I relax.

"Just checking their work." His tone is jolly as he continues to rub me. "I need to be sure you're wet."

He can probably see the wetness on my thighs, so his excuse is flimsy. Not that I care. He can say whatever he wants if he works those clever fingers inside me some more. He caresses my clit with one hand while finger fucking me with the other, and the bliss builds again. My legs tremble as tension coils low in my belly, and all my muscles tighten as I edge towards release. Oh god, he better not stop.

I whimper as he presses hard on my clit and massages my inner walls with his fingers. My breath is ragged, and my eyes shut as I teeter on the brink of coming. Every part of me buzzes with joy as the intensity increases. I'm panting and mewling with each brush of his fingers as he plays my body as only he knows how from years of experience.

When he speeds up his finger fucking, I can't take it anymore and I come, screaming in delight as a soul-shattering orgasm robs me of my senses. The ecstasy continues to crest as he strokes his fingers into my pussy, and stars explode behind my eyelids.

"Ohhh fuck!" Another surge of pleasure rushes over me, and my brain melts. I can't tell where one peak ends and the next one starts, and the orgasm seems never ending as I ride his hand.

At some point I realize he removed his fingers, and my climax fades to soft aftershocks. Jesus, I don't know the last time I came that hard from just fingers, though I can't remember ever being this worked up. I'm so relaxed, I almost forget the other guys are in the room until one of them tugs me to a standing position and turns me around.

I gaze into Aaron's fierce expression, and my heart flutters with excitement. I don't know if I can come again, but it looks like he's not done with me. He picks me up and sets me on the edge of the desk and pushes my shoulders down.

He presses my knees towards my chest as I stare up at the ceiling. No one is asking permission or checking to see if I'm okay, and even though I know I can use Sebastian's and my safeword and all of this would stop, I don't want it to. I'm their sex doll tonight, and I welcome Aaron's meaty cock as he sinks into me again.

Since I still have my shoes on, I know this is probably quite the sight with me on the desk as a sexy dude fucks me. I try to picture it as if I was an outsider watching a porno. Shit, I wish we had this on video.

Aaron continues to plow into me, and when he presses my knees closer to my chest, my brain switches off again. I keep my eyes closed and drift in a daze of hedonism, unaware of anything but the all-over ripples of bliss. At some point, the other guys rotate in and replace Aaron, but I don't care who it is. No one cock is better than another anymore, and it's just continuous rapture.

I'm surprised when I realize no one is between my legs. It's over? I relax and look over at Sebastian, noting the adoration shining from him. My heart pounds, and I'm consumed with passion. I love this man with all of my heart. He's my "one," no matter how good the other cocks felt.

He walks over and holds me steady as he helps me stand up. My legs wobble in my heels, and I would have stumbled if he hadn't been supporting me. I wrap my arms around his waist and tip my head up for a kiss. He brushes his lips against mine, tenderly. Mmm, this is exactly what I need.

I'm still dazed, and murmur, "Thank you."

"You're welcome, love." He kisses me again, and I smile against his lips.

He pulls away from me and turns to the others. "Well, gentlemen, are you ready?"

They all nod while David states, "Oh yeah, I'm ready to come."

All the guys have their cocks out. Oh god, this is actually going to happen. I flush as I think about the vulgarity of what I'm about to do.

Sebastian steps aside and motions towards the floor. "Time for you to lie down and get your reward."

I'm vibrating with desire, and my mind goes blank as I catch David ogling me. He's rubbing himself slowly with pure lust radiating from him. Sebastian helps me kneel on the floor and I stretch out on my back, looking up at the men as they surround me and stroke their cocks.

"You're a beautiful woman," David groans as he tugs on his shaft faster.

A shiver of anticipation runs through me. I'm nervous and excited. Do I dare keep my eyes open? I watch, fascinated, as the guys moan, each one doing what he prefers. David beats his cock furiously, but Brian's hand moves with long and slow caresses. Leo's cock jerks in his fist, and Aaron's strokes are firm and purposeful.

"I'm going to come," David growls, and I watch his hand on his cock until I'm positive he's going to explode.

I close my eyes as he moans, and a splatter of wetness hits my face. David coming is the trigger for all the guys. A chorus of groans and grunts fills the air as their cum jets over my body. I imagine it's just a shower of cum, despite knowing it's probably only a few spurts each; fantasizing that I'm being coated in their seed is utterly filthy. As each drop lands on me, it reinforces the thought that I'm being painted in cum.

I'm lost in the debasement of the moment, and I don't realize they've stopped until I hear their clothes rustling as they put their cocks away.

Aaron says, "Fuck, Jasmine. That was wonderful."

I smile at all the men while they each thank me. I'm too dizzy to stand up, and I drift in a warm, happy place as the men talk in low voices. The office door opens and then shuts, and I feel a presence standing over me. I crack my eyes open. Sebastian and I are alone, and he's staring down at me with a glaze of desire.

"What now?" I ask, my voice barely a whisper.

He takes my hands, helping me get up. "You're a naughty girl, aren't you?"

I laugh and hold on to him so I don't collapse. "You think?"

"Yes, and you look delicious." He glances down at the cum coating my shoulders and chest, gathers some on his finger, and swirls it around my nipple. Oh fuck, that's hot. My breasts ache, and I wish he was sucking on my nipples.

He leads me over to the desk and picks me up, positioning me on the edge again. I spread my knees apart as he stands between them and fumbles with the zipper on his trousers. His hands are shaking, and it hits me that he desperately needs to fuck me. I brush his hands aside and ease Willy from his confinement. I almost giggle when his cock surges in my hand, already wet with pre-cum. Sebastian pulls me closer, trapping his erection against my stomach as he kisses me passionately.

My pussy hums the longer our tongues twirl together, and I moan into his mouth. This experience tonight was amazing, and I need his cock in me to feel complete. I'm the one who breaks off the kiss and I lean back on my elbows.

"Fuck me, Sebastian."

He grins as he positions his cock against my wet pussy. "Yes, babydoll."

With a single thrust, he's buried inside me, and I whimper in delight.

"That's it, Jasmine, take all of me."

He pulls out partway before plunging into me again. His thrusts are deep and hard, and I can tell he's not going to wait for me to come. He's a madman, pummeling into me, seeking release. His desire rekindles mine, and the pleasure builds in layers as I reel towards ecstasy.

As he bulldozes into me, slapping sounds fill the air. It's crazy how wet I am, but five guys toyed with me so I probably shouldn't be surprised. Sebastian's cock is familiar, and him driving into me with an animal fierceness is the perfect finale.

Hunger matches hunger as our bodies collide, and I realize that since none of the other guys came inside my pussy, it's only going to be Sebastian's cum dripping out of me on the way home. For some reason, that matters to me, and the thought of how he only allowed his seed inside me pushes me over the edge. I cry out and shudder from the force of my orgasm as liquid fire streams through my body.

"Oh fuck," Sebastian pants, grabbing my hips for leverage as he slams home repeatedly.

I cling to him as euphoria washes through me.

"I'm gonna come," he groans, thrusting wildly. "Oh, fuck, Jasmine..."

His words bring me back to reality, and I focus on matching his rhythm.

This time it's me making the demands. "Come for me."

"Yes. Yes, babydoll, yes!"

He shudders with release as his cum pours into me, sending aftershocks of bliss through my system as my heart races. I watch his face contort with pleasure while he pumps every last drop into my quivering pussy.

After a few moments, he slows down and holds still as he catches his breath. My heart rate evens out, and my breathing softens as he slips his cock out of me. When I sit up, he engulfs me in his arms and presses his forehead against mine.

"That was unbelievable," he whispers.

I snuggle into him and sigh happily. "I love you."

"I love you, too." He nuzzles my neck affectionately. "Are you ready to go home?"

"Um..." I look down between us, knowing I just got cum smears all over his clothes.

He laughs as if he's reading my mind. "Yeah, we're going to have to sneak out the back."

As he helps me off the desk, and retrieves my clothes from the floor, I'm struck again by how much I love my husband. We just did the filthiest thing I can ever imagine doing, and he's joking around afterwards.

I slip into my dress, and he zips me up. I smile softly, reminiscing about that first night in the bathroom with him. Thank God I was pretending to be a bimbo back then. He's the best thing that's ever happened to me.

Once I'm dressed, he entwines his fingers with mine. "Let's go, baby-doll."

I give his hand a squeeze and head with him towards the door. I'll follow this man anywhere.

The End

Auditioning the Band

Freeuse Wedding Party

Lacey Cross

CHAPTER 1

I scan the crowded dance floor, looking for my absent husband. Dammit, where did Gary go? He was here before I went to the restroom, but now I don't see him anywhere. I wasn't gone that long.

Today is not going how I wanted it to... at all. This is the second wedding we've attended this weekend. Normally I adore weddings, but this is eating up all my free time after several busy weeks. It's been twenty-one — no, now it's twenty-two days since Gary and I've had sex, and he promised me a weekend of pleasure. Fucking weekend of pleasure, my ass. We've been on the go non-stop since Friday afternoon. What in the hell does a woman have to do around here to get boned by her husband?

Sighing, I slowly circle the room, searching for Gary. It's not entirely his fault that it's been so long since we've had sex. I was sick one weekend, then he caught my cold and was sick the following one. Being an adult sucks sometimes, but not always in the good way, and this has been ridiculous. Gary swore he'd make it up to me this weekend. As the night continues, it's looking increasingly unlikely.

Last night I was a bridesmaid in my friend Vanessa's wedding, so I couldn't exactly ditch the wedding early. I couldn't even duck into a quiet corner for some well-deserved attention, since I had duties and shit to take care of. I was hoping for some aggressive cuddling once we got home, but we were both exhausted. The night ended in a soft snuggle pile with our two dogs in our king-size bed, which was good, but not what I wanted. I'm only a guest at the wedding tonight, which meant no responsibilities at the ceremony or before, but the day was eaten up by one monotonous chore after another until it was time to get ready.

I picked my dress carefully. Dammit, I was gonna get laid today, and I knew exactly what would get Gary going. I'm wearing a silky red halter-style dress that hugs my curves in all the right ways, a dress which he's nearly torn off me a time or five before.

My body's been expecting sex all day, and I got desperate enough to try and wheedle five minutes from Gary to just shove it in me and fuck me — anything to ease the ache between my legs. He said he wanted to wait until we had time for a proper fucking. That's my romantic husband for you. I'm not complaining about it, no way. I mean, like, oh no, my husband wants to wait until he can make me come. Poor me.

But Christ, can be it be this century please?

The wedding venue is beautiful, and the ceremony brought back memories of our nuptials. Gary squeezed my hand during the vows, which told me he was thinking of our wedding as well. Everything would have been perfect... if I wasn't so horny.

Once the ceremony ended, I excused myself to use the restroom and ran into my friend Jasmine. She's gorgeous, smart, and the type of woman I'd be insecure around if I didn't know her so well. She's down to earth and a hoot to hang out with, and I consider her my closest friend. When Jasmine told me her husband was using her on a freeuse day *and* he'd already used her multiple times that day, I couldn't stop the stab of jealousy. I tried to play it off like I wouldn't want to be used without coming. Yet I was the thirsty slut who tried to get my husband to do exactly that before the wedding.

Where is that man, anyway?

The wedding band ends the song they're playing, and the singer announces they are taking a break. As people clear the dance floor in search of refreshments, I finally spot Gary across the room. He's standing off to the side of the stage, talking to the singer. I should have figured he'd be with the band since the singer is his best friend, TJ.

What my loving husband doesn't know is I had a date with TJ before I met him. All we shared was a single kiss at the end of the evening, but it was memorable. TJ was young and idealistic and heading out on tour, hoping the band would hit it big. They never quite did, but the band is still together after all these years, through marriages, kids, and divorces. They mostly play weddings, but TJ is at our house often and he said he's happy with his life. And that's really all that matters, right?

He's still incredibly sexy — all sleek muscle on a powerful build. Better yet, both arms have full sleeve tattoos. This makes me wonder what other body art his clothes hide? In my daydreams I play find the tattoos, but it's his hands that rev my engine the most. He has long, thick fingers, and it's easy to imagine them stroking my most sensitive spots.

Yeah, this dude always set my panties on fire. Occasionally I still touch myself and fantasize about our date ending differently. What would have happened if I had invited him in for a nightcap? It's a harmless flight of fancy, and I'd never do anything with TJ. It doesn't stop me from rolling my hips and pushing my chest out as I approach the guys. When TJ catches my eye, the appreciative glint in his warms me. Yeah, I've still got it.

Gary's back is to me so he doesn't see me approach. When I sidle up to him and slide my arm around his waist, the conversation abruptly ends. I only caught a few sentences, but it sounds like they are making plans to do something together. Huh. I wonder what those two are up to? Focus. Gary. Bed. Soon.

Gary leans over to kiss my cheek. "Hey, hot stuff," he says, while TJ murmurs, "Hi Millie."

I give TJ a smile and a soft, "Hi," before playfully punching Gary on the arm and giving him a mock pout.

"I was looking for you everywhere. I thought you hooked up with some floozy and abandoned me."

I didn't really think that, but it's a game we play.

He winks at me, playing along. "You know I've only got eyes for you, babe."

"Damn straight. You're addicted to all of this."

When I run a hand down my hip, Gary laughs and pulls me closer to him. The corners of TJ's mouth quirk as he observes our banter. I've noticed TJ's usually watching me out of the corner of his eye when I'm around him. He's subtle about it, and it's flattering. It might be mean, but I hope he regrets not going for me all those years ago.

The guys pick up their conversation about an old buddy, and I listen for a few minutes before TJ excuses himself to take a break before the next set. Gary has a speculative look on his face as TJ leaves. I'm about to offer him a penny for his thoughts, but he speaks before I have a chance.

"TJ thinks I should take you home and fuck your brains out."

TJ is a good man. My opinion of him rises and I mentally take back my wishes of regret.

"I think you should listen to your best friend. He's obviously smart."

Gary faces me, pulls me against him and smirks. "He also thinks I'm crazy for not tapping your ass every chance I get."

Oh, fuck. That's filthy... and hot. My pussy buzzes and my panties grow damp. Were the guys drinking? There are no empty wineglasses anywhere and I didn't leave Gary alone long enough for him to get tipsy. Do they stand around objectifying me often?

Hell, maybe they do.

My nipples pebble, and I doubt the thin silky layers of my bra and dress hide it. Fuck, why can't I be more like Jasmine? I bet she'd look her husband straight in the face and tell him to use her whenever he wants. I can't get past the idea that getting turned on by my husband and his best friend talking about me like I'm a piece of ass to be used should be wrong. Yeah... I shouldn't like this, right?

My body has other ideas. I fight the urge to rub my thighs together. I don't want Gary to know this is turning me on. But that doesn't mean I can't have a little fun with this. He'll back down at some point.

I walk my fingers up his chest and neck. When I continue past his chin, he pretends to nip at my fingers. Yeah, my hubby is all talk and no action. He's my lovable teddy bear.

I keep my voice light. "So why aren't you? You had the chance earlier, and you didn't take it."

Gary shrugs casually. "I told him I'd rather watch him fuck you."

Oh jeez, as if. I don't bother to hold in my snort. "Why just TJ? Why don't I fuck the entire band?"

Hell, if we're going to play this game, let's play big.

He purses his lips, as if he's considering it. "I don't know. Is five guys too many in one night?"

"Five? There's only four in the band."

When he doesn't answer and captures my mouth for a panty-searing kiss, I melt into him.

Mmm, now this is more like it.

Our tongues twine together, and I press against him. Heh, he's hard. Someone's got a dirty mind and likes the thought of me fucking a bunch of guys. A pulse between my legs reminds me...

Oh yeah, it's me.

The longer the kiss lasts, the more I daydream about four guys kissing up and down my body at the same time. I've never admitted this to Gary, but it's one of my biggest fantasies. I'd love to be fucked by a bunch of guys at once.

I break off the kiss and push against his chest. "Hey, wait!"

"Hmmm?" He nibbles along the column of my neck, and I tip my head to give him better access. A shiver of delight almost distracts me and I lose my train of thought for a moment. What was I going to say? Oh, yeah!

"You never said…" I break off and moan as he sucks gently on my neck. Fuuuck, he's driving me crazy. All I want to do is straddle his leg and grind against his thigh until I explode. It's been so long since I've had an orgasm, it'll probably only take a couple of minutes.

He nips his way up to my ear and gently tugs on my earlobe with his lips. "What were you saying?"

Another shiver runs through me as his breath tickles the sensitive hairs on my ear. More wetness hits my panties. I shift from foot to foot, wishing we were alone. I'm close to not caring. I need to pull it together before he makes me so mindless that I beg him to fuck me in front of the entire reception.

"The band only has four people. Who's the fifth?"

He stops sucking on my earlobe and chuckles. "I'm the fifth."

Oh Jesus. He's so full of horseshit. He'd never watch me fuck the band, but I'm having fun with the fantasy. When he moves his hands behind me and cups my ass, pulling me closer to him, I sigh in pleasure. He seems to like our crazy talk as well.

"I could fuck them and take notes. Audition them."

He kneads my ass. "Yeah, keep a score sheet. Pass or fail."

"Mmm hmm," I moan. "I could be your freeuse slut that you're sharing for the night."

Gary's hand stills. Oh god, did I really say that?

He cups my ass again and his lips crush against mine. His tongue invades my mouth, setting off a sharp wild need deep in my core. Lust burns in my brain. If he screwed me on the stage right now, I'd ignore the crowd and beg for more. We need to go home… right fucking now.

We're both panting when the kiss ends, and he leans his forehead against mine. "Millie, what if I really want it?"

Holy shit balls, he's serious?

My body buzzes and I try to not squeal out a yes. I didn't dream this was a possibility. I never imagined he'd want to share me. My mind whirls with the implications, and I wish I could shut my brain off. For once in my life, can't I just go with the flow and enjoy it? Do I have to analyze everything?

I catch a whiff of his cologne and inhale deeply. He smells so damn good. It's a familiar scent that can relax or turn me on depending on my mood. Today it does both. I wrap my arms around his neck and squeeze him, enjoying our closeness after so many weeks of not feeling connected.

"Do you really want it?"

"Yes."

That simple response sends a thrill through me. Hot damn. A little voice in my head tries to tell me to slow down and think this through. I shove it aside. Not tonight, bitch.

I'm going to take what he's offering.

I give him a slow smile. "Today is a good day for me."

He studies my face for a moment before a lightness settles over his features. "I'll see what I can arrange."

CHAPTER 2

The rest of the wedding reception is a blur. When the band stops for the night, Gary leaves me sitting at a table while he talks to them. Knowing that he's asking them if they want to fuck me is vulgar... and awesome. I'm quivering thinking of it.

When he returns, he smiles mysteriously. "Everything is set."

What the fuck does that mean?

"So it's happening?"

His mouth pulls up at the corners again and for a second I think he won't answer me.

"Yes. My freeuse slut is getting shared tonight."

Ohhh, yes. My mind spins away into fantasies.

I know I'm not really a freeuse slut since this isn't how it works, but it's filthy to imagine I am. Gary could fuck me wherever he wanted, whether that was behind a potted plant in the lobby or underneath the emergency stairs. Heck, the entire band could rail me in the stairway and fill all my holes.

Are they all going to come in me?

I want one of them to blow their load on my face. I've never actually had that done before. Gary prefers my ass or pussy, though occasionally he fucks my tits and glazes my breasts. But never on my face...

I'm not sure how long I daydream about getting all my holes stuffed before Gary tips as head at me like he asked me something. My head spins and I stumble over my words.

"Sorry... what?"

He leans over and kisses my nose. "I asked if you were ready to be used."

"What, now?"

My eyes grow round. Um, where is this happening? I might fantasize about public sex, but I'm not actually into doing it.

"Yes, now. Do you trust me?"

His eyes glow with love and lust. Knowing he really wants this erases any remaining concern.

"Of course I do."

He kisses me softly. "Good girl. Now let's go get you ready. I want to see what you look like being spit-roasted."

Whoa, how long has he been thinking about this?

I try to visualize a guy in my mouth and one behind me, but I can't decide whether I want to suck on TJ or whether I'd rather he be the one fucking my pussy. Then again, maybe I can have both.

Shit, I need to focus. It takes a few moments for me to regain my composure.

"I'm ready."

We both rise. He takes my hand and pulls me towards a side door, walking fast in his eagerness. I rush to keep up. Where in the hell is he taking me?

The side door leads to an alley behind the venue. TJ's van, which they use to haul equipment, is parked close to the exit. As we approach, the back door swings open, revealing the four guys. My lips part and I suck in a breath.

I'm getting fucked in the van?

I've never seen the inside, so I peer closely. The walls are bare with angled brackets that would be good for gripping. A punch of lust hits me when I realize there's a thin mattress on the floor. They covered it with a red plaid blanket.

Uh, do they do this often? Is the blanket hiding a bunch of stains?

TJ must have noticed my expression. "We use it to protect the equipment, and if one of us wants to take a nap."

Uh-huh, likely story. Maybe they take horny MILFS to their van all the time after a wedding. Not that I'm one to judge. I mean, I'm here with them.

Their equipment is nowhere to be seen. Who's watching over the instruments?

Better yet, is this happening with the van doors open or closed?

Where is Gary going to be?

God, this is filthy. Jasmine isn't going to believe the night I'm having. I bet it rivals hers.

My swirling thoughts consume me and I almost don't hear TJ speak.

"Glad you could join us, Millie."

He's formal for how dirty this all is, and I hold in a giggle. The rest of the guys in the band all grin at me and I toss them a soft smile and a tiny wave. I've met them once before, but it was a couple of years ago and I don't remember their names. I don't want to admit I forgot, so I don't ask for an introduction. This makes it more vulgar anyway — getting fucked in a van in a dark alley by strangers.

Gary slides his hand in mine and gives it a light squeeze. "Are you sure you want this, Millie?"

I study him for a second, gauging how serious he is. His expression tells me he needs reassurance that I'm not doing this just for him. God, I love him with all my heart. This is a crazy, amazing step we're taking tonight, but I'm ready.

"Absolutely."

He glances at TJ and nods. "Go ahead."

TJ waves me in. "Let's get this party started."

I hesitate for a second before moving to the opening. Gary steps away and I climb into the cramped space. As soon as I'm inside, I abandon my shoes. I don't need them in here. The van is crowded with the mattress, me, and three other guys, so I kneel on the cold, hard floor. Yeah, the mattress is a good idea. My knees are going to be fucked up quickly without it.

The guitarist and bass player are sitting cross-legged, leaning against a bench-style passenger seat. The third band member, the drummer, is sitting sideways on the bench so he can watch the action. Every few seconds, his hand moves to his lips and I see him pop something bright orange into his mouth. I couldn't believe what I saw.

What the hell? Is he eating mellowcream pumpkin candy? Halloween was weeks ago. What sick fuck still has Halloween candy?

Gary opens the side door and climbs in to sit on the bench seat next to the candy-eating drummer. The guy offers Gary the bag. My husband doesn't even like that type of candy, yet he takes a piece. My mouth waters as I watch my husband chew for a moment. Those damn pumpkins are oddly addicting. Whenever I buy a bag, I can't put it down. But where's my offer of candy? I'm the one about to be fucked by multiple men. I need my strength.

Jesus. They just need some popcorn and then they'll be ready for the show.

I shift to ease the pressure on my knees, and I notice the floor of the van isn't that clean. Okay, maybe this wasn't the best idea. My dress is going to be a mess when we're finished.

TJ grins at me as he shuts the door, shrouding the car in semi-darkness. "We promised your husband you'll get multiple orgasms tonight. I hope you're ready for it."

Wow, Gary told them to make me come more than once? I glance at him and his eyes sparkle in the dim lighting. The floodlights in the alley illuminate the inside of the van so it's bright enough to see everyone, but the details are lost. The darkness makes me feel less like I'm on stage, more anonymous... and yet it also feels far more intimate than I expected.

TJ moves to the mattress and sits on it, then reaches his hand out to me. I take it and squeak when he pulls me into his lap. My ass nestles against the hardness in his pants, and he wraps his arms around me before giving me a quick kiss.

"This is what you wanted, right?"

Um... I dart a glance towards Gary and he's focused on us with a soft smile. Since Gary is still good, so am I. When I nod at TJ, his lips find mine again. I moan against his mouth as his hand moves to my chest, squeezing my breast. My nipples tighten in response and a pleasant buzz fills my mind. Mmm, I'm so ready for this.

TJ rubs his thumb across my hard nipple through the fabric of my dress, and I shiver. His body heat seeps into me, flooding me and bringing my passion to a boil. I wrap my arms around his neck, throwing myself deeper into the kiss. As our tongues war with one another, I wriggle in his lap, trying to get some relief for my aching pussy. The longer we kiss, the more difficult it gets to think.

I want to get lost in this moment.

When he breaks off the kiss, I blink several times to clear the lust haze. I peek over at the guys watching. All of them stare at me with hungry expressions, but Gary is the one I care about the most. The lines of his face are hard, and if I didn't know him so well, I would believe he wasn't happy.

But I do know him that well, and I smile inwardly. I'm looking into the face of my husband, who is so turned on that he's fighting for control.

My pulse accelerates. I'm going to get such a hard fucking when this is over.

Chapter 3

TJ kisses me again. This time, he slides a hand under my dress and between my legs. I spread them open as much as I can as he caresses the skin of my inner thigh. He keeps his other hand around me, holding me still while he explores. His touch is gentle, and I whimper when he reaches the damp fabric of my panties. The pair I'm wearing are just a wisp of lace and cover nothing.

Why did I even put them on? It would have been fun to tease Gary about not wearing any, and also have easy access for when I... get fucked in vans in seedy alleys.

His searching fingers push aside the fabric and slide into my folds. I moan as he lightly grazes my clit with two fingers. Oh god, his fingers are wonderful. He circles my clit with the perfect amount of pressure, and I buck into his hand, wanting more. Somehow, he knows exactly what I need.

TJ chuckles at my reaction and shifts his weight, putting more pressure against my ass with his hardness. My pussy clenches and I whimper louder. He slides his fingers into my pussy and I almost cry out from the pleasure.

TJ's voice is low and husky. "You're so wet."

Fuck. I need his cock inside me.

"Mmm," I moan as his fingers work magic inside me.

"I bet Gary's going to enjoy watching you come over and over again."

That's hot and I feel my need climb. Gary's nodding when I glance at him. I have zero problem with this plan, and I'm ready for him to watch me get fucked by all the guys.

I'm ready to be used.

TJ kisses me again, and I grab onto his shoulders. He alternates between stroking my clit and slipping his fingers inside me, curling them and stroking in an irresistible rhythm. I shudder and whimper, unable to stay quiet. He kisses me until I'm writhing in his lap and moaning so loud I'm afraid anyone walking past will hear me.

When it seems like TJ isn't going to go any further, I take matters into my hand.

Reaching behind my neck, I undo the halter straps on my dress and pull the top down, exposing my strapless bra. Since I'm sitting in his lap, it's difficult to maneuver. Instead of removing my bra, I push it down so my tits bounce free. TJ gives a low hum of satisfaction before taking over and moving his palm to cup my breast and tweak my nipple.

I glance at Gary to see how he's enjoying the show. He's smiling and watching intently. His eyes flicker to mine and I blow him a kiss that makes him smile. I think he approves of my exhibitionist tendencies.

TJ abruptly pushes me off his lap and I land on the mattress with a grunted "oomph." Since I'm on my back, chances are he's going to fuck me, and I gulp. My heart pounds. When he slides the bottom edge of my dress up to my waist, exposing my panties, I can tell shit's about to get real.

"So Millie, you husband told me earlier that you enjoy being called a dirty slut."

Whaaa... Gary told him that? My head spins when Gary laughs.

"Oh yeah, she loves it. The filthier, the better."

I look at Gary again, and he's grinning at me. This is the dirtiest thing I've ever done. Sharing it with Gary makes it better than anything I could have imagined. By comparison, a bit of dirty talk seems positively tame.

All of my attention is on Gary, so I jolt in surprise when TJ rips my panties off.

My brain freezes and I'm sucked into my deepest, darkest fantasy. I've never admitted it to anyone... the van... a dark alley... half clothed... a bunch of men...

Ohhh. Fuck.

My entire body lights up and I become hyperaware of every brush against my skin. My nipples pebble into hard diamonds, and I gasp when TJ tugs on them. I whimper in pleasure, and he continues until I'm biting my lip and squirming.

"Gary, you didn't tell me she likes it rough."

He slaps my tit hard and I moan.

"I didn't know." My husband's voice holds a hint of surprise.

I close my eyes, not wanting to look at him. I never told him because I knew he couldn't do rough. I married a cuddle bear who can fuck me hard, but he'd never get close to hurting me. My secret desires were too obscene to share with him.

TJ grabs my hips and rolls me onto my stomach as he kneels on the mattress beside me. He slips both hands under my stomach and lifts me up, pulling me onto my knees. I'm staring straight at the other band members and a zing of forbidden pleasure courses through me.

TJ slaps my ass hard enough to sting. "Spread your legs, Millie."

My pussy clenches and I gasp as wetness runs down my inner thigh. I position my knees apart, spreading my pussy wide open. I'm never this brazen, especially with someone I've never fucked before, let alone a van full of men, but fuck it. I'm way past caring about anything but getting a cock inside me.

His fingers run across the soft skin of my ass. Then his palm smacks my ass again, and I groan.

"Now, that's a dirty slut."

I clench my jaw to keep from crying out as TJ spanks me over and over. He smacks my ass harder each time before finally sliding his palm over my cheeks. He squeezes my globe firmly and I whimper, unable to stop myself.

I can barely think straight when TJ spreads my ass cheeks wide. His finger traces the crack of my ass down to my pussy, and I throw my head back in ecstasy when he thrust two fingers into me.

"Oh yeah, your slutty wife likes it rough," TJ says, and I mewl in response. "Can you handle it, Millie?"

Oh god. I'm going to come so fast when he fucks me, and I'm going to beg him to fuck me hard. This might be my only chance to fuck someone who can give me the roughness I crave and I want a taste of it.

"Yes, please, fuck me hard."

"Good slut."

His fingers move faster and I buck my hips into his hand, desperate to get his fingers as deep as they can go. I grip the mattress, panting for air. My pussy is sopping wet, and his fingers aren't enough. I sigh in relief when he removes his fingers.

Thank god. I'm finally going to get his cock.

As TJ moves behind me, I look at the other band members. Two men sit with their backs against the seat and both have bulging erections. One of them strokes himself through his pants. Everyone is staying silent, and I meet the gaze of each man briefly. Only the drummer smiles. The other two intensely focus on the action.

Oh god, this is so damn slutty.

TJ wrestles with his clothes for a moment, and when he grasps my hips, I lock onto Gary's gaze. As TJ teases my folds with the tip of his cock and coats himself with my wetness, I fight the urge to close my eyes. I need to be sure Gary is enjoying this.

Gary's face tells me everything. The wild look in his eyes says he's overcome with lust and just as excited as I am.

TJ's cock is larger than Gary's and I can feel him stretching me open as he penetrates me slowly. I moan when he bottoms out and holds still.

Fuuuck. Of course he'd have an enormous cock. I was already fantasizing about him, and this is going to make it worse.

He's not moving fast enough for me. The tension builds until I can't hold back any longer. I rotate my hips, forcing him to knock against me deep inside. Pings of pleasure radiate from my core. My toes curl as the bliss builds without him even moving.

TJ's laugh breaks the silence. "Seems your filthy slut is getting desperate."

"Please." I mewl in distress as he gives a couple of tiny thrusts.

"Please what?"

I need him to fuck me hard. I can get a soft fucking from my husband. My head spins and I close my eyes, sinking down into the depths of depravity.

"Fuck me... Fuck me rough. I need to be your filthy little fuckdoll that you use however you want."

I hear the other band members murmur as if my words surprise them. They probably didn't realize I'd debase myself if it led to a rough pounding.

I don't care what they think. The only person who matters is Gary.

I peek at him. Both his hands are on the back of the seat, gripping it tightly. I bet his cock is aching right now, and I smile softly at the thought.

TJ moves, pushing his hips forward and pulling back.

Oh, thank god.

I grind my ass towards him, moaning loudly as pleasure pulses through my veins. He plunges inside me and I lean down onto my elbows, opening so he can go deeper.

I lose all control when he slams into me, pistoning hard and fast. He's fucking me raw, and knowing that he's going to fill my pussy with his cum is nasty... yet I crave it. I want all the cum in me, no matter where I take it. They can fill all my holes and send me home with Gary a wet, dripping mess, and I'll love it.

TJ pulls out suddenly and I whimper in protest, but then he slams balls-deep inside me again. I cry out and arch my back, pushing against him as he fucks me hard.

"You're a good fuckdoll, taking what I give you."

I squeal in delight as the pleasure mounts. "Yes."

"Do you like knowing your husband is watching his slut get used?"

"God... yes."

And I really do. Gary and I never talked about me fucking anyone else, and I wouldn't agree to him doing the same thing. He's all mine. But this experience is only good because he's the one who asked for it.

"Gary, tell your slut you want her to come for you." He slows his movements and I whimper.

TJ slaps my ass, and I cry out. "Yes! Please let me come."

TJ slams his cock in and out of me, driving me closer and closer to the edge. He reaches around me to pinch my nipple hard and I howl from the intense, painful pleasure.

"Please, Gary. I need to come. Please!"

TJ grunts and his cock throbs inside me. I can tell his orgasm is building, and I desperately try to hold back my own. I squeeze my thighs together, trying to stave off my release until Gary says I can come.

"Please, Gary?" I sob, crazed and desperate.

I latch onto Gary's eyes, and he looks almost as lost as I am. Why isn't he saying anything?

TJ grunts as he hammers into me. "Tell your slut she can come."

The corners of Gary's mouth lift. "Come for me, Millie."

My body goes rigid at his words, and I scream as my climax tears through me. "Ohhhh, fuck!"

Convulsive waves grip me as TJ fucks me through my orgasm. When he comes, he grabs my hips, pulling me hard against him in a last thrust. He shouts out as he explodes, coating my cave walls with his warm cum. He spasms against me, unloading every drop before pulling out and collapsing onto his side.

TJ pants and I close my eyes, sinking further until my head is resting on my hands while his cum runs out of me. It's been years since I've had another guy inside me.

TJ's voice is hoarse. "Who's next?"

Two guys both say "me" at the same time. I keep my eyes closed, not caring who it is.

"Looks like you can fight over our slut." TJ moves away from me.

"We can share. I want to use her mouth." The guitar player has a deeper voice than the rest of them, so I know it's him speaking.

There it is. My husband's fantasy. He wanted to see me spit-roasted. I open my eyes as the bass player moves behind me, and the guitar player kneels in front of me, his cock already out.

"I hope you swallow. I'm going to fuck your mouth real good, and I've been told I'm quite a mouthful."

Oh, fuck. I thought I wanted a guy to come on my face, but now all I want to do is swallow a mouthful of cum.

He better taste good.

He's holding his cock in his hand, moving it towards my mouth. Dang, he's actually impressive. His cock isn't huge, but it's straight with prominent veins that I want to lick. He's going to be able to fuck my mouth easily.

This is going to be fun.

I almost forget the guy behind me until he seizes my hips and slams into me. The bliss spirals and I cry out.

"Ohhhh!"

The guitar player takes advantage of my open mouth and slides between my lips, cutting off my cries. I gurgle around his cock as he slides it all the way in. Every thrust from the guy behind me shoves me further on the cock in my mouth and it knocks against my throat. I've never done this before, and now I can't understand why not.

Goddamn, this is hot.

As I suck him, licking around his shaft, I taste his pre-cum and his musky male scent. I'm so worked up. Nothing bugs me, not even the full bush of hair at the base of his cock that tickles my nose. I just want them both to fuck me and fill me.

They continue like this, ping-ponging me between them. Delight ripples through my body. The guy fucking me hard from behind pushes into me with a smooth rhythm. I moan and whimper around the cock in my mouth, unable to keep quiet. The guitar player is blocking my view of Gary, and Gary better be able to see this. I want to hear how he felt while watching.

"Spank her." TJ calls out. "She likes it rough."

Oh, fuck. A sharp smack on my ass makes me moan. My pussy clenches around his cock.

The guitar player fucking my mouth slides his hands into my hair. He holds my head steady while he face fucks me a little rougher. He doesn't pull out, but keeps sliding in and out of my mouth. Damn, this is intense. I can feel myself getting close to coming again.

"Keep sucking, beautiful. You'll get your reward soon."

The impersonal nature of how they are using me and the dirty talk hits a kink I didn't know I had. I really feel like a fuckdoll.

Yeah, this is fucked up, and yet oh-so-wonderful.

A sharp spike of pleasure ripples down to my toes. I'm getting close. So very close. I wiggle my hips and push back into the guy fucking me while trying to take more of the guitarist's cock down my throat. The guitarist groans as my tongue swirls around his shaft and I suck him in deeper. I feel my core pulsing and relish the sensation for a moment before panic seizes me.

Oh no. No, no, this can't happen. I'm going to come. No one said I could!

Then all thought is erased. Bliss shoots through me, making me squirm, and I give a muffled cry as the ecstasy grips me a second time.

"Ohhh fuck!"

I buck and tremble as I'm assaulted by waves of pleasure. The guy in my mouth still holds my head as his thrusts turn short and quick. He pauses for a second before coming with a groan. The hot spray of his seed coats my throat and it seems never ending.

Damn, he wasn't lying. My throat works around him as I struggle to swallow, knowing it's futile.

The guy behind me howls as he bursts. For a blissful moment, I have two guys blowing their load inside me at the same time. My mind melts under the intensity of the pleasure. I can hardly breathe from the force of it.

When they're both done unloading, they pull out of me. Saliva and cum run down my chin and I wipe it off with my hand before collapsing onto the mattress. This is absolutely filthy.

I love it.

I close my eyes and drift, enjoying the intense relaxation from two orgasms as the guys move around the bus. I'm not paying attention until the drummer whispers close to my ear.

"Get up. We're not done with you."

Ohhhh, I forgot about him. I have one more band member to fuck.

I crack my eyes open and scramble onto my hands and knees as he gets behind me. Instead of slamming into me, as I'm expecting him to, he caresses my sore ass.

"Oh, you poor thing, you're all red."

I melt against him. This is nice. He can keep doing that as long as he wants.

"Now, be a good slut and move over to your husband and give him a little kiss like a good fucktoy."

What's this?

My eyes fly to Gary's. Oh shit, I haven't looked at him in a while. His glazed expression tells me he's so turned on he can hardly think.

The guys move out of my way as I crawl over to Gary. Leaning my arms on the bench, I'm face to face with him.

I give him a cutesy grin. "Hi, love."

He leans forward and brushes his lips against mine. "I love you, Millie."

"That's goooooood." My 'good' turns into a long moan as the drummer slides into my pussy.

My vision tilts and I grip the back of the seat as he jackhammers into me. Gary slides his hands to the sides of my face and kisses me deeply, swirling his tongue with mine as bliss zings straight to my fingers and toes.

I whimper into Gary's mouth as the drummer fucks me vigorously. I'm reeling with each thrust. Kissing Gary while another guy fucks me amps up the pleasure. Gary ravishes my mouth as we suck and taste each other. I'm beyond thinking of anything except coming again, and I'm spiraling higher and higher.

Gary pulls back from the kiss, and his eyes bore into mine.

"Come for me."

I nod frantically. "Yessss."

His eyes widen. I arch my back and scream as I come. My pussy clenches around the guy buried inside me, making him blow his load. He grunts as more cum floods me. He gives a few more thrusts as he empties his balls deep inside me.

When he pulls out, I collapse against my husband, gasping for air. Gary kisses me softly.

"You okay?"

I nod. "Yes."

Gary takes a corner of his shirt and wipes my face clean. I'm covered in sweat and cum, and I'm sure I look a mess. Gary and I exchange dopey grins as he moves his hand away from my face.

"There, all better."

One guy pulls my dress down and I glance over my shoulder. All the band members are smiling at me and I laugh at how satisfied they all look. Damn, I made a bunch of people happy tonight.

"Thank you guys. This was... an experience I won't forget."

A simple thanks doesn't seem adequate, but my head is too fuzzy to say more. Sitting back on my knees, I pull my bra up and adjust the top of my dress, tying it around my neck. TJ moves closer to me.

"Are you sure this was okay? I wasn't too rough?"

TJ's concern warms me. He's a good guy.

"Tonight was fabulous. It wasn't too rough."

"Good." He flashes a wicked grin. "Now tell Gary he better fuck you all you want, or else I'll come and take care of your needs instead."

I give a startled giggle as my pussy clenches. Oh, no. That's hot.

Gary just laughs, as if it's a big joke. "In your dreams, buddy."

TJ snickers with him. "A guy can hope."

The guys talk in low voices as I find my shoes, and TJ helps me out of the van. He squeezes my hand as Gary comes around the side to claim me.

"Thank you, Millie. Crazy night, huh?"

I murmur "Yeah" as Gary says his goodbyes and leads me to our car.

Oh Jesus. What did I just do?

CHAPTER 4

My thoughts whirl and I'm silent the entire car ride home. Is Gary really okay with this? I'm covered in four guys' cum. What if this ruins our marriage?

Gary keeps stealing glances at me, but doesn't speak. When we pull into the garage, he turns off the car and faces me.

"Are you really okay?"

I want to look away, but force myself to meet his eyes. "Yes. Are you?"

He cups my face and brushes my cheek with his thumb.

"I love you more than ever. You're my gorgeous goddess."

The love in his eyes soothes me, and I raise an eyebrow.

"You mean I'm a filthy slut who needs a shower?"

He laughs and kisses me.

"Yeah, but you're MY filthy slut."

I blow him a kiss as I get out of the car. He's behind me as we walk towards the door leading into the house. We're almost there when he grabs me and presses me against the wall of the garage.

"I think you forgot something."

Rubbing my body against his, I can tell his cock is rock hard. I decide to play dumb.

"Oh, yeah... I'd rate the band a 10 out of 10. Would do again!"

He barks out a laugh. "No, not that. But it's good to know."

I tease him some more. "Hmm… I don't think I forgot anything. Boy, am I tired."

I give a fake yawn that turns into a yelp as he uses a knee to spread my legs open. He yanks up my dress and fumbles with his pants, freeing his cock.

"You still have to fuck the fifth man."

I left my ruined panties in the van as a souvenir for the guys, so he's got free access to my pussy.

Gary bites my lip and kisses me deeply. He lifts my leg to wrap around his waist. "Time to remind you who you belong to."

He slams into me, making me cry out from pleasure. I clutch onto his shoulders as he pounds into me.

"Fuck, yes!"

He's like a madman, not caring about me coming. Shit, he must have been holding this in until he found out I was fine.

His hands dig into my hips as he bucks into me, fast and hard. I can hear the wet slap of skin on skin. He's fucking me so hard. I know I'll be sore tomorrow, especially after how many cocks I had tonight. He's knocking me against the wall with every thrust. Dang, he's never been this rough with me before.

It's awesome.

I hold on tight, enjoying the ride as my body quivers. Layers of pleasure build and tension coils low in my belly as every part of my body buzzes. Gary's flushed and puffing as he jackhammers into me.

Seeing his pleasure tips me over the edge. I catapult into a soul-shattering orgasm and I scream out his name as pleasure rockets me to a higher plane.

I'm so far gone, I don't know how much longer he fucks me. The waves of pleasure carry me until he groans and convulses, burying himself deep inside me. His ropes of warm cum bathe my insides as I come back to Earth.

He slows his thrusts and leans against me, letting my leg slide down so I can stand on my own. He stands still, trying to catch his breath.

"Oh god, Millie. I love you."

Wrapping my arms around him, I snuggle as close as I can get. "I love you too."

A cough from the end of the garage startles us both. Oh fuck, he forgot to close the garage door. No one is visible, but the manly voice of our neighbor calls out from the side of the house.

"I saw you guys get home and wanted to return your casserole dish. I'm leaving it out here. You guys have a good night!"

Gary looks at me with round eyes, and I feel the heat of a blush creep up my face. My stomach clenches.

Oh, my God. How am I going to face the neighbor ever again? How much did he hear? And why didn't he wait until morning to return our dish? Dammit!

Gary's loud laugh brings me out of my panic. "Come on, love. Let's get cleaned up and go to bed. You know he's walking home and wishing he could fuck Jennifer against the garage wall."

I grin back at him. Jennifer is a good friend of mine. Maybe I should ask her later if she got unexpectedly railed tonight. If so, I'll tell her she can thank me.

I slide my hand into Gary's. "Let's go. If you're lucky, I'll let you soap me up in the shower."

"Hah, if I'm lucky?"

I give him a saucy grin. "Yeah, I heard you have to do anything I want, or else TJ is going to come over and service me."

Gary grumbles behind me, "He said I had to fuck you, not do anything." I hold back my laugh.

Oh yeah, this is going to be fun.

My pussy hums to life, and I try to push back any thoughts about TJ really coming over to service me.

Yeah... I'm such a slut.

And it's glorious.

The End

Used for Pleasure

Freeuse Resort Weekend 1

Lacey Cross

CHAPTER 1

I recline on a luxurious couch, blinking slowly as I take in the richly furnished living room. I'm attending a baby shower for Sabrina, one of my best friends from high school. She found her wealthy husband through a sugar daddy website during college and it blossomed into love. Now she's expecting her first child and living in pure extravagance.

I hung out with a group of five other girls in high school and we've all stayed close over the years. I turned 32 last month, so we've been friends for a long time. In high school, we nicknamed ourselves the Six Musketeers. We've all taken different paths in life, and Sabrina is now the wealthiest of us.

We're gathered together now, and Sabrina told us to wait in the living room while she grabbed something. My stomach grumbles as I smooth down the hem of my sundress, wondering how long it'll be before she serves us food. She always has the best catered meals at her parties, and I need to fill my belly before we eat cake.

My gaze falls on Tiffany, who is seated on the opposite couch. She lifts her eyebrows at me and tilts her head towards one of the catering staff as he refills her wine glass. She's my closest friend, and I have a pretty good idea of what she's thinking: this baby shower is exactly what Sabrina would plan. It's luxurious yet intimate, with no shortage of caterers to make sure we're happy. And from the sheer number of staff running around, it's clear that Sabrina is paying an arm and a leg for this small affair.

I lift my crystal wineglass off the table and take a sip of the Champagne. Does Sabrina realize that not everyone lives this way? We rarely invite her to our houses because hers is so much nicer for get-togethers, so she might not know this isn't normal for us.

Sabrina waddles into the room with a warm smile, her eight-month pregnant belly happily bulging out from within a designer dress and her blonde hair pulled into an elegant topknot. "Okay, everyone. You ready for the surprise?"

Uh-oh, here we go. Sabrina always goes big when she plans for a party. I bet a stripper is going to pop out and dry hump us while dancing to Pour Some Sugar on Me by Def Leppard—because what else would happen?

Sabrina circles the sofas, handing us each a sleek, black business card with shimmering silver writing. All the card says is "Plaything Resort," along with a phone number and email address. Tiffany and I exchange bewildered glances as Sabrina gracefully sits down, arranging her dress around her like she's royalty.

"This is my gift to you," Sabrina explains. "It's an invitation to an all-inclusive weekend at my favorite private resort. You don't have to worry about anything. Just show up and enjoy yourselves, either on your own, together, or with your husbands."

Sabrina leans back, appearing satisfied with her explanation. We all look shocked and nobody speaks for a few moments.

Finally, I break the silence, voicing what we're probably all wondering. "What is this?"

Sabrina giggles joyfully. "It's a private, freeuse sex resort, silly! It's only open to one group of people at a time. Just tell them what you want and they'll make all your fantasies come true."

What the literal fuck? A sudden surge of warmth courses through me as I picture a horde of men using me. Wow! My husband, Keith, and I recently started living a hotwife lifestyle. He'd totally let me do this.

Glancing over at Tiffany, I can see that she's mulling it over as well, evidenced by the slight flush of her cheeks and the excitement in her eyes. Keith doesn't watch me play with other men so he probably won't want to go. He prefers to stay home and fuck me when I get back while making me tell him all the filthy things I did with the other guy. Assuming Tiffany's husband doesn't want to go with her, maybe she would go with me...

CHAPTER 2

Keith puts my bag in the trunk and pulls me against him for a deep kiss. I've been crazy turned on all week daydreaming about this trip. We've been fucking on every surface of our house for days, but yesterday he only teased me and didn't let me come. He kept thrusting into me slowly, edging me, and then stopping right before I exploded. I'm so damn horny right now, I could ride his thigh and probably come in two minutes.

As his tongue twirls against mine, I moan and consider how I can get his cock inside me before I leave. I just need a couple of minutes, tops.

He murmurs against my mouth, "Ariana, I'm going to fuck you so hard when you get back, your head is going to spin."

Mmm, I like the sound of that, though my head is already whirling. Reaching between us, I rub the hardness in his jeans and purr, "Maybe I'll get so much cock this weekend, I won't need yours."

This gets me the result I was hoping for. He groans and kisses me again, taking his time nibbling my lower lip. His hand slides up to cup my breast, and the gentle pressure makes me whimper.

He growls, "That's not going to happen, baby. Your sweet pussy is all mine as soon as you walk through the front door."

The thought of him fucking me hard once I step foot in the house makes a gush of wetness hit my panties and excitement ripple down my spine. I lick my lips and whisper, "Good. Because you know I'm addicted to your cock."

"You really are," he moans, leaning forward to give me one last kiss.

This is exactly why I'm a hotwife. We've been together eight years—married for five—and ever since I started fucking other guys, our sex life has been off-the-charts wonderful. This freeuse resort will give us weeks of enjoyment when I get back.

The resort is a three-hour drive from our house in good traffic. According to the information the owner sent me, it's 20 acres of private property turned into a secluded paradise. Tiffany and I planned to drive together, but a last-minute work emergency held her up until tomorrow. She's going to drive down separately. I guess I'll have to handle all the sexy men by myself until she gets here.

I spend the drive wondering how it will all work. Am I going to get any warning before they use me? That isn't really how freeuse works, though. They're supposed to just fuck me whenever or wherever they want. As I get closer to the resort, my panties get wetter. Yeah, I'm going to have to change into a clean pair once I get to my room.

Everything about this weekend is a mystery to me, other than that I'm a freeuse toy. Supposedly, a bunch of men are going to use me, but I've made no plans beyond that. When I booked the weekend, I had to fill out a questionnaire about what I would and wouldn't do and give them my safeword. I mainly told them no ass stuff. Keith owns that hole and 'no anal' is the requirement whenever I fuck someone else. Honestly, though, I'm fine with that. I love having one part of me I can never share with anyone but Keith. It gives me that nice, owned feeling that I crave.

When I pull up to a gated entrance, I'm practically vibrating with excitement. The owner emailed me a keycode to get in, but other than that, I don't know what to expect beyond the gate. I tried to pry details out of Sabrina, but she was close-mouthed and just told me to have fun.

The code works and as I drive through the gate, I see a huge, sprawling mansion with a circular drive. A fountain is in front of the entryway, and I park beyond it, next to a set of white stairs and an arched doorway. The house is stunning, but probably a bitch to maintain. That's me, always the realist.

As I get out of my car, a sexy silver fox wearing jeans and a t-shirt walks down the steps. "Welcome! You must be Ariana."

Pulling my bag from my trunk, I nod enthusiastically. "Yep!"

He smiles and takes my bag, and my pussy buzzes as his deep blue eyes appraise me. I wouldn't mind him sticking it in me right now.

His eyes twinkle, as if he knows what I'm thinking. "I'm Chris. We spoke on the phone. Come on in. I just need to see your photo ID and have you sign a couple of forms."

I follow him, and he keeps talking. "Remember, you can always use your safeword. We all know it and will abide by it."

He previously warned me he'd have paperwork to sign, but I wasn't expecting the safeword talk since we already had the conversation about it over the phone. This is kind of awesome, even though I doubt I'll even consider using it. This slut is ready to be filled until I'm dripping with cum from whoever wants me.

Chris guides me to a beautiful mahogany reception desk. He sets my bag down and goes around to the other side of the counter while I fish out my ID from my clutch. As he examines it, his tongue clicks against his teeth. "Yes, that's definitely you. Just sign these forms." His voice is as smooth as the wood of the desk.

As he slides paperwork at me and hands me a pen, a gorgeous guy in swim shorts comes from an archway to the left. The thin fabric doesn't hide his hard bulge and I swallow at the size of his package. Jesus, his cock must be huge. I'd guess he's around my age, with dark hair and tanned skin. His stomach is ripped, and I'd love to run my hands up his chest and see if I can make his muscles jump. I give him a brief smile and lean over to sign the paperwork. The sexy guy walks up close behind me and I hold in a gasp as he pushes my skirt up and yanks my panties down.

Oh my god. We're starting now? Before I can blink, his fingers find my pussy and I bite my lip to stop myself from moaning. Okay yeah, if he keeps doing that, I'm going to come all over his hand.

He strokes my clit with a single finger while plunging his thumb into my pussy, as if he's testing how wet I am. My head is woozy and I stare at the forms dumbly. What am I supposed to be doing again?

Chris points to a line. "Just sign here, please."

Right... signing. The guy removes his fingers from my pussy, and I whimper a little as I scribble my name on the first page. Just as I put the pen to paper for the second signature, the guy behind me grabs my hips and slams his cock into me. His cock is massive and I almost cry out from the intense bliss as he stretches me open.

Fuck! The pen shoots across the paper, leaving a squiggly line, and flies out of my hand as a burst of delight zings through me. I'm being fucked already? I don't know what I expected, but being bent over the reception desk with a dude balls deep inside me within two minutes of being on the property wasn't it. My breathing is shallow and labored as I struggle to keep my moans in check. The guy keeps pumping in and out, making me bite back a scream.

Chris acts as if nothing is going on, picks the pen off the floor and hands it back to me. He points to a line I need to sign. "You missed a spot."

Jesus Christ. The guy in my pussy hammers me against the desk as I try to sign my name. It ends up being a jagged mess, but whatever. Once I sign all the required paperwork, I put my hands flat on the counter to help stabilize me while the guy goes to town in my pussy. The sound of skin slapping skin fills the room, punctuated by his groans of enjoyment. He drills deep, and each whack against me makes me moan.

I barely pay attention to Chris until I notice him snapping a picture of me with his phone. Oh God, that's right. Keith wanted pictures of me being used, and Chris said he would take as many as he could. Chris punches numbers into his phone. Imagining Keith getting the picture catapults me into my orgasm.

I cry out as my inner muscles clench around the guy's cock. The guy grunts and thrusts harder as I writhe under him. He doesn't stop. My whole body shudders as I climax again and then I feel his cock pulsing inside me, unloading spurts of hot cum.

With one final grunt, he pulls out and slaps my ass. "Well done, slut."

I slump over the desk, still twitching, with his cum dripping down my inner thigh as he walks away.

Chris clears his throat. "Once you're ready, I'll show you to your cottage."

I close my eyes and give a silent prayer to whatever god might be listening. I hope I didn't sign up for more than I can handle. Though I literally put my name on the paperwork, so maybe I did.

I'm still adjusting my panties on the way to my private cottage behind the mansion. We pass a lovely pool of sparkling water with sunlight dancing on its surface. A steaming hot tub next to the pool looks so inviting I want to sink into the warm water.

Several men swim in the pool. They smile at me, but don't speak. I'm on edge, expecting any of them to grab me and shove me against the closest hard surface. None of them do—to my disappointment. My pussy is throbbing in anticipation of being used by all these men, and she's getting impatient.

Chris shows me to my cottage and right before he leaves, he bends me over the dresser. Whoa, what's this? Oooh, is he going to use me? Please let him use me! Chris fingers my pussy for a moment, but then stops. Dammit. My brain is fuzzy when he leaves with a cheery, "Have a fun night."

Did he do that just to prove he could? Ugh, I wish he had fucked me while he was at it. I need some cock and I need it now. I take a few minutes to daydream about Chris using me all around the cottage, and once my head clears, I explore my living areas.

The cottage is a simple layout with one bedroom, a kitchenette, dining area, and living room. The bathroom is a generous size, with a shower and separate bathtub. I love the cozy feel of the entire place. I wouldn't mind staying for longer than a weekend.

The property has five cottages in all, and Tiffany and I are each going to have our own. We decided this was for the best since we didn't know if we'd have men joining us in our rooms.

I love Tiffany to death, but I get a little crazy after a few orgasms. I didn't want it to turn into a wild night where I'm tongue deep in her snatch by the end. Our friendship might not survive that. Though, hell, maybe. What happens at the Plaything Resort stays at the Plaything Resort, right? I giggle at myself. Not that it matters. We're both going to have more than enough cock to keep us entertained—I hope.

I find a map of the grounds on the dresser, and I see they have various activities: pool tables, an arcade, a gym, and a sauna. Oooh, I could use the sauna and maybe get fucked in there.

The most annoying part about this weekend is that the guys are using me. I don't get to decide where it will happen. I'm ready to ride every cock I see, but if they don't want to fuck me, they won't. Shit, what if they don't find me attractive?

Most people have a body type preference and maybe I'm not theirs. I'm curvy, with long brown hair, tan skin, and gorgeous brown eyes with thick lashes. Keith might be biased, but he thinks I'm smoking hot. I don't feel like I'm beautiful, although I think my eyes are quite nice. That's just the way it goes sometimes when you're a woman—you struggle to feel sexy unless you look like a supermodel.

Pushing my breasts together, I stare down my cleavage. Okay, so I have pretty fabulous breasts as well. If I want to get fucked, maybe swimming is the way to go so I can flash my tits. Slipping on a hot pink bikini, I grab a towel and some complimentary sunscreen from the bathroom and head to the pool. I feel strangely self-conscious as I make my way to the water, aware of the men watching my every step.

The patio has multiple lounge chairs scattered around. My eyes settle on the one nearest to a dangerously attractive man with dark brown hair and tattoos covering his chest. Two other people are swimming in the pool while the hot guy lays in the nearby chair. My pussy flutters at the thought of him taking me without question. As a rule at the resort, I'm forbidden from asking anyone to fuck me, but that doesn't mean I can't make myself irresistible.

The sun is relentless and I don't want to get a sunburn, so I prop a bare foot on the chair and grab the sunscreen. As I pop open the lid, I'm engulfed by its sweet scent; a combination of coconut and vanilla permeates the air. I breathe deeply and relax. Yeah, this is the life.

As I rub it into my legs, admiring the red polish on my toenails, I notice that the two men in the pool are both staring at me. Taking care to bend over far enough so they can be treated to a sexy view, I slowly apply lotion all the way up my leg. When I untie the straps of my bikini top, the men stop all movement as I face them and apply lotion to my stomach and breasts.

I'm aroused by the many eyes fixated on me. As I apply the cream to my body, I take pleasure in teasing my nipples. The man in the chair next to me is smiling, and I give him a playful look and my most seductive voice. "Would you mind helping with my back?"

His grin widens, and he stands up. "I can do that."

I give him the lotion and turn my back to him, gathering my hair over one shoulder. His warm, firm hands glide down my back, giving me goosebumps. His fingers brush the top indent of my ass and I almost moan as he slides my bikini bottoms down my hips. Hell yeah, my plan worked!

A blonde man in the pool gets out and takes my foot to slide off my bikini bottom, and I step out of them with the other foot. The guys don't talk to me, making me feel like I'm a sex doll they can move around as they please. It's amazing.

My pussy buzzes when I feel fingers graze my inner thigh. I hold my breath as the blonde guy kneels on the ground and slowly caresses up the inside of my thighs, his fingers brushing my swollen lips.

The guy applying sunscreen massages my ass and my head spins as the two men touch me. I've only ever fucked one guy at a time, so having two pairs of hands on me is a new experience. I'm not hating it.

I can't believe I'm getting double teamed with both guys focused solely on me. Now I see why Sabrina said this was her favorite resort. I might not be directing what is happening to me, but I have zero complaints about the joy they're giving me.

The man at my feet runs his fingers along my slit and spreads my labia apart. I got fully waxed before the trip, so I'm soft and hairless for whatever happens. The guy leans forward and kisses my pussy. I suck in my breath as his tongue enters my folds and licks my clit.

Yeah... I'm not seeing how this is about them using me, unless the point is they only use me for my pleasure. I should have trusted Sabrina more. Would she really have recommended this place if she didn't get multiple orgasms?

The guy between my legs murmurs between licks, "Such a sweet pussy."

I moan softly. He's wonderful with his tongue. I shouldn't be surprised that he knows what he's doing—everyone here is probably great at sex since they've had lots of practice. I'm curious to see their cocks, but I have to wait for them to show me.

My toes curl as his tongue delves deeper, and I squeeze my eyes shut, enjoying the sensation. Each flick of his tongue shoots bliss through me. If he keeps it up, I'm going to come soon. With my eyes closed, I don't realize another guy walked up until he speaks.

"I see you warmed the slut up for me. Thank you."

I open my eyes and it's the guy who fucked me over the front desk. The blonde guy between my legs slides away and takes a step back without being told. Dammit. I liked him there.

"I'm Ryder," the new guy says in a deep, gravely voice and my nipples harden into painful peaks at the sexy tone. I didn't know I was going to learn names.

"I'm Ariana," I say quietly and blush.

He laughs. "No, you aren't. You're my fucktoy. The boys drew straws, and I won you. You're mine for the weekend and I haven't decided if I'm sharing you."

Ohhh, shit. Thinking that he won't share me turns me on even more, and wetness leaks down my inner thigh. This is my kind of messed up. Ryder steps behind me, pulls one of my legs up by my thigh. I almost tip forward. The blonde guy who was licking my pussy grabs ahold of my hands. I use him to balance as Ryder slides his cock inside me. Fuuuck, his cock is as huge as I remember and my eyes widen as I stare at the blonde guy in front of me. He's got a spaced out look of lust in his eyes. I think I addled him with my pussy.

When Ryder starts fucking me hard, my mouth pops open in a silent cry. I lean forward and grab the shoulders of the guy that had eaten my pussy, and cling to him as Ryder fucks me harder than I expect. Ryder reaches around with the hand not holding my thigh up and pinches and slaps my nipple. I whimper as he slams into me repeatedly.

"So tight and wet. I could use you all weekend and not let anyone else touch you. Just my hot little piece of ass to use over and over again."

The forms I filled out asked me if I liked dirty talk, and I'd said the dirtier the better. I think they're taking me at my word. I moan loudly as Ryder's cock hits my deepest parts. My pussy tightens around him as Ryder talks in short bursts between each thrust.

"Only nasty sluts come to this resort. You must be a nasty slut."

I whimper when he grasps my hip and whacks against me.

"I bet you're a filthy, cocksucking whore who just wants to be used. That's the type of woman who comes here."

The more he degrades me, the more I sink into a state of submission. Shit. He's right. I am a filthy cocksucking whore.

"Matter of fact," he growls as he pulls out and lets go of my leg and hip. "You're gonna suck this cock right now. Get on your knees, slut."

Oh god. I don't think I'm going to come. I sink to the ground as he moves in front of me and shoves his cock between my lips. He's almost too big for my mouth, but I'm able to get most of him in. The taste of Ryder's cock is salty and sweet, with a hint of musk. As I swirl my tongue around the shaft, I can feel the ridges on his skin that make it incredibly pleasurable when he's fucking me. The taste of my own juices mixed with his is a unique and heady combination that drives me wild.

"You're such a good girl sucking my cock. Suck it faster. Make me come."

I suck him as hard as I can as I bob my head up and down, my cheeks hollowing, as I try to take his entire length. I can hear the wet slurps of my mouth against his skin, and Ryder's soft groans as he slides his hand in my hair. When he shifts his torso to an angle slightly, I'm confused. What is he doing? Out of the corner of my eye, I see the sexy dark-haired guy taking a picture of us with his phone. Fuuuuck, that's hot. Knowing Keith is about to get the picture makes my mind all fuzzy with lust.

Ryder pulls out of my mouth and slaps my cheek with the head of it, causing my eyes to widen. Everything he's doing is making me feel like an absolute whore, and reminds me of my early college years. Back then, I would do anything for a guy as long as he praised me. Being married for so long turned our bed into a place for mutual pleasure, and I didn't realize I missed being used like this.

"We're going to send your husband some great pictures. I bet my cock is larger than his. Does he like seeing his slut sucking on an enormous dick?"

Ryder's cock is significantly bigger than Keith's, but I don't have time to answer him because he slides it back into my mouth and I suck hard again. My pussy is still throbbing from the dirty talk as he fucks me. My nostrils fill with his masculine scent as Ryder's shaft slides deep into my throat. I can taste a hint of saltiness on my tongue, and his coarse hairs tickle my nose.

"Oh yeah, your mouth is so wet and tight. I really don't think I'm sharing you this weekend."

I gasp as he fucks my mouth faster. A thrill runs through me as I wonder if he'll actually be the only cock inside me this weekend. Not what I expected, but I'm oddly okay with this thought. This guy could use me over and over, and I'd thank him every time.

Ryder puts his hands on my head and fucks my mouth harder. He's not hurting me and I'm wooly-headed from being used as his shaft spasms. He groans when he comes, and the splash of cum against the back of my throat almost makes me choke. Since he already came earlier, I wasn't expecting him to have so much. I swallow, gagging slightly as his seed coats my tongue.

Ryder pulls out of my mouth as saliva and cum run down my chin, dripping onto my breasts. I lick my lips and chin clean, and then use my fingers to clean up what fell. Ryder tastes different from my husband, but not bad. Sticking my fingers in my mouth to clean them off, I moan softly.

I'd be willing to take as many mouthfuls as he wanted to give me this weekend.

Ryder looks down at me and smiles. "You might want to go take a nap, slut. I think you're in for a long night."

He signals to the other men, and they all leave me alone in the pool area. I'm a little stunned, but not ready for a nap yet. My legs are wobbly as I get up and slide into the hot tub to relax. Oh my god, this place is insane but fucking awesome. The warm water soothes me, and when I yawn, I realize Ryder is right. I better get a nap.

When I climb out, I fetch my bikini and the sunscreen, and wrap my towel around me before heading back to my room.

CHAPTER 3

The sun is setting when I wake up to a knock at the door. I climb out of bed, and when I open the door, I realize I'm still naked. Oops. Ryder and another handsome half-naked guy are standing there. I blush and stammer, "Hi,"

The half-naked guy is holding a tray of food and my stomach gives a soft growl. Neither of them greets me, and I stand aside to let them in. The guy with the food heads to the kitchenette, and I longingly watch the plate he's carrying until it disappears through the doorway.

I'm about to ask Ryder what's up, but he turns me around and shoves me up against the nearest wall. Oh, I guess this is what's up. My nipples scrape against the plaster and ripples of desire run straight to my pussy. I'm so turned on from getting face fucked earlier, I might come if one of them shoves their cock inside me.

Ryder's hand cups my ass, and I moan. He spreads my butt cheeks apart and sighs. "God, too bad I can't fuck this pretty little ass. I really wanted to come in all my fucktoy's holes."

His words make me wish I hadn't written that anal was off limits. I'm so fucked up, I can easily imagine myself begging him to fuck my ass. I hold in my pleas because I'd never break Keith's trust, no matter how much I want Ryder to take all of me.

He grabs my arms, pinning my wrists to the wall above my head, and pushes his body against mine. His cock is out of his shorts, and he grinds the length of his shaft between the crack of my ass. I moan as he presses harder against me. Holy fuck. I'm not sure I've ever wanted a guy's cock as much as I do right now.

The tip of his cock probes my pussy, and he slams into me. I cry out as he uses my body roughly, keeping me pinned as I sway between him and the wall. His skin is hot against mine and each thrust sends tiny sparks of pleasure through my entire body. When he speaks, his breathing is ragged. "I changed my mind about something, fucktoy."

What's this?

His breath is a warm puff as he continues. "I've decided to share you tonight. We're both going to use you until you're nothing but a mindless puddle on the floor."

Oh god—yes, please. I want to beg him to get started, but I don't need to because he pulls out and drags me to the bed. I glimpse the other guy watching us from the kitchenette doorway as Ryder pushes me back. Squeaking in surprise, I bounce on the mattress as he grips my thighs and tugs me to the end of the bed.

Ryder doesn't wait and puts my ankles on his shoulders and thrusts back into my pussy. I gasp in delight and fist my hands in the sheets. Every nerve ending is on fire as he jackhammers into me.

"You're such a good fucktoy. I'm going to be sad when the weekend ends. I could fuck this pussy forever."

I close my eyes and let the sensations cascade over me as he continues to fuck me and talk dirty.

"I've spent a lot of time today thinking about why you would come here, and I've decided you must be just a whore who loves being used."

His words make me tremble and I whimper and moan.

"Or maybe your husband can't fuck you like this, and you like it rough."

A shudder runs through me. I'd love to say no, but that would be a lie. Keith can't fuck me like this, and I didn't even know I craved it. The bed dips by my head and I open my eyes to find the other guy aiming his cock towards my mouth. I moan, "Yessss," as he slides between my lips. I suck him in deeply, enjoying the saltiness on my tongue and wanting to see how fast I can make him come while Ryder fucks me harder and faster.

"Oh yeah, I bet you're a slutty cum-eating whore, aren't you?"

My moans turn into yelps as Ryder pounds into me. This is amazing and I feel myself nearing an orgasm. Ryder must be able to tell because he reaches between my legs and rubs my clit, skyrocketing me to new heights of rapture. The guy at my head keeps drilling into my mouth. My pussy tightens around Ryder's cock. I'm so close to coming that it's difficult to form thoughts.

"I'm gonna fill your pussy with my hot load. Fuck, this is so good."

Ryder pulls out fully, then slams back into me repeatedly. Everything the men are doing to me turns me on even more. I gurgle around the cock in my mouth, trying to beg them both to use me, but my words are unintelligible.

Ryder's thrusts become more erratic but he doesn't slow down. I scream when his balls slap against my ass. My body shakes and my toes curl as my orgasm rips through me like wildfire.

I cry out around the shaft in my mouth as the guy's cock pulses and explodes, shooting ropes of sticky cum down my throat. Lights flash behind my eyelids and my brain switches off as Ryder continues to fuck me through my orgasm. When he groans and paints my cave walls with his hot cum, I'm floating in a sea of happiness and barely notice.

He slows down, and when he pulls out, I can feel his cum dripping out of me. He lowers my legs and I melt into the bed, curling up on my side. I'm incapable of coherent thought. I'm just one big ball of contentment. The guys murmur together and the front door opens and shuts. I assume I'm alone until the bed jostles. I crack my eyes as Ryder cuddles behind me.

"Is this okay?" he asks as he wraps his arms around me.

I murmur, "Uh-huh."

We snuggle together for a bit as I drift. His warmth on my back is soothing. After a few minutes, he nuzzles my neck and kisses my shoulder.

"I'll be right back."

He gets off the bed and returns with water and a plate with half a sandwich. He holds the glass steady while I sit up, and when he can tell I won't spill it, he lets go. I drink deeply, and then he exchanges the glass for the plate. I lie back down and munch on a delicious turkey sandwich as Ryder climbs behind me and rubs my back.

Shit, I didn't know this place came with aftercare, but then again, I didn't know how intense this would be. After I've eaten my sandwich, he takes the plate and puts it on the dresser and snuggles back against me.

"Are you okay?"

I close my eyes, enjoying being taken care of. "Yeah, this is nice."

"Good," he murmurs. "It's part of your husband's request."

Wow, what? I look over my shoulder at him and he must be able to read the question on my face.

"Your husband called Chris with special requests. He wanted to make sure we took care of you." Ryder grins at me. "Something about you going loopy after multiple orgasms."

I giggle. "My husband knows me."

Ryder yawns, "Now we rest. You have a big night ahead of you." His arm falls across my chest.

My mouth forms an 'O' and I want to ask him what's happening later, but I don't. He probably wouldn't tell me. I'm his freeuse slut tonight and he gets to choose. I snuggle in and drift to sleep with a smile on my face.

I wake up when someone plays with my nipple. I almost tell Keith to let me sleep, but when that someone pinches it painfully, I'm jolted awake and realize this isn't Keith.

"Time to wake up." Ryder pulls on my nipple again and I moan.

I'm not sure what time it is, but it's fully dark outside. I stretch and my pussy throbs at the thought of being used again so soon.

"You have 15 minutes to do whatever you need, and then we're leaving."

Ugh, 15 minutes? I pop up and sprint to the bathroom. I'm a filthy slut who needs a shower and there isn't much time. As the water heats, I brush my teeth lightning fast. I'm in the shower and cleaning off the crusted cum on my inner thigh when Ryder knocks on the door and calls out a five-minute warning. Fuck.

I quickly rinse and step out to dry off. I left my clothes in the bedroom, so I step out there with just a towel on. Ryder gives me a smoldering look and pulls the towel off me. I gasp at his touch as his hand skims over my breasts, and slips under my arms and lifts me onto the dresser.

He pushes my legs open and pulls his cock out of his shorts before sliding into me. I wrap my legs around him and hold on to the edges of the dresser as he hammers into my pussy. The dresser knocks against the wall, creating a loud banging that someone could probably hear outside. Holy shit, this is fabulous.

"Nothing like fucking a clean pussy," Ryder pants.

I bite my lip to hold in a moan as spikes of delight ping up and down my body. There's nothing like being the fucktoy of some dude with a massive cock. I'm close to another orgasm again as his thrusts stretch me out and hit every nerve ending just right. I probably could ride this guy's cock for the rest of my life and be happy.

He speeds up and right before I come, he groans and blows his load deep inside me. Ohhh, no. Goddammit.

I'm whimpering as he pulls out and sets me on the floor. No, no, no. This isn't how it's supposed to happen. My body cries out from the lack of orgasm.

Ryder smacks my ass. "Let's go, slut. You don't need clothes."

I slip on my sandals so at least my feet will be protected. His cum drips down my thigh as I follow him out the door and down a lighted path towards loud music blaring from another building. Inside is a huge room filled with men playing pool around three pool tables. There are more guys than I can count. Oh wow, I didn't know this place had this many guys here.

Ryder leans over and whispers in my ear. "Remember your safeword. I'll be close if you need to use it."

Um... My eyes grow round and he slaps my ass and laughs before addressing the entire room in a booming voice. "I'm sharing my toy tonight with whoever wants her. First come, first served."

Several pool cues drop to the tables and three men advance towards me. A moment of trepidation overwhelms me until Ryder squeezes my hand in reassurance. Oh god, am I ever going to get this chance again? Probably not. A swell of lust and determination drifts over me.

I drop Ryder's hand and embrace the moment, waiting for the men to do whatever they want to me.

Within moments, I'm bent over the nearest pool table with a guy holding my shoulders down while he pounds into me from behind. My face squishes against the felt, and the smell of wood blends with the fragrance of all the men's cologne. The room tilts as waves of bliss ripple from my pussy. The guy inside me doesn't take long to come, and then another man replaces him. He yanks my hair up, increasing my pleasure as he slaps my ass and uses me.

Ryder calls out, "She likes it rough, boys, so don't go easy on her."

Fuck, what did I put on my forms again? I said I liked it rough, but what else did I say? Hands pull me off the table with the guy's cock still buried in me, and I find myself bent over sucking on another guy's dick while the guy behind me keeps drilling away. Every thrust from behind shoves me further on the shaft in my mouth. Luckily, this guy's not too huge, but he's large enough to tickle my throat with every stroke.

The guy explodes in my mouth and it's so much cum that it dribbles down my chin and onto the floor. The cum is salty and slightly metallic, with a slight hint of sweetness. I try to swallow as much as I can, but when he pulls out, a gush of liquid leaves my chin a mess. Another cock slides into my mouth and I moan at how filthy this is. This one's a little bigger than the last guy, and my mind goes fuzzy as two of my holes are filled and used.

At some point, the guy behind me comes, and they lay me on my back on the edge of the pool table. One man fucks my pussy while another guy stands to the side and I suck his cock. Multiple men hold my legs open and when one guy plays with my clit; it's too much and I cry out with my climax.

Sharp pleasure runs from my fingers to my toes and the guys don't stop using me. They fuck me through my orgasm and then my next one. Through it all, Ryder keeps up the dirty talk, telling me I'm a whore and a cum-guzzling slut. This is one of the top 10 greatest sexual experiences of my life. I'm floating in a haze of bliss, not caring who is using me or how many of them come on me. I just want all of them to find fulfillment tonight.

I lose count of my orgasms as the men switch around, shoving me against the walls as they pound into me. They bend me over every piece of furniture in the room as they all take their turn with me.

Time blends together until I find myself on the floor with three guys standing and jerking off over me. I close my eyes, open my mouth and stick out my tongue, hoping that some of them will hit my mouth. Warm drops rain down on me, and at least one guy's cum paints my lips. When the noise of them jerking off and their groans die down, I lick the salty cum away and slip into a state of pure joy.

When I come back to my senses, Ryder has me in his arms and he's carrying me towards my cottage. He sets me on the bathroom counter and pulls out his phone.

"Say cheese for your husband."

Oh god. I think of how sexually satiated I am and giggle. I know I look happy in whatever picture he just took.

He starts the shower and helps me stand up. I'm surprised when he enters the shower with me.

"Just stay still," he murmurs.

God, this guy is nice. He rinses me and uses a loofah with body wash to clean me up. My pussy aches, and he's gentle when directing the handheld sprayer between my legs. When we're done, he dries me off with a big fluffy towel and carries me to bed. The aftercare provided here is what really makes it a fabulous experience.

I'm too exhausted to do anything but murmur my thanks. As soon as my head hits the pillow, I zonk out.

In the night, I wake up with Ryder in bed with me, and feeling secure, I fall asleep again. I blink awake several hours later with birds chirping through an open window and someone knocking on my door. The side of the bed that Ryder is on is cold, so I can tell he's been gone for a while.

My pussy gives a small twinge of protest as I get out of bed and pad towards the doorway. I'm feeling overwhelmed by last night's experience and trying to process my emotions as I pull the door open. Keith is standing on the other side. A sudden joyful shock hits me, and I burst into tears for no reason. He pulls me into his arms, smothering my face with kisses.

"Oh baby, I couldn't stay away. You were so gorgeous in all the pictures."

I cling to the love of my life and kiss him passionately. As our tongues entwine, my nipples harden and I realize I'm naked, but he's not. I need his cock inside me, NOW. I pull at his clothes, and he helps me tear them off.

We fall into the bed together, a tangle of limbs, and when his cock slides into me, I sigh from the thrill and the feeling that I'm right where I belong. Last night was more intense than I ever imagined it would be, but he's the only man for me.

We surge together frantically, as if we can't get enough of each other. He's on top of me, and his lips are everywhere. His fingers brush against my clit while we both try to get his cock deeper inside of me. Keith knows exactly how to make me come, and it's not long before I'm shuddering around his cock and crying out with my climax.

He follows quickly, coming with a roar as he unloads more cum than I've gotten out of him in a long time. It feels like he's never going to stop coming as my orgasm recedes and then peaks again. When it finally ends, I'm shivering with tiny aftershocks of pleasure when he pulls out and rolls onto his back.

"Holy fuck," he groans, and I giggle.

Entwining my fingers with his, I give him a soft smile. "I'm glad it was you at the door. I didn't know how much I needed you until that moment."

He shifts onto his side and kisses my fingers. "I know, baby. This was the plan all along. I told them to give you an amazing night, and I'd take over on Saturday. You're MY freeuse slut today."

Sliding into his arms, I give him a deep kiss. His cock twitches against my belly and I giggle again. I think I'm going to enjoy being just his today. After all, there's still one hole left that hasn't been used yet.

If I play my cards right, maybe I'll go home tomorrow with all my holes filled after all.

AFTER USED FOR PLEASURE (BONUS STORY)

I'm naked and bent over a patio table close to the pool at the Plaything Resort while my husband Keith drills me from behind. My head swirls, and I try not to feel embarrassed when I see my best friend Tiffany walk past with two men in tow. She grins and gives me a tiny wave and two thumbs up. Looks like she finally made it to the resort. She missed a fun party last night.

Keith smacks my ass, bringing my attention back to him, and I hold in a gasp. The sting from his hand quickly turns into pleasure. Damn, he's good. He pins one of my shoulders against the table and holds my hip with his other hand as he thrusts into me. He fucks me so hard his balls slap against my clit with each plunge. I moan at the sensation, pushing back into him, wanting more of his cock. My nipples scrap against the metal table, sending a burst of pleasure straight to my clit, and I shudder.

"Ariana, you're such a slut," he growls as he thrusts into me. "I bet you loved having all those men fuck you last night. I saw the pictures. You looked like a cum-drunk whore."

I whimper in response as he holds me in place while he slams into me. I love when he talks dirty and uses me this way. He's been fucking me off and on all morning, ever since he got to the resort. I'm his freeuse slut today and he decides what happens to me. I've lost count of how many orgasms I've had. My whole body is sensitive from being fucked so roughly last night, and now he only has to touch me and I'm close to coming again.

I hear several male voices walking towards us. Oh great, they're probably wanting to go for a swim. I can't see them, but when they're almost upon us, they stop talking. They probably fucked me last night, but it doesn't stop the flush of humiliation.

"Hey guys!" Keith calls out to them. "Any of you want a ride on my freeuse slut?"

Ooooh, what? A chorus of "yesses" sound out as Keith pulls away from me. He turns me around to face him, and I stand with my legs spread. He pushes two fingers into my pussy, making sure they get nice and wet before pulling them out and holding them in front of my face.

"Suck them," he orders.

I obey, opening my mouth so he can push his fingers in. I taste myself on him and lick them clean. When I'm done, he keeps a firm grip on my shoulder to hold me steady.

"Go ahead, boys," he says in a voice that sounds way too jolly for what is happening. "Do what you want with her."

Earlier I was overwhelmed, but after spending half the day with my husband, I'm ready to embrace multiple cocks again. I just didn't know Keith would want to watch someone fuck me. He never has before.

There are four guys, and two of them pick me up and lay me on the table, pushing my knees towards my chest. One guy gets between my legs; he's a familiar face from last night. He slides his cock up and down my wet slit, and I groan as he sinks into me.

Keith moves to stand to the side, and I can tell he has the perfect view of this guy's cock thrusting in and out. Fuck, that's filthy. My entire body vibrates with lust as I keep my eyes on Keith. He is rapt and can't look away at the action between my legs.

"Yeah, that's it," Keith murmurs. "Fuck that pussy harder."

My inner muscles contract at his words and the guy hammers into me harder and faster. I hold on to the edges of the table as my tits bounce around. Oh god, this is so hot.

Another guy comes up to my head and slides his cock between my lips. Having two guys stuffing me while my husband watches makes me feel like the ultimate freeuse slut. They're only doing this because he wants them to, which makes this experience even more amazing.

The guy in my mouth fucks me slowly and I'm too busy to watch Keith anymore. I have an eyeful of this guy's junk, and I gurgle happily around his shaft as he drills into my throat. I can't do anything but lie there and take it in both holes.

When the guy between my legs comes with a shout, I feel his warm seed filling me up. The world tilts as I orgasm right after he does. The cock in my mouth muffles my scream, and my entire body spasms as bolts of electricity turn me limp from ecstasy.

Another guy replaces the one between my legs, and I barely notice as he slides in. They can do whatever they want to me; I'm loving it all, and every stroke is exquisite pleasure.

The guy in my mouth jerks and comes with a groan, his cum spraying the back of my throat. I'm not able to swallow it all. When he pulls out, saliva and cum run down my cheek. The guy fucking my pussy has one hand on my thigh and one hand on my tit and uses me hard and fast.

"Oh, fuck yeah." Keith sounds enthusiastic. "That's it, slut. Take it all."

He's obviously enjoying the show. God, I love that man.

Keith moves closer to my head, but he's still focused on the guy fucking me, so I can tell he's just trying to get a different view. The fourth guy moves to the table with his cock out and rubs the tip against one of my breasts. I gasp when he smacks my nipple with it. The guy in my pussy slows down and his longer strokes take me close to another orgasm.

Keith caresses my cheek. "Are you going to come again?"

I don't think I have a choice. The pleasure builds until it crests and my eyes roll back as a wave of bliss washes over me. My pussy tightens around the guy inside me, and he groans loudly as he follows me over the edge.

The guy between my legs pulls out and rubs his cock against my pussy lips, smearing his cum along them. He steps back and the fourth guy grabs my hair, putting his cock between my lips. Guess he's done poking my breast. He shoves it into my mouth as far as it will go and holds it there while he groans loudly, then blows his load.

When he finally pulls out, cum dribbles down my chin again, making me an even bigger mess.

Someone hands Keith a towel, and he wipes off my face while the other guys sound like they're straightening their swim trunks.

"Thanks for letting us use your slut," one of them calls out.

Keith grins at me while he replies, "You're welcome. It was fun to watch."

The guys jump into the pool as Keith helps me sit up and wraps his arms around me. He kisses my forehead and I inhale his musk, letting the scent soothe me. He strokes my back as I shiver from aftershocks of pleasure.

"I love you so much, Ariana. There won't be any other men tonight. I just wanted to see that once."

I hug him close to me and smile into his chest. Whatever he decides is fine with me, but if later he wants to share me and watch again, I'm more than willing.

The End

Used for Amusement

Freeuse Resort Weekend 2

Lacey Cross

Chapter 1

An old crystal sun catcher hangs in the window from a fraying string. Its colors create a rainbow on the headrest of the couch. If my friend Katie moved a few inches, it would be on the back of her head. My gaze keeps coming back to the bright sparkles of light, and I admire the twinkling colors. The sun catcher seems out of place among the elegant décor, yet it must have some special meaning to Sabrina, my high school friend, who is hosting this small baby shower.

Sabrina is the first one of us to get pregnant. She's wealthy, and she loves hosting parties, so I was expecting a big to-do when I got here, but she only invited our close-knit group of friends from high school. Including Sabrina, there are six of us here.

Katie and I drove here together; I wanted time alone with her to ask her for some advice about my marriage. Katie married her high school sweetheart and has been married for 14 years. I've only been with Sean for five years and our sex life has slowed down recently. He still thrills me in the bedroom, but we're busy, so we have less time to connect. I want to find out if Katie has any advice on how to keep the spice alive in a long-term relationship. We were too busy catching up on life and I didn't get time to talk to her on the drive here. I'm hoping to bring it up on the way home.

Sabrina left the room to get something to show us. Sabrina's super sweet, and is utterly adorable at eight months pregnant. Just being around her puts me in a good mood because she's clearly happy and living her best life.

A swarm of catering staff circles the room, which seems odd now that I think of it. There's at least a one-to-one ratio of catering staff to guests, which is excessive for a baby shower. They're all incredibly sexy men as well. What are the chances of that? Maybe they aren't actually a catering crew and this is about to turn super raunchy when they all rip off their clothes and dance for us. That dark-haired guy across the room could come gyrate in my face while wearing just a banana hammock and I certainly wouldn't complain.

The guy notices I'm looking at him and he brings over a bottle of Champagne. Oooh, that's right. Come over here and service me. God, I've been such a thirsty slut lately. I need my husband to fuck me into oblivion tonight.

My body tingles as the dark-haired server refills my glass and I catch the eye of my friend, Ariana, sitting on a couch across from me. I tip my head towards the server and Ariana gives me a knowing look. Yeah, she's thinking the same thing I am. There's no way these sexy beefcakes are just servers. I know strippers aren't a typical baby shower thing, but if someone was going to hire some, it would be Sabrina.

As I take a sip of Champagne, I grin at Katie and try to get her to smile back at me. She's looking grim for someone at a baby shower, and I wonder why. She needs to lighten up before the live entertainment starts.

Sabrina finally joins us again. "Okay, everyone. You ready for the surprise?"

I sit up straighter. Oh hell yeah, bring on the strippers! Sabrina waddles around the sofas and hands us each a business card. I'm momentarily disappointed. Um, this isn't a stripper. When I examine the card, I'm baffled. It says "Plaything Resort" on the front and has a phone number and email address on the back.

I look over at Ariana and I can tell she's as confused as I am. Sabrina sits down and we all have to wait while she adjusts her dress around her. She's really playing this up—but that's why we all love her. Nothing is ever dull with her around.

She smiles and laughs. "This is my gift to you. It's an invitation to an all-inclusive weekend at my favorite private resort. You don't have to worry about anything. Just show up and enjoy yourselves, either on your own, together, or with your husbands."

No one says anything, and I turn the card over and read the name again: Plaything Resort. Who or what is the plaything?

Ariana breaks the silence. "What is this?"

Sabrina giggles. "It's a private, freeuse sex resort, silly! It's only open to one group of people at a time. Just tell them what you want and they'll make all your fantasies come true."

Oh fuck, there is no way Sean would go with me—or let ME go. This is totally wasted on me, but could you just imagine—a bunch of guys who look like the sexy caterer all over me? Mmm, yummy. My body heats and I'm probably blushing. Okay, so even if I'm never going to use this card, I can at least seduce my husband tonight.

I don't have time to talk to Katie about my declining sex life on the drive home. We're too busy discussing the Plaything Resort—or rather, I'm discussing it, and Katie is on a tirade.

"I can't believe Sabrina offered that to us. I told her the only person who would like it was Ariana because she's a hotwife. Why in the hell did she think any of us would want this? We're all happily married."

Huh, so Katie knew about that already. I'm driving and trying to keep my attention on the road while my mind whirls. "Yeah, and it's not like Sean would let me go, even if I wanted to."

"Exactly!" she bursts out. "That lifestyle is fine for Ariana. I just hope Sabrina didn't actually pay for this. She's going to have wasted a bunch of money when no one goes."

Katie continues to talk about the disgusting, perverted things that probably happen at the resort. Every point she makes sounds wonderful to me. A resort where people are there just to please me? My panties grow damp as I imagine a cock in my mouth, one in my pussy, and a guy sliding in the backdoor. I'll be the freeuse toy for a bunch of men any day as long as my husband agrees to it. All those orgasms...

Katie interrupts my thoughts. "Can we turn the air conditioning on? It's warm today."

"Yep." I turn the dial and the cool air blasts us. Oh yeah, that's good. I was getting a little hot under the collar.

When I pull into Katie's driveway, she turns to me. "I'm sorry. I've been ranting, haven't I?"

Her eyes are glassy, and she's just as flushed as I feel. Dang, she really hates this idea. To hell if I'm going to admit I'm ready to open my legs and tell a bunch of men to come and get it.

I give her a smile. "It's fine. I don't know what Sabrina was thinking, either."

Yeah, Sabrina was just trying to be an amazing friend. Too bad I won't be able to experience this once-in-a-lifetime opportunity. Katie thanks me for the ride and I can tell she's miffed. Her poor husband is going to get an earful tonight.

I'm not sure what I'm going to say to Sean. We've talked in the past about him sharing me because Ariana is a hotwife and loves it, but the conversation wasn't ever serious. As I daydream on the rest of the drive that he wants to share me, I'm getting more and more turned on.

When I get home, I find out that Sean's got a headache. There will be no seducing him tonight. Damnit, now my body needs to understand we're not getting plowed by Sean while fantasizing about other guys' cocks.

I wait until the next morning over breakfast to tell him about the offer, and keep my tone light. "Hey love, I forgot to tell you the crazy gift Sabrina gave us at the shower."

He's eating his favorite apples and cinnamon oatmeal and reading something on his phone. He pauses and looks at me. "She gave you a gift at her own baby shower?"

"Well, there's usually party favors or prizes from games, but this was a lot bigger than that."

I can tell he's only half interested because he glances at his phone again. "She didn't try to give you a puppy again, did she?"

Sabrina once tried to give me a golden retriever puppy because she was buying the brother. The condo we live in isn't the best location for a big dog, so I declined. "No, not a dog. She gave me a voucher for a weekend at a sex resort."

That gets him to stop looking at this phone. "A what resort?"

"It's a freeuse sex resort. We can go together or I can go alone." I can tell he's digesting this information.

"Who is the freeuse person? You or them?"

Why is he asking questions? He is supposed to laugh it off and say how Sabrina is nuts.

"Uh, I think I am—or the person who goes. She said you go and they make all your fantasies come true."

He grins. "What if my fantasy is to use someone else?"

My mouth almost drops open while my pussy buzzes. Um... can it be me, please? A vision of him using me wherever he wants around the condo pops into my head and it takes a moment for me to remember he asked a question. Okay, I need to focus.

I laugh lightly. "The invitation was to ME, and I want to be the one used. She said couples could go together if they wanted to."

"Huh, interesting." He goes back to looking at his phone.

That's it? That's all he's going to say? I'm slightly disappointed, but drop the conversation. It's not like I expected him to say we should go.

Sean presses his body against mine as he fucks me on the washing machine—or half on it. He found me doing laundry, kissed the back of my neck, and somehow that led to this: my panties are on the floor with me laying halfway on the washer with my legs wrapped around him. My hands are over my head, gripping the control panel. I hold on for dear life as my husband fucks me harder than he has in weeks.

It's been two days since I told him about the offer and he never mentioned it again, but it's all I can think about. A weekend surrounded by beefy guys all there to use me as much as they want? That sounds like heaven on Earth to me. I've been turned on and trying to seduce him, but we've been busy like usual. It seems someone finally took the hint.

We move in perfect harmony in a dance we've done hundreds of times in our five years together. My skin glistens with a light sheen of sweat, and my breath comes in gasps of pleasure. His hands explore my curves under my nightshirt, sending jolts of bliss shooting through my body.

"Tiffany," Sean moans as he thrusts harder and faster. "I want you to go to the resort."

Ohhh! My heart skips a beat., and I cry out, "Yessss," as a wave of rapture ripples to my toes.

Sean pulls on one of my nipples and I groan. I love when he does that. He switches to pinch the other nipple and I moan again. He knows exactly how rough I like it. Pings of delight shoot through my body and I clamp my legs around him harder, trying to draw him inside me as deep as I can.

"Sean, I need to come."

He chuckles, "Not yet. I want to watch you squirm and writhe in pleasure."

He tugs on my legs, and I loosen them as he pulls out. I whimper and bite my lip to stifle my cries so the neighbors in the condo next to us don't hear me. When I can tell he's going to flip me over, I let go of the washing machine and help him. Setting my feet on the floor, I bend over and grip the top as he slides inside me from behind.

"Fuuuck," I moan loudly, and slap my hand over my mouth to muffle any further sounds.

He drills into me, hitting every sensitive spot as his hands grasp my hips. I feel like I might burst from the pleasure.

"You want a bunch of guys using you, don't you?" His voice has a low growl that always gets me more worked up when he uses it.

I nod and whimper as I arch my back.

"Tell me, Tiffany."

My eyes roll back into my head and I remove my hand from my mouth so I can moan, "Yes. I want all those men to rail me."

He groans, "I married such a filthy slut." He pounds away, wrapping his hand around me to brush against my clit. His fingers tease my swollen nub, and I whimper in delight. My head spins as I speed towards my orgasm.

I can't keep quiet any longer and start begging, "Please. Can I come, please?"

"Not yet, slut."

His deep voice sends a shiver down my spine as he hammers into me. I love it when he talks dirty. It's always been a part of our relationship, and it's one reason I hooked up with him. I've always had a voice kink, and Sean's sexy voice hits all my buttons—but him talking dirty really lights my panties on fire.

"I need to come," I beg.

He slaps my ass, and I gasp, almost coming right then from the surprise.

"I'm not done with my slut." He twists his hand in my hair, pulling my head back. "Don't even think about coming."

I moan as he fucks me hard and fast. I close my eyes, surging against him as the bliss threatens to overwhelm me. My toes curl against the linoleum and my thighs quiver with pleasure. I imagine there's a train of guys on my ass and it's someone else's hand pulling my hair. I chant, "Fuck me. Fuck me, harder," as he slams me against the washing machine.

Just when I think I can't take any more, he spanks me again and groans, "Come for me, slut."

My body goes rigid as my pussy spasms. I moan as my orgasm takes over. I feel a gush of warmth between my legs. Oh fuck, that's me. I don't care that I'm making a mess as the rapture consumes me.

He releases my hair and pulls out, and I'm so far gone, I almost don't notice he hasn't come.

"Get on your knees."

I open my eyes and look over my shoulder at him in confusion. My brain is so fuzzy, I couldn't even tell you my own name right now.

"On your knees," he repeats, his voice hard.

Oh! My legs feel weak as I sink to the floor. He stands over me, with his shorts around his ankles, stroking my wetness onto his cock. He has a crazed look in his eyes and I can tell he's beyond reason and needs to come. I love it when Sean loses control. It brings out the animalistic side of him and that's when things like getting fucked against the washing machine happen.

"Open your mouth. I want you to imagine how many cocks you're going to suck at the resort."

Oh fuck, yes. I part my lips and stick out my tongue as he slides his cock between my lips. He moans as he thrusts into my mouth and I suck on him, loving the taste of my juices on him. It's always extra dirty when he fucks me first and makes me clean him off.

I envision some other guy's cock in my mouth and moan around his shaft. Knowing that a bunch of men can pick which hole to use for the weekend makes me crave the debasement of being just a toy to be used. How many loads of cum will I take? I hollow my cheeks and suck on Sean as hard as I can, desperate to make him come. I want him to give him as much pleasure as he gave me.

He groans, holding my head as he forces his cock into my mouth as far as it will go. I gasp a little and he releases me, sliding in and out of my willing mouth.

"Oh god, that feels good, baby. Suck my cock."

He's back to calling me baby, which means he's really close to coming. I hold on to his legs and bob my head, deep throating him.

He growls, "Faster, baby."

I work my head up and down as quickly as I can, sucking his cock down to the base.

I moan around him and caress his balls gently, knowing it usually makes him come. He cries out with his orgasm and his cock spasms in my mouth as the first spurt of cum hits the back of my throat. I swallow quickly and then swallow again, hoping he's not done yet. He's still twitching inside my mouth and I use my hand to milk his shaft, getting every drop out of him.

"Mmm, fuck," he pants as I lick and clean him up.

When he gives a final all-body shudder, I can tell he's finished. I sit back on my feet and grin up at him. "You sure you want me to go?"

He looks down at me with utter love and devotion. "Yeah, baby. I want you to go."

Mmm, hell yeah. Guess this means I'm about to become a hotwife.

CHAPTER 3

I arranged to go the same weekend as Ariana. We were going to drive together, but there was a work emergency that held me up for a day. Ariana went without me, and now I get the awkwardness of showing up alone. I wanted to hide behind her and make her check in for us. Plus, now I only get to stay one night. I was supposed to have had multiple orgasms by now.

I'm annoyed and stressed on the three-hour drive. As I pull up to the iron gates at the resort, I punch in the keycode the owner gave me. Sean decided not to go with me. The idea of me fucking someone else turns him on, but he's not ready to watch it yet. I respect that since I wouldn't want to see him fucking another woman. I'm just thrilled he's willing to share me at all.

I drive slowly down the lane, gawking out the window at a gorgeous mansion with a fountain in front of it. Fuck a duck, this place is stunning. Now I'm even less amused by the cruel twist of fate of the work emergency on the ONE weekend I actually had plans.

I park my car next to Ariana's, but I don't get out immediately. I need a minute to gather my courage. If I wasn't so desperate for a bunch of guys to use me, I would have just canceled. I don't like to travel alone like this. I'm shy and I need someone with me to talk to strangers. This just goes to show you how much of a slut I am since I'm willing to leave my comfort zone for cock.

The owner, Chris, seemed nice, though. Before I could register for the resort, he and I talked on the phone about consent and safewords, and to go over a questionnaire I had to fill out about my sexual limits. I assured him I'm excited for the weekend.

God, I really do want this. My body tingles with sexual tension as I climb from my car. I smooth down my flowered sundress and grab my bag.

A masculine voice behind me makes me jump. "Welcome, Tiffany. Glad you could make it!"

Shit, where did he come from? I turn, and a gorgeous older man with salt and pepper hair grins at me. He's fit, wearing a white button-down shirt and shorts that show off his toned legs. A jolt of lust runs through my body as his deep blue eyes twinkle at me. Okay, yeah, he could use me if he wanted.

"H-hi," I stammer and my face grows even warmer as my pussy gets more wet.

He takes my bag from me, and I wordlessly let go of it. As I follow him up the stairs to the entrance, I admire his legs again. I need to stop eying the owner. He probably doesn't play with the guests.

He leads me to a reception desk and sets my bag on the counter. "I have some forms for you to sign."

Two guys walk in, smile at me, and lean against the wall. Uh... what's this?

"I just need to see your ID."

"Oh, sure." I fish out my driver's license from my bag while keeping an eye on the two men. They're wearing swim shorts, tank tops, and no shoes. They're both super sexy, and I catch the taller one's eye. He winks at me and I bite my lip.

Chris hands my ID back to me and slides some paperwork and a pen towards me. The guys against the wall stand there while I quickly sign all the forms.

"You're all set, Tiffany. Just remember, everyone here knows your safe-word and will abide by it."

Just hearing him mention my safeword makes my heart rate speed up. I have zero intention of using it. I want all the cocks I can get stuffed into every hole.

"Thank you." I smile at him, and try to look friendly, despite how nervous I am. I'm sure once I get a few cocks in me, I'll loosen up.

Chris tucks the papers into a folder and gestures to the guys against the wall. "They'll show you to your cottage."

I pick up my bag, dropping my ID back in it, and one man steps forward. "I'll take that for you."

"Thanks. Lead the way."

I follow them through the mansion and out some French doors onto a breathtaking deck. It's midday, and the sun is shining. It's one of those perfect days where there's a refreshing breeze and it's not too hot to be outside. The guys don't say anything, but they pause at the edge of the deck right before we step down onto a stone path. I'm busy looking around at the lovely bushes past the deck when the taller one bends me over the railing.

Oh shit, this is really happening. I can feel wetness leak into my panties, and I gasp as he grabs my hair and yanks it back, causing my head to snap up. Fuck, I love it when someone tugs on my hair; it was something I wrote on the questionnaire of likes and dislikes.

"This is your first time here, isn't it?" he growls in my ear.

I nod and whimper in delight. God, his voice is so sexy.

He pulls my hair again and I can't help the moan that escapes me. "Use your words."

I gasp out a yes, and he slides his hand down my back and caresses my ass through my sundress.

"I'm going to fuck your sweet cunt."

I whimper again and wiggle my ass at him. *Oh yes, please fuck me.*

He yanks my dress up over my ass, nudges the hem of my panties to the side, and rubs my clit. I'm already so wet from thinking about what would happen this weekend, he could slide his cock right in.

I moan out in pleasure, and he laughs. "You're eager to be a freeuse slut, aren't you?"

Yes, yes, I am. I want all these men to use me. I don't respond to him, and instead rock against his hand.

He slides two fingers inside me and fucks me for a moment. My head spins while I hold on to the railing. This is exactly what I need—a guy taking what he wants from me.

I whimper in protest when he pulls out. "I'm not sure I'm going to let you come. I might just keep you desperate for every cock and never satisfied. We're going to go slow and enjoy you over and over again."

What? That's not what I want. I don't have time to protest because he pulls his fingers out of my pussy and shoves them into my mouth. I suck on them hard, moaning as I swirl my tongue and taste my wetness on him.

"Good girl, you're a good sucker. You're going to be a fun toy to break in."

I groan as his fingers leave my mouth, and he slides them back into my pussy.

"You're already soaked, like a good little slut."

I requested dirty talk on the forms I filled out, and this is fabulous. He keeps thrusting his fingers in and out of me until I'm on the verge of an orgasm. He removes them fully and I whine in protest.

"Come with us," he says, as he pulls me upright. I stand on wobbly legs and I can feel my wetness coating my inner thighs. He leads me to the path and my high-heeled sandals click on the stone walkway. The second guy is next to me, still carrying my bag. He gives me a sexy grin as he looks me up and down.

"You're gorgeous," he murmurs.

My heart skips a beat. This is all happening so fast. I try to smile back at him, but it comes out as a nervous grimace. "Thank you."

He reaches over and tugs on my arm, and we both stop walking. I squeal as he squeezes my breast through my dress.

"Oooh, nice tits."

The tall guy stops walking and watches us while the shorter guy palms my tit. I can't help but push my chest into his hand. I've been horny as fuck for days and I'm ready to be ravished.

He leans in closer and whispers in my ear. "We're going to use you all night because you're a slut who wants this."

He's right. I am. My pussy is aching for him to fuck me right now. He releases my breast, and we walk again, this time closer together. I can sense his hungry gaze on me and my body vibrates in anticipation.

I smell the pool before it's in view, and the guys pause and usher me to go first. The tall one speaks. "Your cabin is just past the pool. Keep following the path. We're right behind you."

Oh yeah, they are so going to bend me over something whenever they want. Why else are they behind me? When the pool comes into sight, a broad grin lights up my face. It's Ariana! And she's bent over a table while her husband fucks her. I didn't know Keith was coming. She looks dazed and happy. I give her a little wave and two thumbs up. You go, girl—get that cock.

CHAPTER 4

When we get to my cottage, the men follow me inside. The short one sets my bag on the bed as I poke my head in every nook and cranny of the one-bedroom cottage. It's cozy and decorated with light blue tones. There's a large bathroom with a separate shower and a massive tub that could fit four people. I doubt I'll have time to take a bath with only one night here, but I could imagine plenty of fun ways to use a bathtub of that size. The kitchenette, dining area, and living room are small, but fine for my needs.

Once I'm satisfied with my inspection, I turn to the men. Both of them are leaning against the wall again. This must be part of their performance. Mmm, they really are gorgeous. Both of them are muscular and tanned. I'd love to run my hands under either of their shirts and see if they have six-packs. I suspect they do. Yeah, okay, I'm ready to be used. The rules for the resort are that I can't ask for it. I have to wait for someone to do whatever they want to me. Someone better fuck me soon.

The taller one grins at me. "I'm Max." He gestures to the other guy. "And that's Arlo."

"Nice to meet you both." I'm still smiling nervously and can't help the flush on my cheeks as I gaze up at them with wide eyes. My voice cracks as I add, "I'm Tiffany."

Oh god, they already knew my name from when Chris said it during check-in. I blush even harder and dip my head to hide my embarrassment. I probably sound stupid.

Max steps close and tips my chin up. I meet his gaze and my body hums to life. There's a hardness in his eyes that makes me shiver. This is a guy who'll enjoy using me.

He gives me a crooked smile right before he spins me around and shoves me against the nearest wall. My cheek is against the textured plaster and I get a surreal feeling, like I'm living in a porno. Does this actually happen to people outside of movies? He pins my shoulder to the wall with one hand and pulls my dress up over my ass with the other, just like he did on the porch.

I gasp in shock when he shoves my panties aside and thrusts two fingers into my pussy. Jesus, would he stop with the finger fucking and just give me his damn cock? I moan and gyrate against his hand, trying to get friction on my clit.

His breath is warm in my ear. "So this is how tonight will go. Earlier, we drew straws, and I won, so you're mine. I have to decide if I want to share you."

My head spins at his words. Um, wait. Do I get a vote in this? I came here to be used by a bunch of men, not just one hot guy.

Max continues. "But since I share everything with Arlo, he's an exception. He gets to use you without my permission."

I moan and rotate my hips, imagining one of them in my mouth and one in my pussy. I wanted someone in all my holes, but I'd be okay with two. My entire body is on fire and I desperately need a cock inside me.

Max stops fingering me and drags me to the bed. I fall onto my stomach on the mattress and he grabs my hips, forcing me up on my knees. Ooooh, it's going to happen! My pussy buzzes in anticipation as Max slides my underwear down my legs. He leaves my sandals on and bunches my dress up around my waist, exposing my bare pussy to his view. Since I figured there would be more guys between my legs than normal, I tidied up the lawn down below before this trip and left just a small landing strip. I'm glad I took the time. I'm feeling sexy and ready to be fucked.

Max whistles. "Arlo, come see this pretty little pussy we get to fuck."

Oh god, wait. I didn't consider how I would feel with multiple eyes examining me at the same time. In my head, it was one-on-one with multiple men in a row. Lowering my face to the bed, I try to hide my flaming cheeks in my hands as Arlo stands behind me. I try not to squirm, knowing they're both examining my pussy. Wetness leaks down my inner thigh, and my stomach tenses with a mix of desire and humiliation from being examined so closely.

Arlo swipes a finger up the middle of my pussy lips. I moan and wiggle my ass against his hand, silently begging for more. He laughs as if he's delighted with my response as he slides his finger in, filling me up.

I sigh in pleasure, but he quickly pulls his hand away, leaving me feeling empty again. What the hell, man? Why are they only toying with me and not fucking me? Are they trying to drive me insane? A zing heads straight between my legs and I'm aching to feel a cock slide inside me.

Max slaps my ass cheek hard, and I jump in surprise. "Are you going to be a good slut for us?"

I pant as the heat from his hand fades and I become more aroused by the second. "Yes," I gasp out. "I want to be used."

Max takes hold of my hair and yanks my head back, pulling me up on my hands. I cry out with painful pleasure and I almost come from the rough treatment. My entire body throbs with desire. God, I'm a mess right now.

I feel Arlo's hands rubbing the spot on my ass cheek where Max just spanked me, and I moan again. Shit, I'm going to beg soon.

As Arlo strokes me, Max says, "You're so fucking wet," right before he sinks his cock into my pussy, filling me up as he slides in to the hilt. He's got a long, thick cock, and he pings all my nerve endings as bliss almost overtakes me.

I cry out in delight as he uses my hair as reins, keeping me upright on my knees as he makes me ride his cock. This is exactly what I came for—a hot guy taking what he wants from me, using me for his gratification.

He fucks me vigorously, and I can feel my breasts bouncing underneath my sundress. So much for my strapless bra having good support. I try to rock backwards to keep up with his thrusts, and I'm quickly working up a sweat. I feel myself edging close to an orgasm, but right before I come, Max groans and I feel his warm cum bathe my inner walls.

He lets go of my hair and slides out of me while I collapse onto the bed. Nooo, what? Arlo brushes my hair out of my face and smiles at me. "We'll see you later."

I'm dazed and my pussy twitches as the two men leave me. When the door clicks shut, I moan and close my eyes as my entire body cries in protest of the stolen orgasm. I'm not sure I'll survive the night if they don't let me come.

I gather up my panties from around my knees and pull them up, smoothing my dress down over my ass. As I sit on the edge of the bed, his cum leaks into my panties. I take a moment to recover. I think Sabrina's idea of a good time differs slightly from mine.

Once I can think again, I dig my phone out of my bag and text Sean.

Tiffany

> I've been toyed with twice so far without coming.

I include a pouty face emoji. He's quick to respond.

Sean

> Poor baby. If they send you home unsatisfied, I'll take care of you. I promise.

Awww, yeah, that's why I love him. I'm about to reply with a kissy GIF, but a picture of his hard cock pops up with a message underneath.

Sean

> With this.

Desire flutters in my core, and I admire the prominent veins on his shaft. I can tell it's from today based on what he's wearing. Oooh, I can have fun with this since he didn't see my pussy after I shaved. I quickly take off my panties and climb onto the bed, pulling my dress up and spreading my knees so the camera on my phone has a graphic view. It's awkward but I'm satisfied with the result. My pussy lips are wet and swollen from being used, and I can see Max's cum dripping out of me. I send a message with my picture.

Tiffany

You'll take care of this?

His response is immediate.

Sean

Yes, now go find a cock to make you more of a mess. I want some good stories when you get home.

He gets the kissy GIF from me, and I tell him I love him. I set my phone on the bed and spring up, determined to find someone to fuck me. I'd seen Ariana down by the pool—maybe there are more men there and I can tempt them to use me?

I brought a bikini so I'd be ready for anything. As I'm changing, I spot a map of the grounds on the dresser and examine it. The game room intrigues me, but when I see they have a sauna, I know I've found where I want to go first. If no one fucks me on the way there, at least I can get some relaxation out of the night.

I abandon my sandals for some flip-flops and set out towards the pool. The sauna was close to it, and I'm curious whether Ariana is still around getting fucked by her husband.

As I walk, I admire the luxurious landscaping and manicured paths. This is an elaborate resort for only one group of people to enjoy at a time, and other than not having an orgasm yet, this place is ideal for a weekend away to unwind.

When I reach the pool, I pause to take it all in. There is a hot tub, lounge chairs, and a full-sized diving board on one side of the pool. A small crowd is gathered around the table that I last saw Ariana bent over. Curiosity gets the better of me and I skirt along the edge of the pool area, hoping no one notices me. What I find makes me smile with delight.

Two guys are using Ariana while Keith and two other men watch. Ariana is on her back and her pussy is on display for everyone to see. One man is between her legs, while the other guy is thrusting his cock into her mouth. Damn, that's hot.

I'm tempted to stay and see what happens, but as I listen to her moans, I feel myself heating up. It's probably better if I don't get turned on watching my best friend fuck a bunch of dudes. Though... maybe it's too late?

I'm still wondering if I'm forever going to be visualizing her being railed by the pool as I step into the sauna. It's empty and I sigh in disappointment. The men are too busy fucking Ariana to be in here. Oh well, time to relax.

After a few minutes, the room is full of steam and I'm thoroughly hot. I'm lying down on one of the long benches with my eyes closed. When the door opens, I peek through my eyelashes and hold in a smile when I see Max and Arlo stroll in. They're shirtless and wearing just their shorts.

They say nothing to me, so I stay on my back as they pick out benches next to each other across from me. As I watch them, my pussy tingles again. They are both hot as sin and have chiseled bodies. Arlo has more muscle on his frame than Max, but they're both broad shouldered with trim waists. I can clearly see that their cocks are hard underneath their shorts, so why aren't they fucking me yet?

Arlo turns to look at Max. They smile and shrug in some sort of silent communication, then rise and walk over to my bench. Arlo works on turning the heat and steam off, while Max straddles my chest, hovering over me, and points his cock towards my mouth.

"Open up. It's time to really see how well you suck cock."

I moan as the head slides between my lips, his thick length filling my throat. He smells like citrus body wash, so I can tell he showered recently. I swirl my tongue around his shaft, trying to maximize his pleasure. This was the part I craved—a guy just taking what he wants without asking me.

Max puts his hand on the wall behind me so he can lean in and fuck my mouth. My pussy grows wetter with each stroke. Arlo peels my bikini bottoms off and then settles between my legs. He pulls my knees up so he can sit on the bench close enough to my pussy to rub the tip of his cock along my slick folds. I moan around Max's cock as pings of bliss radiate through my body. Please god, I hope they fuck me long enough for me to come.

Arlo sinks into my pussy as I whimper. Fuuuck, this feels so good. I wrap my legs around Arlo and then reach up to grip Max's thighs as he steadily drills into my mouth. Arlo is thrusting up into me hard and fast, and I clench around him, trying to keep him inside me.

Max's cock twitches on my tongue and he pulls out, rubbing the head across my lips. I lick and suck on the tip of his cock, enjoying the taste of his pre-cum.

He groans, "You're a good cocksucker."

I moan and nod, flicking my tongue against the sensitive underside of his head. When he stands up, I'm disappointed. I wanted him to blow his load into my throat.

In what seems like a choreographed routine, Max sits on the bench behind my head and lifts my shoulders as Arlo leans back until he's flat on the bench. Max helps me sit up and straddle Arlo. As soon as I'm stable, he pushes my shoulders down until my face is close to Arlo's.

Arlo smiles at me, and gives me a cute, "Hi," before pulling me into a deep kiss. Our tongues swirl together as the door swings open, letting cool air in. I can't see who it is, but another masculine voice greets us.

"Hey, you guys want a third?"

Max replies with a laugh. "Only if you brought lube."

My pussy clamps down around Arlo and my toes curl from pleasure. Hell yeah, we want a third. I've always been too shy to contemplate doing anything wild like this. That's what makes this freeuse resort so wonderful. I don't have to even talk to the guys and they're fucking me.

My head whirls as my tongue duels with Arlo's. I almost don't hear the new guy's response.

"I actually have some."

Oh god, no way is this random. He didn't just walk in here carrying lube. My body ignites as I hear the cap opening a second before someone's finger rubs cold moisture around my asshole. I moan as the person works the lube into me. Yeah, I don't care if this was planned. This is fucking awesome.

When the person removes their finger, the tip of a cock replaces it. I break off my kiss and glance over my shoulder. It's Max.

He holds onto my hips, smiles at me, and starts sinking in. The pressure is painful but feels so damn good. My eyelids flutter and I sigh as Arlo thrusts his hips up, fucking me and forcing Max's cock further into my ass. Motion by my head makes me focus. The new guy's cock is by my lips.

Oooooh, all three holes at once! They really listened to what I put on the forms. I open my mouth and suck on the new cock greedily while Max's cock stretches my ass open. I've never had two men—so three at once is mind blowing. Time slows down as the men use me. I close my eyes and let myself experience the pleasure through all my senses.

The room is still warm, and our bodies are slick with sweat, which only makes this seem dirtier. Max uses my hips to control my motions as he strokes in and out of my ass. Each thrust forces me to grind down onto Arlo's shaft. They're both big and fill me completely. I squeeze around them as I moan from the euphoria of being thoroughly used.

The guy in my mouth speeds up, and I wrap my fingers around his shaft to help hold his cock steady as he face fucks me. When he applies pressure on the back of my head, I open my mouth wider and take him in as deep as I can until he hits the back of my throat. I gag, but quickly recover.

Our moans and groans, along with the wet slapping sounds of our bodies colliding, fill the small room. My head spins from how erotic everything is. As my rapture builds, my heart races and my entire body hums from the approaching orgasm. This is beyond anything I've experienced before and the ecstasy builds in layers until I can't take it any longer.

I scream out around the cock in my mouth as an intense release shoots pleasure from my fingertips to my toes. The waves of rapture keep coming as I ride the cocks in my pussy and ass, mindless about anything other than the bliss their cocks create inside me.

Max groans, "I'm going to come," right before he plunges into my ass one last time and explodes. His coming triggers Arlo, and Arlo's cock pulsates for a moment before filling my pussy with warm cum.

The third guy's cock twitches against my lips as he rasps out his climax, spurting his load into my mouth. I swallow what I can, but it's too much for my throat and some streams out of my mouth. When he's done coming and pulls out, I try to catch my breath and my panting turns into a moan as Max withdraws from my ass.

I'm limp from my orgasm, but I can feel myself tightening around Arlo in an effort to keep him inside me longer. It seems to work because he hasn't pulled out yet and is still breathing heavily from his own orgasm.

When he grimaces, Max picks me up off of Arlo's cock. He cradles me in his arms as the new guy helps him open the door. Max carries me out in the cool air and I take a few deep breaths. Okay, yeah, it's good to be in the fresh air. He sits down on a chair by the pool and settles me into his lap. The new guy hurries over with a bottle of water. I'm not sure how he got it that fast, but I don't care.

He hands me the bottle without a cap and I take several deep sips, washing down his cum. I'm sure I look like a mess. I'm naked from the waist down, with cum and saliva running down my chin. Yeah... I don't care.

When the new guy can tell I'm finished drinking, he takes the bottle from me while I cuddle against Max's chest. Max rubs my back and I float in a happy daze as the breeze cools me down.

When he breaks the silence, his voice is husky. "You're a very naughty girl."

"I wanted to be fucked." I giggle and nod against his chest in emphasis.

He leans in, his mouth close to my ear. "We're not done with you yet."

A thrill ripples down my back as he stands up, still holding me, and walks over to the edge of the pool. I get no warning before he jumps into the water with me in his arms. I scream, but close my mouth before I hit the water. When we come up for air, he laughs while I grin at him. I guess this will get me clean. He swims up to me and propels me towards the edge of the pool.

When my back hits the rim, he kisses me deeply as he takes off my bikini top. He tosses it behind him, and I almost protest that I might lose it, but realize it doesn't matter. Hell, my bottoms are probably still in the sauna.

The murmur and laughs from a group of men head this direction. I try to break off the kiss to see who it is, but Max pulls me tighter against him, not letting me escape. The group greets us and several guys jump into the pool. My body hums to life, wondering what's about to happen.

Max finally stops kissing me, and I barely get time to look around the pool before he spins me and boosts me up. I'm bent over the edge with my ass out of the water.

"Come and get it boys, the freeuse slut is open for business."

Ohhh, god. This is dirty. Being treated like a fucktoy makes me crave being one. I lay the side of my face on the concrete and embrace the moment as someone positions themselves behind me. There's a ledge under the water, and it's wide enough for the guys to stand on and fuck me.

The guy at my ass grasps my hips and lines his cock up with my pussy. He sinks into me slowly while Max stands next to me. Max runs his hands between my chest and the concrete so he can tweak my nipples. I whimper at the pain, and my pussy tightens around the cock inside me. Oh god, the stories I'm going to have to tell Sean when I get home. I daydream that Sean is jerking off tonight as he imagines what is happening to me. The reality is so much better than anything I thought it would be, and Sean is going to love hearing about my slutty adventure.

As the guy slams into me, Max talks in my ear, "You're such a slutty cumdumpster whore, taking all these loads."

I whimper at his words and my mind goes blank. I am a whore. Only the most depraved sluts would want a bunch of strangers to use her without the promise of an orgasm. Max continues to call me filthy things, and every sentence sinks me further into the mindset that makes me want to be exactly what he claims.

It's almost a surprise when I orgasm. As the waves of ecstasy crash into me, the guy in my pussy groans with his release. He fucks his cum back up into me for a moment before pulling out. He's immediately replaced by someone else.

Ohhh, god. The new guy's cock is thicker than any I've had yet, and I'm panting by the time he's fully inside me. When he starts thrusting, it short circuits my entire body. I shiver and cry out as another orgasm overwhelms me. When I come down from the peak, I'm lightheaded and utterly relaxed.

He drills into me a few more times before roaring as he comes. After he pulls out, it's just a line of guys. I have no idea how many guys fuck me. One guy doesn't even use my pussy; he just slaps the head of his cock against my clit repeatedly while he jacks himself off until he erupts against my cunt.

More cocks rub against my bare skin while I float in a dreamlike state. My pussy aches, but it feels good at the same time. When someone comes around in front of me, I let out a tiny laugh, knowing they're going to demand I suck them off. Max grins at me as he kneels and positions himself so his cock is by my head.

I lean up on my forearms and take him into my mouth, sucking him slowly while the other guys fuck me and force me to take Max in deeper. It feels incredible to be used like this. When he comes in my mouth, I swallow what I can before he pulls out.

Someone else takes his place, and then another, until my mouth is full of cock and my pussy is dripping from all the loads of cum I take. I don't know how many orgasms I have. When the guys eventually stop, Max pulls me into the water and holds on to me while I float on my back with my eyes closed. I experience a moment of pure joy while I'm weightless in the water. The connection with Max makes me feel safe.

After a while, he pulls me into his arms and carries me out of the pool. I snuggle against his chest and keep my eyes closed. I open them again when we're entering my cottage. Max takes me into the bathroom and stands me up. I sway and lean on the bathroom vanity while he rubs me with a fluffy towel. I'm dopey from pleasure, and all I can do is smile.

He grins back at me, and when I'm dry, he bundles me up in a robe and leads me to the dining room. I sit down and he fetches me a tray of meat and cheese rolls from the fridge, along with crackers and cold apple juice. This seems planned also, and awesome.

Max watches over me as I eat. When he can tell I'm finished, he carries me to the bed. He lays me down, snuggles behind me, and wraps his arms around me. "Do you want me to stay the night?"

I shiver as I come down from the intense high of being fucked by so many men, and I'm grateful for his offer. "Yes, please stay."

He kisses my ear and whispers. "I'll be here, so relax and sleep when you can."

As he rubs my back and shoulders, I let my mind drift over the evening. Ohhh, this is so damn nice. I almost feel like crying. This moment right here might be the best thing about the resort.

After a while, exhaustion overpowers me. Right before I fall asleep, I imagine Sean's reaction when I tell him about tonight. I can't wait to get home and share it with him. This really was a once-in-a-lifetime experience.

I fall asleep with the biggest smile on my face.

After Used for Amusement (Bonus Story)

As soon as I walk through the front door of my condo after my night at the Playtime Resort, I drop my bag and keys to the floor.

"Sean, I'm home!"

I remove my shoes and strip off my stretch pants and panties, not caring where they land. Where's my husband?

I've got a cock to ride.

I yank off my shirt and sports bra and leave them on the floor as I prowl the condo for Sean. Our place isn't big, so there's nowhere he can hide.

I find him naked in bed, his thick, firm cock ready for me. My nipples harden and wetness drips down my inner thigh.

He grins at me with hunger in his eyes and strokes his cock. "Hi baby."

Oh, it's game on.

I give him my most seductive purr. "Ready to hear how many guys fucked me?"

He groans out, "Yes," and continues stroking his shaft slowly.

I climb onto the bed at his feet and crawl up his body, hovering my head over his cock while I stare up at him. "They called me a whore, and I let them use me however they wanted."

As I speak, I lean down and kiss the tip of his cock, swirling my tongue over the head.

Sean moans and his breath hitches. "How many times did you come?"

I look up at him with a twinkle in my eyes as I take him into my mouth and suck on the tip, twirling my tongue along the underside. I'm so excited to tell him, I can hardly stand it.

"Lots," I say as I pull his cock out of my mouth to talk. "They used me until I could barely move. I lost count of the orgasms."

Sean groans and pushes the tip of his cock back into my mouth while his hand moves up and down his shaft. My pussy clenches around nothing and reminds me I need his cock inside me. I love giving him blow jobs, but today I need him deep inside me.

I stop sucking on him and crawl up his body the rest of the way, kissing him deeply while I straddle him and reach a hand between us and guide his cock to my wetness.

When our lips part, he whispers, "How good was it?"

I sink down on his length and we both moan. I sit up, twining my hands in his as I rock against him. "So good," I hiss out as a bolt of pleasure runs down my spine. "I was being used by guys in every hole at once."

Sean's eyes go wide. "Every hole?"

Mmm, oh yeah, my husband is gonna like this story. I roll my hips faster. "Yeah, I'm a slut — a freeuse slut — who had three cocks in me at once. Filling me with so much cum it was running out of me. You saw the picture. That was just one guy's cum. Imagine that multiple times over. So many cocks."

Sean groans as his eyes flutter closed while he concentrates on me fucking him. Our pleasure builds with each thrust of our hips. I clasp my hands tighter against his as I bounce faster.

"At one point, they had me bent over the side of the pool as they lined up to use me."

His hips buck into me hard, and I cry out with pleasure. "Fuck Sean, by the time they were done with me, I was dazed and didn't know my name. I've never had that many orgasms in a row."

Just remembering all those cocks inside me last night edges me closer to my orgasm. I can tell Sean is close to coming too, so I squeeze my inner walls around his cock while I grind down on him hard and fast. I might have taken all those cocks and had more cum inside me than I could contain, but Sean's cum is what really matters. No matter how corny it sounds, he's the one I want to fill me up for the rest of my life.

His eyes pop open and he stares at me. He grits his teeth as his body tenses right before he roars out, "Fuck, Tiff!" and then bucks up into me one more time before he explodes inside me with a sexy groan.

He shivers as I close my eyes and lose myself in pleasure, riding him hard and fast, seeking my release. I rock against him and let go of his hands so I can put one on his chest and move the other to reach down and rub my clit. And then it happens — my orgasm crashes into me and I cry out with ecstasy. It feels like every nerve in my body is on fire while my pussy spasms around Sean's cock. I keep bouncing on him as the waves of pleasure peak and recede.

When I finally come down, I slump against him as the room spins. We're both panting, sweaty, and smiling. Ever since I got the invitation to the freeuse resort, our sex life has been great. When we first got together, we fucked like rabbits, but over time, we got busy. This resort seems to be the jolt our marriage needs.

I roll over to the side of him and snuggle up against him. Last night was so exhausting, I'm asleep within moments.

I wake up with a mouth on my nipple. I arch and moan as I crack my eyes open and smile down at Sean.

"How long were we asleep?"

He sucks harder on my nipple, making me gasp before letting it pop out of his mouth. "Long enough for me to be ready to use my freeuse slut."

My pussy flutters from his words as he rolls me onto my stomach. Oh fuck, he knows I love this position. He pulls my ass cheeks apart, and I gasp when he brushes a finger over my asshole.

"How many guys fucked this?" he asks as he runs his fingers over it again and again, coating it with wetness from my pussy.

"Just one," I moan out as he continues to tease it with just his fingertip, then add, "I think."

I honestly don't know for certain. At the end there in the pool, they could've been doing anything to me and I wouldn't remember. I'm expecting him to fuck my ass, so I'm surprised when he covers me and slides into my pussy.

Oh, fuck, fuck, fuck. This feels so good. I wiggle my ass at him as he pumps his cock in and out, filling me up while he grinds against my ass cheeks. He grabs my wrists and pins them to the bed and whispers in my ear, "I'll reclaim that hole later. Right now I need to fill my pussy up again."

"Yes," I mewl out as the pleasure almost overwhelms me. I love it when he says my holes are his and gets possessive — and it's true. I might have fucked so many men last night that I lost count, but Sean owns all my holes. I'm his slut.

As he works himself up to a fever pitch, his moans and the endless pleasure switch my mind off. I drift in a haze of bliss, just wanting him to use me and take whatever he wants. I don't even need to come, though if he keeps fucking me, I know I will.

After several minutes, his cock pulses inside me and his warmth spills into my pussy again, triggering my orgasm. I cry out, "Ohhhh, god," and clench around him, milking every drop he has to offer.

He slams into me repeatedly as he unloads ropes of thick, sticky cum. I swear I feel him coating every inch deep inside. Ripples of pleasure run from my fingertips to my toes as he groans with his last thrust.

When we're both done, he rolls onto his back and practically drags me half on top of him. I am a limp noodle as I snuggle against him.

"Fuck," he says, squeezing me tight, "that was hot."

I can only purr in agreement. Maybe not tonight, but I am looking forward to him claiming my ass again.

I think I'm going to enjoy being a hotwife.

The End

Used and Teased

Freeuse Resort Weekend 3

Lacey Cross

Chapter 1

I stare down at the sleek black business card in my hand. My stomach muscles tighten, and my thoughts race. The card is deceptively simple for something I know holds a lot of meaning. All it has on it are the words "Plaything Resort" in shimmering silver along with an email address and a phone number. I know exactly what this is, but I thought my very pregnant friend Sabrina wasn't going through with this hairbrained idea?

Sabrina explains to the small group that's gathered for her baby shower that it's a freeuse resort where you go to be used sexually by strangers. I barely listen. I've heard this all before. Two months ago, Sabrina took me out for lunch and told me she wanted to gift everyone a weekend at the resort. She's gone multiple times and loved it.

I don't know what the hell she's thinking. We're all married. It's not like I'm going to go home and announce to Trevor, my adoring husband of 14 years, that I'm going to go be fucked by a bunch of hot studs at a resort all weekend. This is a colossal waste of Sabrina's money.

The shitty thing is that it's all I've been able to think about since that lunch date. Trevor is my high school sweetheart, and we married after we graduated. He's the only one I've ever fucked. Sure, I've been curious about what I missed since I didn't have any slutty college years, but I have a good life and I'm not about to ruin it for a weekend of fun.

I even told Trevor about Sabrina's plan. He laughed and said she was crazy. I tried to assure him I wouldn't go if she followed through with it. That just isn't what married people do. We don't fuck other people—well, unless you're Ariana. One of my friends is a hotwife, and she sleeps around, but that's different because she has her husband's blessing.

Trevor said I sounded like a prim schoolmarm, and he's been teasing me about it ever since—trying to get me to admit I find the idea hot. Well, news flash: of course it's hot. A resort where men do whatever they want to me and I'm just there for the pleasure? But that isn't real life. This doesn't just happen. I've got a husband, three kids, a full-time job, and a house to clean on the weekends. No one has time to be off gallivanting for an entire weekend. Trevor is going to laugh when I tell him Sabrina went through with her stupid plan.

Sabrina's baby shower is a small, intimate affair. It's Sabrina and the five of us who have all been friends since high school. I look around the room to see if everyone else is as shocked by this offer as I am. Hell, I'm not shocked. I'm annoyed. I don't need or want this temptation.

My friend Raven is sitting next to me. When she folds the business card and shoves it in her jeans pocket, I almost protest. You don't just fold it like that! I try to catch her eye, but she's lost in thought, staring off in the other direction. I'd like to know what she thinks about this, but I'll call her in a few days since there's no opportunity to talk openly at the party.

By the time the baby shower is over, I'm feeling downright pissy. Why did Sabrina even give us the temptation? Is she trying to ruin our marriages? I should just rip the card up and toss it in the trash. Except I have a knack for remembering numbers, and that phone number's already burned into my brain.

Another one of my friends, Tiffany, drove me to the party, and I feel like I'm ranting the entire way home.

"I can't believe Sabrina offered that to us. I told her the only person who would like it was Ariana because she's a hotwife. Why in the hell did she think any of us would want this? We're all happily married."

Tiffany seems distracted. Her wistful voice tells me she's not convinced this is a horrible plan, even when she replies, "Yeah, and it's not like Sean would let me go, even if I wanted to."

"Exactly!" I burst out. "That lifestyle is fine for Ariana. I just hope Sabrina didn't actually pay for this. She's going to have wasted a bunch of money when no one goes." Am I the only one who understands this resort isn't a good thing? "I bet if you left it up to a bunch of men to use you, they'd all just keep fucking your ass. Who wants an entire weekend of ass-fucking?"

An unwanted ripple of lust runs straight to my pussy and my body heats as I imagine a beefy guy bending me over and sliding his cock into my ass. Oh god, this is so wrong.

"Can we turn the air conditioning on? It's warm today." The cool air blasts over my heated cheeks, and I continue my tirade. "I bet if they weren't using your ass, they'd just be demanding blowjobs all weekend. Plenty of guys can get pussy, but can they get all the blowjobs and anal they want? I don't think so."

I try to picture Trevor using me all weekend, and my panties grow damp as I imagine myself on my knees waiting for him to get home from work. Yeah, in my dreams. I don't need to be fantasizing about this. Everything was fine until Sabrina handed out the business cards.

By the time Tiffany drops me off, I realize I went a little overboard. Ugh, I didn't even find out what was going on in her life. I'll call her in a couple of days to catch up. Giving her a smile, I apologize and head into the house. I'm half miffed and half so damn horny I'm ready to rip my husband's clothes off and ride him to glory.

If he's alone, I'm going for it.

CHAPTER 2

The house is quiet when I walk through the door. My mother took the kids to a craft fair today, and Trevor had some landscaping he wanted to tackle in the backyard. Mmm, maybe he'll be all sweaty from doing manly things. My pussy clenches at the thought, and I try to push away the image of him shirtless and shimmering with a sheen of sweat. Instead, I focus on the business card in my purse. Should I call the number and see if they'll refund Sabrina's money? Or better yet, just burn the card.

I slip off my shoes before stepping out onto the back patio, and I spot Trevor's shirt draped over a chair. He's lying on a lounge chair with his eyes closed and sunglasses on. It looks like he finished working.

Oooh, should I stroll up and offer him a blowjob? I bite my lip as I imagine crawling between his legs. The thought sizzles through my body, and I almost do it.

Wait, that doesn't get his cock inside me. Our backyard is secluded, so this is the perfect time to climb on his lap and fuck him. Then we both get satisfaction.

He raises his sunglasses to the top of his head as I approach. He smiles but doesn't say anything. I feel emboldened and want to make sure I get his cock inside me.

"Hey stud," I say as I straddle him and rub his chest. "You're all sweaty."

He shifts his position so my pussy comes in contact with his growing erection through his jeans. "Yeah, I've been working hard while you were off having fun."

I know he's teasing me, but that doesn't mean I can't play with him a little. I caress his abs and dip my fingers into his shorts, purring, "While you were working hard, I've been thinking about you all day."

His cock twitches against my palm, and he reaches up to stroke my cheek. "Yeah?"

"Yeah." I remove my hand from his shorts and moan as I grind against his hardness. "I've been imagining all the nasty things you could do to me."

"Like?"

He trails his fingers along the hem of my shirt, tugging on it. I smile and lift my arms so he can pull it off. I'm wearing a pink sports bra, and his gaze darts to my breasts as I remove it.

His voice is husky. "Tell me."

I sit up straight, sliding back and forth over his cock. "Well, for starters, we could have a freeuse weekend, and you could use me all you want."

That gets his attention, and his eyes take on a predatory gleam. "You want to be my freeuse slut for a weekend?"

The idea of a bunch of guys at the resort using me has me all hot and bothered, so why not have fun with Trevor instead? Just because I'm not going to the resort doesn't mean I can't get my freeuse weekend.

"Yeah," I whisper as I move down so I can rub my breasts against his chest and kiss him. "We'll clear the house, so it's just you and me, and you do whatever you want."

He abruptly breaks off the kiss and sits up, causing me to shift backwards. "Seriously?"

Uh-oh, he doesn't like the idea. Heat rises to my face, and my chest tightens. I quickly try to backpedal. "Jeez, I was just joking."

"No." His hands grip my hips tightly. "Don't do that. Tell me what you want."

I try to stall for time while his cock swells underneath me. Oh wait, maybe he *is* interested. "What do you mean?"

"I'm curious how it would work."

I bite my lip as my pulse races. I have a few seconds of indecision and then sigh. Fuck it. I should be able to tell him my fantasies, and maybe we can use this to spice up our marriage.

"Sabrina got us weekend passes to that freeuse resort I was telling you about. But since I can't use it, I was thinking we could have our own private weekend with me being your freeuse slutty wife."

His eyes sparkle, and his fingers dig into my hips. "And what would I have you do?"

"Anything and everything. I'd be yours to use," I moan as I grind against his cock again.

"Hmm," he says and then grins. "Why don't we just go to the resort?"

My nipples harden, and pleasure zings straight to my pussy. Um...this is not what I was expecting. "What?"

Trevor pushes me off of him but then rises and scoops me up into his arms. I cling to his shoulders and admire the way his muscles ripple underneath my hands.

His tone is matter-of-fact. "We could use a vacation, and what's better than a sex resort vacation?"

Oh my god, I think he's serious. My heart pounds, and my pussy floods with wetness. "But it's for me. The guys would use me. You'd want to be there?"

Are we really having this conversation? This is nuts.

He carries me down the hall and into the bedroom, tossing me on the bed. My stomach flutters from pleasure when he crawls over me. "Hell yes," he says. "If my wife is going to get fucked by a bunch of other men, I want to watch."

As his lips descend, I arch my body against his. Even just discussing this is fucking hot. Hell, I better get him to commit to this before he changes his mind. He brushes his lips against mine, and I moan, "Okay, but only if you're sure."

"I am," he murmurs against my lips. "I want to see how slutty my wife can get."

Wow. I'm not sure what to say, so I reach up to grip his shoulders and search his eyes. "Are we insane?"

"Yep," he says and then rolls us so I'm on top. "Now, show me how badly you want this."

Trevor's always been so laid back, but now he's ordering me around and taking control? This is great. As his fingers move up to cup my breasts, I shiver and grind against his hard cock, moaning from the friction of the fabric of his shorts. I need him inside me.

As if reading my mind, he rolls us again and pushes up on his knees to stare down at me. When he unbuttons my shorts, I lift my legs in the air and hold them closed in front of him as he pulls my shorts off my legs, along with my panties.

"Just remember, you're mine, no matter how many guys you fuck."

My breath catches in my throat. This is so hot. I nod and then spread my legs wide in invitation. "Yes... yours."

With a groan, he lowers his mouth to my pussy and licks a long stripe up to my clit. Fuck, yes. My thighs settle on his shoulders as he sucks on my sensitive bud. His hands move up to hold my nether lips open while he devours me. Sharp spikes of pleasure swirl in my core, and I close my eyes as his tongue works its magic.

We've been together since high school, and I've never slept with anyone but him. Sex has been a little rote lately, but today is different. I've never seen him like this. He's like a junkie and I'm his fix, but he still can't get enough. As he moves two fingers into my pussy and curls them, joy zips through my body. If just talking about going to a freeuse resort does this for us, sign me up for the real thing.

As he finger fucks me, his tongue swirls around my clit, and my entire body hums with pleasure. My body is singing, and all the blood rushes to my pussy as he takes me over the edge. I cry out as my orgasm crashes into me, writhing against his mouth while he holds me down and continues to lick me through the pleasure.

When I come down, I'm a little lightheaded. Jesus, it's been far too long since he's gone down on me until I came. He kisses his way up my body, and I shiver in anticipation. His mouth finds mine, and I taste myself on his lips as I wrap my arms around his neck. He made me come, so now it's his turn to be pleasured.

I push on him, rolling us again so I can straddle him. When I sit up, my wet pussy rubs against his hard cock. "Mmm, I want your cock in me."

As I glide up and down his shaft, he moans, "Fuck, yeah."

His firm hands grasp my hips as he pulls me closer. I move with him until the head of his cock pushes against my slick entrance. His breath hitches as I slowly sink down onto him, and I roll my hips in pleasure. A sigh of bliss escapes my lips as his hard length fills me completely. Every nerve in my body lights up with pleasure. It's been far too long since we've been playful like this, and today feels like coming home.

I gyrate my hips faster, fucking myself on his cock as my orgasm builds. How did we let things get stale? This is what it's all about—enjoying ourselves and letting our pleasure take over.

It doesn't take long before the pleasure overwhelms me again. By the way he's flexing his hips to force me to move faster, I can tell he's close as well.

When his cock pulses and he explodes, I follow him over the edge. I scream as the waves of rapture crash over me and the pleasure consumes me like wildfire. My body trembles with pure ecstasy, and I fuck him through my orgasm.

When we come down, we collapse into each other, chests heaving. My pussy spasms in aftershocks of pleasure as his cum drips out of me. God, that was amazing. As I lie down next to him, he pulls me against his chest. "Holy shit," he whispers.

I'm breathless and can only nod as we cuddle. Holy shit is right. I can't believe we're going to the resort.

Together.

Chapter 3

I call to make the reservations at the Plaything Resort the next day. The resort owner, Chris, is a friendly guy, and afterwards he sends me questionnaires to fill out. The forms ask about my likes, dislikes, my hard nos, and my safeword. I didn't even have a safeword until now.

Trevor and I go over the paperwork together, and it's an eye-opening experience. My husband is one kinky bastard. He basically wants me to get as much dick inside me as possible, and he doesn't care which hole.

Yep, it's going to be an ass-fucking weekend. Even my husband wants to see it.

After we send the forms, Chris calls and speaks to us both on the phone, separately, to go over expectations. He checks to see if we have anything we want to discuss that isn't on the paperwork. I get the feeling he's making sure we both want to do this, and I appreciate the effort. It's probably to prevent a brawl if one partner can't handle the other letting loose at the resort. I don't see this being a problem for us. Trevor is almost like a changed man. He's all over me every day, fucking me all over the house.

The only thing left is to clear our schedule for the weekend. My parents agree to watch the kids and thankfully don't ask too many questions about where we're going. As far as they know, we're taking a weekend to reconnect. Which if you think about it, we are—if you count my pussy getting pounded by a bunch of other cocks while Trevor watches as reconnecting.

Our trip isn't for three weeks... three looooong weeks. Ariana and Tiffany schedule their weekends before ours, but they're close-mouthed about what happens when they're there. They claim they don't want to ruin the surprise.

In the days leading up to the trip, Trevor's sex drive is through the roof. He even fucks me while I'm brushing my teeth one morning. He just walks into the bathroom, presses his cock against my ass, and the next thing I know, I'm bent over the vanity with him balls deep in my pussy. I'm loving life.

After we drop the kids off at my parent's house, it takes two hours to get to the resort. Trevor is driving, which is good since I'm a distracted mess and getting wetter with every milepost we pass. I've been a bundle of excited energy for weeks, and I can't believe we're finally on our way. I don't know what to expect other than a bunch of guys using me, but I'm ready to embrace my sluttiest side. Blowjobs and ass-fucking for everyone!

When we pull up to the iron gates at the entrance of the Plaything Resort, I read off the gate code Chris sent me, and we drive slowly through. The lawn is beautifully manicured, and I daydream about several muscular men working in the yard every morning. I bet it's a bunch of college-aged guys who are looking for some freeuse pussy in their downtime. My nipples harden at the thought of eager younger men. I've always been more attracted to older men, but I suppose I could handle a weekend of athletic young men with lots of stamina pounding away at my pussy... if I have to.

We park on a circular drive next to a large fountain. As we get out, a yummy silver fox in cargo pants and a button-down shirt strolls up. I barely have time to gawk at him before he's followed by two sexy, muscular men in shorts and t-shirts. They both look like they're in their mid-twenties, and their biceps are huge. I bet their stomachs are flat. Oh yeah, I lay odds that those two could fuck a woman for hours and barely work up a sweat.

When the older man speaks, I recognize his voice as Chris. "Welcome, Katie and Trevor!"

I give a shy, "Hello," as I sneak peeks at his sexy companions.

Chris helps Trevor with the bags and chats about the drive. I'm way more interested in the hotties, and I walk over to the fountain and pretend to examine it so I can study the men from the corner of my eye more easily.

Chris calls out to me, "Oh, Katie?"

"Yes?" I have to force myself to stop staring at the eye candy to answer.

"As a reminder, we all know your safeword and will abide by it. Don't be afraid to use it. We're here to serve you."

I smile at Chris, and my core flutters when he says they'll serve me. I like the sound of that.

Before I can respond with my thanks, one of the hot guys steps up behind me and bends me over the side of the fountain. I grip the edge, and my face is right above the water. Wait, how did he get over here without me seeing him? Is he a ninja? My pussy pulses as he holds on to my hips and grinds his cock against my ass.

As if a stranger bending me over the fountain is the most normal thing in the world, Trevor casually says, "Katie, I'm going to check in real quick. I'll be back."

My, "Okay," turns into a gasp as the man pushes my sundress up to my waist and slides my panties down to my ankles.

The other younger guy speaks from my left. "Hey, I want some too."

Oh fuck, are they going to double team me right here in front of the resort? Is this place THAT raunchy? Is this who I am? Am I going to let myself be spit-roasted in the driveway where anyone could walk past?

As the older man slides his fingers into my pussy, the younger one moves beside me and pulls his shorts down to free his cock—his thick, gorgeous cock. Fuck, this is happening. They really *are* going to double-team me out in the open... and I want it. For one weekend, I want to be the slut who takes it in every hole and allows herself to experience everything.

Wetness floods my core, and I mentally let go of any expectations for this weekend. I'm here to be used. If they want me, they can have me.

The man behind me removes his fingers from my pussy, and I hear the rustle of fabric. He positions the tip of his cock against my pussy and pushes into me slowly, stretching me with his thickness. Oooh, god. I gasp at the unexpected size of his cock as pleasure ripples down my spine.

"Fuck, yeah," the guy standing next to me says as he strokes himself and watches. "That's it, slut. Show me how much you can take."

Oh, I'll take anything and everything you want to give me. This is going to be an awesome weekend.

The older man swings my hips, making me face the younger guy. Yeah, I can see where this is going, and I welcome it.

"Suck his cock."

Mmmm, yep. I can't believe Trevor is missing this. This is the first cock, other than my husband's, I've ever had inside me, and I'm about to have another in my mouth. This is so fucking dirty.

As the man behind me leisurely thrusts into me, I grip the other guy's shaft and lean forward to lick the head of his cock. His pre-cum tastes different from Trevor's—more of a metallic tang—but it's not unpleasant. I'll willingly swallow his load.

He holds the sides of my head as I engulf the tip of his cock, sucking him deep. This is more fun than I was expecting. Each time the guy in my pussy thrusts in, it forces the guy in my mouth deeper inside.

Wait, is this the welcoming party for everyone who visits? Do we all get railed in the parking lot? That might be why Ariana and Tiffany didn't want to spoil the surprise.

The two men continue to fuck both my holes as delight spirals me close to an orgasm. Movement from the corner of my eye tells me when Trevor returns. He leans on the car and gives me a thumbs up. If I wasn't in the throes of passion and had a cock buried in my throat, I would have laughed at his gesture.

The guy behind me speeds up, and knowing he's about to come tips me over the edge. I cry out around the cock in my mouth as waves of bliss ripple from my fingers to my toes. As I spasm, he groans and stills, pumping his cum deep inside me.

When he pulls out, the other guy withdraws from my mouth as well. "You want this cum, don't you?"

"Yes," I whimper as my pussy twitches around nothing.

He grips the back of my head and pulls me towards him as he strokes his cock. I close my eyes and stick out my tongue a second before he grunts, "Take it," and shoots his cum over my tongue and lips.

As his warm seed drips down my chin, I lick my lips and swallow as much as I can. I was right; he doesn't taste bad. My head swims as the men help me stand up.

"Welcome to the Plaything Resort," one of them says, and the other chuckles as they walk off.

My panties are at my ankles, and I've already taken two loads of cum. Oh shit, what if this was a mistake? Is Trevor shocked? I turn towards him quickly, being careful not to trip on my panties.

He's next to me in a flash, smiling and pulling me against his chest. "Damn, baby, that was hot."

Oh, thank god. As I snuggle against him, Chris approaches with a clipboard. "Did you enjoy your welcome?"

I can only nod, too wooly-headed from pleasure to speak.

Chris continues, "Do you want someone to escort you to your room?"

Trevor replies to Chris while I pull up my panties. "Nah, we can find it with the map you gave me. Thanks."

Before we head out, Chris has me sign a few documents Trevor couldn't sign for me. They're all forms we discussed over the phone, so I quickly add my name and Chris waves us off.

My darling husband grins at me and takes me by the hand as he leads me down a path around the main house. I scan the area as we walk, expecting someone to jump out of the bushes and pin me against the wall of the house. I don't think I'm crazy to feel this way based on what happened within two minutes of stepping foot on the property. Talk about a warm welcome. Hell, I didn't even get their names.

The Plaything Resort has five guest cottages, so groups can visit at the same time. I could have come here with one of my friends, but I honestly didn't want to feel like someone I know was watching me. Like, 'oh hey, I'm the biggest slut ever! Don't mind me.' Yeah, no thanks. Even if they're here for the same reason, it would be awkward. The only friend I would have felt comfortable coming with is Raven. But her husband isn't the sharing type, so I doubt she'll ever use her free pass.

When we enter our cottage, I barely have a chance to look around before Trevor pushes me against the wall and pins my hands above my head. Oh, hello. What's this?

His lips lock on to mine and devour me, kissing me like it's the only thing keeping him alive. I moan into his mouth and writhe against him, loving the way he takes charge.

He trails his lips down my neck and releases one of my hands so he can unzip his jeans. He pulls out his cock and then shoves my panties down. Oh, hell yes.

As soon as my panties hit the floor, I step out of them and wrap my legs around him. He lifts me, pressing me against the wall, and groans as he sinks his cock into me. I'm still sensitive from the previous guy fucking me, and I cry out with pleasure.

God, yes. It's been a while since we did it against a wall. I'm loving how this resort is bringing out Trevor's wild side. When I slip my arms around his neck, he clasps my hips tightly and slams into me. The pleasure is overwhelming, and I whimper as I arch into him. I need his cock as deep as it will go.

We're both moaning as we fuck like we haven't seen each other in days—it's wild, savage, and glorious. It doesn't take long for me to come all over his cock. As bliss washes over me, he pulls out and sets me on the floor before spinning me so I'm facing the wall.

Holy hell, he's a madman.

Trevor slams into me from behind, and my cries echo through the room. He reaches up with one hand to grip my breast through my sundress, rolling my nipple between his fingers while he reaches down with the other hand to rub my clit. When he bites down on the side of my neck, my orgasm peaks again, sending jolts of ecstasy through me.

"Fuck," he roars against my neck before his cock jerks inside me and he fills me with cum.

He collapses into me, pinning me against the wall as we catch our breath. Jesus, I think he fucked my brains out. When he pulls his cock out, wetness splashes on my inner thighs, and I giggle.

He laughs with me and helps me stand before cuddling me against his chest. "Damn, babe, this is going to be an awesome weekend."

"Mmm hmm." I can only agree. This is starting out fabulous. I was riding high on a wave of adrenaline, but now I'm tired. I bury my nose against his neck, breathing in the comforting, familiar scent of him. "What was that all about?"

He hugs me more tightly. "Just having a little fun with my freeuse slutty wife. I hear she wants to be used all weekend."

Mmm, I'm liking this trip even more now. I tip my head up, and he gives me a soft kiss.

"Well, your freeuse slut needs a shower after being used by three men."

I give him a playful push, and he releases me with a laugh as I collect my overnight bag. The bathroom is huge, with a jacuzzi tub and a separate shower. I'm not sure how this weekend is going to play out and I'm excited, so I speed clean myself in the shower. I don't want to miss any chance to get a cock in me.

I'm wearing a robe and towel-drying my hair when I join Trevor back in the bedroom. He's relaxing on the bed and looking at a map of the grounds.

"Hey babe, what do you want to do tonight? They have a pool, a hot tub and sauna, or a gaming room. It looks like they have some walking trails around the property also, if you want to go for a nature walk."

Now he's just being silly. No one is going to find me and use me on a nature walk. The rule of the resort is I can't ask to be fucked. I have to wait for the guys to take whatever they want, whenever they want it.

Wait, what if they don't want to fuck me? Oh god, that would suck. At least I have Trevor, who seems horny enough today. He'd give me a good boning if no one else did.

Trevor lifts an eyebrow. "So... what do you want to do?"

Oh, shit... "Um, how about the hot tub? That sounds relaxing." I saw the hot tub through the bushes on the way to the cottage, so I know it's in a central location. There's bound to be men passing by it.

Trevor grins. "That sounds good, but I want you to go skinny dipping."

Oooh, easy access for the men. "Sure, whatever you want, hon."

I blow him a kiss and shrug the bathrobe off my shoulders. I'm already naked underneath it.

As I toss it aside, he whistles. "Damn, you're sexy."

As I walk towards the bathroom to brush my hair, I wiggle my ass for him. I make quick work of my long, brown hair, pulling it up into a high ponytail. It's just going to get wet again in the hot tub, so there's no point in doing anything special with it.

I stare at myself in the mirror before leaving the bathroom. I'm flushed, and my eyes sparkle. Every inch of my body feels hypersensitive, and my nipples are dusty pink pebbles. Yeah, I'm ready to get fucked again.

CHAPTER 4

Whoever maintains the landscape of the resort does an amazing job. It's lush and pristine but not overdone. It feels like we're in our own private sanctuary, and it's absolutely perfect for a weekend away.

The landscaping also keeps us from seeing anyone on our walk to the hot tub. Strolling around without clothes on is liberating, and my pussy is soaked by the time we get there. This is more erotic than I imagined it would be, and for the first time in my life, I'm able to be as slutty as I want. Having my husband encouraging this behavior is the ultimate fantasy.

Since I'm already naked, I don't have to do anything but kick off my flip-flops and slide into the hot tub. Sighing, I let the jets massage my body. This is the life.

I'm hoping someone comes to fuck me sooner rather than later. If this is my one chance to fuck as many guys as I want, I need a swarm of cocks using me. I want to be like that meme of the woman getting hotdogs thrown at her face, except with real cocks.

Trevor climbs in, and I cuddle against him as the hot water surrounds us. Two men walk by, and when they see me, they pause and stare at the tops of my breasts floating above the water. My nipples harden from their hungry gazes.

After they start walking again, Trevor laughs. "That was pretty awesome."

Awesome? They didn't climb in here and use me. What the fuck? I try to keep my voice neutral. "Maybe they'll come back to fuck me."

Trevor cups one of my breasts as he looks in the direction the men went. "I bet you're right."

We relax in the hot water for a while, but I'm antsy. My body is humming with lust. Where are my cocks? God, I really am a slut.

I giggle at myself, and Trevor gives me a questioning look. "What?"

I try to hide my grin as I shake my head. "Nothing."

"Hmm, you sure about that?" He reaches for a breast and tweaks one of my nipples, and I giggle again.

This playful side of Trevor is wonderful. I turn so he can't see my face. "You wouldn't be interested."

"Baby," he says as he wraps his arms around my waist and pulls me closer to him, "you know you're going to tell me, so you might as well just say it."

Mmm, he's right. When I turn back, his lips are waiting for me before I can tell him how much of a slut he married. As our tongues duel, he pulls himself out of his swim shorts and drags me onto his lap. I straddle him, and he thrusts up into me, filling me with his thick cock. Oh god, this is exactly what I need. Who needs a swarm of cocks if you've got a god for a husband? I'm sensitive from so many orgasms already today, and I close my eyes as the pleasure builds.

The jets and warm water relax me as the waves of bliss start at my core and zing through my body. I picture a bunch of hot college guys fucking the hell out of me, and the fantasy sends me over the edge. I cry out and shudder as my orgasm peaks. My pussy clenches around his cock, milking him, and he groans as he explodes inside me.

When we come down, I'm limp from utter relaxation and not paying attention to my surroundings. I'm surprised to see three guys slip into the hot tub across from us.

Two of the men lounge in the bubbling water, but the third one pulls me off of Trevor's lap. "My turn."

My pussy tightens from his hungry gaze, and he pushes me back against the side of the hot tub and spreads my legs. Oooh, this is perfect. As he positions his cock at my entrance, the other men watch us silently. It's odd to be on display, but so fucking hot.

When his cock slips into me, he's thick and long, and he has to work himself in slowly. By the time he's completely in, the other two guys have their hands in the water. By their arm movements, I can tell they're stroking themselves.

As the man pumps into me, he squeezes my breasts, pinching and pulling my nipples. I moan, almost delirious with pleasure as I spread my arms and hold on to the side of the hot tub for stability.

I've had four loads of cum in me so far today, and I'm about to get a fifth. This right here is probably why Ariana and Tiffany were close-mouthed. I'm not sure I'd be able to describe this resort to anyone either. They're using me, but also somehow doing the exact perfect thing to please me. I must have revealed more in those questionnaires than I realized.

The guy between my legs slams into me repeatedly, and I stop thinking about my friends. I'm chanting "Oh god," as the pleasure builds.

When the guy speeds up, I know he's going to come soon. He grunts and growls out a loud, "Fuck," and pumps his hot cum deep inside me before letting go of me and moving away.

My head spins from the lack of an orgasm. Wait, I need to come!

Another one replaces him. I'm spun around and bent over the side of the hot tub. I turn my head and lock eyes with Trevor as the guy behind me fingers my asshole.

Wait, he's not going to try to assfuck me right now, is he?

He sighs, "Too bad I don't have any lube," and rams his cock deep into my pussy.

"Ohhh, fuuuuck," I cry out as he hammers into me. Oh shit, oh shit, oh shit.

As he pistons in and out, I lose myself in the waves of rapture. The guy before him warmed me up, and within moments I come all over this guy's cock, spasming violently as bolts of electricity zing through me.

He groans and fills my pussy with the sixth load of cum. When he pulls out, my head lolls to the side, resting on the edge of the hot tub as I sink down into the water. Oh god, I think they've fucked me senseless.

I barely notice it as the men pull me out of the hot tub and wrap a towel around me. Within moments, I'm cuddled in Trevor's lap in a chair. I rest my head against his shoulder as he rubs my back. Trevor chats quietly with the guys, but I'm floating in a bubble of relaxation and don't understand their words. I come to a little when Trevor stands up and carries me to our cottage, only then realizing the third one didn't fuck me. Bummer.

He sits me at the dining table and rummages in the tiny fridge. "They left food for us, and I just need to heat it up. Here, drink some water."

He opens a water bottle and hands it to me. Sipping dutifully, I fight the temptation to lay my head on the table. I'm totally fine, and I don't want to freak him out. I'm just limp from pleasure. As Trevor heats our food up in the microwave, I space out.

When he sets a plate in front of me, the smell of mashed potatoes and gravy perks me up. Did they make this just for us, or are these leftovers from a meal? Not that it matters. I'm so damn hungry I'd wolf down a peanut butter and jelly sandwich if it was in front of me. The roast beef and potatoes are like the finest ambrosia to my stomach.

Trevor sits down next to me with his own plate and digs in. "How are you feeling?"

"Mmm," I respond as I take another bite. "I'm good. Where are we going after we eat?"

He laughs and shakes his head. "Baby, we're done for the night. We're going to snuggle and get some good sleep."

I open my mouth to complain and then shut it as I yawn. Yeah, his plan sounds lovely. I can get more cocks tomorrow.

After I finish the meal, my eyelids are drooping, and Trevor helps me to bed. He snuggles up behind me, wrapping his arms around me and pulling me against him. Yes, this is what I need.

Right before sleep takes over, I whisper, "I love you."

Trevor murmurs, "Love you, too, babe."

CHAPTER 5

I wake up early the next morning with nervous energy running through my body. How many cocks will I get today? Please let it be a ton. Who knows if Trevor would ever want to share me again. I need to take this chance while I have it.

After a quick shower and breakfast, I toss on a cute pair of ass-hugging shorts and a blouse. I'm wearing panties but opted to forgo a bra. I want to be comfortable and keep all my clothes easily removable, so I choose to wear slip-on sandals.

We stroll around the grounds, admiring the gardens. Every time we pass a secluded area, I still expect guys to jump out of the bushes to use me. To my disappointment, no one does. I'm already a wet mess just imagining getting fucked. I need an actual cock inside me.

It doesn't help that my annoyingly sweet husband is using every opportunity to brush against me, and he keeps stealing kisses whenever he feels like it. I'm vibrating with sexual tension and in a constant state of arousal. It's messing with my head, and every time I see a guy, I try to imagine what his cock looks like.

Maybe there are some guys using the sauna or working out in the gym? Yeah, we really need to find them. I haven't been assfucked even once yet. This is wrong. Where's my swarm of cocks, dammit!

My lusty thoughts are making me feel like a complete whore, and it's fabulous. Every woman should have a weekend like this at least once in their life. I'd like it to come with a few more cocks, though, please.

I'm still glad Trevor came with me. He's in a great mood and keeps teasing me about how many men I fucked yesterday. Hell, I'm surprised Trevor hasn't used me yet this morning. Every time I look down at his shorts, he's hard.

Ooooh, wait. I know how his mind works. He's waiting on purpose. He wants to be the last guy who fills me with cum on this trip. That's so romantic in a filthy way, and oh-so Trevor.

We tour the grounds until it's lunchtime and then visit the main house for our meal. The kitchen serves us a delicious salad that isn't too heavy. It would be the perfect lunch for an afternoon of wild sex, but that is seeming more unlikely. What the fuck is going on?

After lunch, we pass several men who smile and say hello to us, but no one tries anything with me. Every time someone approaches us, my pussy zings with delight, thinking that I'm finally going to get fucked. When it doesn't happen, the letdown is *real*.

Trevor keeps glancing at me and smiling, like he can read my mind. Shit, he probably can. He knows how much I hate—and yet love—being horny without release. It's like the ultimate edging and makes me even more crazed by the time he screws me. But really, what's a girl got to do to get fucked around here?

After another hour of wandering the grounds, I'm fed up. FINE, if no one is going to fuck me, we might as well find something fun to do.

"Honey, I want to go to the game room and see what that's all about."

He takes my hand. "Sure."

When we walk in, there are five guys sitting around a gaming table playing cards. They look up, and two of them rise and approach us. Oh Jesus Christ, finally. I've been waiting all freaking morning.

Trevor gives me a reassuring squeeze of my hand before letting go. The absence of his touch leaves me feeling vulnerable, but I'm distracted when the men flank me. I quickly look them over; they each have lean muscular bodies and long hair, like classic surfers. One is blonde, and the other is brown-haired. Mmm, getting fucked by hot surfers isn't something I ever thought about before, yet the way my pussy lights up tells me it's now my number one fantasy.

The blonde guy moves behind me, and I feel hands on my shoulders. I gasp as his fingers stroke my back, delicately tracing along my curves before sliding under the fabric of my shirt. His fingers dance around my nipples, pulling and tugging, as I moan and press into his hands. I want to beg him to fuck me, and I have to bite my lip to stop myself. Shit, I need to remember I'm not allowed to ask.

The brunette stands in front of me and then kneels down. He removes my sandals and then peels my shorts and panties down my legs. Thank god, I'm finally going to get a cock in me soon.

No one is talking to me, and it's making me feel like I'm just a hole for them to use. Am I even a person to them? Is it messed up that it's turning me on more?

The brunette lifts one of my legs and places it over his shoulder, which shocks me. Why are they trying to give me pleasure? Shouldn't I be bent over a chair while they use every hole?

"Ohhhh god," I moan as the man in front of me fixes his mouth on my pussy.

He licks and sucks, sending tingles throughout my body. Holy fuck, why am I complaining about him eating my pussy? If this is what they want to do, I'm not protesting. This is so fucking amazing.

As the blonde nibbles on my ear, he whispers, "You like being used, don't you?"

"Yes," I whimper, as the brunette starts fucking me with his tongue, driving me wild with lust. Who wouldn't like this?

I close my eyes as the pleasure builds and lean against the guy behind me. He's kissing my neck and playing with my nipples while the man kneeling in front of me is alternating between licking my clit and sticking his tongue into me as far as it will go.

Within moments, the brunette's expert tongue drives me over the edge. With a scream, I climax, and the guy moans against my clit, sending vibrations through my core. I shudder and spasm as the pleasure washes over me, and I ride his tongue through my orgasm.

My legs are shaking when he stops licking me and moves my thigh off his shoulder. One of them removes my shirt. I'm so mentally fuzzy from my orgasm, I'm not sure who it is.

Being naked in a room full of men shocks me back to my senses, and I feel a moment of panic. My eyes dart around until I find Trevor. He had moved to a couch against the wall while I had a guy tongue-deep in my cunt. His smile reassures me, and I can see the outline of his erection through his shorts. He's clearly enjoying the show. Any lingering tension drains from me as I grin back at him.

I've been wanting this all day, but the reality of this many men and knowing they might all fuck me is a little more intense than I expected. I'm thankful, again, that Trevor is with me. This experience wouldn't be as enjoyable if I was worrying he was going to be upset when I got home.

I'm so focused on Trevor and my inner thoughts that I'm surprised when the men pick me up and carry me over to the poker table. Ooooh, sexy powerful men carrying me is a nice fantasy fulfillment. The day is definitely looking up.

They set me down on the tabletop, and a pile of poker chips dig into my back. It's a small table, so my lower legs hang over the side. The surfer guys scoot their chairs aside to make some space and take their places next to me.

The man by my head speaks. "Winner of the next round gets to fuck it first."

My pulse quickens and the room spins when I hear them address me as "it," like I'm an object. Ohhhhh fuck. Suddenly, my day makes sense. They're doing this based on my answers to their questionnaire regarding my desires, kinks, and expectations for this weekend. What had I written? That one of my dirtiest fantasies was to be nothing more than a hole that men would use for their own pleasure. My nipples harden and every nerve ending zings alive.

This is what I want.

They deal the cards and play around me as if I'm not even here. I close my eyes as a warm fuzziness seeps over me. It feels as if I'm in a trance. These guys could do whatever they wanted to me. I *am* just a toy. Mission accomplished.

As I'm zoned out, they occasionally pull at my nipple. When someone smacks my breast, I gasp and open my eyes. Looking around, I can't tell who did it, and they go back to ignoring me. My eyes flutter shut as I feel the wetness between my thighs increase.

Finally, the round ends. One of the competitors rises in triumph and takes his place between my legs. I watch him pull his cock out of his pants. It's already hard and bobbing in front of him.

Two strong hands take hold of my ankles and force them apart while tugging me down the table until my ass is at the edge. Two other men grasp my wrists and pull them above my head; I'm completely immobilized. My eyes widen as my breath catches in anticipation of the first thrust. This is a fun game.

The rational part of my brain knows I can use my safeword and they would stop, but a sense of helplessness washes over me anyway. This feeling is something I can never get from Trevor. He's dominant, but lovingly so. He'd never be able to treat me as if I was a hole to be used. If this is the level of catering they do for all their guests, I'm not surprised Sabrina loves this place.

The guy between my legs thrusts forward, filling me with his thick cock. Despite being wet and ready to be fucked, the invasion still surprises me. He stretches me out, pinging every nerve ending deep inside.

"Ohhh," I cry out.

My back arches from the bliss, pushing my breasts up and making me tug at the hands around my wrist. Being reminded I'm helpless makes me shiver in delight as the guy fucks me slowly. Nothing is happening like I imagined. It's so much better.

As his thrusts pick up speed, he reaches up to play with my nipples, tugging and pinching the sensitive nubs. Fuck, I'm already close to coming. As the pleasure builds, I cry out and writhe against the hands holding my wrists and ankles.

As the waves of rapture crash over me, the man fucking me grunts and shoots his cum deep inside me. I swear I can feel his cum painting my insides. When he pulls out, a gush of wetness splashes on my thighs and runs down my crack to the table. Fuck, this is dirty.

The men release my ankles and wrists, and everyone sits down again.

"Next round," someone announces. "Winner of this one gets to choose the hole."

Someone shuffles the cards, and two others play with my sensitive nipples as if I'm just something to toy with while they're bored and waiting. My body shivers with delight, and I feel a perverse pleasure as the men twist my nipples almost painfully. I didn't know how much I would love being treated like a sex doll. Anyone could walk in here and use me, and I'm such a whore that I'd let them. This is amazing.

Wait, where is Trevor?

I lift my head and realize they positioned me so Trevor is directly across the room with a clear view of my pussy. He's probably not close enough to see the wetness leaking out of me, but I imagine for a moment that he is, and I shiver with desire.

While the two guys play with my tits, another one folds and moves between my legs, sticking his tongue inside me. He's cleaning up his friend's cum? The filthiness of what he's doing, plus how wonderful his tongue feels, almost makes me orgasm. This keeps getting better and better.

When the dealer wins, the man between my legs moves out of the way. The men grab my wrists and ankles, and I feel a tingle of anticipation. The dealer probes my pussy with the head of his cock. His girth isn't as wide as the first man's, but I can tell it's longer when he slides in. He reaches a spot that none of the other men this weekend have reached, and pleasure swirls in my core.

"Fuck, it's tight," he groans.

Every time someone says something that makes me seem like a sex doll, it pings a long-dormant part of my brain and makes me more compliant. If they wanted to fuck me all night long and never let me come, I'd beg them to use me and cover me in cum. I really am a filthy whore.

The dealer brushes my clit with his finger while he fucks me. I'm so sensitive, I'm crying out from pleasure with every touch. The winner's cock throbs and he roars, "Fuuuuck!"

I peak again, screaming out and pulling against the men holding my wrists and ankles. Waves of bliss crash over me as a burst of wetness coats the cock inside me. The dealer moans loudly and blows his load, jerking with his pleasure as he fucks his cum back up in me. When he finally pulls out, another gush of cum mixed with my juices sprays my thighs. Fuck, this is so hot.

Everyone releases my wrists and ankles, and they all sit down again.

"Third round, same deal."

I'm blissed out and barely able to follow what's going on as the game starts. One of them folds quickly and moves between my legs like last time. He licks and sucks until I climax again, and my body continues to tremble from pleasure after he stops.

The game is noisy with lots of groaning at the end, so it must be a close win. This time, instead of taking ahold of my wrists and ankles, multiple men lift me off the table and carry me towards my husband on the couch.

They stand me up in front of him. Cum slides down my thighs, and I bet I look an absolute mess... yet I've never felt more desirable than I do at this moment.

I feel a little punch-drunk, and I give him a goofy grin. "Hi."

Lust burns in his eyes, and the corners of his mouth tip up. "Hi there."

A hand applies pressure to my shoulder. Oooh, are we going to give my husband a close-up view of the action? I sink to my knees and eye Trevor's hardness under his shorts. At least this is proof that he's still enjoying watching his wife be the biggest slut ever.

Trevor reaches down to stroke himself through his shorts, surprising me. His voice is thick when he speaks. "Do you know what time it is, baby?"

I don't care what time it is as long as I get more cocks in me. I lick my lips in anticipation and shake my head. "No?"

He slips his hand into his shorts and pulls his cock out. "Time to get over here and use that mouth for something other than moaning."

I gasp in surprise, and my nipples stiffen to sharp peaks as my pussy hums with approval. Dang, I didn't know Trevor would be comfortable with his cock out in a room full of guys, but I love it. I eagerly crawl forward as he spreads his knees. Leaning on his thighs, I wrap one hand around the base of his cock while slowly taking the tip into my mouth.

As I sink my lips around my husband's shaft, one of the card-players kneels behind me and rubs his cock up and down my wet slit. I have a moment of clarity and think about how this would look if I were watching it. I bet this would make a fabulous porno, but living it is better than any video ever could be.

When the guy plunges inside me, he stretches me out, filling every inch of me. I moan around Trevor's cock and try to give him the best blowjob of his life. He deserves an amazing orgasm for letting me come to this resort.

The man pumps into me from behind, his fingers digging into my hips as he thrusts deeply. Trevor cups the back of my head and uses my mouth. He's being more aggressive than he's ever been before. Fuck, this is amazing.

As the pleasure builds, the man plowing me speeds up and groans. The room fills with the wet sounds of our fucking. The card-player is enthusiastic, and within minutes, I climax again. My body convulses, and I gag a little on Trevor's cock. My husband grasps the sides of my head, forcing me to stop sucking on him until he can tell I'm back in control. I'm such a dirty slut, and I love it.

As I slide his cock back into my mouth, he pets my hair, and a warm fuzziness steals over me. The next cock to press against my pussy gives me a momentary shock as he slams into me. It's the thickest cock I've ever had, and I moan from a pleasurable pain as he stretches me out. He doesn't give me time to adjust when he pulls out all the way and plunges back in. The intense pleasure makes my mind go blank.

Time blurs as the men take turns behind me. I don't know how many times I orgasm, but at some point, Trevor groans and unloads a huge mouthful of cum deep in my throat. I swallow every drop and clean him up like the cum-drunk slut I am.

After that, it's open season on my mouth and pussy, and the guys move me around like I really am a fuck doll, positioning me however they want. I think I suck on two more cocks, and at least one man comes all over my breasts. No one hardly speaks to me, and they just do whatever they want for as long as they want.

At some point, they move me back to the gaming table, and the huge guy is plowing away at my pussy. My eyes are closed, and it's one continuous moan of pleasure as he fucks me. This time when I come, it's so powerful I see stars flash behind my eyelids and I immediately zone out again.

The cool night air against my skin revives me. I'm in Trevor's arms, and he's carrying me back to our cottage. Oh god, it's over? As soon as we walk in the door, I start shivering and feel like I'm going to cry.

Trevor sits on the side of the bed, holding me and kissing my forehead. He rocks me gently and rubs my arm while he soothes me. I don't know what's wrong with me, but I need this connection with him.

Eventually, I calm down enough to look at him and say, "Thank you."

He chuckles and hugs me more tightly. "No, baby, thank *you*."

He lays me down and leaves me briefly, returning with water and two sandwiches. "Eat this, baby. They left it in the fridge for us."

I'm relaxed and dazed as I slowly nibble on the sandwich. When I've eaten a good portion and had some water, he gets in bed and wraps me up into his arms.

"Baby, you were so gorgeous and brave. That was fucking awesome."

I nod against his chest and snuggle closer. "Yeah, it was."

"You make the hottest freeuse slut ever."

"You're the best husband ever." I giggle and then sigh as he strokes his fingers down my spine.

His voice rumbles through his chest. "So, that's a wrap for the weekend. Is my freeuse slut satisfied?"

I lift my head so I can see his face and nod. "Oh yes, more than satisfied."

Sighing, I close my eyes and sprawl half on top of him, feeling every muscle in my body melt. I'm not sure I'd be up to anything like this again, but occasionally fucking another guy while my husband watches would be fun. I'll talk to him about that after we're home and we've processed this experience.

Right before I drift asleep, I realize no one fucked my ass. I sleepily murmur, "The guys didn't use all my holes."

Trevor's soft laugh makes my head bounce on his chest. "That was on my list of nos. That's MY hole."

That's my romantic husband. His wife can be the biggest slut ever, but he's reserving my ass. I kiss his chest as happiness swells inside me. Mmmm, yeah, I'm fine with this.

AFTER USED AND TEASED (BONUS STORY)

It's been three months since my incredible weekend at Plaything Resort, and it definitely changed my marriage for the better. I've never had a closer, more intimate relationship with Trevor, nor have I ever felt so desired and sexy. Our bond has skyrocketed to heights I could never have imagined.

Since we got back from the resort, Trevor has convinced me to have sex with one of his friends while he watches. He told me it's erotic to see the pleasure on my face while another guy fucks me. This arrangement seems like a win-win to me.

Right now, I'm in bed, naked and dripping wet, while I wait for Trevor and his friend Jasper. The fucked up part is that Jasper used to be married to Trevor's sister. It's been a few years since they divorced and it's not like Trevor and Jasper are related, yet it still seems wrong... which only makes it hotter.

Even though I enjoyed myself at the resort, I'm apprehensive about doing it in our bedroom. It's not as anonymous or impersonal since this person knows Trevor and me personally. I worry it will make things awkward. But I trust my husband, and he wouldn't arrange this unless he was sure it would end up with everyone happy and satisfied.

When Trevor walks in alone, his eyes smolder with desire when he sees I'm naked.

"Mmm, damn, babe. You look good enough to eat."

His words send a wave of warmth through me. I've never doubted that Trevor finds me hot, but hearing his compliment tonight gives me the boost of confidence I need before fucking Jasper.

"Thanks." I'm laying on my stomach, and I wiggle my ass at him.

"I left Jasper in the living room. Are you ready for him?"

Ohhh, it's show time. My pussy hums to life and I imagine Jasper fucking me and filling me full of cum.

My, "Yes," sounds breathy with excitement.

He grins and calls Jasper in. When I see Jasper, my pulse speeds up. His gaze skims my body before he focuses on my ass. Trevor reaches over, tracing his fingers down my back and over one of my ass cheeks.

"Baby, Jasper is going to use your pussy. I'm going to watch and jerk off. Once Jasper leaves, you're all mine. You're not allowed to talk unless you need to use your safeword. Got it?"

What's this? Oh fuck, he didn't tell me he was going to give me instructions not to talk. Delight pings my brain and I nod, already mentally sinking into a warm fuzzy place where I just want to obey and be a good girl.

Trevor gives me a reassuring smile as Jasper undresses and stands at the end of the bed. He takes a hold of my hips and pulls me back, forcing me onto my knees. I rest my forehead on the backs of my hands, stretching my pussy open and presenting it to him.

Jasper whistles. "Ready for me, freeuse slut?"

Oh god, he's using the resort nickname Trevor gave me. My husband has been calling me that more often since the weekend at the resort and I love it. I'm not supposed to talk, so I remain silent, and I shiver with delight as Jasper probes my entrance with the tip of his cock.

Trevor takes a seat in the chair next to the bed and rubs himself through his jeans. Shit, that's hot. I love how my husband enjoys watching me with other men.

I gasp as Jasper sinks his cock into me. I'm wet enough that he slides in easily, but his cock is thicker than I expected. Dang, I never knew Jasper was packing such a monster in his pants. I bet Trevor knew, and that's why he chose him. I peek over at Trevor and see him intently watching the action. The chair is angled so he can see Jasper sliding inside me — that's how my kinky husband rolls.

Jasper takes hold of my ponytail and tugs, sending a zing of pleasure through me. He grabs my hip with his free hand and starts fucking me. With one hand in my hair and the other on my hip, I feel like he's riding me. I'm just his dirty slut being used however he wants.

Movement from Trevor makes me look in his direction, and my eyes widen as my husband pulls his cock out from his jeans. He strokes himself slowly, and I can tell he's taking his time so he won't come too quickly.

Jasper's cock feels wonderful, and the tug of his hand on my ponytail sends sparks throughout my body. A tingle of excitement flutters through me, and I arch my back and rotate my hips to take him in as deep as possible. He increases his thrusts and hits a spot inside me that drives me wild. Holy fuck, how does he do that?

I moan from the intense pleasure and meet every thrust with one of my own. Jasper has a bruising grip on my hips, and I welcome the pleasurable pain.

Trevor's pupils are dilated, and his cock is hard, glistening with pre-cum as he strokes himself faster. I love how Trevor is embracing this experience, and knowing he's having fun increases my pleasure.

Jasper slams into me harder, and the ecstasy builds until it's almost unbearable. He lets go of my ponytail and moves his hand around to my breast. When he pinches one of my nipples, it sends me over the edge. I cry out as an orgasm crashes over me, and I come apart. Joy radiates throughout my body. Jasper keeps fucking me through it, and another wave builds up inside me. I climax again with a scream, and Jasper roars before filling me with his seed.

My mind blanks for a moment while Jasper spasms against my ass, making sure I get every last drop inside me. When he pulls out, cum drips down my inner thighs.

I collapse onto the bed and roll over as Jasper puts his clothes back on. "Thank you, Katie. You're a great freeuse slut."

My husband's ex-brother-in-law just walked into the house, used me, and now he's leaving. I've never felt like such a slut. This is amazing.

Jasper thanks Trevor, and both men leave the bedroom. When Trevor returns, he's hard and ready to go. He climbs on the bed and moves between my legs.

"Fuck, that was so hot, babe."

I nod and spread my legs wider. He pushes his cock into my pussy and slides in easily from my combined wetness with Jasper's cum. Pleasure spirals in my core and I sigh at how wonderful my husband's cock feels.

"You're so sexy, and I was afraid I was going to blow my load too soon. But, baby, I want to make sure you get all the cum you want."

I groan as my pussy tightens around his cock. Hearing Trevor describe me as a cum-slut is so fucking hot — mostly because it's accurate. He knows how much I love feeling his cum dripping out of me long after he blows his load.

Trevor pumps into me, and I wrap my legs around his waist. He reaches down to play with my nipples as he fucks me. My husband talks dirty the entire time.

"Yeah, my freeuse slut, that's it. Come all over my cock. Jasper came inside you, and now I'm going to fill you up. I'm going to use my cum-drunk slut until you're covered in my cum."

The filthiness of his words makes me shiver in delight, and the stimulation on my nipples sends me over the edge again. When I come apart,

Trevor groans and shoots his cum deep inside me. Shoving in to the hilt, he grinds against me as he spurts his seed.

After he pulls out, Trevor kneels over me and milks out the last few drops of cum over my stomach. When he finishes, he cuddles up next to me on the bed while I make tiny circles on my stomach with his cum, rubbing it into my skin.

I'm a glorious, debauched mess, and I feel absolutely amazing.

Turning to Trevor, I grin at him. "So... when can we do this again?"

He laughs before kissing me deeply. Our tongues twirl together and aftershocks of my orgasm ripple through me. When we break apart, Trevor brushes a stray strand of hair off my cheek.

"How about next weekend?"

I give him a soft kiss on the shoulder and purr at him, "Mmm, sounds lovely."

Oh yeah, I might be an insatiable cum-slut who wants to be used, but I think my husband is just as kinky as I am. We've changed over the last 14 years, but it's wonderful to know we're changing together.

This is going to be fun.

The End

USED FOR HIM

FREEUSE RESORT WEEKEND 4

LACEY CROSS

CHAPTER 1

My friends and I smile at each other, but my gaze quickly drops to the ground. I wish I could fully enjoy this moment since this should be a joyous occasion. Sabrina planned this swanky baby shower for herself, and it was sweet of her to do that since she's the one we should all be treating like a pregnant goddess.

My thoughts keep drifting to Austin and our marriage, and it's difficult to relax and set my worries aside. It feels like the magic is gone. We've been together for seven years and finally tied the knot a year ago, and now we haven't had sex in a month. Where did the passion go? We used to fuck like rabbits all the time, but now it seems like it's gone.

I'm just as horny as ever, and I've offered to suck his cock whenever he wants, but he keeps saying he's exhausted. What sort of guy is always too tired for a blowjob? I know it's not because I suck—heh—at giving them. He was more than willing to be the recipient of my world-class blowjobs for years. The worst part is I know he's watching porn and jacking off. Why isn't he talking to me—or better yet, fucking me?

"Relax," Holly, my closest friend, mouths at me from a couch directly across from mine.

I fight the urge to stick my tongue out at her and smile instead. Okay, time to focus on this party. The baby shower is a small, intimate gathering.

There's six of us, counting Sabrina, and we've all been friends since high school. We're relaxing in Sabrina's luxurious living room while a catering company serves us food and bubbly. I bet the couch I'm sitting on costs more than six months of my mortgage—and there are three couches in the living room. Sabrina and her husband are over the moon for each other, so I know she didn't marry him for his money, but she sure found herself a perfect sugar daddy.

Katie is next to me, and a crystal sun catcher hanging in the window casts a pretty rainbow on the couch behind her. Every time she moves, it almost touches her head. I love crystals, and that small rainbow brings me comfort. Life can't be all bad when there's beauty in the world.

Sabrina leaves the room for a few minutes, and when she comes back, she hands out business cards. Are we about to play a game? I'm intrigued by the sleek black card with shimmering silver words that say 'Plaything Resort', and I'm not paying attention to what's going on until Sabrina speaks.

"This is my gift to you. It's an invitation to an all-inclusive weekend at my favorite private resort. You don't have to worry about anything. Just show up and enjoy yourselves, either on your own, together, or with your husbands."

I twirl the card between my fingers. Oooh, maybe a vacation is just what Austin and I need. I'll bring a bunch of sexy lingerie and—

"What is this?" Ariana breaks into my thoughts by directing the question to Sabrina.

When Sabrina giggles in response, I have a hard time holding in my grin. She's got such an adorable laugh. "It's a private, freeuse sex resort, silly! It's only open to one group of people at a time. Just tell them what you want, and they'll make all your fantasies come true."

Wait, what the hell? My heart pounds as I stare at the business card, and my panties grow damp as I imagine multiple men fucking me non-stop for a weekend. Why is she giving this to us?

Austin has joked about me being with other guys a few times, but I'm sure he wouldn't really want that. Sure, we're going through a dry spell, but that doesn't mean I need other men to fill the void. I should buy a new toy. That might help, since the lack of sex is making me think about dry humping the nearest hot guy. One of the men on the catering staff is attractive, though his legs are kind of scrawny. I bet I could find some real hunks at the resort who have thick, muscular thighs to ride. Mmm, yeah, that sounds perfect.

Shit, I need to get my mind out of the gutter. Austin and I had some pretty wild times before, but this freeuse resort makes anything we've done seem tame. Sabrina said we could go there on our own or with our husbands. *Yeah, as if Austin would go with me.* He barely wants to fuck me himself. Why would he want to watch other men using me? Can I just go without telling him?

My stomach muscles tighten, and I sigh. What the fuck? I will not cheat on my husband. I need to talk to him about how I'm feeling and what I want.

Holly stares at me, as if she's trying to figure out what's going on with me, and I give her a bright smile. I'm not faking this very well. I need to do better.

The rainbow on the couch catches my eye again, and I study the crystal in the window. Something about the crystal is off. The cord it's hanging from is frayed. Why have an old crystal in a decadent living room?

This isn't the right time to ask Sabrina about it, so I push it out of my thoughts as I fold the business card and tuck it in my pocket. The gift of a weekend at the resort is a nice gesture, but I'll never use it. The card is going straight into the trash when I get home.

CHAPTER 2

I try to forget about the business card for the next week and even go as far as throwing it away in the trashcan in my home office so Austin won't accidentally see it. There's no way I'm going to talk to Austin about a freeuse resort.

It's the middle of my workday and I'm fixing lunch when my cell phone rings. When I see it's Holly, a rush of happiness makes me smile. I haven't talked to any of my friends since the baby shower, and Holly always knows everything about everyone. She'll give me any juicy gossip.

"Hey, Hols, what's going on?"

Holly launches right into talking about the baby shower. "So get this... Sabrina just called me to invite me to lunch tomorrow. I get the feeling it's about the resort. She's totally crazy if she thinks I'm going to that place. She knows Carlos and I are trying to get pregnant."

I laugh. Sabrina is batshit crazy if she thinks any of us are going to the resort—well, except maybe Ariana. Her husband lets her fuck other guys, so that's their lifestyle.

I try to placate Holly. "I doubt she expects you to go."

She gives a "hmm," like she's thinking. "I don't know about that. Everyone else is going. Are you going?"

Wait... what's this? "No! Are you sure everyone else is going?"

"Yep. That's what Sabrina told me."

She's got to be wrong. "There's no fucking way Katie would go. Trevor would throw a fit."

Holly giggles. "Trevor is going with Katie."

"Oh, wow. That's wild."

We chat a little longer and then say our goodbyes. I'm still reeling from the news that everyone else is going to the resort. That can't be true. I'm sure Holly misunderstood. Shit, I don't have time for this. I need to get back to work.

All afternoon, I daydream about fucking a bunch of beefy guys. That would make up for lack of cock for the last five weeks. We used to have sex at least three times per week, so that's three multiplied by five weeks... yep, I'm going to need fifteen orgasms. We won't count the ones I had by myself—those are freebies.

Austin is picking up teriyaki chicken takeout for dinner since neither of us feel like cooking. I'm still distracted by my filthy thoughts when Austin gets home with the food. Normally I'm talkative, but I'm lost in my daydream while we eat. I feel his eyes on me, and I smile at him to show him nothing is wrong—well, nothing *new* is wrong.

When he's finished, he sets his fork down and studies me. I blush and feel guilty, as if he can read my thoughts and knows I'm fantasizing about other men with thick cocks pounding away at me.

"So... what's wrong?" he finally asks.

Ugh, I don't know what to tell him, so I lie. "Nothing. I'm just a little tired today."

He nods and collects our dirty plates. When he turns back to me, he says, "Anything going on at work?"

"No, it's not work." I sigh, and in an impulsive moment I blurt out, "Why aren't we having sex?"

Oh god, I can't believe I just said that. I can feel my face flush, and I fidget in my chair. What if I don't want to know the answer? I needed to prepare for this conversation.

He comes over and kisses me on the forehead. "I'm sorry, Raven. I love you."

Well, that was a non-answer if I ever heard one. He takes the dishes to the sink and is quiet for a moment, so I'm surprised when he continues. "I thought things would be different."

"Different?" I suddenly feel like I'm tiptoeing through a field of landmines, and I wasn't told there was a battle going on.

"Yeah... marriage."

Oh fuck, he's not happy. My dinner rebels in my stomach and I'm confused, so I snap at him, "Austin, we lived together almost six years before we got married. What did you think was going to be different?"

He shrugs. "You don't seem like you'd be interested in... things."

My face heats and I know I'm a bright pink. "Like what?"

He hesitates for a moment and then shrugs. "Never mind."

"No, what is it?" He can't just say that and not finish the thought.

He sighs and moves to the kitchen table and sits down. "The idea of you fucking other guys. I thought you'd be interested in doing it, eventually."

My mind goes completely blank for a second before something clicks. "Are you talking about those jokes you always make?"

"They weren't jokes, Raven. Or, I didn't want them to be."

"Why in the hell would you think I'd want to fuck other guys?" I explode. He doesn't know I *was* thinking about it sometimes.

He looks surprised by my incredulous tone. "I don't know. It's just a fantasy. I thought you'd like the freedom."

Everything feels surreal, and I'm quiet for a moment before finally saying, "I'm confused."

He takes my hand. "It's just something I thought about. I thought we could do it together or something. I didn't know how to bring it up."

Something that feels dangerously like excitement stirs in my gut. "You want to watch me fuck other guys?"

He smiles, and the twinkle is back in his eyes. "Or watch *them* fuck you."

My mouth drops open. "Wait. Sit here. I'll be right back."

He nods, and now it's his turn to look confused. I dash into my home office and dig in the trash for the black business card. Butterflies dance in my stomach when I come back into the kitchen and put it in his hand.

"What's this?"

"That..." I give him a saucy grin as I slide into the chair across from him again, "...is our ticket to a freeuse resort for a weekend where you can watch tons of men fuck me. Do you want to go with me?"

He plays with the folded card, and I'm surprised when he frowns and his face flushes like he's upset. "When did you get this, and why didn't you tell me about it before?"

"Sabrina gave this to me at the baby shower. She gave one to the whole gang. I didn't tell you because I didn't think you'd want to do it." I reach across the table and take his hand. "I threw it out. I just hadn't emptied the can yet."

He thinks about that for what feels like an eternity before he says, "You didn't think I'd want to do this, but did *you* want to do this?"

My husband is the love of my life and it shouldn't be difficult to talk about my dirtiest fantasies, but I'm still bashful about admitting I want a bunch of guys to fuck me. Biting my bottom lip, I nod sheepishly and then giggle. "The thought has some appeal... just a little."

"Just a little?" He raises his eyebrows at me, and I feel myself blush as I lower my eyes to the table.

A neediness builds in my core and I fight the urge to squirm. "Yeah, just a tiny bit."

"Well…" He rises, tugging me up with him. "It's a good thing you didn't toss out the trash yet."

His eyes blaze as he lifts me and deposits me onto the kitchen table. I can't even ask what he's doing before his lips crash down on mine passionately, his tongue gliding into my mouth as he pins me against the dining surface.

"Austin, what's got into you?" I gasp in surprise as he yanks my pants and panties off. He spreads my legs and then steps back to observe me. Oh god, this is dirty. It's odd to feel laid bare for him like this, and I want to move my hand to cover my pussy, but I force myself to let him look.

"I'm going to fuck you," he growls. "Right here on this table. I want to watch you writhe and plead for more."

His cock is rock hard, straining against his pants, and I whimper as he yanks his zipper down and pulls it out.

I can feel wetness dripping from me, and I can't resist teasing him. "You like the idea of watching me fuck other guys this much?"

"Oh yeah, baby. But I'm going to like it more when you beg me to let all those other guys fuck you."

He steps forward and pushes into me without warning. His cock stretches me wide open as he pounds away at me. I gasp and moan from the intense pleasure, my legs splayed as wide as I can get them as he fucks me hard and deep. The table wobbles, and I'm afraid it's going to collapse, but he keeps fucking me, his eyes on mine the entire time.

Pings of delight swirl in my core. I'm ready to beg him to let me go to the resort. "Please, Austin, please let me go."

He continues to talk dirty. "You want them to line up and fuck you hard and deep?"

Each word makes my mind spin. I'm so close to an orgasm. "Yes, oh god, yes. I want to be used and fucked until I can't walk."

"Good girl," he growls. "I want you to come for me and think about all those men filling you full of cum."

The moment he says that, I imagine men coating me with cum, and I explode around him, crying out, "Ohhh, god!" My pussy clenches and milks his cock as he fucks me through my orgasm.

When his cock pulses, he groans and a warmth fills me as he unloads deep inside me. He keeps fucking his cum back up into me as the pleasure turns to soft ripples of joy.

Jesus Christ. Who is this man?

As I pant and try to catch my breath, he pulls out and tugs me up for a kiss. "Now we can go to the resort, and I'll watch them fuck you senseless."

I grin as my pussy clenches in anticipation. "Oh yeah. We're going to have the best time."

I can't wait to be a plaything for all those sexy studs, but I'm only doing this because Austin wants it. I'm not going to complain if my husband wants me to fuck a ton of other guys. Nope, not me.

CHAPTER 3

"Sign these forms and then you can be on your way to your cottage."

Austin and I are at a counter checking into the resort. The owner, Chris, is a silver fox, and we've spoken over the phone several times in the last few weeks to go over all the details of the resort. I wasn't expecting Chris to be so sexy. I wouldn't mind it if he bent me over this counter right here and welcomed me to the resort.

Oh god, maybe it's wrong to think about the owner like that? I peek at Austin, feeling guilty and hoping he doesn't guess what's running through my head. Austin is looking around, checking out the décor, and I relax. It's all good. My husband doesn't know how wet and ready I am to spread my legs to the first guy who wants me.

I give Chris a quick grin before signing my name in all the required spots. It's been wild since we decided to come here. Austin made a fairly good dent in the fifteen orgasms I was owed as he fucked me all over the house. Anytime one of us started talking about the resort, it ended with his cock inside me. Not that I'm complaining.

I'm still standing firm on the idea that I only want to be here because Austin wants it. Now that we're finally here, I'm a horny, nervous ball of energy. I don't know what to expect other than I told them I wanted to feel like a slut for the weekend. Just admitting that out loud felt like I was at a self-help meeting.

"Hello, I'm Raven, and I'm a slut."

Except hopefully instead of donuts and coffee, I'm going to get cocks shoved into every hole.

Chris interrupts my silly daydream. "Raven, as a reminder, everyone here knows your safeword and will abide by it. Don't hesitate to use it. Plenty of women do."

My eyes grow round as my pussy hums to life. They might push my boundaries to the point where I use my safeword? Holy fuck, why is that idea hot?

Chris takes the forms I just signed and shows us a map of the grounds. He circles our cottage and my mind wanders while Austin talks to Chris about the amenities. I'm so distracted by the idea of a bunch of guys using me it's difficult to concentrate on anything else.

Wait, where are all the men?

We filled out questionnaires about what we like and don't like before we came, and I said I wanted all cock. I thought it was lovely that they offered the lesbian experience, but I need to be stuffed with some long, hard sausages... sooner rather than later. They should have offered me a cock as a door prize as soon as I set foot on the property. One of the rules here is that I can't ask to be fucked. I have to just wait for someone to use me. Well, I'm an impatient slut, and I need cock.

As the conversation with Chris winds down, a beast of a man walks in from an archway. He's got massive muscles, tons of tattoos, and long curly black hair. He's barefoot, and all he's wearing are shorts. His massive thighs make my pussy throb. Oh yeah, he could be my demigod, and I'd ride that thigh... my brain freezes for a second, and when it kicks on, I start mentally singing the "You're Welcome" song from Moana. Mmmm, I'd say thank you to that guy if he fucked me.

Chris and Austin say their goodbyes, which focuses me back on what we're doing. As we head out the archway to pass through the villa to get to the cottages, I give the demigod the side-eye. He didn't say hello or even acknowledge us. This place is weird, and yet, that turns me on even more.

As we step out onto the back patio, I sense a presence behind me a moment before I'm shoved face first against the wall.

The demigod's deep voice addresses my husband. "Hey, sorry man, I'll be just a minute."

I drop the bag I'm carrying a second before he yanks up my skirt and pulls my panties down just past my ass.

My heart pounds so loudly in my ear that I almost don't hear my husband say, "No problem."

As the demigod shoves his thick cock into me, I cry out, "Yes!"

He fills me completely, and my body hums with pleasure. I moan and whimper as he plows away at me. I've been turned on for days thinking about this trip, and I assumed I'd come as soon as someone fucked me, but my orgasm eludes me.

The demigod grunts, and his warm seed coats my insides. Oooh fuck, I didn't come. I shudder and cry out in distress when he pulls out. I'm panting, and can't think of anything except coming.

The demigod turns to my husband. "Sorry about that, man. She's just so damn hot I couldn't resist."

My husband just grins as the guy walks away. I'm left standing there with my skirt bunched up, my pussy dripping cum, and my body aching for more. What sort of shitty door prize was this?

"Hey," my husband says, touching my shoulder. "Let's go to the cottage and get you cleaned up."

I'm still horny and I want to come, but I don't argue. There's nothing else to do. He helps me pull up my panties, and I pick up my bag. Our cottage is a short walk from the main building, and I can feel cum leaking out of me with every step. I love the feeling, and I'm giddy as I skip ahead of Austin.

The sun is warm, and the grounds are gorgeously maintained. It's the perfect paradise to spend the weekend. Halfway to the cottage, I can smell the pool... but I don't see any men on the path. Dammit, where are they? I need someone to come fuck me so I can orgasm. This time I'm certain I will come within moments of a cock sliding inside me.

A splash of water and laughter from at least two men tells me where I can find them. Raw need pulses through me, and lust takes over. I need to orgasm.

I stop in my tracks, forcing Austin to stop with me. "Honey, I want to go swimming."

Austin smiles. "Sure, let's put our stuff in the cottage and change into our suits."

More laughter from the pool area rings out, and a yearning deep in my core makes me do something crazy. I drop the bag I'm carrying and pull my shirt over my head, exposing my white bra. "No, now."

He glances at my breasts, and my nipples harden. When I reach behind me and unclasp my bra, sliding it down my arms, he laughs. "Okay, let's go."

I don't know what's got into me... heh, or maybe it's the opposite. It's what's NOT in me that is fueling this craziness. I've never been an exhibitionist, but as we stroll into the pool area, a naughty zing heads straight to my pussy when three pairs of eyes focus on my tits. A fourth guy surfaces from underneath the water—okay, make that four pairs.

Hell, if all eyes are on me, I'm going to make this good. I will not wait around and hope someone wants to fuck me. I'm going to make them want to. Carpe diem, motherfuckers.

The men stare at me in silence, and I have a moment of hesitation. Am I really going to be this slutty? Austin sets our bags on a nearby patio table, and when I glance back at him, he's got an encouraging smile... and a hard bulge under his jeans.

A tingle runs down my spine. His support is all I need. I inhale deeply and hold it as I close my eyes. I count to three. When I exhale, I let go of all my preconceived notions of how I should act. I'm here to experience pleasure with a once-in-a-lifetime opportunity. It's time to embrace my sluttiest self.

I open my eyes and give the men a sultry smile. It's game time.

Swaying my hips, I unzip my skirt and let it drop to the ground. My white panties contrast against my golden skin, and I feel so fucking naughty as I turn away from the guys and bend over at the waist to unbuckle my sandals. The fabric of my panties stretch across my ass as I remove them.

Austin moves and sits in a chair next to the table he set our bags on. He leans back as if he's ready to enjoy a show. I'm going to give him one.

When I straighten up, I spin around to face the pool again. All eyes are on me as I hook my fingers into the waistband of my panties. I move my hips in a slow circle, teasing them with my body, and I feel a rush of power as one guy licks his lips.

In one quick movement, I pull my panties down and step out of them, tossing them at Austin. He catches them and brings them to his nose, inhaling deeply. Yep, that's why I love the guy. He's watching me give a strip tease for other guys and enjoying it.

A slight breeze caresses my skin while the man closest to me, a sexy redhead with adorable freckles, swims closer to the side of the pool. He crooks a finger at me and smiles. "Come on, baby. Let's get you wet."

"But I'm already wet," I purr at the guy I've now dubbed Freckles.

His eyes narrow, and a glint of lust makes me shiver. "That wasn't a request."

Oh fuck, Freckles is a dom. I love it when a guy commands me to do things. I lower myself into the pool. The water is warm, but I still suck in my breath from the temperature change. Freckles moves in front of me, and I can see his erection under the surface. My pussy hums with approval, and I feel like a sexual goddess. I'm turning these men on. It's their choice whether they fuck me, and their hungry gazes tell me they want to.

Freckles pulls me into his arms and kisses me hard. I wrap my arms around his neck as my tongue slides against his. He reaches down and cups my ass, squeezing it, and I moan into his mouth. This isn't exactly freeuse, since I walked up, stripped, and basically offered myself to them. But just knowing these guys have permission to do whatever they want still pings the part of my brain that craves being used. Sure, I made this moment happen, but I don't know what they're actually going to do.

His hands roam over my body, and he tweaks my nipples before pushing me against the edge of the pool. The concrete is rough, but I barely notice as he spins me around and bends me over the side. The cool air rushes over me, and my pussy throbs. I want him to fuck me so badly.

A couple feet under the surface of the water, there's a ledge that runs the perimeter of the pool. It's too low for my toes to touch when I'm bent over the side like this, and I'm thinking it's also too low to sit on comfortably. It doesn't make sense until Freckles stands on it, putting him at the perfect height to press his cock against my entrance. I cry out in delight when he sinks into me with one swift motion. Pleasure shudders through me, and I moan as he pulls out and slams into me again. Jesus, I really am going to come fast.

He fucks me harder and faster, sending jolts of bliss through my body. When he reaches around and circles his thumb around my desperate clit, I scream out, "Oh god, oh god, oh fuck!" My thoughts vanish as wave after wave of pleasure crashes through me—my body trembling as he continues to fuck me.

It doesn't take long before he groans and blows his load inside me. As he pulls out, I sag against the wall, panting. The orgasm was exactly what I needed to quell my horniness.

When Freckles moves away, I expect one of the other guys to replace him and slide his cock inside me, but a voice from the deck startles me.

"I see you guys are enjoying my toy."

What? I blink, and it's the demigod who fucked me against the wall talking as he strolls up to us. There's a hardness under his shorts, and I swallow a pool of saliva in my mouth. I know exactly what his cock feels like.

I consider protesting that I'm actually Austin's toy, but a fuzziness steals over me. No, he's right because I'm everyone's toy. They all can use me however they want, and I'll love it.

I glance over at Austin, and he looks as dazed as I feel. At least he's rock hard underneath his jeans. Mmm, I'll take care of that later.

When I look at the demigod and admire his shoulders, the truth of what I'm doing smacks me in the face. My body tingles, and my pussy clenches, wishing there was a cock inside me. I keep telling myself that I'm only here because Austin wants it, but that's not true. I want to feel like a complete whore and have a bunch of men use me. The fact that Austin wanted to see it was just the icing on the cake. I really am the slut I wanted to be.

The demigod kneels down next to the pool and reaches out, stroking my cheek. "Are you ready to be my good girl?"

Oh god, yes. I nod, and he stands and pulls his magnificent cock out of his shorts. It's thick and veiny, and it's pointing straight at me.

He reaches for me. "It's time to get out of the pool."

Since I'm still bent over the edge, it doesn't take much to climb up. Water runs down my legs, and I wonder how much of it is me and how much is the pool. The demigod guides me to a chair before sitting down in it himself.

His voice is like silken steel. "Get on your knees and suck my cock."

Shit, I'll do whatever he wants if he uses that tone of voice. I kneel in front of him and wrap my hand around the base of his cock. It's hot and smooth, and I feel a rush of power again as I lick the tip. The demigod leans back and closes his eyes as I take him in my mouth and suck.

As I bob my head, I can hear Austin moan behind me. I turn my body slightly so I can get a side view of Austin. He's rubbing himself through his jeans. I can't wait until he fucks me tonight.

The demigod grips my hair and fucks my mouth faster. I relax my jaw and let him use me. I'm nothing but a plaything for him.

Movement from behind is the only warning before another guy pulls on my hips, bringing my ass up. His fingers run up and down my pussy, and I moan around the demigod's cock as I realize I'm about to get fucked.

The man behind me murmurs encouragement and praises as he slides his thick cock inside my wet depths. "Good girl. I'm going to make you come so hard. You won't even remember your name."

Mmm, yes, please. My entire body is still tingling from my last climax, and I was ready for another round of pleasure. This new man may not be as big as Freckles or the demigod, but he's got some good moves that make me moan with each thrust.

The demigod grips my hair and fucks my mouth harder and faster. I'm so wet and horny. I want to come with him, but I'm not there yet.

The guy fucking me reaches around and rubs my clit as he whispers, "Come on, baby. Come for me."

I lose it, and my body shudders as I orgasm. The demigod groans and spills his seed into my mouth, and I swallow it as waves of bliss assault me. With the guy pounding against my ass behind me, and cum dripping out of the corners of my mouth, I truly feel used. This is what I came for.

The demigod pulls out, and the other guy continues to fuck me. I whimper when he says, "You're such a good little slut."

The mix of praise and degradation sends me over the edge, and I come again, clenching around him as he pounds away at me. I'm in a sea of pleasure when he finally comes with a groan. His warm cum coats my insides, and I feel it dripping out of me.

After he pulls out, I collapse onto the ground, exhausted and spent.

The demigod kneels down and strokes my face. "You're so beautiful when you're used. Just wait until tonight. There'll be more where that came from."

I blink at him, unable to process his words fully. My pussy spasms as a thrill runs down my spine. That sounds amazing. I've barely been here an hour, and I already feel like I'm being taken to the next level of pleasure. I can't wait.

He smirks as he stands up and pulls his shorts up. "Let's go, guys. She needs rest for later."

Oooh, what's happening later?

The men laugh as they get out of the pool and head off.

Austin kneels down next to me and strokes my cheek. "Are you okay?"

I smile at him. "Mmm, yes. I'm wonderful."

He helps me up, and I sway a little. When he steadies me, his hands roam all over my body, touching me where the men did. I can tell he's so horny that he's almost mindless. Ohhh, he needs me.

Reaching between his legs, I stroke his cock through his jeans for a moment before fumbling to free it. He helps me with his jeans, and when his cock is free, I push him down into a lounge chair. He watched all those men fuck me, and now it's his turn.

I'm so damn wet from the other guys' cum mixed with my juices, and I get a dirty thrill knowing that Austin is going to add his load to the rest. Straddling his waist, I sink down on his cock, and we both moan as he fills me.

He murmurs, "Fuck baby, you feel so good."

I lean in to kiss him. Our tongues mingle as I ride him slowly. I don't have to hurry, and I want to savor every second. Soft pleasure swirls in my core. I'm enjoying the loving moment with him. I crave being used, but I need times like this as well. This is the only man who matters to me, and

I'm so fucking lucky that we talked through our problems. Who knew that I just had to fuck a bunch of other men to spice up our love life again?

He groans, and when his cock spasms inside me, I speed up my movements. It's time for us to come. I ride him hard and fast, and he grips my ass, rocking me against him. It only takes a few moments before I explode around him, crying out as a white-hot pleasure ripples from my fingertips to my toes.

Within moments, he yanks me down onto his cock and moans as he unloads spurt after spurt of cum inside me. I collapse against his chest with a giggle. God, what a day so far. We haven't even made it to the cottage.

We rest for several moments before he finally murmurs, "You're the sexiest thing I've ever seen."

His words make me giddy, and I grin at him. "I hope you liked that as much as I did."

"Oh yeah, baby. I loved it. Now let's go get cleaned up."

CHAPTER 4

The property has five cottages, in case people want to come in groups. I'm glad we came alone. I'm not looking for an orgy. Plus, it's nice to have this be all about me.

It doesn't take us long to unpack and scope out the small living area. There's the bedroom, a nook with a kitchenette and dining table, plus an enormous bathroom. The nautical decorations throughout the cottage remind me of vacationing on the coast. Somehow, it fits, even though we're not anywhere near the coast.

There's sandwiches in the fridge for us, and as soon as I eat and shower, I pass out. When I wake up, the sun is setting, and Austin is next to me on the bed, watching me.

I didn't get dressed after my shower, and my pussy flutters as I see the desire in Austin's eyes. It would be easy to push him onto his back and ride him again, but I'm curious what the demigod meant earlier about me needing rest for tonight.

I lean in, kiss Austin softly, and ask, "What're you thinking about?"

"You." He grins and lightly trails his fingertips down my spine, causing me to shiver with delight. "I was wondering what you're doing here."

I laugh and lean into his touch. "I'm here to be used, silly."

"Do you like it so far?" His eyes flash and his hard cock brushes against my leg.

"Mmm, yes. Did you enjoy watching all those men fuck me?"

"Oh yeah. It was hot, and I was horny as hell. I wanted to fuck you while they were using you."

His words send a tingle through me, and I kiss him deeply before whispering, "You could join in..."

He shakes his head. "Not this time, baby. I want to just watch you."

This time? I didn't consider doing this beyond the weekend, and the thought makes me warm and fuzzy all over. "Okay, then. What should we do tonight?"

He laughs and pulls me off the bed as he gets up. "You need to put on that pretty sundress I saw you pack. Chris said they're setting up a sound system on the patio for dancing tonight."

Hey, he knew all along what we were doing tonight? I smack him playfully. "You could have told me about the dancing."

He mock-flinches. "Um, weren't you listening when Chris talked about it?"

Oh. Right. I was too busy being a super slut and imagining other guys fucking me. "Um, no. I guess I wasn't. That sounds fun!"

He grins and smacks my ass. "Now go put your dress on. We don't want to be late."

I love it when he gets all commanding. It's not often, but when he does, I melt.

The sundress is made from a soft cotton with a light blue floral print. I don't bother with a bra or panties. Let's be honest here, they're probably going to come off at some point. I only brought a couple pairs of shoes, and I go with my comfortable ballet flats—just in case I actually dance.

He dresses in his jeans and a t-shirt, and when we're both ready, he leads me to the patio. While we were sleeping, someone transformed the patio into a lovely oasis with fairy lights and tables and chairs scattered around an open area that I assume is the dance floor.

I count at least ten men, plus Chris. Lively music is playing through the outdoor speakers, and people are laughing and talking as we approach. Wait, did they plan this just for us? On the questionnaires we filled out, I said I like to go out dancing on the weekends, but I didn't expect them to use that information. Either way, this is pretty awesome.

Chris comes over to us and pulls me into his arms. "I claim the first dance."

Whoa, I didn't expect that. He moves to the middle of the dance floor, and as I press against him, I can feel his hard cock. He whispers in my ear, "Welcome to your slutty party," before spinning me out of his arms and making me laugh.

We dance, and after Chris, another guy takes his place. Then another and another. It's heaven as I get lost in the music and the rhythm of their bodies against mine.

At one point, Austin joins us, and I'm sandwiched between the two of them, loving every second of it. The men all take turns with me, and I lose track of who is who. They're all sexy, and I want to fuck every single one of them.

The night progresses, and their hands get more bold as they caress my butt and breasts. Each new set of hands on my body turns me on even more until I'm in a haze of lust. When the demigod takes me into his arms, it's suddenly like I'm in my own private Dirty Dancing movie. His thick thigh is between my legs, and I'm grinding on him mindlessly, wishing his cock was inside me.

Wetness coats my inner thighs—yeah, I probably should have worn panties—and I'm practically a puddle of bliss waiting for someone to use me.

When the demigod pulls me to the edge of the dance floor until my back is against the railing of the deck, I know it's time. He kneels in front of me, pushing my dress up, spreading my legs, and putting one thigh on his shoulder. Wait, he's going to eat me out here? In public? I've never done anything like this in front of other people.

His tongue swipes along my folds, and I gasp. Holy fuck. His fingers dig into my hips as he licks and sucks on me. I almost close my eyes from the pleasure, but when I glance around, I see all the men staring at me. Ohhhh, fuck. An immediate wave of embarrassment quickly turns to delight. They aren't looking at me and judging me. They're all admiring me. I'm the guest of honor at this gathering, and they're all waiting for their turn with me.

When the demigod slides a finger inside me while sucking on my clit, I moan and have to hold on to the railing to keep my knee from buckling. Pleasure radiates through me, and I'm so close to coming. The men gather around us, watching, and I feel like a queen. The demigod works me with his tongue and fingers, and as my orgasm approaches, I'm desperate to come with all these eyes on me.

Thinking of how this looks from the men's point of view pushes me over the edge. I close my eyes and cry out, my body shuddering as the waves of pleasure overtake me. I tremble as he keeps licking me through my orgasm, and I'm wooly-headed when he finally slides his fingers out of my pussy.

"Mmm, you're such a good girl," he growls at me before he stands and kisses me hard.

I can taste myself on his tongue, and suddenly I don't feel like just a slut—I'm a complete whore. I just orgasmed in front of a group of guys and my husband, and now I'm sucking my own essence from the demigod's tongue. Yep, I'm a whore, and it's amazing.

My body hums with bliss as he steps away, and Freckles moves in front of me. He spins me around and leans me over the railing. He fumbles with his fly, and my head spins as I wonder how I got here. It was just a few weeks ago that I thought something was really wrong with my marriage. Now everything is beyond wonderful.

My body buzzes as he gets his cock out, and then he's inside me, fucking me hard and fast. I hang onto the railing as he whacks against me, and the wood digs into my palms. I love every second of it.

Within moments, he groans and unloads inside me, and it's not long before one of the other guys takes his place. This time I'm facing him and leaning on the railing with my legs wrapped around his waist, practically suspended in the air as he fucks me. It's like they think I'm a gymnast, but for tonight, maybe I am. I'm willing to be their pretzel if it gets me all their cum.

They take turns with me, and at some point, I lose my dress. I'm on all fours, sucking on one guy while another drills into my pussy from behind. This is crazy in the best of ways. Everything is one continuous wave of pleasure. Every cock feels good, every brush against me sends sparks of pleasure down my spine. I'm hypersensitive to everything.

After what feels like an eternity, I think the party is winding down, but the demigod approaches me again. I'm on my knees, and I give him a dopey grin. "Hi."

For a brief moment, it looks like he's about to smile, but a hard mask falls over his face as he pulls me up and bends me over the table next to Austin.

"Oh, hi to you too!" I give Austin my cutest smile and blow him a kiss. He's not afraid to smile back at me.

When I hear a pop-top like someone is opening a bottle of lube, I glance behind me, startled. Uh, what's going on? The demigod drips lube in the crack of my ass, and I close my eyes and moan. Ohhhh, god. I don't know why I wasn't expecting someone to fuck my ass. I said on the forms they could use whatever hole they wanted. And yep, they're going to use me all right.

The demigod rubs his cock against my asshole for a moment before pushing the tip of his cock inside. I tense up, but then I remember to breathe and relax. The lube helps him slide in, and I moan as he stretches me out. After a few moments of rocking back and forth, he's buried to the hilt inside me.

It feels so different from when Austin fucks my ass. I don't know if it's because the demigod is so much larger or because I'm in a completely new position. But it feels good, and I want more.

As he fucks my ass slowly, I moan and writhe underneath him. I feel so slutty and used. It's wonderful. I didn't realize it, but this is what I needed. Having every hole used somehow makes the night complete. I'm a whore who just got ganged by multiple men, and I'm going to be dripping with their cum while I sleep with my husband.

When the thrusts against my ass become harder and faster, I moan from the pleasurable pain and push back towards him. I'm desperate for him to come inside me. I've had so many orgasms tonight, I don't even need to come again. It's about being fucked and used, not the orgasms.

He groans and spasms as he fills me with his warm cum, and I can feel it leaking out of me as he pulls out. He slaps my ass, and I yelp from surprise.

"We're done with you."

Austin helps me stand up, and he pulls me into his lap. He kisses my forehead, and Chris sets a bottle of water next to us as the guys melt into the darkness.

Austin strokes my back. "Are you okay?"

I smile and nod, feeling exhausted and sated. "Yes. That was everything I wanted."

He kisses my forehead again, and I cuddle against him while he opens the bottle of water and I take a few sips. When he can tell I'm not as loopy from pleasure anymore, he helps me up and leads me down the lighted path. As we walk, I can feel the cum running down my legs, and my pussy tingles.

Once we're in our cottage, Austin starts a shower for me, but ends up pulling me into the shower with him. We wash each other, laughing and teasing as the warm water cascades down our bodies.

"Raven, you are so fucking beautiful. I loved seeing you used by those men. I'm glad we came here."

"Me too, honey. This weekend has been everything I needed. And I think you enjoyed it too."

He grins and kisses me. "Oh yeah. I enjoyed watching all those men fuck you. But do you know what the best part is?"

"Mmm, what?"

He turns me around and presses my breasts against the cold tiles of the shower. As his cock slides inside my pussy from behind, he groans. "Knowing that when they're done with you, you're still mine forever."

"Ohh, yes. I'm all yours."

As he fucks me slowly, my mind spins. I'm sure tomorrow I'm going to get used just as much as I was today. I don't think I'll end up using my safeword. This was amazing.

But beyond just the pleasure, the resort is a turning point in our marriage. I can feel it. We're going to be stronger than ever. I'm so fucking glad I asked him why he didn't want to have sex with me that night.

Plus, I'm a complete slut, and I can't wait to do something like this again. Maybe next time Austin will join in on the gangbang. But for now, it's just me being a whore for my husband. And that's okay.

After Used for Him (Bonus Story)

After breakfast, Austin and I head to the game room and have an hour of fun until the demigod — a gigantic beast of a man — shows up with two other guys. They don't need to ask to fuck me. I'm their freeuse slut for the weekend.

I'm playing pinball when the demigod yanks down my shorts and slides his cock into my wet depths. This is what I'm here for, to be used by multiple men.

He growls in my ear, "Keep playing the game; if you lose, we'll fill you full of cum and leave you wet and needy. You're nothing but a cum dumpster for us."

Fuck, this is dirtier talk than anyone did last night. Yesterday they treated me like a goddess they wanted to please, but today it's different. I'm their filthy slut to use however they want.

I bounce against the machine, feeling wetness running down my inner thigh as the lights flash and bells and whistles ring. All I care about is the thick cock drilling me from behind and the orgasm that's approaching like a freight train. Of all the scenarios I imagined might happen today, this wasn't a possibility.

The demigod wraps an arm around me and pinches my nipples. I cry out when white-hot pain shoots through me, and I slam my fist against the side of the pinball machine. The buttons beep and click as I try to track where the ball is going — well, the ball in the machine. The demigod's fucking me so hard, I can feel his balls hitting my clit with every thrust.

One guy beside me, a muscled blonde from last night, strokes himself and watches the action at my ass. He's fluffing himself to stay ready for his turn in me. This is so fucking hot. I love knowing I'm about to get filled with so much cum that I'll be leaking all day.

A pinball shoots past the paddles and into the hole. Shit, I'm not paying attention. Every stroke of the demigod's cock practically makes my eyes roll into the back of my head from pleasure. How am I supposed to play?

I set up another ball and try to follow its trajectory as it bounces against the walls of the machine. Fuck, it goes straight into the hole again. My body trembles as my orgasm approaches, and the demigod thrusts harder and faster.

The pinball machine hums with the force of his pounding, and it chimes as I get a high score. It's all meaningless at this point, but I can barely think straight, anyway.

The demigod grunts as his cock twitches inside me, filling me with his cum. Noooo, oh god. I need to come. He pulls out, and before I can say anything, the muscled blonde takes his place. He flips me around and I lean onto the machine, wrapping my legs around him. When he immediately fucks me hard, each thrust sends pleasure rippling from my fingers to toes.

Wait, where's Austin? My head whirls as I search for my husband. Relief floods through me when I spot him behind the three guys, lust blazing in his eyes. Thank god; he's still enjoying himself.

The pinball machine shakes as the guy slides deep inside me and the movement makes it hard to concentrate. The dancing last night was perfect, but this right here? This is the stuff of legend — what did I do at the freeuse resort? Oh, you know... just got plowed on a pinball machine by three studs.

Yeah, this is awesome. The third guy who hasn't fucked me yet starts playing with my nipples. I close my eyes as pleasure washes over me. The freedom to be the biggest slut in the world is the reason this resort is so amazing. Once I let go and embraced my inner whore, I was free to have the most incredible experience of my life.

As the blonde guy fucks me to the edge of my orgasm, my body trembles with my impending release. I just need another minute and I'll come.

My vision blurs from pleasure, but the blonde guy comes before I do. He groans and releases his load into my pussy. As he withdraws, I'm sticky with cum and covered in sweat. Oh fuck. This weekend has been incredible so far, but I need to motherfucking come.

When the third guy stops playing with my nipples, he has a gleam in his eye. He pulls me off the pinball machine and bends me over the pool table that's nearby.

"It's time for the slut to get another load," he growls as he slides his cock into my sopping wet pussy.

Mm, yeah. I'm in the mood to take all the cock I can get. If this is my last day here, I want to go home sore from all the cocks slamming into me.

As the guy plows me against the table, I see Austin standing to the side, stroking himself through his shorts as he watches. He looks happy and horny. I love him so much, and coming here might have changed our lives.

The dude fucking me unexpectedly slaps my ass and I yelp.

He's fucking me hard, but barely sounds winded. "Concentrate, slut. It's time for a game."

Huh? A game? What kind of game is he talking about? He fucks me even harder, and a gush of wetness runs down my leg as I close my eyes. I don't want to play a game. I just want to come.

He slaps my ass again and I whimper. "Open your eyes. It's time to play pool. Make your shot and I'll keep fucking you. Miss it and you lose."

Ohhh, fuck. He's serious. He didn't say what happens if I lose, but I don't want to find out. When he slows down his movements, I push back against him, trying to get him to fuck me harder again. He holds my hips in place and doesn't move. I bite my lip and groan in frustration.

Shit. Fuck, okay. I stare at the pool balls set up on the table. The green felt is rough under my palms. I'm barely holding on, and I can feel the guy's cock pulsing inside me. I have to hurry.

He stays still as I knock two balls into the side pocket. Yes! He pulls out and strokes himself, keeping his cock right against my dripping pussy. I arch my back and aim for the tricky angle shot. As I hit the cue ball, the seven drops into the side pocket.

He shoves his cock back into me and groans, "Changed my mind. Taking too long. Need to come."

Oh, thank god. He fucks me hard, and I grip the side of the table as pleasure builds in layers. Right before I come, he groans and explodes deep inside me. *Noooo, fuck!*

I whimper as he unloads ropes of sticky cum before pulling out and milking the last few drops over my ass. Does this mean I lost?

He smacks my ass and growls, "Bad luck, slut. Guess you have to wait to come now."

Damn it. I'm horny and frustrated and stare in disbelief as the three guys walk away. He didn't tell me what would happen if I lost, but I guess I just found out.

Austin steps up beside me, stroking his cock through his shorts. I take over for him, gripping him tightly and kissing him passionately.

He murmurs, "God, you are so fucking hot. I'm not going to last long when I fuck you."

A thrill shoots through me as he slams me against the pool table and bends me over it. He better last long enough for me to come. That's all that matters.

He rips his shorts down, and his cock springs free. As he slides into me, I moan and relax. Yeah, this is what I need.

He pistons into me, and I whimper. "Faster, honey. Please, I need to come."

He picks up speed, pounding harder until his balls slap against me — god, he feels so damn good. The pressure builds until he reaches around to rub my clit. Stars burst behind my eyes.

I scream out as pleasure wracks my body, and he thrusts deeper and harder before groaning and letting loose a torrent of cum deep inside me. I ride the waves of rapture as he whacks against me, unloading everything — and it seems like a lot for a guy who came twice yesterday.

He collapses on top of me, both of us panting heavily. Wow, that was incredible. This morning, I woke up thinking nothing could surpass last night, but I was wrong. I've never felt so liberated and free. I just got treated like a sex doll and fucked against a pinball machine and a pool table. It was wonderful.

"Come on, babe. Let's get you cleaned up and relaxed," Austin murmurs in my ear.

My stomach grumbles loudly, making us laugh as Austin adds, "Plus some food."

I kiss him softly. Yeah, this slut needs some nourishment to keep her energy up. Something tells me I have a lot more loads of cum to take today.

The End

USED AND TREASURED

FREEUSE RESORT WEEKEND 5

LACEY CROSS

Chapter 1

"Relax," I silently mouth to my best friend, Raven, who is sitting on the couch across from me. There's a tension radiating off of her I can't identify, but she needs to loosen up. This is supposed to be a day of fun.

I'm attending a baby shower for Sabrina, one of my high school friends. There are six of us here, including Sabrina, and the event is meant to be lighthearted. I've perfected the art of pretending to be fine, so no one knows I'm not enjoying myself. I don't want Raven to ruin it.

Everyone else's lives seem wonderful, but Carlos and I have been trying to conceive for three years with no success, and it's starting to take a toll on us. I'm 33 and always assumed I'd have a minimum of one or two children by now, but life doesn't always follow our plans. I fell in love with Carlos, and we later found out he has sperm mobility challenges. It sucks, but that's how the cookie crumbles sometimes. He's the love of my life, and I wouldn't trade him for all the babies on earth.

Sabrina leaves the room to grab something, and I try to get in the mood for the festivities. We have presents to open and cake to eat. I need to get out of this funk.

Golden afternoon sunlight streams through the window, causing a crystal sun catcher in the frame to cast a dazzling rainbow across the couch. Whenever Katie shifts her head, the sparkle captures my attention. I swear it's mocking me for my hidden sorrows. Yeah, well, I have a good reason for my mood, so the sun catcher can shove it.

Sabrina waddles back in and says, "Okay, everyone. You ready for the surprise?"

I struggle to contain a sigh. She looks so unbelievably adorable with her enormous belly. Why can't that be my life? When we first arrived, I promised myself I wouldn't focus on the sadness, but jealousy is a hard mistress, and Sabrina has a glow of joy all around her.

I fantasize what it would be like to be her as she navigates around the couches, handing something to each of us. She has everything I want in life: a wealthy husband, a baby on the way, luxurious vacations, and a beautiful home. Except that I'd rather have Carlos instead of her husband—not that there's anything wrong with him. He's older, and he's great to her. But he's not my incredible, lovable Carlos.

Sabrina stops in front of me, and when I move to take a black business card from her, she keeps hold of it until I look up at her. She gives me an intense gaze as she eventually releases the card. That was... strange.

When she settles in on the couch, she announces, "This is my gift to you. It's an invitation to an all-inclusive weekend at my favorite private resort. You don't have to worry about anything. Just show up and enjoy yourselves, either on your own, together, or with your husbands."

A thrill runs through me as I examine the black business card with silver lettering that reads 'Plaything Resort.' Hell yeah, a free vacation! But why would I go to an exclusive resort without my husband? We can't really afford trips. This could be just what I need to relax and enjoy time with Carlos.

"What is this?" Ariana asks, and I want to shush her. Don't look a gift horse in the mouth. Take the free vacay and don't ask questions.

Sabrina's giggle is silvery and light. "It's a private freeuse sex resort, silly! It's only open to one group of people at a time. Just tell them what you want, and they'll make all your fantasies come true."

Suddenly, the card in my hand feels like a venomous snake and I want to toss it on the table. That's a hell no. I'm not going to fuck other people while I'm trying to get pregnant. Meanwhile, my traitorous pussy lights up at the thought of multiple guys lined up to pound me raw. What is that called? Running a train on someone?

I shift my legs to ease the growing ache between them. Fine, I'll admit that the idea of fucking multiple guys at once is appealing, but it's a fantasy that won't ever happen for real. Once Carlos and I began trying to get me pregnant, I discovered I have a huge kink for cum. I love being fucked without a condom and feeling it inside me. Just knowing I could get pregnant whenever Carlos blows his load inside me—even if it's unlikely—excites me and makes me crave more of his cum.

My mind races as I try to concentrate on the party instead of dreaming of rushing home and pouncing on my husband, begging him to fill me. God, I can envision an entire resort filled with men, their only goal to fuck me and give me multiple loads of cum. Although I won't be going to the resort, it'll give me plenty of fantasizing material.

CHAPTER 2

As soon as I arrive home from the baby shower, I kick off my shoes and hurry to the bedroom. Carlos is home, deeply engrossed in a computer game in the room that will eventually become a nursery. I hastily toss the business card on the nightstand as I shed my dress, desperate to find Carlos so he can fuck me senseless.

Carlos looks up from his computer as I stride into the office, naked. "Hey, doll." He gives me a lascivious grin and eyes my breasts. "How was the baby shower?"

I pounce on him and straddle his lap. "Let's talk later. I need you inside me NOW."

His lips curl up, and his eyes have a devilish sparkle as he lifts me onto the desk. Mmm, nice. Something prods the soft flesh of my ass, so I reach back and shift the keyboard away from me.

"What happened at the shower to get you all riled up?"

I grab his belt buckle and pull it open. "Oh, nothing much... just Sabrina offering us a weekend pass to a resort where a bunch of guys will use me. Like, for sex. It's called freeuse."

He chuckles, "I know what freeuse is," and crushes his lips to mine. He kisses me hungrily and moans into my mouth. The way he's kissing me reminds me of when we first started dating. It's been a while since

I've seen this level of passion from him. I wiggle against him, my pussy throbbing with desire. We don't need to talk anymore. It's like we can read each other's thoughts as he licks and kisses the delicate spots on my neck. I'm so incredibly turned on, I'm going to come quickly.

He pauses from kissing me as he finishes tugging his pants down, and I murmur, "Where do you want to come?" It's been months since I offered him any other choice than my pussy, and his eyes light up in eagerness. My heart warms and a wave of love for him sweeps through me.

I want to do things that will make my husband happy again. It doesn't matter if he wants to come on my face or in my mouth. I don't need to get pregnant this very second. Maybe we should take a breather for once and stop worrying?

Without responding to me, he spreads my legs wider and thrusts into me, sending me over the brink to a fast, powerful climax. "Fuuuuuck," I cry out as he hammers home. My legs tremble, and I lean back on my hands for stability.

He watches my tits bounce as he fucks me, and pings of bliss ripple through me. I study his face. I adore how his nostrils flare and his lips harden with determination. This animalistic need has been missing from our marriage for a long time. I should straddle him in the office more often.

As he continues to pound into me, I cry out in delight. I rock my hips to meet his, wordlessly encouraging him to come for me. I let go of all the fears and worries that have been clouding our sex life for so long as I enjoy my husband in this moment.

"Please, Carlos," I whimper, "I need your cum."

As if my words turn him on even more, he picks up the pace. "I'm gonna fill you with my cum, baby," he groans.

This is the extent of our dirty talk, even though I've told him I'd like to be called a slut and he could be rougher to me. But today it doesn't matter. Everything he's doing thrills me.

He whacks against me a few more times, grunting as he pumps into me and releases his seed. Feeling his warmth coating me tips me over the edge again, and I moan as ecstasy rushes over me.

Once our high fades, we lean against each other and catch our breaths. As his cock softens inside me, he withdraws from me and falls back into his chair.

"I feel used," he chuckles.

I give him my best saucy grin. "Good, that was the plan. I needed a good fucking after imagining a freeuse resort full of men."

He laughs again before his expression turns serious, piercing me with a look that makes me feel like squirming. What is he thinking?

"You know, Holly, you could go if you wanted."

My mouth drops open for a moment before I recover. "No, I couldn't. I don't want to risk a condom breaking."

He kisses me softly on the lips and then on the forehead. "So don't wear a condom."

Huh? Is that a joke or something?

He must sense my confusion because he sighs and hugs me tenderly. "It's a free trip, and we could skip fertility treatments."

Whoa, wait a minute, what's going on? I shake my head at him, confused, and push out of his arms. "No… I don't want that."

I thought the plan was to try IVF with his sperm in a few more years, when we're making more money and can save up for it. Why is he offering this now?

He shrugs. "It was just a thought. I'm fine with keeping you all to myself, though the idea of you getting fucked by other guys is hot."

He embraces me in a hug, and my head spins. As he steps back and puts on his pants, I shove the thought away. He's crazy. I'm not going to a freeuse resort to get pregnant. I hop off the desk, determined to forget about the dang resort.

Chapter 3

The resort is all I can think about for the next week. Once Carlos put it in my head that I could go and get pregnant, it took root in my mind like a stubborn weed. I can't dig it out. I need to find something else to occupy my mind so I don't become obsessed.

When my phone rings, I see it's Sabrina, and I'm curious what she wants. I answer, "Hey girl, how are you feeling?"

She giggles on the other end of the line. "Enormous and tired. I didn't call to chat about me, though. I want to find out if you and Carlos are going to use the pass to the resort."

Oh God, hearing Sabrina mention the resort makes me imagine a ton of men using me. I squeeze my legs together as desire sweeps through me. Shit, I really need to stop thinking about this.

Taking a deep breath, I keep my voice casual. "Nah, we're not going."

She hesitates for a moment. "That's too bad. Most everyone else is. I thought you'd have fun."

"Everyone else is?" What the hell? My pussy clenches, and an unexpected stab of jealousy knifes me in the gut. I didn't think everyone else would go. I mean, Ariana maybe, since her husband shares her.

Sabrina giggles. "All but you and Raven so far."

"Even Katie?"

Sabrina's laughter intensifies. "Oh, Katie is going all right, AND Trevor is going with her."

Whoa... I try imagining Katie being a complete slut, and I just can't picture it.

Sabrina interrupts my thoughts. "Want to go for lunch tomorrow? I'll treat. We need to chat."

The solemnity of her words leads me to believe it's urgent, so I quickly agree. We talk about the logistics of her picking me up at work tomorrow before hanging up. She totally wants to talk me into going to the resort, but why does she care?

I spend the rest of the day in a dither, and not even a phone call with Raven can clear my thoughts. Raven informs me she won't be attending the resort either, so I guess it's just me and Raven holding firm. I go to bed frustrated with desire for the unknown men at the resort. It doesn't seem fair that all my other friends are getting this chance. Why them and not me?

At work the next day, I can barely concentrate and I'm walking through a haze. My mind churns. I can't wait for Sabrina to pick me up for lunch. We usually do our lunch dates at an upscale sandwich shop around the corner, so I'm surprised when she arrives in an elegant BMW that looks like it cost more than I can make in two years at my job.

She greets me with, "Hey, girl." We chat about the weather and other trivial topics on the short drive. Instead of the sandwich shop, she takes me to an exquisite sit-down restaurant for lunch. I'm glad I took an extra hour of personal time off work. I figured she might want to talk for a while.

She's quiet as we walk in and when we're seated, she studies me intently for a moment before saying, "You should go to the resort."

I immediately bristle. "I don't want to risk a condom breaking, and I'm not sure I want to fuck someone other than my husband."

She leans back in her chair and caresses her baby bump, giving me another meaningful stare. "The resort did wonders for me and Luis."

This gets my attention. "How so?"

The waiter arrives to take our orders, stopping the conversation briefly. As soon as he leaves, Sabrina explains. "Luis had a vasectomy before we got together. Even after reversal surgery, we tried for several years with no success, so we went another route. He knew about the resort and one weekend there during my fertile times, and 'boom' here we are."

She pats her belly for emphasis, and my mind races. I never considered asking Sabrina how she got pregnant, assuming it was the traditional way with her husband. I'm even more in awe of Sabrina and Luis now. "Wow. Why didn't you mention this before?"

Her laughter is delicate, like a wind chime. "You didn't ask. Plus, I needed time to become comfortable with the idea of telling anyone I had a weekend gang bang and got pregnant. But the outcome has been more than rewarding."

Our food arrives, and I attempt to absorb the information. I'm not sure how to respond to her, so we switch topics while we eat. When we're finished, she pulls out a tiny box from her purse and places it in front of me.

"This is for you."

Curious, I open it up. It's the sun catcher that was hanging in her living room. I didn't get a good look at it before, but the frayed string tells me it's old. Why is she giving me this?

She reads the confusion on my face and offers a soft smile. "It's for good luck. My cousin gave it to me after she became pregnant, and I brought it with me when I went to the resort. It's been passed around for years."

"Wow," I murmur in amazement. "Don't you want to keep this?"

"No, please, take it. If it helps you and Carlos achieve your dreams, that would make me happy."

Touched beyond words at her gift, I whisper a humble, "Thank you." Though I don't believe in magic, the fact that this trinket has accompanied other women through their struggles makes it precious.

After giving me time to think, she speaks again. "If you decide to go to the resort, I have another request."

Raising an eyebrow in surprise, I wait for her to continue.

"Let me organize the weekend for you. You deserve something special."

Special... like ten cocks inside me? My cheeks flush with embarrassment as my pussy throbs. Am I really considering this? Going to a sex resort is insane, but there's something in my mind nagging me to not pass up this opportunity.

"I'll talk to Carlos."

She reaches over and squeezes my hand. "I hope it works out."

CHAPTER 4

The resort is more beautiful than I imagined it would be. As Carlos drives away after dropping me off, a shiver of desire runs down my spine. After having lunch with Sabrina, I talked to Carlos about me taking a weekend at the resort. That led to a round of passionate sex while I begged him to let me go. It took us a few weeks to organize it and wait for my fertile period, but here I am. Carlos wanted to drive me here and pick me up afterwards, and I'm thankful for that—and also that he didn't stay long.

The owner, Chris, clears his throat, and I turn to him. "Ready to check in?"

"Yep!"

I follow him into a gorgeous house, admiring how sexy he is. He's the perfect example of a silver fox, and I briefly wonder if he fucks the guests. I mean, I would if I were him. Why not? I imagine him shoving me against a wall and using me. My nipples harden in anticipation. Shit, I need to focus and not drool over the owner.

After I show him my ID and I sign the forms, I get brave enough to ask. "So... do *you* ever make freeuse of the guests?"

I blush after I ask him. Fuck, I hope he does. Please say yes.

His eyes sparkle as he winks at me. "Only the male ones."

Well, now. I laugh, delighted and disappointed. Guess I can get that thought out of my head.

Once I finish the paperwork, he takes my hand and tenderly kisses the back of it. "I promise you won't even think of me once the guys are done with you."

My stomach flutters with lust, and I bat my eyelashes flirtatiously at him. "I'm holding you to that promise."

He flashes me a mischievous grin as he leads me away from the reception area to my cottage. The grounds are curiously quiet. I expected there to be throngs of men eager to use me.

The cottage is small and cozy yet furnished luxuriously. He sets my bag on the bed and prepares to leave. "Remember, everyone knows your safeword and will abide by it. You agreed to let Sabrina schedule your time here, but I still want you to know we've crafted every detail for your pleasure."

Oh God, what *did* Sabrina ask them to do? I give him a soft, "Thank you," and he leaves. I slip off my sandals and check out the cottage, uncertain what I should do. Am I supposed to just wander around looking for people to fuck me?

There's a side nook with a kitchenette and a dining table, and the bathroom is huge with a separate shower and enormous tub. On the vanity is a note next to portable speakers.

```
Holly,
Please take a few minutes to relax and draw
yourself a bath. Press play for the music.
You're going to want to be relaxed for tonight.
Julian
```

Who is Julian? I expected the note to be from Chris, but he probably would have just told me to take a bath while he was here instead of leaving a note. I have no idea what to expect this weekend, but the thought of being relaxed appeals to me.

I turn on the water and add some vanilla-scented bubble bath. While the water is running, I unpack my bathroom supplies and line them up on the vanity. I pull the sun catcher from Sabrina from my toiletries bag, holding it up and admiring it in the lighting before setting it on the counter. Maybe it is magic, and this will be my lucky weekend.

Quickly stripping down, I press play on the speakers, and soft jazz music fills the room. Ohhh, this is going to be great.

Right before I step into the tub, I catch a glimpse of myself in the mirror. My blonde hair is up in a messy topknot, and my cheeks are flushed from excitement. My breasts are full and aching, and my dusty pink nipples are pert, begging for someone's mouth. I wish I wasn't taking a bath alone.

The water is heavenly as I ease into it. Ahh, this is the life. I use a soft washcloth and caress my belly and breasts as the music and warm water soothes me. This really isn't how I expected my weekend to begin, but I'm not hating it. Now I just need a guy to join me. Slipping a hand between my legs, I gently rub my pussy, enjoying the tingle of pleasure.

A light tap on the door doesn't even surprise me. Oooh, is this my guy? I remove my hand from between my legs before calling out, "Come in."

A stunningly fit, thirty-something man steps into the room. His short brown hair and tantalizing five o'clock shadow make my pussy hum. He's wearing nothing but boxers and I can see the outline of a thick cock through the fabric. Oh yeah, he's yummy.

He perches on the edge of the tub and leans over to kiss me softly. "I'm Julian. I'm glad you followed my orders."

Mmm, his orders... my pussy pulses with anticipation. If his orders include things like bubble baths, I'm willing to follow anything he says.

"I hope you enjoyed my music selection," he murmurs, and then reaches into the water, rubbing a hand over my breast, teasing my nipple with his finger. I gasp as pleasure zings between my legs. Is it crazy that I'm letting a guy I don't know touch me?

Yeah... maybe, but it feels fabulous. I sigh softly as he continues to explore my body, squeezing my breasts and caressing my belly.

His voice is deep when he speaks. "This weekend will be enjoyable for everyone as long as you let yourself relax."

I'm not sure I'd call what he's doing to me relaxing. Every moment is making me more desperate for a cock inside me. When he slips a hand between my legs, I spread them to give him better access and jest with a breathy moan, "We could spend the entire weekend in here, and I'd enjoy it."

His husky laugh makes me think even filthier thoughts. He can do whatever he wants to me as long as he keeps touching me like this. As his fingers brush against my clit, I bite my lip to hold in a gasp. Pleasure washes over me in a tidal wave.

"Don't hold back," he orders.

I moan and lift my hips into his touch. He presses the palm of his hand against my mound, and I groan from euphoria. I close my eyes and focus on his fingers exploring me. When he slips two inside me, the stretch of his thick digits makes me cry out. I writhe in the tub as an orgasm builds, water sloshing as I rotate my hips to get his fingers in deeper. He teases me until I finally moan loudly as bliss crashes down on me, making my legs quiver with pleasure. Ohhh, god.

When he can tell I've come down from my high, he helps me out of the bathtub and gently wraps a fluffy towel around me, making me feel pampered and cherished. Yep, I'm relaxed—mission accomplished.

I'm shy and unsure of what to do next. As he towels me off, I ask, "So, um... now what?"

It's a little odd to have just been finger fucked by a man I don't know, yet it somehow feels natural. Yeah, I can't explain it and I choose not to overthink my emotions. All I want is to have fun and to enjoy being used all weekend. That was just the start.

"Now..." He takes my hand and leads me out to the bedroom. "You get a massage."

My eyes widen at the sight of candles flickering around the room and an inviting massage table set up near the bed. Did he do this before he joined me in the bathroom, or did someone else set it up? Hell, who cares?

I let the towel drop to the floor, and I climb onto the table, face down. As soon as I settle in, another man enters the room from the kitchenette. He's younger and hot, with a full sleeve tattoo—something I've always found attractive on men. Mmm, yeah, he revs my engine as well.

The new guy remains silent, and they both apply oil to their hands before starting the massage. Julian focuses on my upper body and neck, while the other guy rubs my feet and calves. I melt into the table as they expertly stroke every muscle of my body and work the kinks out. They take their time, kneading every part of me as I moan with delight. I've had massages in the past, but I've never had two people work on me at once. This is truly something else.

As I feel one of them spread my butt cheeks and rub close to my pussy, I start to suspect this is more than just an ordinary massage. His fingers penetrate my pussy as the other guy massages my foot. Mmm, so good. I grind against the hand inside me. It's thrilling to be touched and teased all over. The sound of moaning bounces off the walls, and it takes a moment to realize the noise is coming from me. My eyes drift shut, and I concentrate on how glorious this feels, being taken care of like this. So far, this is the best spa resort ever.

When the guys stop touching me and help me roll over, I don't even grumble at the lack of fingers in my pussy. I want them to play with my breasts—no, I *need* them to touch me. I'm aching, and only a cock in me or a mouth tugging on my nipples is going to satiate my hunger.

As soon as my back is against the massage table, Julian fondles my breast with his powerful hands, and I suck in a breath when he twists my nipple. Fuuuuck... yes. When I glance down, I can see his bulge pushing against the thin material of his boxers. They look ready to rip apart and unleash the monster hidden underneath.

I part my knees so Tats—the pet name I've chosen for him—can explore my pussy. Julian bends over and flicks his tongue around one of my nipples while Tats proves he's a wizard with my clit. He spirals his finger around the sensitive bud at the perfect speed until I'm bucking against his hand and moaning like a dirty slut. Pleasure coils in my belly, and my head thrashes when the sensation is almost too much.

"More, please," I beg. I want one of their cocks inside me.

Julian stops sucking at my breasts, and Tats shifts away as Julian pulls me to the edge of the table. He positions my ankles over his shoulders, and I gaze up at him with pleading eyes while my heart races. My body is bursting with intense need as I wait for him to fill me. I'm so fucking wet and ready for him.

Julian chuckles at my desperation. "Does our Goddess want my cock?" he asks.

Their Goddess? I could get used to this. "Yes, fuck me, please," I beg, praying he'll put me out of my misery. Freeuse is maddening. I'm used to having more control, and someone needs to just fuck me.

Julian guides his cock to my pussy while Tats laughs. I want to grumble that I'm not finding this so funny, but Julian distracts me with the bulbous head of his cock teasing my entrance. He eases into me with one smooth motion, and I give a deep-throated groan of satisfaction. Finally!

Tats smirks as he watches me, wrapping his hand around his impressive length, and starts rubbing. Julian strokes into me, deep and slow, while gazing at me like I'm the most exquisite creature in the world. The heat in his eyes as he thrusts faster causes my back to arch off the table, pushing against him to get his cock even deeper. I wasn't expecting anything like this, and I close my eyes, losing myself to the moment.

My orgasm sneaks up on me, and I gasp as my body trembles from the growing euphoria. Fuck, fuck, fuuuuck, it feels soooo good. When my orgasm hits, waves of bliss ripple from my fingers to my toes.

Julian groans, "Is my Goddess ready for me to fill her pussy full of cum and get her pregnant?"

What? Oh fuck. "Yes," I moan, and writhe against him, desperate for him to come.

"Good, I'm going to pump my seed into you and breed you until your pussy is overflowing."

Ohhhh shit, yes! That's what I want to hear. His thrusts quicken and he clutches my thighs. When he shudders and groans, his warmth fills me. He continues to fuck me, unloading everything he's got until I'm a boneless, quivering mess.

As he pulls out, he whispers, "That's a good girl," and I know I've made the right decision to come here. I arrived not even two hours ago, and I'm already soaring high from pleasure. This weekend is going to be life-changing. I can tell.

As soon as Julian steps away, Tats helps me stand up and then he bends me over the table. Oh hey, guess I'm getting fucked some more. As Tats slides into me from behind, he fists the topknot in my hair and pulls my head up so he can whisper in my ear.

"Want to know the difference between me and Julian?"

I can barely think while he's slowly fucking me, and I peep out a, "What?"

He sucks on my earlobe for a moment, and his breath is a warm puff in my ear. "I'm not as nice as he is."

What does that mean? He applies pressure and shoves my shoulder back down to the padded bench, and I grip the sides as he relentlessly pounds into me. Ohhh, okay, I know what he meant now. Fuck, he's good.

"You see..." he huffs out. "Julian likes to treasure his women and breed them softly."

Uh oh. My brain blips out when I realize where this is going, and he continues. "Where I like to take a woman and turn her into my breeding whore for the weekend."

Oh... my... god.

He's in a frenzy, and he digs his fingers into my hips as he fucks me harder than I ever have been before. I'm loving every rough moment as the rapture builds in layers. It's going to be a good one when I come.

Tats lets go of my hip to slap my ass, making me scream out. He growls, "And breeding whores beg for what they want. So, beg."

Beg for him to fill me? What happens if I'm not good at it? Shit, I better try. "Please," I start off timid, not sure if that's enough. "Fuck me and come in me. I want you to get me pregnant."

I peek at him over my shoulder to see a smug smile cross his face. "That's it?" he teases.

Ugh, he wants to make me crazy. I tighten my grip on the edges of the table and moan louder, "Oh god, please fuck me harder."

That earns me another satisfying smack on my ass, and I whimper in pleasure. Delight rockets through my body and my mind lets go.

I pant out, "Fill me up... just keep filling me up. Breed me like a filthy whore."

Hearing those words out of my mouth fills me with shame. I've never wanted to be called a whore before, but I'm so desperate for his cum that I called myself that. Humiliation and excitement war inside me while my brain whirls in pleasure. I love every degrading moment of what he's doing, and I hear myself begging, as if I have no control over what I'm saying.

"Breed me," I babble. "Please, cum in me over and over again. Give it to me."

He slams into me without mercy until my pussy clamps around him. I explode from rapture as he erupts with a primal grunt. He keeps fucking me as he unloads ropes of sticky cum and I'm shivering from a continual wave of bliss. It seems like forever before he gives one last thrust of his hips and stops.

When he pulls out, my pussy flutters, and I moan at the loss of his cock. Tats wastes no time before he pulls me from the table and forces me to my knees. "Time to clean me up," he commands and pushes his cock between my lips.

Fuuuuck, he wasn't lying when he said he wasn't as nice—and I still love it. I suck on his cock, swirling my tongue around it to clean him off. Tasting myself on him makes me feel like the filthy whore I called myself.

When he pulls out of my mouth, I'm half mindless from pleasure. Tats grins, "See you later for more of that," and walks out the door.

Jesus, what just happened? That was beyond amazing. My chest heaves as I try to make my brain function again. Eh, who needs to think? Apparently not me. All I need is my mouth to say whatever dirty thoughts pop into my head, and my pussy to take whatever cock a guy wants to shove into me. I guess a massage with two hot guys turns me into a super slut. Carlos is going to love this story when he picks me up.

Julian lifts me up into his arms, and I cuddle against his hard chest, smiling into his neck as I breathe in his woodsy cologne. He carries me to the bed and leaves me there for a moment before returning with a bottle of water, peanuts, and a banana. Mmm, room service is nice. He climbs into bed behind me and rubs my back while I nibble on the snacks and sip water. The aftercare is soothing.

He doesn't make small talk but simply holds me while I eat and process everything. When I'm finished, he urges me to lie down next to him. "Rest now, then more sex later."

My eyes flutter closed while his comforting arms are wrapped around me. Rest now... mmm... yes... more sex later... sounds like the perfect plan. This is the best baby-making resort ever. They'd get a five-star review from me. I smile and drift to sleep while snuggling him.

When I wake up, it's dark outside the windows and the candles are blown out. I'm groggy, so it takes a moment to realize what woke me. Julian is spooning me and nuzzling my neck while his hand pinches a nipple. His cock, pressed against my ass, makes me shiver with need. Oh yeah, this is why I'm here.

Before I arrived, I filled out questionnaires about what I liked and didn't like. Chris and I talked on the phone, and he said even though Sabrina had some requests for me, he still wanted to know what I desired. One thing I wrote down is how I love being woken up by sex, so this is perfect.

Without a word, he rolls me onto my stomach so he can cover me and thrust his cock into me from behind. I moan out a loud, "Yessssss."

He murmurs, "Time to give my Goddess her bedtime breeding," as he pumps me full of his hot cum.

Fuuuuck... what? I quiver around him as his warmth coats my insides. He didn't fuck me long enough for me to come.

"Good girl." Somehow the praise makes my lack of orgasm better. He strokes my back and I yawn, still tired. I've been so excited about the trip, I haven't been sleeping well and the relaxation is making me even more groggy.

Yawning loudly again, I ask, "What are we doing tonight?"

He chuckles. "Nothing outside of the cottage. You need rest for tomorrow."

Huh, what's happening tomorrow? I don't voice the thought and snuggle my head into the pillow. I murmur, "Sounds good," as I drift off.

Twice during the night, I wake up. At some point, Tats joins us, and they take turns with me. By the time I finally get solid sleep, I'm so full of cum I can feel it dripping out of me. This resort is wonderful.

Chapter 5

When the sun streams in my window and wakes me, I stretch and savor how loose my muscles are. After spending hours on end being fucked yesterday, I'm surprised I'm not sore, but I feel refreshed and ready for more cum.

Julian peeks his head from the entryway to the kitchenette. "Is my Goddess ready for breakfast?"

Oooh, another day of being a Goddess. "Yes, please."

"I'm making food. It will be a few minutes."

Oh good, I have time. I sneak off to the bathroom to make myself slightly more presentable. When I see the mess of my hair in the mirror, I can't stop the laughter. Jesus, I need a shower and a hairbrush.

I'm not sure how long I've got before food is ready, so I skip the shower and settle with cleaning my teeth and brushing my hair. When I join Julian again, there's a covered silver tray sitting on the dining table in the nook. Julian is dressed and holding the chair out for me to sit in. After I'm settled, he removes the dome and reveals a mouthwatering feast, and my stomach rumbles.

He winks. "This isn't my only surprise today."

My excitement ratchets up another notch. What do they have planned for me? I'm easy to please, and I'd be happy with another day like last night.

He has a plate for himself, and while we eat, I try to probe him for details. "So… what're we doing?"

Julian gives me a secretive smirk. The mischievous glint in his eye is sexy as hell, and I shiver as I imagine all the filthy things they could have planned. "Eat and find out," he challenges with a hint of authority that makes my pussy wet.

I take another couple of bites and try a different tactic. "Why am I your Goddess, but the other guy said I'm his whore?"

The corners of his mouth twitch. "Do you really want to know?"

I nod quickly, curious where this is leading.

"Chris talked to your husband, and your husband said you wanted him to talk dirtier in the bedroom and he's never been able to. He suggested we call you a whore and see how you react."

My body lights up with desire, and I set my fork down while my mind whirls. Carlos arranged this? I didn't even know he talked to Chris when I wasn't around. Fuck, my husband is awesome.

"Eat up." Julian waves his fork at me. "We've got big plans, and my Goddess needs her strength."

Oh, right. I need more cocks in me. When we're finished eating, I take a quick shower and marvel, once again, that I'm not sore. I've had more sex since I've arrived at the resort than I have in any twelve-hour period before, but clearly my pussy is made for a marathon of cocks.

When I'm all done in the shower and dried off, Julian is waiting for me with a cup of coffee and a blue sundress to slip on. It's simple with spaghetti straps, but it's not one that I brought with me. I'm not surprised that it's exactly my size. Dang, they're even supplying clothes for me.

It doesn't escape me that I'm missing a certain piece of clothing, and I arch my eyebrow at him. "No panties?"

That wicked grin of his is back, and he shrugs. "Panties will just get in the way."

Okay then. I gulp down the coffee and slip on my sandals before following him out the door. We stroll along a path, heading towards a wooded area. I have no idea where we're going, but my pussy tingles at the thought of fucking more guys. Tats eventually joins us, and I eye the large tote bag he's carrying. I can't see what's in it, but it's bulky, so it has to be several items.

When we reach the tree line, I follow them down a wooded path. As we get deeper in, the sunlight dims. Jesus, how big is this resort? We walk for several minutes before the guys stop next to the trunk of a gigantic tree.

Julian smiles and says, "Turn around."

My heartbeat quickens. What's he going to do to me?

He places a soft, black cloth around my eyes and ties it at the back of my head to blindfold me. Ohhhh damn, are they going to lead me to a secret location and they don't want me to see their hideout?

After they've checked my vision with their fingers and determined that I can't see anything through the fabric, he gives my ass a playful spank, and I gasp in surprise, then giggle.

One of them pulls my hands together in front of me, and when I feel rope wrap around my wrists, my brain almost shuts off. They're tying me up? My breathing quickens, and I remember discussing one of my dirtiest fantasies with Carlos. I told him I sometimes daydream about being tied to a tree and ravished.

The guys remain silent, pushing me back against the large tree. My wrists are quickly bound to an overhead branch. I desperately pull at the rope, feeling vulnerable when I realize escape is impossible. All my senses heighten: the scent of dirt and pine fill my nostrils, and I can feel a breeze against my skin. When I hear twigs snap as though someone is approaching us, I whimper with anticipation.

Finally, someone speaks, and I jump when it's a voice I don't recognize. "There's the filthy whore, all tied up and ready to be bred."

Damn. Just hearing someone say that is enough to drive me wild. My body hungers for cock, and my legs tremble as I bite my lip, desperate to keep myself from crying out and begging someone to fuck me. This is far beyond anything I anticipated, and instead of being afraid, I feel myself opening up and surrendering to the experience. I'll be their breeding whore as long as they fill me full of cum.

Someone moves close, and I recognize Julian's scent. He trails a finger from my lips down my neck and then cups my breast, teasing my nipple through the sundress.

His breath is warm on my neck. "We're going to give you what you want. My Goddess is going to be a beautiful pregnant mess when we're done with you."

Ohhh fuck. "Please," I gasp and strain against the rope holding me up.

He kisses my neck. "Remember your safeword if you need it."

Jesus, is he crazy? I will not need it. This is my ultimate fantasy. I squirm my hips, trying to tempt them to touch my pussy, and I feel like I'm floating away on a cloud of bliss. It's surreal that I'm tied to a tree waiting for complete strangers to breed me.

Two sets of hands explore my body, and when I hear more twigs snap, I strain my ears, trying to guess how many more men are heading this way. It sounds like more than a couple.

My clit pulses with need at the realization that I don't know what's going to happen. But it's more than just that. I also have no control. I don't have to make any decisions. The guys are going to do what they want to me, and I'm at their mercy.

My head spins as someone lifts the bottom edge of my sundress and I hear the snip of the scissors parting the fabric before I even feel the cold metal against my skin. My entire body freezes as my dress falls open, exposing my tits to the cool air. The world disappears, and I'm hyper focused on every sensation in my body.

Strong, callused hands grip my thighs, forcing my legs apart, and my breath hitches as a thick cock impales me. I squeal from pleasure as shocks of delight ripple along every nerve ending in my body as he stretches me out. "Ohhh god."

The bark bites the skin on my back as I arch against the tree and clench my pussy around the cock in me. Not knowing how many people are here and how many cocks I'm going to take before they're done with me makes everything more intense. I wiggle against the bindings and wrap my legs around the guy's waist as he supports my ass and plows into me.

I get the sense that people are crowding in to get a better look, and a momentary spike of embarrassment rushes through me at being on display. Holy fuck, this is real. This is actually happening to me.

Fingers pull on my nipples, and I groan, overwhelmed with a storm of emotions. The guy whose cock is inside me still has his hands on my ass, so it's not him playing with my tits.

I moan out, "More," while tilting my head back and pushing my breasts out. I can only imagine what this looks like, and I get lost in the visual as I imagine a line of guys with their cocks out, stroking and waiting to use me.

A tongue swipes at my nipple and then sucks. Mmm, fuck, that's good. Someone's got my other nipple, and I try to buck against the cock in my pussy, but between all the hands on me and the guy holding me steady while he fucks me, all I can do is squirm as they continue to torment me. The guy on my right kisses a line up my neck and nibbles on my ear while tweaking my nipple.

When he speaks, I know it's Julian. "How does it feel to know all these men are ready to breed you?"

"Fuuuuck," I moan in response, unable to form a complete sentence. My mind is a swirl of colors as pure ecstasy courses through my veins.

The guy between my legs groans loudly, and he holds himself still while his cock spasms and unloads inside me. He pumps a few final times before slipping out of me and moving away.

My feet barely touch the ground before a new pair of hands grips my ass and a new cock replaces the emptiness with a fast and hard thrust.

The voice from the guy inside me growls, "Is the whore ready to be bred?"

It's Tats. Yes, yes, yes. I part my lips to beg, but he swallows my words with a blistering kiss that sets fire to my soul. His mouth commands mine to obey and, as our tongues entwine, I become a madwoman. I can't get enough of him, and his kiss sets off a sharp, wild need. I want him to fuck me as hard as he can.

When he stops kissing me, my "Please... oh god, please," is a breathy mewl. I'm willing to beg for all their cum and be their whore that they can use all night long. I thrash my head and cry out, "Breed me, put a baby in me. Make me your breeding whore and fill my hole with your cum." I'm rewarded with a smack on my ass.

Tats increases the tempo of his thrusts until I'm just about to explode. My thigh muscles tense, and I sway my hips, trying to force him in as far as he can go. Someone pulls at a nipple harder, and the combined pleasure of Tat's cock and the guy playing with my tit sends me over the edge. My orgasm hits me harder than I expect, and I scream out with my release and flail at my bindings as my body convulses with waves of delight.

My mind is gone, and my entire focus is on my pleasure as electricity burns in my veins. I still haven't recovered when Tats groans as he comes hard, sending a rush of cum into me to mix with my juices and the other guy's seed. It seems like he's unloading ropes and ropes into me, but time has lost all meaning as the ecstasy keeps spiking. He fucks me slowly until the pulsing of his cock stops and then he slowly withdraws, leaving me empty and aching for more.

The desire to submit to these strangers fills me as my orgasm dissipates. They can use me however they want, for as long as they want. I'm ready to be the ultimate slut.

When Tats moves away and my feet meet the ground again, the dirt against my soles makes me realize I lost my sandals. Limp with pleasure, I barely notice different hands touching me until they spin me around and press me against the tree face first.

The bark grazes my nipples as the new person pulls my hips back and lines the tip of his cock against my entrance. This guy doesn't seem to be in any hurry as he pushes into me slowly, one glorious inch at a time. I'm so wet that I can feel moisture dripping out of me. Fuck, this is filthy—no, it's me who's filthy, and it's marvelous.

I'm in an awkward position with my arms above my head and my breasts against the tree, but I don't care. It's not painful, and I'll take a little discomfort for all this cum. The new cock fucks me slow and steady until I'm a quivering mess and another orgasm builds.

He whispers in my ear, "You're being a very good girl and taking our cum like a good little freeuse slut."

A spark of awareness travels down my spine when I realize this guy is giving me the exact degradation that I love. "Yessss," I moan. I want to hear it all. I want to be praised for being a good breeding whore, and I want them all to tell me I'm a slut and a cumdump.

I feel myself sinking into the deepest recess of my mind where I really am just a freeuse fucktoy. It's not just about breeding anymore. I want them to come all over me—not just in me. If this is my chance to have a bunch of guys fuck me, I want to be delirious with ecstasy and covered in cum at the end.

His strokes change and become more forceful. "Do you want my seed, slut?"

I whimper, "Yes. God, yes." And I do—I want him to paint my womb with his cum, and I'll keep taking and taking until there's nothing left for him to give me.

My mind floats in a haze while he works me over with each punishing thrust of his cock. As he finally empties into me with a deep guttural growl of satisfaction, I revel in the joy of being a vessel for all these guys' seed. I want more.

Another man takes the last guy's place, and each thrust forces me up to my tippytoes. He's a little rougher than the last guy, and I quickly spiral towards another orgasm. I scream as my entire body is wracked with an almost painful pleasure.

As waves of delight ripple from my fingertips to my toes, it triggers him to explode. He unloads inside of me, adding even more cum to what's already there, and each whack against my pussy makes a wet sound. I'm beyond caring, and I'm floating high as a kite with joy.

He pulls out of me, but before I can adjust my stance to regain my footing, another cock slides into my slick entrance. Oh fuck, are they really all lined up and waiting for their turn to breed me?

Bliss ripples from my core, and each solid thrust sends me reeling. I writhe under him, wild from the pleasure and the exhilarating helplessness of not being able to do anything but take every load. My mind is craving even more. I want everything. I want every inch of me covered in cum and dripping with it.

I lose count at how many times I'm fucked, and the pleasure becomes an unending orgasm until I realize someone is untying me from the branch. My wrists are still bound when I'm shoved to my knees. The change of position makes me put my elbows on the dirt and lower my head to my hands as someone slides inside me from behind.

A hand grabs my hair, and another cock presses against my mouth, begging to be let in. I open my lips, and the cock sinks into my throat while the guy behind me slaps my ass.

In the background, I can hear chatter. The guys are talking together like it's a social gathering, but a few guys are yelling encouragement and praising the men for filling me up and making me take all their loads. Them talking about me like I'm a piece of ass makes me feel like the ultimate fucktoy.

The person in my pussy grunts out, "Here it is... take it." As he blows his load deep inside me, the guy in my mouth growls and pulls out to shoot cum all over my face and in my hair, just like I wanted. It's hot and sticky and so satisfying.

When the cock inside me pulls out, his cum runs out of me, leaving a wet trail down my thighs. Someone else quickly takes his place and pounds into me.

I'm still blindfolded, so I have no idea who any of these people are. For a fleeting moment, I wonder what Carlos would think if he saw me here now, completely debased, being gang fucked. Would he even recognize me?

Hell, I don't even give a fuck. I'm on a different plane of existence from all the orgasms, and I'm a million miles away from reality as I take each load in my pussy and mouth. I lose count of the cocks I suck on and swallow down what's offered. Time loses all meaning and all I can do is exist in a bubble of pleasure.

When my final orgasm rips through me, the pain is sweet and exquisite. I collapse into the dirt, trembling, while cum trickles out of my well-fucked pussy and pools underneath me. I can't move, and I'm content to lie there in filth. Even if someone had asked me what I wanted this weekend, I wouldn't have known how to ask for this. It's absolutely perfect.

I hear some guys saying goodbye, and two firm hands untie my wrists before helping me up, so I'm standing. When my knees threaten to buckle, he swoops me up into his arms. I can tell it's Julian.

I rest my head on his shoulders as he carries me. I don't even care that I'm still blindfolded as I float in a haze of pleasure. This place is the most spectacular resort ever.

It feels like barely any time passes before I can tell we're entering the cottage. He speaks to someone in the room. "She needs to be cleaned off. We'll be right out."

Oh god, more guys are here to use me?

He carries me into the bathroom and sits me on the counter. I hear the bathroom door close and the shower start up before he removes the blindfold.

It's a struggle for my vision to readjust to the brightness, but I can make out the concerned expression on his face. I must look like a complete mess after being used, and I try to run my fingers through my tangled hair but make little progress. "Hi," I smile up at him and laugh. "That was fun."

Julian's concern eases, and he reaches to rub his thumb over my cheek. "My Goddess needs a shower."

A shower sounds good. I stretch, wincing as my pussy protests. Now that I've come down from my high and the sex endorphins are wearing off, I can tell that parts of me are sore. They didn't hurt me, but I was so thoroughly used there's no way I won't be a little sore tonight. Maybe the warm water will help loosen up the aches and pains. Julian is fairly filthy also, and my lips twitch. "Come on, you too."

I hold out my hand and wait for him to take it. Julian helps me off the counter and into the shower, where I stand under the spray and let him clean me. As he scrubs my hair, I turn my head up to the water to rinse off, enjoying the pampering. "Thank you for looking after me."

Julian kisses me gently and murmurs against my lips. "Anything for my Goddess."

A knock at the bathroom door makes me giggle. "Are there guys out there waiting to fuck me?"

Julian calls out, "We're almost done," and then grins at me. "Your pussy is prized among us."

His silly non-answer warms me, and I enjoy his playful mood. When he turns off the water and towels me off, I feel refreshed and slightly energized. If there really is a group of guys out there, I could take them.

He slips a robe over my shoulders and brushes my hair. When I'm clean and presentable, he kisses me on the forehead. "Wait here for two minutes and then come out."

What does he have planned? If it involves candles and another massage, count me in. Except I'm the freeuse slut, so really count me in for anything.

Julian leaves briefly and surprises me when he comes back immediately. He hands me a bottle of water and a packet of trail mix. "Almost forgot this. Eat and drink for two minutes and then come out. You're going to need your energy." He winks at me and then leaves again.

Hmm... two minutes? I lean against the counter and open the water bottle and take a drink before attacking the trail mix. Shit, I really am hungry and didn't notice. I pick up the sun catcher and play with it as I munch and daydream about the experience in the woods. How many guys fucked me? It would be funny if it was only three guys. At some point, all the cocks blended together and I couldn't distinguish size differences. Heh, I'm such a slut. This little sun catcher doesn't need to be magical with how much cum I took.

Wait, how long has it been? I set the water bottle and half-eaten packet of trail mix on the counter and open the bathroom door. The lights are dim, and the candles are lit again. See, I knew it!

Except there's no massage table. Instead, my husband is sitting on the edge of the bed, looking nervous.

I squeal and launch myself at him. "You're here!"

Carlos catches me in a hug and falls backwards on the bed with me on top of him. "Of course," he whispers and kisses me deeply. "Chris talked to me about what they had planned, and there's no way I could stay home all weekend."

I kiss him all over his face, and my knees slide to either side of him as my bare pussy comes in contact with his hardness through his jeans. Mmm, someone is turned on.

When he gazes at me, the look of love in his eyes makes me realize how glad I am he joined me. "This was so fun." I beam at him while I slowly undulate my hips, teasing him as my pussy drenches his jeans. I need him. I need him now.

He wraps his hand behind my head and pulls me down for another kiss while he lifts his hips. His bulge is pressing against my clit, and I moan out loud. Fuck, that feels good.

I sit up so I can reach for his belt buckle and undo his pants to give me better access. As I slip my hands underneath his boxers and free his cock, his erection springs forth. Oh, yum, he's hard as steel and leaking pre-cum.

When I position him between my legs, he moans and holds my hips to guide me down onto his length. He slides in with ease as my pussy swallows him whole and my body sighs in relief. Fuck, having him here feels right. I pause for a moment to relish the sensation of him deep inside me before I rotate my hips.

I'm grinning as he grasps my hips. "Ride me, baby," he commands while squeezing me to encourage me to move.

Oh, that's so hot. I put my hands on his chest to brace myself and rock forward and back as I build to a faster tempo. Carlos closes his eyes and relaxes under me, letting me take what I need and use him.

After the day I've had, watching him surrender to the pleasure I'm giving him is the hottest thing ever. I tilt my head back as I climb higher and higher while his cock hits the perfect spot inside me. I cry out, "Oh, Carlos, oh, shit," as I explode.

It's as if everything I did today compounds and suddenly bursts inside me like a dam breaking. Pleasure and release combine in an overwhelming feeling of liberation, and tears roll down my cheeks as I tremble from bliss.

I grind against him and milk his cock until he groans and shoots his cum deep inside me. I pound against him a few more times, making sure I get every drop before melting to the bed next to him.

"Holy fuck," I moan as tiny aftershocks of delight ripple through me. Is there such a thing as too many orgasms?

Carlos rolls onto his side and runs his fingers through my hair. "God, I love you so much."

I turn to cuddle against him while he wraps his arms around me in a loving embrace, making me feel cherished. I close my eyes and whisper, "I love you, too."

We lay there in silence for a few moments, basking in the afterglow of our orgasms. When he kisses me softly, I smile against his lips and murmur, "We have a lot to catch up on."

He laughs. "I bet we do." As he caresses my hip, he asks, "Did they treat you right?"

I look up into his eyes and give him my best saucy grin. "Oh yeah, and did you know you just got fucked by a Goddess?"

He kisses me passionately and murmurs between kisses , "Yep, and I'm the luckiest man alive."

When he breaks off the kiss, I snuggle against him more tightly and yawn. Yeah, after a nap, I'm going to fuck him again and see his reaction when I tell him how the guys used me. But first, this breeding whore needs some sleep.

EPILOGUE

The sun catcher sits on the counter next to the pregnancy test as Carlos and I wait the required two minutes. It's obvious before the time is up, but we wait just to make sure the second line doesn't disappear.

It doesn't.

I squeal as Carlos crushes me against his chest and kisses me passionately as my body floods with excitement.

The sun catcher worked its magic!

AFTER USED AND TREASURED (BONUS STORY)

Note: This bonus story takes place at the freeuse resort after Carlos joins her.

As I sleepily open my eyes, Carlos's arm is wrapped around me and his fingertips gently stroke my back. When my husband notices me stirring, he leans over to give me a kiss and whispers softly. "Did the Goddess get some rest?"

I stretch out leisurely and yawn as the memories from earlier come flooding back. My pussy clenches as I recall the afternoon spent getting filled with all that cum.

"Mmm, yes," I answer with a grin. "Very nice."

He raises an eyebrow, and a hint of color appears on his cheeks. "Tell me everything that happened today."

I bite my lip and run my hand down his chest, tracing the lines of his muscles until I reach his growing erection. "Well, when I first arrived at the resort, there was a note in the bathroom telling me to take a bath and listen to music. During the middle of my bath..."

As I describe every naughty detail of my day, Carlos's breathing quickens and his cock throbs against my fingers as I caress him. When I finally finish telling him about being fucked while blindfolded and how many times I came, he groans and thrusts into my hand.

"What if I told you..." he says breathlessly, "that I want to watch you get fucked by a guy tonight?"

Oh, hell yes. There's no way I'd say no to that, but can my husband handle watching someone make a total mess of me? I peer up into Carlos's eyes and find nothing but pure desire reflected there.

"Just one guy?" I grip his cock and he moans. I can't resist teasing him, and he shudders while closing his eyes as I pump slowly up and down its length.

After a few moments, he gasps, "Any number you want."

Mmm, that's the correct answer. I laugh and pull my hand away. "That's good because I'm the freeuse slut and who knows how many guys will line up."

I roll out of bed and beckon him up with me. "Get up, lazy bones. We need to find a guy to fuck me."

Carlos laughs with me as he climbs out of bed. Yep, this is going to be fun.

As we exit the cottage, I'm wearing shorts, a tank top, and sandals. The first person who pulls my shorts off will discover I am not wearing panties. We follow the path towards the pool. While I scan the area for potential guys who could fuck me, Carlos puts his arms around my waist and teases the skin above my shorts' waistband. It tickles so much that I giggle as we pass by the wooden building with the sauna.

When we come around the corner, my eyes light up when the sauna door opens and Tats emerges. I never found out his real name, but he fucked me roughly yesterday and I nicknamed him Tats. Holy fucking hotness, his body is drool worthy. Along with his full sleeve tattoo, he also has tattoos disappearing into the towel around his waist. Mmm, I didn't notice those before, but I was busy being pounded against the table.

Oh shit, I don't want Carlos to see me drooling over a hot guy. I take a quick look at my husband from under my eyelashes, and to my surprise, there's a twinkle of lust in his eyes. Alright, maybe he's okay with me checking out an attractive guy.

As if in some silent communication between the men, Carlos lets go of my waist, and Tats closes the distance between us. He places his palm on my hip, sending waves of heat radiating straight to my core. I stifle a whimper of need as he pushes me face first against the wooden siding of the sauna.

He tugs at the drawstring of my shorts while running his lips along my neck. "How's the breeding whore tonight?"

Ohhhh, fuuuck. I don't answer and tilt my head to the side, exposing more skin, and shiver in delight when he bites my neck gently. He shoves his hand inside the front of my shorts to cup my pussy. I can feel wetness drip from me and soak his fingers as he slips one digit inside me, thrusting it in and out. My knees threaten to give way as my body responds, tightening around his finger.

I turn my head towards Carlos, and he's leaning against the building, watching us intently with hunger in his eyes as he caresses himself through his shorts. Holy shit, that's hot. I wanted to make sure my husband was okay with watching me being used, and clearly he is.

Tats presses his body against mine, forcing me into the wood and creating a tantalizing friction through the cotton of my tank top. As he removes his finger from my pussy, he circles my clit. I moan loudly as he creates electric jolts of bliss in my core.

I almost object when he moves his hand away, but he doesn't leave me empty for long. With one swift movement, he drags my shorts down to my ankles, exposing me. Cool air flows against my slit, and I can feel my inner thighs becoming slick from arousal. After all the sex I've had in the last 24 hours, I'm surprised I can still react so intensely to anyone's touch, but I'm a wet mess and ready to beg for someone to breed me.

Tats spreads my legs further apart with his foot against mine, and I reposition myself to help him. In one smooth movement, he thrusts inside me, filling me all the way up before pausing for a moment. Ooooh, god. His cock feels incredible as it stretches me out. I grind against him while pushing my ass up to give him deeper access.

I have no control, and he firmly holds my hips in place. When I cry out in frustration, needing to move, his low chuckle is right in my ear, sending tingles of excitement through me. "Hush, little whore, and take your breeding."

Ooh fuck, yes please. He pulls his cock out all the way before slamming back into me. I cry out in pleasure as he pounds me against the siding. With how fast he's fucking me, I might not come—and yet, somehow, it's okay.

I shake in delight as he uses my body to satisfy himself, and I keep my head turned towards Carlos so I can watch the emotions play across his face. My husband has a hungry look in his eyes and the tent in his shorts tells me I might get another round with my husband's cock after Tats is finished with me.

Tats continues to fuck me vigorously and growls, "Tell your husband how much of a whore you are."

I moan as I can feel myself edging closer to orgasm, but I bite my lip to stop myself from answering. Oh god, his dirty talk drives me wild.

"Look at him," Tats orders. "Your husband wants to know how much you enjoy taking my cock."

There's a command in his tone that makes my insides flutter and tremble. Oh shit, I want to please him and give my husband the show he deserves. When I stare at Carlos, the raw intensity of need I see there cranks my excitement even higher as I whimper, "I'm such a filthy whore, I love letting any cock use me."

Tats grunts loudly in satisfaction and brings his hand around to rub my clit in fast circles. Within moments, I explode around his cock and cry out as pleasure ripples from my fingertips to my toes.

I clench around the cock inside me, and Tats groans as he fucks me so hard he's knocking me against the wall. When he comes, he roars out as he spills thick ropes of cum deep inside me.

He jerks a few times before pulling out, and I collapse against the building for support, completely boneless and delirious from pleasure. Tats slaps my ass and I flinch from the unexpected pain, then giggle.

Without another word, Tats picks his towel up off the ground, wraps it around his waist, and whistles as he walks away.

My husband steps closer to me, places his hands on my waist, and swipes a finger around my wet hole while scooping up cum. I groan loudly with pleasure when he puts his finger in my mouth for me to suck on. Oh fuck, that's hot.

When I turn to look at him, there's an impish smile on his face. "Lets see how many more men we can find to fuck you."

Yeah, I married a keeper.

I wrap my arms around my husband, kissing him deeply before retrieving my shorts from the ground and pulling them back on.

If my amazing husband wants to watch me take more loads of cum tonight, who am I to complain?

The End